"In Levesko's debut novel, a deep-thinking young man ponders life and love in Paris and beyond…Alex's journey from irresponsible unfocused youth to a more thoughtful maturity will resonate with anyone who's struggled with questions of how to live in the world…an overly philosophical novel at times, but one that captures the turmoil and excitement of the late 60s."

—*Kirkus Reviews*

Also by Ed Levesko

Long Time Passing
A la Fin du Jour
eddies in life
Umbra (English)
Umbra (French)
Point of No Return
10 West to Venice
Where Justice ends
The Guitar Player
La Nuit Blanche

www.edlevesko.com
edlevesko@gmail.com

At the End of the Day

At the End of the Day

Ed Levesko

Copyright © 2000 by Ed Levesko

ISBN: 978-0-6158-3169-5

Ed Levesko, Publisher

P.O. Box 144
Culver City, CA
90232
U.S.A.

edlevesko@gmail.com
www.edlevesko.com

To my son, David-Alexandre, whose love I value above all else.

August 1998
Venice, Italy.

Only the historical events and people in this book are real, the rest is fiction.

But life takes sudden twists.

Sophocles

Fifth Century Athens

At the End of the Day

ONE

The envelope was postmarked Kabul, Afghanistan, and was addressed to me in Paris. There was no date stamped on it as to when it had been mailed. Inside, there was a letter in small, neat, delicate, writing—a woman's handwriting. It was dated June 3, 1968, about two months earlier. It read:

> *Dear Alex,*
> *I apologize and regret to be the bearer of tragic news. Chris is no longer; he died three weeks ago here in Kabul. I thought you would care to know what happened. He always thought very highly of you and among his papers, I found your address. I pray that my letter gets to you and finds you in good health. I am terribly sorry I did not write sooner, but I do hope you will understand.*
> *Yours truly,*

The letter was signed: *Anne.* No last name, no return address, no other additional details were given. Nothing about what he had died of, or how.

My good buddy Chris, gone! What a shame—damn shame. Good old Chris. Man, life truly is impenetrable. All kinds of memories suddenly came rushing back to me. How long had it been since I thought about him?

In the last postcard I received from him, he wrote he was on his way to India. Anne must have been the English girl he was supposed to go with. I immensely regretted how lax I had been in trying to keep in touch with him.

Sudden news about a friend's death shocks your soul. Part of you dies and the ache and emptiness in your heart are made worse when you are left to wonder how it happened. You want to stop your life, go back and do the things you did not do and say the things you should have said.

The heart suffers from remorse. The personal disappointment at not having been the person you thought you were or the friend you should have been is devastating. It makes you feel like a fraud. It shatters the idea you have of yourself.

There are two inescapable and simple truths in life: birth and death—no room for ambiguities. With the sad news coming on the heels and in contrast to the other things that had happened and which were presently shaping my life here in Paris, it got me thinking about the tricks the cosmos plays on us and how paradoxical life is.

We never know when the good or the bad will come knocking on the door. All we do is ponder and wait. About the only certainty we can count on is the total uncertainty of it all.

I had met Chris some sixteen months earlier in Athens, Greece, through Cleo, in the late spring of 1967. Cleo, born in Egypt of Greek parents, had opened up a boarding-house for errant tourists, mostly Americans.

Chris's father had emigrated from Greece to America eventually settling down in Ohio, where he had gotten married and where Chris was born and raised. Cleo and Chris, though citizens of other countries, always thought of themselves as Greeks.

After an all-night drive from Yugoslavia, I arrived in Athens early one morning and went to the American Express office to replace some lost traveler's checks, wire money to a friend in Istanbul, and pick up my mail.

My plan was to stay in Athens for just a couple of days, as my final destination was the island of Hydra. Through the efforts of Milo, a friend in Paris, I was on my way to meet an Italian film-producer who had hired me to help him write a script for a film he wanted to make.

Upon returning from a recent visit to Japan, I had written a rather whimsical story about sumo wrestling meant to poke fun at how serious the Japanese are about this old and very traditional all-male sport. The producer had read it, liked it, and wanted me to work with him.

I was surprised that anybody knew or was even familiar with the story. Anyway, this was going to be my first foray into that strange and murky world of celluloid and make-believe.

I was looking through my mail outside the American Express office when I struck up a conversation with an American couple who had also just arrived. They were on their way to Cleo's and suggested I go with them since I, too, needed a place to stay while trying to get in touch with the Italian producer.

When we got to Cleo's, breakfast was being served on a terrace at the back of the small building overlooking a vacant piece of land where an excavation was taking place.

Two young soldiers with their M-16s lazily draped over their shoulders were standing by the site. Greece was then under the control of a clique of Army colonels.

They had organized a *coup d'état* and had installed a military junta. Greece's king had fled to England, and rumors had it that the junta would not let him come back. In the meantime, the king was supposed to be plotting to get rid of the colonels from his forced exile in London.

Cleo was a handsome woman, probably in her late fifties, who radiated an Old-World charm that made it possible to like and trust her. She told me she did not have a single room available just then, but that if I did not mind sharing a room with another American, I was welcome to stay.

Sharing a room with someone I did not know, however, was not high on my priority list. I had also left Paris because I did not want to continue sharing quarters with my girlfriend.

"Cleo, you're asking me to share a room with a total stranger who is not even female." She got a kick out of my saying that. "Let me get some breakfast first, and then we'll see."

The modern city of Athens reminds me of Burbank, California—bland. Like Burbank, it is made up of apartment buildings without distinguishing features. Both cities seem to be missing something;

4

however, it is in the ancient ruins that Athens is different. Nothing can prepare a first-time visitor for the majestic beauty of the Parthenon or the other ancient monuments still standing in the city.

The chattering of the crowd that early morning at, Cleo's, got me thinking about the other Americans sitting there. Everyone seemed to be in high spirits. I felt old among them, though I was just a few years older than they were.

A European friend of mine has a pet theory about most Americans and the way we behave with strangers when we first meet them. He says those first few minutes are critical due to our tendency to tell people we have just met the story of our lives, without being asked, after which we seem to run out of topics of conversation.

It makes us look frivolous, immature and self-centered, he argues. He also claims that most Americans know the rest of the world through a distant, benign, but pervasive television watching.

That is how we remove ourselves from life's realities. It is also how we construct our own view of the world: Through the narrow confines of television viewing. We do not read books or newspapers. We are oblivious of others in the world. It does not seem to impact us at all.

We are what he jokingly calls "the best-informed-ignoramus-citizens around." We exhibit a self-centeredness blinding us to the place we occupy in the world. It deforms not only our view of it but also our place in it. But he still loves the U.S., he says.

Around me, I could hear all sorts of comments and ideas from the people sitting there. All I had to do was close my eyes, and I was back in the States at a crowded college cafeteria during lunch hour. Everyone was making plans. Plans about everything!

The bits of conversation that drifted my way spoke of a great sense of adventure, excitement, youthful enthusiasm, and curiosity about the world at large. I was not totally convinced my friend's criticism about Americans was fair.

I found myself reflecting upon the many reasons why I came to Greece. It was true I was going to attempt to write a film script for this producer, and that my girlfriend and I had had enough of each other. It was also true that lately I had been feeling restless and in a bit of a rut.

I guess my ennui was an accumulation of many things that individually did not amount to much. When I added them up, however, it resulted in a sense of annoyance and a longing to make some changes in my life—though I was not sure just what kinds of changes were necessary.

I needed to filter my restlessness through a different prism, hoping it would help me understand what was happening. I was looking for simpler things, different things.

A change of geography and atmosphere or *ambiance,* as the French would put it, might help me clarify the confusions and contradictions, presenting me with new ideas, new perspectives.

Soon just about everyone left the terrace except for a man sitting at a corner table with a dog by his feet, and a man and a woman sitting at another table. The man with the dog ordered a couple of fried eggs, which the waiter brought him.

After smelling them, he shook his head and sent them back. A few moments later, the waiter brought him another pair of eggs. The man smelled the eggs and seemed satisfied. He then placed the plate by the dog.

At first, the dog did not bother looking at the plate. Finally, it got up, sniffed the food, looked at the man, and shook its head clearly indicating: No! The man moved his head up and down sternly indicating: Yes!

Dog and man stared at each other without moving. It was a standoff! After a few moments, and with weary energy, the dog began eating ever so slowly while giving the clear impression his heart was not in it.

The dog finished and licked the plate very delicately. The man then took a piece of toast, and after spreading butter and jam on it put it on the dog's plate. The previous routine was repeated with the dog finally eating the toast with the same weary lack of energy.

Only when it was done did it acknowledge the man by wagging its tail furiously. I had the strange impression that, in the game they were playing, the roles of master and pet had been reversed.

The woman from the couple got up and walked over to pet the dog. She was tall, probably in her forties with certain hardness to her looks, yet when she spoke, her voice was soft and very pleasant. There was something asymmetrical and incongruous about her demeanor, as the voice and looks did not seem to come from the same person.

She said her name was Mary, and her friend was Evan. They came from Australia. She also added that while she and Evan were sharing a room, they were not lovers but just friends.

I could not guess why she felt the need to explain that. The man with the dog said his name was Stewart, the dog's name was Percy, and they came from England. Cleo came back a few moments later to find out what I had decided.

The breakfast and the prospect of having to go out and look for a hotel had made me tired, so I told her I would be willing to share the room with her other guest after all.

"His name is Chris. He's American, but you can't meet him because he's in jail."

Her voice and manner suggested she was not comfortable sharing too much information with me.

"He's a good boy, and I'm very worried about what may happen to him," she added.

"What did he do?"

"He didn't do anything. It's this damn fascist government," she said, with a sense of disdain in her voice.

"Have you tried the American Embassy? That would be his best bet."

"The American Embassy . . . a den of incompetents?"

A frown appeared on her face and she looked at me as if I had suggested something foolish like tying up a hungry dog with a long chain of freshly made beef sausages.

I told her I had a couple of contacts in Athens who could perhaps help, but what I really needed was rest. Once my head was clear I would try to give her a hand.

6

She said she understood and then took me up to the room I would be sharing with this jailbird. I went to sleep right away, which was somewhat unusual for me.

It was past noon when I woke up. Though I travel a lot, and have slept in countless strange rooms, I still cannot get used to waking up in unfamiliar surroundings. The building seemed very quiet. After taking a shower, I went down to the terrace.

The man was still sitting at the same table as earlier, and playing solitaire while the dog rested by his feet. I had the impression they had not moved at all. Cleo and a man were sitting at another table. She invited me to join them for lunch.

I had given some thought to helping her friend Chris. A few years ago, I had met a Greek guy in Bangkok, while I was in the Army, who had told me he knew everyone worth knowing in Greece, and to look him up if I ever came to Athens. His name was Demetrios. I still had his address. The only problem was that he happened to be a mercenary.

The thought of calling on him to help Cleo's friend get out of jail was kind of dubious since I did not know the details of the incarceration. I also did not know how Cleo would react to the news about Demetrios, and what he did for a living.

I decided to keep some details to myself and see how things worked out. We had a long and leisurely lunch, during which the conversation was of no consequence, topped off with some wonderful strong coffee and a cognac.

"What about this Chris, why is he really in jail?" I asked her.

"It was a silly incident. It was the government's fault. He doesn't deserve to be a prisoner. I'm worried about him."

"How bad is it?"

"He insulted some government officials using bad words."

Since a military government was in charge, this had caused problems for Chris with the authorities; however, Cleo did not seem interested in giving me any more details.

"I told you, I know someone who lives here in Athens. He said he had some connections. He might be able to suggest a way out of this—that is if I can find him," I said.

"I have asked some people here to see if they can help, but they're afraid. You would be a nice man if you try to help Chris."

She gave me a big smile and held my hand, which was kind of surprising. I showed her Demetrios's address.

"You'd better get a taxi to take you there. I'll pay for it," she added.

"You don't have to do that."

She then gave me walking directions to the nearest post office, as I needed to send a wire to my Italian producer informing him I was in Athens. At the post office, I did manage to make myself understood in a mixture of French, English, and hand gestures.

The woman behind the counter reassured me the message would get to Hydra. Maybe today, maybe tomorrow, but it would get there.

Athens was sticky and humid at that hour of the day, with very little traffic. But I was able to get a taxi, and the driver had no trouble understanding where I wanted to go. It turned out he had lived in Atlanta for a couple of years and spoke English. The first words out of his mouth after he found out that my home was in San Francisco were:

"Frisco! Then you know Thanatakis?"

"No, I don't know him."

"You don't know Thanatakis?" He was surprised.

"No, who is he?"

"He's my cousin."

It seemed normal to him that I should personally know his cousin or about his cousin if I had lived in San Francisco.

"Everybody knows him!"

"Well, I've never met him."

I could tell he was clearly disappointed I was not among his cousin's best friends.

"I'll give you his address because when you go back you must meet him. Tell him I sent you."

"OK. Before taking me to where I'm going, I want you to drive by the Acropolis."

"Why?"

"I want to see it."

"This is the time only for tourists. If you want to be like the rest of the Americans who come here and visit the Acropolis and think they are now experts in Greek history, you're crazy."

"I want to see it, and I know something about Greek history, too."

"Typical. You think you can look in the Yellow Pages or buy a Sears and Roebuck catalogue and you know everything. What should I call you now: Professor?"

"The Yellow Pages and Sears and Roebuck don't sell history or travel guides. Anyway, why are you busting my chops?"

"No normal person drives by to see the Parthenon at this time of day." He was very adamant. "If you want to see other tourists you go there, and you'll see them with their stupid Kodaks, and hear their vulgar, loud talk. If you want to see the Parthenon, you must see it early in the morning or at night with a full moon shining on it. Now, *that's* something."

"I have no idea when the next full moon is going to take place. And even if it is this evening, I want to see the Parthenon now. But if you don't want to take me, I'll get another taxi to do it."

"The problem with you Americans is that you don't know the difference between a hole in the ground and your own assholes," he said.

Then he started to mutter in Greek as we drove wildly over to the Parthenon. After we got there, I saw how right he was. The place was swarming with tourists and their ubiquitous Kodak cameras.

"Happy now?" He asked.

He was obviously relishing his victory over me, after which he drove to Demetrios's place at what can only be described as at Formula One, Grand Prix speed. He now seemed in a happier mood as he started to hum a song.

"Where are you staying?"

"Oh, you wouldn't know it."

"I know everything!"

"It's a small place called Cleo's."

"I know it. I'll come to see you later," he said, as if I had invited him to do so.

I dismissed his idea and paid the fare. He refused to take a tip and probably burned off half of his tires when he drove away. He had dropped me off in front of a modern building, several stories high, on the outskirts of Athens. The apartments each seemed to occupy entire floors.

Looking at the expensive cars parked on the street it occurred to me that whoever lived on that street was either in the shipping business or the drug business—or both.

I thought the cars would certainly have brought joy to the heart of any run-of-the-mill Beverly Hills car-thief on the prowl. For a moment, I hesitated; I was not sure what the hell I was doing there.

I crossed the street and looked at the directory. Of all of the names listed, two of them were in English. Demetrios's was one of them. Finding his name so openly listed surprised me.

If you are a mercenary, the last thing you want is to have people know where you live. His neighbors most likely did not know what he did for a living.

I pressed the buzzer a couple of times. Finally, I heard a woman's voice as if I had woken her, then a man's-tired voice. After I identified myself, there was some hesitation from the man.

I imagined him going through a mental Rolodex looking for the name, finding it, and matching it with some hazy memory, then concluding I was not a visitor from hell—from a best-forgotten past—coming back to collect a personal debt.

Demetrios had not changed much from what I remembered. He sported the same big hairy chest and the strong arms and hands he once boasted he used to kill men. He was wearing a golden-colored robe that was much too small. It made him look like a half-naked bear, which made me laugh.

Right behind him was a very attractive young woman with a classic Greek profile rubbing the sleep from her eyes. She was wearing a robe—probably his—that was much too large for her.

"Alex, you bum, where have you been?" He had a big smile on his face.

"I'm sorry I woke you up."

It suddenly dawned on me that no self-respecting Athenian would be expecting or receiving visitors at the siesta hour.

"It's about time you showed up."

He gave me a bear hug as if I was his lost cousin from America. It felt as if he was expecting my visit. This was a crazy idea, as he had no way of knowing I would show up.

The apartment was large, bright, cool and comfortable, tastefully decorated with antiques mixed with African sculptures and safari trophies.

The whole set up sort of jolted me because mercenaries deal with death; however, the apartment was anything but deathlike. The living room offered a wonderful view of the sea.

"Meet Helen, the most beautiful wife in the whole world," Demetrios said, turning to the young woman who smiled a shy, embarrassed smile. I shook her hand.

"Welcome," she said, then excused herself and left the room.

He was genuinely happy to see me and immediately poured a couple of double whiskeys. We toasted to life and Greek women. Helen came back a few minutes later carrying a tray of sweets, some strong Turkish coffee for Demetrios and me, and his robe, which she placed right next to him.

She had exchanged his robe for a lovely, feminine and stylish one that gave the impression she was wearing very little under it, but it was not cheap or vulgar. As she sat next to him, he absent-mindedly started to stroke her legs.

"Things have surely changed," I said. "The last time I saw you in Bangkok you were staying in that rat-infested firetrap, remember?"

"Bangkok! I love Bangkok," he gave out a big loud laugh that shook his entire body. "That's where we met," he said to Helen. Her smile seemed to suggest she was familiar with the story.

"Yeah, I loved Bangkok, too."

"But you didn't like Vietnam?"

"I hated it. I can't say that it was an exhilarating experience."

I did not know why he had mentioned Vietnam. He looked at me and seemed about to say something, then looked at his wife and shrugged his shoulders.

Maybe the look on her face told him that it was not a pleasant subject to be discussing. I certainly avoided it if I could help it. She probably saw it on my face.

I was uncomfortable, and I did not know if it was the simple fact that I was not sure what I was doing there. Or that I suspected Helen knew that I knew she was half-naked under her robe, or that Demetrios was partially showing his private parts through the small robe he was wearing.

From deep within the apartment, I thought I heard a baby cry, though I was not sure. Demetrios wanted to know what was going on with my life: Was I working as a journalist as I had once told him I was going to do? I said I had not done it for a while.

"There are too many guys calling themselves journalists. Vultures are what you call them, right," I said. He laughed when I reminded him of that. "My aims are simpler now. I just want to make a few bucks."

"You don't want to save the world from bad guys anymore?"

His own words seemed to amuse him, as he had once accused me of having my head up in the clouds. He was happy to learn I had been hired by an Italian producer to write a film-script, and he wanted to know the details. My friend Milo had convinced the producer to hire me.

I had been surprised when he did because I did not consider myself much of a writer, more of a hack really. On the other hand, I was willing to work for cheap. Demetrios greeted this part of the story with hearty laughter that made his large stomach shake.

"I wrote an article about you," I said.

"You did?" He looked at me, surprised.

"Yes. Remember you asked me to do it?"

"Yeah, you didn't forget." He turned to look at Helen. "So now I'm famous!" he said, laughing. She smiled.

"Can I read it?"

"I don't have a copy with me. But when I get back to Paris, I'll mail you a copy."

"You promise?"

"Yeah, I'll send it to you."

"You're still a *masterpiece*," he said.

This was a joke between us. Greek men constantly use the word *malaka* or "masturbator" to address each other. Demetrios had changed the word the first time we met and had called me a "masterpiece" instead of a "masturbator".

He had been concerned about my "American puritanical sensibilities," he explained. I had told him to shove it "where the sun don't shine." After laughing and hugging me, he had declared that, for an American, I was OK.

I now explained the situation about Chris. He listened, his face emptied of emotion. His eyes held a neutral look. For a moment, I thought he had not understood. He put his glass down, refilled it, and signaled to me to do likewise, but I declined.

Then another young woman suddenly appeared in the room. A minute ago, she was not there; I blinked, and there she was. It was almost as if a magician had made her materialize out of thin air.

She was carrying a small baby who was perhaps about three months old. Now I understood why I had heard a baby's cry a few minutes earlier. The young woman could have passed for Helen's sister. An innocent yet not so innocent beauty about her made me hesitate to look in her direction.

There was, also, something mysterious, fleeting, wistful and indefinable about her. It was as if she was there, yet she was not. That made her attractive and forbidden at the same time.

The way she looked at me with her dark penetrating eyes felt like she could read my mind. She scrutinized me, looking not at me but through me, questioning why I was there, my secrets, my desires, who was I?

Something passed between us. It was pleasant, but unnerving. No woman had affected me like that before. I had the strange sensation of being in the presence of a woman of many secrets, mysteries, and hidden truths. The effect was hypnotic, magical, ephemeral—and odd.

"This is my cousin, Iris," Helen said.

"*Vous parlez français, Monsieur ?*" Iris asked.

"*Oui.*"

Iris's serious demeanor and her use of formal French to ask if I spoke French, sort of took me by surprise. I do not know why. We shook hands. Her hand was warm and slightly damp.

"*Enchantée,*" she said.

"*Moi aussi.*"

Of course, I was enchanted to have met this sloe-eyed beauty.

She handed the baby to Demetrios, who started making faces. The baby cooed and gurgled in response. He handled the baby with a great deal of care and fatherly love.

In Demetrios's big hands the baby seemed fragile, naked, tiny—almost like a toy. I could not help thinking what he had said about using his hands to kill people.

Both women looked at the doting father with pleasure. He handed the baby to Helen, who immediately put the baby to her breast. For some mysterious reason her breast seemed to glow in a nice, warm, strange way.

It was as if she had a light inside it. Iris then left the room as softly as she had come in, and I felt agitated, though I could not tell exactly why.

Watching Helen nurse her baby and seeing the bond between mother and child made me feel disconnected, alone, rootless. The whole world belonged to me but I belonged to no one.

No one claimed me. I also wondered if I would ever be lucky enough to find a soft and comforting breast to rest my weary self on.

Demetrios got up and left me in my reverie alone with Helen and the baby. The only sound heard in the room was the baby suckling happily. Mother and child had eyes only for each other.

Demetrios came back. He had changed into street clothes and had strapped a small revolver to his waist. A crazy thought ran through my head: How dangerous is it going to be to get this Chris character out of jail?

Demetrios stood right next to Helen, watching her and the baby. He said something, and she gave him a big smile.

"Come, we pay someone a visit," he said to me.

I said goodbye to Helen and followed him out of the apartment. His brand-new Jaguar had the latest gadgets. He slipped a cassette of the Beatles into the deck and with the sound of "All You Need Is Love" going full blast, we tore out of the garage.

"We're going to see the ex-chief of police," he shouted over the music.

"We need the new chief," I shouted back.

"The old chief is related to the new one, very convenient." I got a look that one gives to the uninitiated. He smiled a cobra smile.

I asked about the present political situation in Greece, and he answered that he did not want to talk about politics. As far as he was concerned, politicians were the scum of the earth, and they should all be shot without mercy.

"I can be satisfied to kill a few for peanuts," he said, and he laughed again.

"Are you still freelancing?"

"We do not talk about it."

I felt detached sitting next to him as we drove through Athens. My thoughts drifted to Cécile back in Paris, and I wondered if she had gone to see her old ex-boyfriend.

It seemed every time we had a quarrel or she went into a funk, I would not see her for a few days. She always went to stay with her ex.

At first, it had surprised me—until she explained, it had nothing to do with sex. They no longer had or wanted that kind of relationship.

It had more to do with seeking comfort in old surroundings with old friends when things got wacky. Thinking about Cécile I made plans to wire Milo instructions to give her some money—she could use it.

Then I wondered about Demetrios's wife. Where did he find her? Did she know what he did for a living? I wanted to ask him about Iris, too. Maybe later, I thought. We were driving erratically around Athens. It was almost as if we were trying to shake a tail.

He had said to me that in his line of "business" you had to pretend to be "cool"—the words he used back in Bangkok—when in fact all of your senses were constantly focused in making sure there would be no surprises waiting for you around the next corner.

"This is no throw of dice. You want to know results before you enter room," he had said.

"How do you do that?"

"People have it, people don't. When you don't, you don't know because you're dead before you know you don't have it."

His English seemed tortured, but I understood what he meant. Today, however, he did not give the impression that we were being shadowed. Perhaps, it was just an old habit, a tic; though, in the kind of business he was in, I suppose it never hurts to be on the alert—one gets to live longer.

Then he talked about the new baby and Helen. He also mentioned that he had two other boys much older from a previous marriage, shouting all this over the din of the Beatles' music.

He did not get to see his sons much because his ex-wife did not want them to have much contact with him. Of course, whenever he was late with the monthly-check, she let him know right away.

"Don't get ever married," he said.

"Wait a second; this is your second marriage."

"I'm a romantic fool," he said, and laughed aloud.

I did not remember that he had mentioned his sons when I met him in Bangkok. He did not provide many details about how he had become a mercenary. He said he had spent a great deal of time in Africa, where the CIA had recruited him.

Although he never mentioned the name, the way in which he referred to the "outfit" left no doubt he was talking about the American spy agency.

He had gone to Vietnam and had done several short tours. "Going fishing," was the expression he used to describe what he did there. Demetrios did not preach politics and never pretended he was doing God's work. The people he was paid to kill deserved to die. Period.

He had also said that by staying in his line of business the chances of collecting his old-age pension were next to none. It was not fatalistic or morbid as much as accepting that such a reality came with the job.

"One morning you get up, it's the last time you see the sun," he had said.

"And it doesn't bother you?"

"That's the life," he said, and shrugged his shoulders.

Surprisingly, he did not think he had any personal enemies. He loved the whole world! I never knew if it was his or my own warped sense of humor that made me believe he really did not have any enemies.

"Of course, he doesn't. He has exterminated them all," said the editor—in a typical editor's sarcastic fashion—of a magazine, I had submitted the story about Demetrios. I hated the bastard for saying that.

The business with Chris intrigued Demetrios. I told him I knew very little other than he was an American whose father was Greek and who was in jail because he had insulted the junta.

"So, what about Chris, this *malaka*? You're working on a story? Is that how you want to make money?" His voice was filled with suspicion.

"No, it's just a case of wanting to help a fellow American. Besides, Cleo is troubled by it, and she struck me as being a nice lady who wants to help a friend."

13

We drove into a small square with outdoor cafés and tables all around it. We stopped. While he went into a café to make a phone call I sat outside, drank a beer, and listened to the sounds of Greece around me. The memory of an old professor I had in college came to me.

He was a Greek scholar teaching a course in classical mythology. His method was unorthodox, really off the wall. We studied the *Iliad*, but we did it backwards. He started with the end first.

"In ancient times everyone knew the story," he had said. "The ancient Greeks recognized that the magic and beauty of the poem, the drama, were in the journey it took us through and not in the outcome. That's why it is as fresh today as it was then."

Most of the class did not quite get the idea at first, but we went along out of fear that if we did not, he would flunk us out. Very often, he got us to assemble at some place other than the classroom and, usually, the meetings would be held at night.

One time, we met just before dawn in his backyard, drank champagne, and quietly watched the sun as it emerged from the shadows of the night.

He challenged us to imagine, as the ancient Greeks had done, that the sun was the god Helios in his golden chariot traveling across the vault of the sky every day.

Miraculously, the professor got everyone to come join him so early in the morning, but we were never the same afterward. We had experienced something new, mysterious, everlasting, and powerful.

Nobody complained after that. And we met everywhere! In parks, warehouses, football fields, restaurants, churches, parking lots, libraries, courthouses, hospitals, synagogues, gas stations, supermarkets, coffee shops—you name it. We even met at a mortuary; that was spooky. The *Iliad* is also about death, he reminded us.

Once, we met on the beach around midnight. It was a beautiful, clear evening, the sky filled with shiny and distant stars. As we sat on the sand surrounded by darkness and sounds of waves softly lapping the rocky shore, he started to recite parts of the *Iliad* in classic Greek.

The professor had said the poem had been kept alive, in those ancient times, through the tradition of oral storytelling. As I was looking up at the sky and listening to the words, the story of the Trojan War became alive in a way I had never experienced before or since.

It felt like we were right in the middle of it, filling our imaginations with poetry, fantasy, and magic.

The theme of the *Iliad*, stated at the beginning of the poem, has to do with the wrath of Achilles, the great Greek warrior who refused to fight for the Greeks.

A young maiden, Briseis, who was part of his war booty, had been taken away from him by Agamemnon, the chief of all of the Greek warriors. Achilles got pissed and refused to fight. The Trojans took advantage of the situation and wreaked havoc among the Greek ranks.

The remarkable thing about the professor reciting the poem was that in the sounds of the words—even though we did not understand them—in the drum-like music of those ancient words, one got the entire sense of the story.

It resonated with the personal drama of war, of men engaged in a giant struggle, brutal, deadly, and larger than their lives. It was loud, rumbling, deep, and warlike, filled with passion, overflowing with the fury of revenge, the brutality of the battle, and the agony of dying.

The professor said the *Iliad* was for everyone across mankind's history because of the human emotions it portrayed. In those ancient words, as he recited them, we imagined an Achilles larger than life, like a caged animal in his tent, enraged, fuming at what he perceived an injustice done to his honor, dignity, and manhood.

Achilles only goes back to fight the Trojans after his friend Patroclus is killed on the battlefield by Hector, the great Trojan warrior. Achilles kills Hector, after which the Greeks were then able to win the Trojan War.

Somehow, the sounds of Modern Greek I heard, as I sat in the café waiting for Demetrios, did not resemble the deep, rumbling, rolling sounds of the classical Greek I remembered when the professor recited the poem that night, at the beach—sounds that made such a lasting impression on me.

"We must leave, but I will meet you later," Demetrios said.

He was standing right next to me. I had not heard him come back. It was uncanny how he moved. One would have thought a man his size would not be so nimble. To say he was not light on his feet would be like saying a ballerina had lead feet.

He said he needed to go alone to a rendezvous and would come by Cleo's later to take me to eat the best-tasting lamb chop sandwiches in this part of the world.

"I will have news about that *pusty*, Chris," he added.

Pusty was also another word Greek males use constantly when addressing each other. It is derogatory. He dropped me off at the hotel. Cleo was happy and relieved when she heard about Demetrios's efforts.

I thought it best to keep certain facts about him to myself, as I did not want to have to give a lot of explanations. I reminded her that he was an old professional acquaintance of mine.

"Do you think he can get him out?"

"If anybody can, I think he can."

Suddenly, I felt tired. I had not come all the way from Paris to get some miscreant I did not even know out of jail, to find Demetrios, to be rattled by a young woman, or to eat lamb chop sandwiches—even if they were made out of ambrosia.

I went up to my room to rest. Sometime later, Cleo came to tell me the Italian producer was calling.

The voice on the phone was of someone suffering from a cold. He was friendly, and expansive with a clipped British accent, and said they were not quite ready for me.

He would get in touch in a couple of days. Before hanging up, he asked that if I needed money to let him know, and he would arrange to have his banker wire it.

Afterward, I decided to call Cécile in Paris but realized I did not know where she would be. Instead, I called Milo.

He was out so I left a message with his housekeeper for Milo to give to Cécile—I knew she would be calling him—and to please tell her I was fine. I also asked Milo to give her some money. I knew this would upset her because she was always accusing me of wanting to buy her affection and loyalty.

She argued this was a way for me not to face my own shortcomings. In a sense, she was right but not completely. I was sharing the money because I wanted to and not because I was trying to bribe her.

Cécile and I have lived through some interesting times. She has never wanted to settle down with anybody. She once said, I was probably a good candidate, even if I was American, too self-centered, irresponsible, and unwilling to commit to love or to life.

According to her, I was always drifting out of step with life's rhythm, and it was by my own choice, never wanting or needing anybody, excluding and secluding myself from life.

"If I'm all of those things, why do you stay with me?"

"Parce que je t'aime et je suis folle," she said. "And I'm also crazy about you."

When I was leaving for Greece, I had asked her to come with me. She said no.

"You know you don't want me to go with you."

"That's not true."

"Why didn't you ask me to go to New York with you?"

"Because you say you hated New York the time we were there."

"That doesn't mean you shouldn't ask me to come with you."

"But if I know you're going to say no, what's the point of asking?"

"You have to be chic, polite and have good manners."

"I'm chic and polite and I do have good manners."

"Excuses, excuses . . . typical male behavior."

That she was unhappy when we had been to New York—the very reason I had not asked her to come with me this time around—has never been part of her reproach.

She had gone on to argue the only reason I was asking her to come to Greece now was out of guilt and dishonesty—it was a sham. It was not. It is hard to try to guess what anybody thinks, what Cécile thinks, or what any woman thinks.

Female companionship has never been a real problem in my life. The trick, my friends have always said, is to find the right one and hang onto her. I would like to know what the sign is indicating just who the right woman is. In the abstract, one could argue any woman can be right for any man.

After the phone call to Milo, I went back to my room. Sometime later, there was another knock on the door. It was the taxi driver.

"I told you I'd come to see you," he said. Actually, I was glad to see him again. He said he was getting off his shift early tonight.

"I have come to invite you to eat the best lamb chop sandwiches in the world!" he added. I started to laugh. What is it with these *malakas* and their lamb chop sandwiches?

"Someone else has already invited me, but you're welcome to join us."

He seemed a bit disappointed and upon leaving made me promise to wait for him, as he would be back in a couple of hours. Suddenly, I had this crazy urge to call Demetrios's house secretly hoping I could talk to Iris.

Helen answered the phone. She said that Iris asked about me, and she laughed and thought it was all very charming and innocent.

I lied when I told her that I had hardly paid attention to Iris other than to notice that they resembled each other, and that they were both very attractive women. The last statement was no lie, and I could tell she was pleased I said it.

She repeated they were cousins, that Iris was visiting for a few days, and that she came from Crete. Women from Crete are very passionate and strong, she said.

I was not sure why she said it and was on the verge of asking but decided it was better to ignore her words. Whatever her reasons were, it was none of my business.

We spoke in French, and she explained that she and Iris had lived in Paris for a couple of years as students. She attended the Sorbonne—my old Alma matter--and Iris the school of *Sciences Po*—Institute of Political Science. We talked about several Parisian cafés I knew very well, which were also favorites of theirs.

"*J'aime beaucoup le Café de La Paix à L'Opéra,*" Helen said.

I told her I also loved the *Café de la Paix*. I had spent many lazy hours sitting on its terrace watching the world go by while nursing a glass of wine.

She added she had not heard from Demetrios, and she did not expect to hear from him. Most of the time he did not tell her what he did she said, somewhat, wistfully.

The conversation with Helen lifted my spirits. Afterward, I felt a strange and happy sensation knowing I had made an impression on Iris. I wondered how people could go back and live in some small village in the middle of nowhere, especially after living in great cities like Paris.

What did it take to do that? I tried to see myself returning to Daly City where I grew up, back in California, but I did not see how I could do it.

After dark, I went down to the terrace. The air was sweet and warm. The moon, not quite full, hanging in the sky was surrounded by transparent white clouds.

The terrace was crowded, and the talk seemed to be about museums, excavation sites, old ruins that had been visited and catalogued—sweet memories to be stored away for those inevitable and future dreary days when living would turn into a blur and life would be filled with longing, regrets, sadness, and the inescapable cynicism.

Memories to be recalled when existence would overwhelm us with its bitterness, disappointments, and failures. When the heart, lonely, and in sheer desperation, searching for love and happiness, would long for the dreams that made it pure, that had sustained it.

For when life, in her inexorable march toward an outcome no one understood, would no longer be as happy, carefree, and innocent as everything was on this particularly spring night.

The couple, Karen and Ron, whom I had met that morning at the American Express office, came by to say hello. They were very cheerful. They came from Kansas City; had met at the university, and were now engaged to be married.

Both sets of parents had decided to spring for a prenuptial honeymoon trip just so the lovebirds would know for sure marriage was for

17

them. So far, everything was working out as planned. There had been some minor squabbles but nothing major or drastic.

"We're going to prove to our folks we're adults," Ron said.

"Yes, that we're responsible and made for each other," she said, and hugged Ron.

"Your parents must be pretty understanding," I said.

"They have no choice. This is the 60s, the Age of Aquarius," she replied.

Their lives had been scheduled down to the last detail. They would have good jobs. Ron had studied accounting. She was going to be a teacher. Karen would get pregnant when she became twenty-five years old—two kids was the limit—then she would stay home while Ron continued earning the bucks.

Later, there would be a big house with a white picket fence, two fabulously well-behaved children, and money for the kids' private schools and for the parents' retirement.

Their purpose in coming to Europe now was to scout locations for that golden future retirement! Actually, it was all very innocent and sweet. They were twenty-two years old, though Ron was younger by a couple of months. Spain and Italy showed great potential. They had no opinion yet about Greece.

When I suggested that France would not be a bad choice, they responded they did not like the French, though the food was better than in England. When I also suggested that back home there were some really nice and interesting places to consider they agreed, though the prospect of retiring in the States did not seem to thrill them.

They asked if I knew of a good restaurant not too far from Cleo's hotel. They were leaving early the next day for Crete so it was going to be an early dinner, then to bed. I told them they probably knew more about Athens than I did.

They had visited the place whereas I seemed to have spent most of my time since arriving trying to get some guy I did not even know out of jail.

"This is very interesting," Karen said.

Ron said it was his turn to call the States, so he left to make the phone call.

"Are you a bounty hunter?" She asked a moment later.

"No. What makes you think that?"

"I don't know . . . something. So, what do you do?"

"I'm in the 'leisure business'," I answered, hoping to humor her and because I did not know what else to say. Besides, I always find that people who ask what you do right after meeting them are never interested in finding out anything else about you—who you are. All they seem to care about is listening to the sound of their own voices.

"And what is that?"

"You know, 'ladies of leisure' kind of thing."

"That's it, I knew it!" She said it as if she had just won a bet. She was looking at me in such a strange way that it threw me for a loop.

"I told Ron I thought you were either working for the CIA or in some kind of funny business," she added.

"What kind of funny business?"

"Something illegal, not very Christian," she answered. I started to laugh, but she did not seem to appreciate my levity.

"What made you think that?"

"I don't know. It's just a feeling . . . the way you act."

"And how do I act?"

"I have a sense about these things. I don't know if I would trust you," she said as if this had been on her mind for a while. Her attitude was a bit amusing.

"Why would you not trust me?"

"I can't put my finger on it. You're not like Ron."

"How is Ron?" I asked, unsure if it was the right thing to be asking.

"Well, I don't mean he's better than you. I can't figure you out. And I'm very good at figuring people out."

"There isn't much to figure out. Anyway, about the 'ladies of leisure' business, I was just trying to be funny."

"I think you're serious."

"Come on, I'm not."

"I don't know," she said, mistrust in her voice. "You escape me."

I laughed. Without Ron around, she seemed very different. Poor Ron, I thought, he is going to have his hands full with her.

The taxi driver then joined us. He had changed clothes and had apparently taken a bath in some kind of men's cologne for he reeked of it, and he was a charmer.

In no time at all, he had Karen laughing and listening intently to his wild adventures while living in Atlanta.

It was clear he had set his sights on her and was not about to let go. A couple of times I tried to interject that Ron was taking too long with the phone call, but it did not seem to make any difference.

Karen had found a guy who was wooing her probably in a way she had never been wooed before. Silently, I sat listening to their talk. They did not take much notice of me.

She had changed. She no longer seemed the naïve, young, innocent, American abroad. Even her laughter had changed. It was throaty, sexy, filled with feminine mystery, excitement, and desire.

It was no longer the laughter of an immature girl but was now the laughter of a young woman who perhaps, for the first time, sees herself as an object of desire to strange men. The metamorphosis was surprising and intriguing.

"You must be a dancer," he said.

"How can you tell?" Karen was obviously flattered.

"Oh, it's a feeling I have."

"Well, I'm a good dancer but Ron is not."

"We will teach him," he said and took her hand and kissed it. She was enthralled by his *Scaramouch* gesture.

The taxi driver really knew the game, and he played it with zest. One had to admire him for his audacity. I had to accept, however grudgingly, that here was a guy quite good at seducing impressionable young women.

Karen was responding to his charm shamelessly—a combination of innocence and decadence—attracted by the forbidden fruit all mixed up

19

with what mom said not to do. It did not seem too farfetched to imagine they were going to jump each other's bones at any moment.

By the time Ron came back, Karen and the taxi driver were playing footsie under the table. He had placed his hand on her thigh, caressing it, and she did not seem to mind. I had to hand it to the taxi driver. I also had to admit Karen had fooled me. She introduced the taxi driver to Ron. His name was Manos.

He stood and shook Ron's hand. By way of introduction, Karen told Ron that Manos knew some great places to eat and dance, and she now wanted to go out and have fun.

"We have to get up early in the morning," Ron said.

"Please. Manos will teach me how to dance to Greek music."

"You too must learn to dance to Greek music," Manos said to Ron and pretended to dance by himself. We all laughed.

I saw how pleased Karen was to find herself between two men competing for her affection, ready to do battle to be the chosen one. She already knew who would walk away with the trophy because it is always the female's decision. It has been thus since the beginning of time.

They asked me to join them, but I told them I was waiting for a friend, that perhaps we could get together later in the evening.

Manos wrote something on a piece of paper, handed it to me with a kind of prizewinner look in his eyes, and they left. He no longer seemed interested in taking me to eat "The best ambrosia-like food in the world!" I laughed. The night might turn out to be interesting, indeed.

Cleo came by later and said Demetrios had called. He had some news, was coming to see us, and wanted me to wait. Clearly, he had charmed her.

He did not show up until late in the evening. Two tall, beautiful, and classy young women, Lisa and Robin, accompanied him. They were twins who came from Minnesota by way of California. All three of them were in a jovial mood. He immediately started kidding me about Iris, his wife's cousin.

When I asked him why he had not brought her along, he said the only place he had permission to take her was to church on Sundays. The other bit of news was that the twins knew Chris, our jailbird. I wanted to know the details but Demetrios wanted to go and meet Cleo.

I told him she was probably in bed. He insisted we wake her up. I was not sure what the protocol was, though I did not think Big D., which was what I started calling him, was too interested in protocol. So off we marched to Cleo's private quarters. She was not surprised to see us.

We all crowded into the small bedroom. Demetrios acted toward her with all the deference due someone of position and status. He promised he would get Chris out of jail that very night.

With exaggerated politeness, he said he was giving her his word of honor. Tears appeared in her eyes. Demetrios's eyes were also glistening. The twins looked embarrassed, uncomfortable, and I just wanted to laugh.

"You must come with us," Demetrios said to Cleo.

"No, I will cry and embarrass everyone. All I care is that Chris will be coming home tonight," she said, with the seriousness of a parent anxiously waiting to be reunited with a wayward child.

When we got to the police station, a rather nondescript building, I was not surprised to see Demetrios behave as if he owned the place. He greeted the policemen as old friends, shaking hands and kissing them on the cheeks in typical European fashion. The cops, however, had eyes only for the twins.

Demetrios talked to the man in charge who apparently did not know what was going on. It was obvious he had not been given the word. Though I could not understand the conversation, I could sense the man was not amused and certainly not interested in releasing anybody.

"He doesn't believe me." Demetrios said to me, somewhat perplexed.

"Why not?"

"He's got no balls," he answered in a low voice.

Demetrios went back to talk to the man who still resisted the idea, and after arguing some more Demetrios seemed to convince him to make a phone call and tried to give him the paper with the number.

However, when the cop looked at the paper, he reacted as if Demetrios was handing him a piece of radioactive material or a message directly from hell.

The man did not want to touch it. He kept shaking his head, while Big D. kept pushing the paper toward him. You could see on the man's face that he was looking at his future, carefully weighing not making a phone call, against the outside chance the crazy character he had in front of him was telling the truth.

He got up from his chair and walked toward the door as if he had had enough of the whole affair. He stopped, turned around, and glanced at the other cops in the room looking for support. They all looked at him as if to say: It's your balls; you make the decision; you are the boss.

The man was not happy. I could see little beads of sweat on his forehead. The other cops also got very tense—the twins were forgotten for a moment.

Demetrios winked and smiled at me, obviously getting a kick out of what was going on. The cop walked back to his desk and after waiting a moment, he picked up the phone, very gingerly, and dialed. The phone conversation was probably over in about thirty seconds. The man was relieved.

His worried air was slowly giving way to having a great burden lifted off his shoulders. He smiled, maybe at his own good luck. The other cops started eyeing the twins again. Everything went back to normal. Big D. walked up to the man and kissed him on both cheeks. The man was smiling and embarrassed.

"Now we are brothers," Demetrios said to me, laughing, but without much conviction.

I had to admit, in spite of my own cynicism about these things, that the day would end with some kind of victory for Cleo and even Chris, whom I had now come to think of as someone I knew. The officer barked some orders, and two of his cops disappeared into the back of the building.

Then one of the twins reached into her oversized tote bag, pulled out a bottle of French cognac, and tried to hand it to the officer. He did not want to take the bottle.

There followed an animated discussion among all the Greeks. It was a divided camp. Some of the men seemed willing to take the cognac while others were reluctant. Demetrios served as the referee.

The whole incident was humorous for clearly the twins, the cognac, and the bonhomie—all were parts of a show Big D. had put together and it had worked.

Some glasses were finally produced, and we went on to toast to the love and friendship between Greeks and Americans when Chris walked into the room.

My first impression was that he would rather be sleeping. He was about my height, six feet tall, with a lean frame that made me think he might be a boxer. He was not a bad looking guy, and his eyes narrowed a lot when he looked at us.

He was wearing crumpled inmate clothes, his shoes had no laces, and he had no belt for his pants. He was holding them up with both hands. He was a bit bewildered, and his face was bruised. It was obvious he had been beaten up.

The twins were taken aback by his appearance. Demetrios walked over and gave him a bear hug. Then he started to talk to him in Greek. *Pusty* and *malaka* were the only two words I could identify. Big D. was giving Chris a lecture!

It was like the older brother giving the younger one a piece of his mind. Chris said something defiant to Demetrios and Big D. started to laugh. The other Greeks picked up the laughter.

Soon we were all laughing, passing the bottle, and drinking from it—except for the twins. Then the head cop went to a closet, took out Chris's civilian clothes, and handed them to him.

That was probably what made him really believe he was getting out. Another cop handed Chris the bottle of cognac, and he took a long drink. The Greeks cheered and clapped. One cop escorted Chris out of the room to show him where he could clean up.

When he returned, Chris had showered, shaved, had changed back into his civilian clothes, and looked respectable. His hair was slicked back, and he had a big smile on his battered face.

He embraced the twins then walked over to shake my hand firmly. We shook hands with the cops then walked out of the room, down a long corridor, and out of the building. Even the two cops standing outside shook Chris's hand.

I was walking behind Chris, who had one girl on each arm, when I heard him say one of the cops standing outside had also been among the ones who beat him up.

I had been thrown in jail once in Africa. It is not one of my fondest memories. While covering a local guerrilla war, Gilles, a Belgian photographer working with me, and I were arrested by government forces.

We had been crossing back and forth from guerrilla territories often, we thought we were safe; however, these guys evidently had not seen us before, or maybe they were just looking for live targets.

We could hear the soldiers laugh and talk among themselves as they stopped to reload their weapons. The shooting went on for about ten minutes—a lifetime for us—then suddenly stopped.

The next thing we knew, we were surrounded by soldiers who were pointing their AK-47s directly at us. It was hard to tell who was in charge, because they were jostling and shouting half angrily, half mockingly at us.

I was pissed. I saw that Gilles, one of the coolest guys I have worked with, was also pretty pissed and was not about to take any shit from them. But there were more of them, they had guns, and there was no doubt they would kill us without a second thought.

So, I half-whispered to Gilles to keep quiet. He was not a happy camper, but he kept his cool.

They blindfolded us, and after a long walk, they shoved us into separate rooms. They pushed me into a corner and ordered me not to move or talk or I would be shot. I knew the threat was not an empty one.

The stench in the room was overwhelming. Then the blindfolds were removed. A tiny, naked, lightbulb hanging from a long electric cord was the only source of illumination.

After I got used to the semi-darkness, I saw that the room was large, filthy, dingy, sinister, nauseating, and deadly—like a morgue. I also realized I was not alone.

There were about two dozen or so males in the room, although I could not tell their ages. They did not act as if they had seen me at all; not a sound or a look came from them.

Though I had been to the African continent before, this was the first time I had actually covered a revolution. I always thought reporting on civil wars was something particular and peculiar to certain individuals.

I never saw myself as part of this fraternity. The standard wisdom says war correspondents are the guys who can take the horrible things humans do to one another. I never considered myself that tough.

What I was looking for was the rationale as to why people commit genocide. My painful Vietnam War experiences had only added to my confusion, despair, and did not contribute a damn thing to clarify the nagging questions: Why do we kill each other?

Where is our so-called moral imperative? I thought there had to be something, some complicated element in our psyche that while not justifying the butchery would at least help explain it.

I was searching for some insight about humanity but mostly about myself because I did not want to accept one basic and brutal truth: Humans can get used to anything, even the gratuitous killing of others. It was not just individuals killing other individuals, but groups, countries, killing others.

Not too long ago we had witnessed wholesale slaughter of innocent people simply because they were different or had a different religion. And the perpetrators were not Martians bent on killing others.

I did not want to accept that we kill each other because we want to. There really is no other reason behind it. Man's inhumanity to his fellow man is just another virus plaguing our daily human existence.

It does not take a genius to recognize that pathological hate is pernicious, contradictory, and deeply embedded in our genetic code. It belongs to us all.

In some screwy and creepy way, it makes us human—not the nice kind but human, nevertheless. We live in this mire of human indifference but I insisted in trying to find a clue, a reason, something to justify its ugly and depressing reality.

The more I looked the more I realized that no amount of agonizing, reflecting, or reporting on the terrible suffering humans inflict on other humans would make any difference. It would not change anything.

The sun would rise and set every day; seasons would come and go; the universe would go on existing; humans would continue killing each other. Nobody really gives a rat's ass about why we butcher each other; we just do it that is all. We are programmed for violence from birth to death.

To search for an explanation or a solution to such behavior is hopeless. It is an exercise in total futility because in the final analysis brutality and the slaughter of man—by his fellow man—are among the most characteristic of human traits.

An old man, a boy of about twelve years of age, and I ended up being the only ones left in that room. Throughout the night, the guards came, took the others out, and never brought them back. This was always followed by muffled gunshots echoing in the distance.

Who were the boy and the old man? Were they related? What was going through their minds? How were their hearts feeling? They sat right next to each other but never said a word.

Once, when the guards were not looking, I saw the young boy reach over and hold the old man's hand trying to give him some comfort.

The old man took the kid's hand and kissed it. It was a gesture of such pure human beauty and innocence; an act defying the putrid, ugly, and vicious atmosphere that surrounded us.

Then the guards came back at dawn. Why always at dawn? The beginning of a new day should always be happy, glorious, carefree, filled with hope —not with the stench of death.

The guards were talking very loudly and as they went to the old man first, he got up and blew his nose. The boy got up and very softly talked to the guards, mixing his own language with his broken English.

I can still hear the young, soft voice saying they should let the old man go. He had a right to his old age! It was not an argument or a plea but stating a fact, a cold logic belying the boy's young years. He explained the old man was no threat to them; he should be allowed to go free.

Perhaps due to the lateness of the hour or that the guards only needed another kill to complete their quota before their shift ended, they did not take the old man. They took the boy, instead.

Before he left the boy pissed in a corner. The image of this young boy casually relieving himself before being murdered was so evil and disconcerting. They all marched out of the room, the young warrior leading the guards on a mission—his own execution!

My ridiculous hope that they would let him go was soon shattered by the awful, deadly, and much too brutally familiar and depressing sound of guns breaking the early morning's silence.

They threw the old man, Gilles, and me out of jail soon after. Through a partially opened door, I saw a courtyard with many bodies piled on top of each other.

The old man just kept on walking down the dusty road without ever looking back in our direction. The guards returned all of our possessions; nothing was missing. They even gave us back the film they had taken out of the camera. They made a great fanfare out of returning our belongings.

Gilles and I had not been allowed to see each other that night. The room he was placed in was also emptied of people, he told me later.

"I hated what those pricks were doing," he said. "Man, I wished I had had a gun. I would have wasted all those sons of bitches. You know, I think I will become a farmer. At least you get to see things grow instead of seeing life destroyed."

Several days later, Gilles and I went out and got very drunk and finally talked about what had happened. It was not much of a conversation. We had been close but the event in Africa was the beginning of our drifting apart. We never worked together or saw each other again.

I have always regretted we lost touch. I often wonder if he did become a farmer. The truth is that neither one of us found a way to comfort the other over the grief and the guilt we felt about what we had witnessed—nor how powerless we had been to prevent it.

As I was walking out of jail with Chris, the image of the young boy came back so hauntingly clear. The guards had not treated him with impatience or disrespect.

In fact, the distinct impression I had when they all marched out of the room was that he was leading them and not the other way around. Clearly, he had talked the others into replacing himself for the old man.

So many times, I wish I had made an effort to talk to the boy. It is a regret without limits. It is not that I was not afraid—I was. But I could have made an effort. I am not talking about nobility, certainly not my own.

Could that have made any difference? Maybe trading places with him—probably would have gotten all of us killed, but still . . .

I knew the guards standing nearby would not have allowed me to talk to the boy. Their threats to kill me were very real, but at least I could have tried. To tell the boy it was not what someone his age should be doing.

To take him aside and ask how he had achieved his force of character? What had he seen in his short life that made him act with such foolish bravery?

Deep in my own heart, I knew the young boy had traded his life for that of the old man. What kind of courage does that take? What was he hoping to accomplish? Did his youth and innocence blind him to what was going to happen?

No, he had made a choice, and it was an amazing moment of truth for someone so young. Not a word was exchanged between the boy and the old man. Were they related? It was a muted and deadly farewell. It was not fair.

I had felt empty, but not angry. The whole event had seemed so ordinary, senseless, and banal. There really was no angle as to why people kill. They just do it as calmly as the boy peeing before being murdered. You could at least argue the boy had a physical need: his bladder was full; he needed to evacuate.

The boy's memory is fresh in my mind. Who was he? He was somebody's child; he was humanity's child. It was so heinous, so disgraceful that human beings could inflict such vile acts on other humans. The good always seem to die young.

The evil had not surprised me but had left me numb. Primo Levi had once written of his concentration camp experiences: "The worst survived, that is, the fittest; the best all died."

Very often the memory of that young boy would come back and overwhelm me when I least expected it. It faded in and out of my psyche like a harsh and jumbled radio signal that I would never be able to triangulate.

Here I was, a free man, walking down the street accompanied by two beautiful women and wanting to believe that the world is just a fine place to be, while Chris and Big D. were ambling ahead of us arguing in Greek. We were on our way to get something to eat.

How absurd life is!

I had told Big D. about Manos, the taxi driver. He had taken the paper that Manos gave me and said nothing.

"How did you end up in Greece?" I asked the twins.

"We visited it once with our parents when we were kids," one of them said.

"So, we came back to see what we missed," the other added, laughing.

"And have you found what you missed?"

"That's the big question," one of the twins said.

"We're still looking," the other one said. "We'll probably never find it, but it's fun to look for it."

There was a nightclub owned by an American woman and Chris, like the twins, had stumbled upon it a few nights ago. That is how the three had met. They got to be friendly with the owner.

Demetrios knew the owner, and when he came by early this evening, Big D. met the twins and discovered they all knew Chris. Lisa and Robin had decided to accompany Big D., on a kind of a dare, when he told them about Chris—not really because they were worried about their fellow American.

Chris had struck them as someone who could take care of himself. It came as a bit of a shock that he was in jail. When I said I did not know Chris at all, that this was the first time I had met him, the twins thought I was a nifty guy to have gotten him out of jail. I reminded them that Big D. had done it.

"What about you, what do you do?" one of the twins asked.

Unlike earlier in the evening when Karen had asked the same question, I was not bothered by it.

"I'm doing it." The twins laughed "A girl I met earlier today thought I was a pimp."

"The charmed life," one of the twins said. It was my turn to laugh.

"Actually, I'm going to write a film-script for a producer, so maybe it is like being a pimp."

"Oh, you're a writer," the second twin said, somewhat impressed.

"Writing a film-script is not really being a writer."

"I disagree," said the first twin. "You still have to write the words down."

"So, the producer can change them later because they don't fit the color of the leading lady's hair," I said. They appeared to think my words were funny.

The present situation had a surreal sense to it. Less than thirty minutes ago, we had been trying to get someone I had never seen before out of jail. Now we were on our way to get something to eat, commenting and laughing about the whole episode.

It was as if it had been the most natural thing to happen at this time of night in a strange city. One of the twins then suggested that I should take them to meet the producer.

She added, a bit facetiously, he might like them enough to give them a part in his movie. I kind of liked the idea of me showing up towing a couple of beautiful women. It might impress the hell out of the producer.

The restaurant was crowded and smack in the middle of it were Manos, Ron, and Karen.

There was a small band playing typical Greek music that struck me as sounding like Middle Eastern music.

Ron was sitting at a table while Manos and several other men, with Karen among them, were dancing. This was unusual, as most Greek men seem to dance with other men. And if it is a woman, it is most likely a foreign tourist.

Karen saw me, stopped dancing, and came over to embrace me. She was deliciously tipsy and having a wonderful time. A waiter appeared out of nowhere, and soon we were squeezed around a small table.

Through the din of the music, I made the introductions. Ron was less tipsy than Karen was, but he also appeared to be enjoying himself.

Big D. was soon on the dance floor. I had to marvel, once again, at a man his size being able to move so gracefully. The music ended with a fast beat and crescendo, and the whole room erupted into loud cheers and laughter.

Then Big D. walked over to the table, picked up a dish, and with a great deal of relish dropped it on the floor. The dish shattered into many pieces, and soon the whole crowd was throwing dishes on the floor.

It was crazy watching seemingly normal people smashing dishes on the floor, kind of frenzy, with some of them dancing over the broken pieces, while the café's owner stood by with a silly look on his face as if it was the most natural thing in the world taking place.

It was strange and fun, but there also was an edge to the crowd. High tension was in the air. It felt as if it would take very little to push the crowd in a dangerous direction.

Suddenly, three policemen walked in, and the crowd became abruptly silent, as if a switch had been turned off—a sharp contrast to how noisy it had been just a few moments before. The tension, however, remained.

The policemen went to talk to the owner, and from the look on his face, it appeared they were giving him a stern lecture. Most of the people in the restaurant gave the impression they would have preferred to be on another planet.

It reminded me of the room back in Africa and the men waiting to die. When the cops left, the crowd became lively again. Big D. said the whole thing had to do with the junta not wanting people to keep their traditions.

In Greece, it was traditional to break dishes on the floor as a sign of joy, madness and freedom. When the junta took power, they tried to abolish this appetite for joy and liberty in fear of the free spirit of the people.

A new law had been passed, though it was not enforced all the time, that the public no longer had any right to smash dishes on the floor. But Demetrios did not think the cops were interested in arresting over a hundred people, many of them tourists. It would not look good as foreigners brought in much needed cash.

Greece was now keen on changing its image as a fascist state. The need for revenue would override the need to control people's lives. In true revolutionary fashion expediency prevailed over ideology, and money became more important than orthodoxy.

The music started again and soon the twins became the focus of attention for many males in the room. Several of them came by the table and asked the twins to dance. At first, they refused but eventually relented when Big D. and Chris got on the dance floor.

Soon, we had the twins and Karen dancing in the middle of the floor with several men around them, having the time of their lives. I noticed that one of the twins was a graceful dancer.

Chris did not seem much worse for wear from his ordeal. It was obvious that his jail-time had not crowded his style. He was having a wonderful time as if nothing had happened to him.

Perhaps, this was his denial period or he really did not give a shit whether he stayed in jail or not.

I did not know exactly why either, but his attitude pissed me off, which was the reason that when he came over to ask me to join them in the dance, I told him to go fuck himself!

By then he and I had put away many glasses of *retsina,* the smelly and rancid-flavored liquid resin from the grapes. It is indeed the dregs of the wine, and it took getting used to.

However, once the initial shock was out of the way, one could actually get to like the stuff and get very drunk in a short time. Chris started to laugh, and before we knew it we were both laughing.

"You really *are* a masterpiece," he said. "Thanks for getting me out."

"You should thank Cleo and Big D."

"He calls you a 'masterpiece' and you call him Big D."

"Well, he's a big guy, isn't he?"

"Yeah, he is. So where is Cleo?" Somehow, he expected me to know her whereabouts.

"Sleeping."

"I know she's sleeping. What I mean is how she is?"

"How in the hell should I know?"

"She likes you," he said, after a moment's reflection.

"No reason why she shouldn't."

"I mean she just doesn't trust too many people."

"So, she's succumbed to my charm because I'm a likeable, trustworthy sort of guy," I said, not so sure I was going to like Chris after all.

"She has to like and trust you; otherwise, she wouldn't have asked for your help."

"Are you related to her?"

My question surprised him.

"No."

"So, what's the big deal about you?"

"There is no big deal. I just got my ass in trouble for opening my mouth too much and too loudly, I guess."

"That will do it every time."

"I hear you're in the movies."

"You've heard wrong," I said, wearily.

"Robin told me," he said, more to reassure himself than me.

"What's up with the twins?"

"Why, what's there to be up about?" His voice was distrustful.

"I don't know. Any plans about getting into their knickers?"

He sucked in some air and held it in, and then let it go with a loud hiss before answering. "I would like to, though that would be screwing up a good friendship."

"Oh, that's funny, very funny and clever."

"Well, I'm a funny, clever, sort of guy."

"*Touché!* Boy, you missed your calling."

"So why did you do it?" He asked after a moment of silence, apparently not wanting to discuss the twins anymore.

"Do what?"

"Get me out of jail?"

His words now seemed to have a distant interest. I did not have an answer. In fact, I had no answer for many of the things that were now shaping my life. So much had taken place on this one day. Paris and Cécile seemed very far away—almost lost in another life.

As I sat there, half drunk, their images in my mind were like a train moving along its tracks at a very fast speed in the middle of a dark night. Cécile and I would probably never get back together.

The whole relationship had lost its magic and momentum. Now, it was just staggering toward its inevitable end like a drunken sailor looking for a place to crash. We were no longer the same people, and it made me angry, sad, and resentful.

Cécile and I had met back in Paris at a wedding party we had both attended. When we first talked, I actually disliked her because like many French females she knew she was beautiful, arrogant, opinionated, sophisticated, difficult, elegant, full of herself, and did not have much patience with lesser mortals like Americans.

"*Je suis Française,*" she said, stating the obvious and certainly making fun of me.

"You could have fooled me," I said, trying to humor her. "I thought the French were polite, open, kind and loved Americans."

"Who told you that?"

"A little bird."

"Well, your bird is not very intelligent," she said, but she did smile.

"I guess not."

Her attitude did not take away the fact that she had one of the best pair of legs in Paris. Even in the dead of winter, she always wore dresses. I thought that no female had the right to have such superb legs. It was a blessing and a curse.

In typical female fashion, she complained men always looked at her legs first. They never took the time to figure out what she had between her ears.

"I want to insure my legs," she said to me one day.

"What?"

"You know like the famous American movie star Betty Grable."

"How do you know about that?"

"I read about it somewhere."

"Now you want to be a movie star?"

"No, never. I just want to insure my legs. They are pretty, no?"

"They are beautiful."

"It's true?"

"Yes."

"OK, I will insure them. *Un million de dollars pour les jambes magnifiques de Cécile,*" she said, laughing.

"Cécile, you *are* crazy," I said. On the other hand, maybe it would not be a bad idea for her to insure her legs for a million bucks.

When guys ignored her legs, it was the worst insult heaped upon her femininity. You were damned if you did and damned if you did not. To be out with Cécile was probably akin to being a drug dealer. All the guys wanted to score.

She was crazy about jazz. When I found this out, I told her that as an American my opinion of her improved a lot, that there might be some kind of saving grace to being French after all.

"*Quel chauvin,*" she said.

"What? I'm not a chauvinist, and look who's talking."

Her father was musician, and his love for jazz had been instilled in her from an early age. He had been a minor recording artist in Paris, but his only claim to fame was a couple of recordings he made with Django Reinhart, the great Gypsy guitar player.

Her most precious possession was a large collection of 78-rpm records of the great American jazz figures, of the early twenties, that she had collected while a college student in Washington, D.C.

Cécile and I used to spend long weekends with friends just listening to those old records. Among them was a favorite of mine recorded by Reinhart and the violinist Stéphane Grappelli.

Some of her fondest memories were of herself as a child standing at the recording studio listening to Grappelli playing old jazz standards, Broadway tunes, and repeatedly practicing his scales.

A couple of weeks after we met, someone gave me two tickets to an Ella Fitzgerald concert. So, on a wild hunch, I got Cécile's phone number and called to invite her to go to the concert. The idea appealed to her, but I could also sense she was not particularly crazy about going with me.

To try to impress her, I told her a story of something that had happened to me some time ago.

Quite by accident, I ended up sitting in the balcony of a small theater at the American Center for Students and Artists on Boulevard Raspail by myself, while Ella and her ensemble were rehearsing for a TV show, she was doing later that evening.

It was the middle of the afternoon, and the place was deserted. The center was a kind of refuge for students and artists. I had gone upstairs to catch a few winks, and I ended up catching something simply amazing.

For over an hour, I sat listening to Ella and her group rehearse all the numbers for the show. In a magical way, she was singing to me while I sat in the dark like a little mouse, making no noise, just listening. It was a thrilling moment.

I remember thinking it was a shame I did not have a tape recorder with me. When they finished, I wanted to stand up and applaud but, of course, I did not. Anyway, my story did not seem to have impressed Cécile at all. To my invitation, she said no, but she did ask me for my phone number.

Maybe her asking for it was a consolation prize to me for turning down my invitation. So much for my hunch, I thought. Then, a few minutes later she called and said she had changed her mind.

"Was my Ella Fitzgerald story that did the trick?"

"You made that story up, didn't you?"

"No, it did happen."

"I love Ella, but I was more in the mood for Nina Simone."

"Well, let me call Nina and see what I can work out."

"Do you know her?"

"Sure," I said and I laughed. "We go a long way back. I know I can talk Nina into replacing Ella tonight, just for you."

"You're that good?"

"Absolutely!"

"Americans are so full of it."

"How many Americans do you know?"

"A few."

"I was hoping to be the only one."

"What an ego," she said, laughing.

"So why did you change your mind?"

Her answer was that I had no right to ask such a question. As a woman, she had the right to be difficult and change her mind. That is the first lesson to be learned about women, especially French women. The second lesson: Never ask a woman *why* she changes her mind.

"Those are the two best lessons in life," she continued. "Learn them and you will never have trouble with women."

From the evening of the concert, we became inseparable. It seemed she never left my apartment. I remembered those days so well because while we were together, we lived as intensely as only two people who are in love can live.

Much later, love—this rather strange, inexplicable, and powerful emotion that makes us believe that everything is possible, that invades our souls more than anything else in our existence—got tangled up with life and its vicissitudes. Everything went to hell after that.

So, in spite of my alcohol-filled mind, I wanted to give Chris a clear answer to his question, but I could not. Somewhere, I had lost the thread, and I did not know how to find it again. What I was doing now was navigating in all directions going nowhere, going around in circles.

First, I blamed me; then I blamed Cécile; then I blamed Cécile and me; then I blamed everybody else. Finally, I ran out of people to blame. I was beginning to get sober from thinking too much.

I glanced over to see Karen and Ron holding hands while Manos sat right next to Ron looking at him with envy.

"I didn't get you out of jail. It was Cleo and Demetrios," I finally said to Chris.

"True, but if it hadn't been for you nothing would have happened."

"Bad timing."

"Boy, talk about being funny."

"OK. I have a right to one good deed in my whole life."

"Only one?" Now he was mocking me.

"Yes, and I think I just blew it."

"Shit, you're probably looking for an angle so you can write about it and make money off me."

"Not really. No one would want to buy the story or even read it."

"What do you mean?" He was put off by my words.

"It isn't interesting," I said just to bug him.

"Boy, I'm glad I'm not your enemy."

"Oh, don't take it personally."

"You really know how to hit below the belt."

"I don't know about that. Anyway, your story hasn't enough gore."

"First, it wasn't interesting. Now there isn't enough gore?" He sounded disappointed.

"That's why I've got this movie gig."

"I'd hate to see when you're really pissed off."

"Then. . . I'm much nicer."

"You know, I'm going to like you even if you are a royal pain in the ass," he declared after a moment of silence.

"Suit yourself," I said, and we both laughed at our own drunken silliness.

Big D. came and sat with us. I had seen him drink a lot, but he looked just as sober as when we walked into the restaurant earlier. He wanted us to go to his place for a nightcap. I did not want to go. Eventually, I relented when everybody said I was being a party pooper.

Helen did not seem surprised to see us showing up at such a late hour. Soon, food and drinks were produced and the party continued. Ron and I were talking when Iris walked in the room.

I had forgotten all about her and when I saw her again, I knew I was in trouble—deep shit trouble. By the way she glanced at me, I could tell she understood that in my mind I was undressing her. Watching her body language told me she knew precisely what I was thinking.

It felt like we were doing a sexual but mental minuet; no, it was more like this long-silent-sensuous-filled-with-desire tango. During which the rhythm of the couple's dancing and pairing would lead to something unique, thrilling, and unknowable.

My sentiments were probably all due to the alcohol now sloshing around inside my brain. I was in that strange state of mind: drunk but not totally wasted, when feelings and ideas are sharp, pure, as when in the middle of the night we are thinking about some decision we need to make.

And it all seems perfectly clear and feasible until the morning arrives, and we discover all we have done is burn and waste billions of brain cells for nothing.

I walked out to the balcony because I needed some fresh air. The twins were beautiful and so was Helen. Even Karen was holding her own, but Iris was different. It felt as if Iris was testing me, daring me to enter her world before she vanished, but it also felt like she did not care one way or the other.

I could see that Chris, Ron, and Manos were paying attention as men pay attention when they see a woman who encompasses all of their male fantasies and more—a woman who is also unattainable—fleeting may be a better word.

At first, I thought it was the drinks and the late night. But when I looked at Chris, Manos, and Ron, I also sensed we were all reacting to something different. Attractive women surrounded us, yet Iris had an aura about her: intense, cryptic, voluptuous, wispy, there, not there.

With her, it seemed like anything would be possible because in some mysterious way she could guide a man through the labyrinth. It also seemed terrifying, removed, and distant. Perhaps, a better description would be that she was challenging me to ignore her—as if that were an option.

It is always a mystery the effect some women have on men. Manos came out and joined me on the balcony. He still smelled of the cologne of the earlier evening.

"Who in the hell is she?" he asked softly.

"Helen's cousin."

"I'm in love!"

"I thought you were in love early in the evening," I said, trying to humor him.

"Puppy love. This is for real."

"Watch out for Big D."

"Fuck him. A man could kill for her."

He was serious. I was getting sober while in another way I was also getting strangely intoxicated. Many ideas ran through my head and none of them made sense. I had to get away from this place, from her. However, why did I feel so damn vulnerable?

I was not looking for romance or sex because I saw them as complications I could do without for the time being. The whole sentiment was getting confusing. Big D. came out to the balcony.

It was a warm evening with the moon perched high in the sky, playing hide-and-seek with the clouds. Manos, Big D., and I stood on the balcony quietly watching the moon, each lost in private thoughts.

I wanted to be alone with Iris, talk to her, and have her explain what had never been explained to me by any woman before. I wanted to stop feeling so restless, anguished, and weary. I wanted to be somewhere else, really. Manos went back in.

"I think I'll call it a night," I said to Big D.

"Chris is OK."

"Yes, I think so."

"Well, maybe a little crazy."

"Who isn't?"

"I'm not," he said very formally.

"I'm sure you did crazy things at his age."

"Not that kind of crazy."

"By simple deduction all Greeks are crazy—just like the English."

"I prefer to be crazy than to be English," he said, smiling.

"I don't blame you. What did you say to Chris in jail?"

"I told him to keep his mouth shut."

"He wasn't pleased by that."

"He's a *malaka*."

"All of you guys are a bunch of *malakas* and *pusties,* anyway."

"Thank you," he said, and laughed.

"That bottle of cognac was a nice touch."

"Twins' idea."

"Really?"

"Yeah, anyway we got him out."

"So how did you do it?"

"Somebody owed me a favor. It was nothing."

"Yeah, I guess it wasn't."

When you are a mercenary, the only favor others owe you is because you got rid of their enemies. I was going to ask him what kind of favor it was but decided against it.

"Let's just hope he stays out," he said, without much conviction in his voice.

I brought the glass to my lips and took a long drink. The alcohol burned my throat.

"I've got to go," I said.

"Why don't you stay here for the night?"

His invitation came from so far out of left field that I really thought I had not heard it right. I was alone, and there was no one waiting for me anywhere. I looked at Big D., yet I could not tell why he had extended the invitation. It was something spontaneous. He saw my hesitation and smiled.

"For old times' sake," he added.

"OK, but only if you lend me your toothbrush."

He laughed aloud and went back into the room. Suddenly, I felt as if a great burden had been lifted off my shoulders.

TWO

I woke up from a deep sleep. My watch showed I had only been sleeping for a couple of hours. The apartment was very quiet. I glanced around the room to get my eyes used to the darkness and the different shapes that assaulted me in my half-awake, half-asleep state.

As I tried to get my bearings, I suddenly realized I was not alone in the room. Then I thought maybe I was having a dream; but, no, Iris was there! Her perfume told me that.

Earlier in the evening, after the others had left, Demetrios, Helen, Iris, and I had sat in the living room and talked a little bit. I sat across from Iris and from time to time, I got a strong scent of her perfume, but it was not so much the scent as her presence that affected me.

Iris and Helen spoke English, but they wanted to speak French and of Paris. I could tell that Big D. felt left out of the conversation. Soon, he excused himself after gently telling them to let me get some sleep.

It was at the beginning of September, a few years ago, when I arrived in Paris for the first time; it was in the evening. I was going to stay with a friend. From the airport terminal at Les Invalides, I had asked the taxi driver to take me on a short tour through the traffic up the Champs Elysées avenue, to L'Etoile, go around and back down the avenue and past Place de la Concorde, and on to the right bank of the Seine. We passed the Louvre, its imposing façade classic and mute.

Though these sights were familiar, through photos and films, seeing them for the first time I felt the thrill of discovering something ageless and wonderful. The trees still had leaves, and there was a feeling of hope and excitement in the air. It was on rue Le Regrattier, in the middle of l'Île Saint Louis, where my friend Gary lived.

From that first night, I loved Paris! It was the culmination of personal circumstances and crazy dreams—dreams that always seemed too far away and destined to be realized by others but not by me—that had eventually brought me to Paris.

Gary, who is a photographer, had lived in Paris for a couple of years. After catching up on the news of people we knew, and my freshening up a bit, we took a walk along the Seine toward Les Halles, the central market for the entire city.

The weather was perfect—sweet, soft and warm. The lights of the city burned an enchanting blaze welcoming strangers like me. The sights and sounds of the city I encountered were pure pleasure.

Coming out of Gary's building and turning immediately to the right, we came upon one of the great cathedrals in the world: Notre Dame. Like many people who are not religious, I am attracted to religious buildings.

Finding myself in front of Notre Dame gave me a sense of delight and spiritual pleasure. The great lady loomed in front of us half-enveloped in lights and shadows. We walked around the building looking at its majestic shape. Gary said that seeing this splendid cathedral every morning gave him all the necessary fuel, in his heart and soul, to carry him for the rest of the day.

As an artist trying to understand, trying to find his inner voice, seeking the place where he fit, searching for his uniqueness and spirituality, Gary said that living in the shadow of this great monument made it a bit easier to believe in humanity one more day.

Though he soon had to go back to the States, for family reasons, his heart and soul would always remain here in Paris.

We walked to Les Halles, a giant open market located right smack in the middle of the city spread over many streets where Parisians had been doing their shopping for ages.

It was attractive and charming in what so many of us think of as uniquely French, and immediately revealing how important food is to them.

The streets were filled with people of all kinds, shapes, colors, and status. It was a carnival, the Fourth of July, and New Year's Eve all happening at the same time in one huge urban setting.

We saw muscled guys carrying carcasses of beef on their shoulders and dainty little old ladies tenderly caring for the flowers.

There were vendors extolling the uniqueness and qualities of their products with zest and warmth. And lots of people out for a stroll or happily chatting away, waiting to enter a cinema or a restaurant. This was a world exuding humanity, warmth, style.

Gary and I walked around admiring the variety of fruits and vegetables, the fresh fish, the great variety of wines, and the cheeses with their pungent smells coming from all corners of France.

It was a wonderful feast for the eyes, for the nose, and for the soul—a giant bazaar of comestibles to eat and wine to drink, in the restaurants, in the bistros, on the sidewalks. It was an incredible *ambiance* of the rich pleasure of edibles being tended to with affection and seriousness.

We were to meet Gary's American girlfriend and a couple of other friends. What I remember most about that night was an incredible feeling of excitement, of wellbeing, of freedom. Spiritually I felt that Paris was home! It is a feeling that has never left me. I am always saddened when I leave Paris and so happy when I come back.

We went into a small restaurant and found Gary's friends waiting for us. The place was crowded, filled with sounds of happy people chatting away and revealing how much they honor and respect their language. I could hear it that evening.

I read, somewhere, that the French are born wealthy in language. It is a patrimony handed down to them by their ancestors. It is the only country, to my knowledge, that has a television show about their language and its uses.

You see these sages with their dictionaries ready to triple verify that the word being used is correct, proper, and corresponds to normal usage and tradition—and the program has a huge following among the general public.

There is also a story that the French Academy, the venerable institution that protects the purity of the French language, is presently working on the letter D of the alphabet to make sure that the words under this letter are correct from all points of view: usage, syntax, grammar, pronunciation, spelling, history.

They intend to check all of the letters of the alphabet. Yes, the French are indeed very serious about their language. And they have every reason to be so.

They are people who also think as much about their souls as they think about their stomachs. People who have produced Voltaire, Matisse, Sartre, and who also invented *champagne, croissants* and *soupe à l'oignon.*

I knew I would love Paris forever! It was Thomas Jefferson who said, "Every man has two countries: his own and France."

"Let's celebrate this beautiful city," Gary said that evening when I first arrived in Paris. "Nothing matches her. She's special and magical as Hemingway so eloquently put it in *A Moveable Feast*—one of the novels he wrote about Paris. So, we must thank the gods for allowing us to be here maybe even die here."

We drank a toast to that. My first evening in Paris remains in my memory as fresh and immediate as if it happened yesterday. Paris helped me discover a sense of the past, of history, of human things that had been and could no longer be again.

It was in Paris where I came to realize man's need for a spiritual life; a spiritual life that must bring him understanding and solace to help sustain him in his despair, loneliness, and sadness when the heart was broken and hope seemed just another empty word.

It was also about coming to terms with knowing who he really is, his station in life—his needs, his own mortality, and his place in the scheme of things—in spite of the total absurdity of his existence. Paris does that to you.

Gary's personal, romantic, sentiment about Paris was of a woman he had loved a long time ago. She was young, lovely, innocent, and ageless—would remain so in his heart forever.

Because of this feeling he always needed to go back and find her, see her, touch her, be with her, if only for a short time, but it was enough so that he could go on and continue with his life—never feel lost. I understood those sentiments.

I was not lost in Paris. I never experienced the sense of being an outsider, of not belonging. Yes, I was a stranger but never an outsider. When I was in London, I was an outsider. No matter how long I stayed there, I would always be an outsider.

Iris stood against the light as it filtered in from the street through the partially opened curtains. As my eyes became used to the half-light, half-dark surroundings, I was not sure how I was supposed to react to her presence.

I could not make out her face. She walked to my bed and stood right next to it. Then she sat, and I pulled the covers back. She hesitated for a moment, took off her nightgown, and got in right next to me.

Her body was cool, and she was shivering. I tried to give her warmth from my own bed covers. We did not talk. We just lay there quietly listening to each other's breathing.

Soon, she was breathing softly and regularly as if she had fallen asleep. I had no desire to make love to her. It felt good just to be right next to her. Her body was lovely, relaxed, and resting comfortably.

It seemed the visit meant something else, something I could not grasp, and I was mystified by the strong sense of peacefulness and wellbeing that washed over me.

After a long interval, slowly, I lifted the covers, got up, turned on the small lamp by my side of the bed, and stood looking down at this mysterious, sleeping Aphrodite.

For a moment, it felt as if I was the intruder and not she, and it occurred to me that Iris might be playing a game, but she was sound asleep.

I looked at her face, her throat, long, and soft, which ran down to lovely firm breasts any woman would envy. The sun had not touched them as it had the rest of her body and the small nipples stood out like two beautiful pink, grayish pearls.

Her stomach was firm, and it slid into the curve of thighs and in the middle, a small triangle made more prominent by its soft, dark color. The long legs appeared to go on forever. Watching her, I wanted to take in all of the details: the tiny birthmark right next to her belly button, the lusciousness of her breasts, and the full mystery of her sex.

I watched her for a long time because I was afraid if I closed my eyes this apparition would vanish. It did feel like I was in a dream. After a while, a sense of tiredness came over me. I got in the bed carefully so as not to disturb her and soon slumber made its sweet appearance.

I woke up late in the morning. She was gone. Again, I thought it had all been a dream, but the strong scent she had left on the pillow told me otherwise. I got up, and on the night table, there was a small piece of folded paper with a simple line written in French: *Tu ronfles.*

It made me laugh. I do not know too many guys who do not snore.

In the French language, there are two ways of addressing people: the *vous* and the *tu*, formal and informal. In a meeting between a man and a woman for the first time, traditionally the *vous* is usually employed.

However, once some degree of intimacy is established, the *vous* is replaced by *tu*. Iris had used *vous* when we first met, now she was using *tu*. My luck sure as hell seemed to have improved, I thought.

But I also had to admit when it came to women, I knew very little. Boy, talk about the fates tempting you.

I walked out onto the balcony. Helen, Demetrios, Iris and the baby were there. Demetrios had given me one of his robes to wear, and I must have looked ridiculous for he started to laugh.

"*Pusty*, you need to eat more of your hot dogs if you want that thing to fit you," he said.

How am I supposed to act, I wondered. What is the game plan? Many thoughts ran through my head regarding the previous hours but in the end, I decided to act as if the whole thing was normal.

Iris did not act embarrassed. Big D. and Helen showed no sign of anything being amiss. The talk was about the previous evening's events.

I was still marveling at how the whole business with Chris had ended on a happy note. What about the taxi driver, had he gotten anywhere with Karen? He had also been taken by Iris's presence to the point of saying a man could kill for her. In the bright morning light, I saw, again, how right he was.

"What's next?" Demetrios asked.

"I don't know. I need to get in touch with the producer that I'm supposed to be writing the story for."

"Cleo called this morning to say your mysterious producer would be calling here today," Helen said.

"Cleo called here?" I did not know why that surprised me—maybe because I did not hear the phone ring.

"Yes," she answered.

"She called to thank us for getting that pusty out of jail," Demetrios said.

"Did he really insult the government?" Iris asked.

"Yeah, but it wasn't that important," he answered.

Iris looked at me, and suddenly I wanted her. She knew that in my mind I was undressing her. She started to blush and quickly got up on the pretext of making more coffee. Helen and Big D. were occupied with the baby so they were not paying much attention to anything else.

Pretending I wanted some water, I went into the kitchen while Iris was preparing the coffee. I was kind of embarrassed by my horny behavior. On the other hand, she could not claim total ignorance or innocence.

I stood behind her without touching or making a move. Slowly, she turned around and put her fingers on my lips.

"You shouldn't think those thoughts so early in the day," she whispered, smiling.

"I can't help it. How did you know what I was thinking?"

"It's easy to see."

"It's your fault."

"It is not," she said, laughing. "You make me blush."

"So, what do we do?"

"I don't know," she said slyly.

We walked back to the balcony. Now I was the one blushing. I was afraid it would be obvious. Iris seemed to be in control of herself. The phone rang, and it was the Italian producer calling.

He wanted to find out when I would be arriving in Hydra. We set a time for the following day. I would take the ferry leaving early in the morning that took about three hours to get there.

The next thing I had to figure out was: How can I stay in the apartment one more night without being invited? I had to find a reason and only one was available, yet I could not share it with anybody.

Helen came to my rescue by suggesting I stay with them that night, and that Demetrios could take me to the pier in Piraeus early next morning. I was very surprised by her suggestion and hungrily agreed. I did not dare look in Iris's direction.

Cleo sent all of my belongings by taxi later making me promise to come by and see her after my return from Hydra. After a long and leisurely lunch, everyone got sleepy and we decided that a siesta was what we all needed.

I went back to my room. Then I thought I should write a letter to Cécile and was considering what to say when Iris walked in. It was so unexpected. Talk about the gods screwing with your head. She smiled, embarrassed, shy, and full of mystery.

This is risky I thought. So, I immediately looked toward the door. She understood. She shook her head then locked the door. Our lovemaking was long and tender. I wanted her to have as much pleasure as I did.

I was completely overcome by passion, lust and tenderness for her. That afternoon, I got to know every inch of that lovely body and it was mine to do with as I pleased. I could not get enough of her.

Iris was a nymph, Aphrodite, Helen of Troy, the mother earth—all there for me. I was full of questions. She would listen and give me a smile, which seemed to say there was no reason why I should be asking her anything.

She was with me, we were together, and that was all that mattered. Sometimes, it is hard for me to accept the simple things in life. When I asked her to come with me to Hydra, she threw back her head and laughed.

"I'm serious."

"You're mad."

Yes, I was crazy—crazy about her.

Later, she left the room as quietly as she had entered it. I was not sleepy anymore so again tried to write a letter to Cécile. My head had been full of ideas about what I wanted to tell her before Iris came into the room, but now I discovered I could no longer think of anything to say.

What was this thing with Iris all about, anyway? And the way it had happened? That was most intriguing—very unexpected.

What had prompted her just to walk into my room, and twice in a row? I had not quite asked her about it because I was not sure if it was the right thing to ask. I suspected she would not have told me. So, what was she looking for?

What was it? Carnal excitement? Lust? Pure, raw sex? Curiosity? What the French call: *Le goüt de l'étranger,* or what I call the taste of the forbidden fruit. But it did not seem that way. Maybe I should not worry too much about it. Life *was* screwy lots of times. No pun intended.

Riding those thighs in wild ecstasy was wonderful, but I was also looking for something else. I wanted some answers to life. Iris had burst upon it just at the very moment when my own turmoil was pushing me in several directions and all of them confusing.

I had known some great women and some less great. So why should this one affect me so differently than the others? I wished I knew the answer.

The phone rang somewhere. Its muffled sound brought me back from my reverie. A moment later, there was a knock on the door. It was Helen.

"It's Chris. He wants to talk to you."

She did not appear to suspect anything. I felt relieved.

"I'm inviting everybody to dinner tonight. You, too, *pusty.*" Chris sounded very cheerful.

"Why?" I asked just to give him a hard time.

"That's the least I can do."

"No, that's the most you can do."

"You know, I think you're right," he said, laughing as the line went dead.

I like jiving with Chris, and was grateful, for without him I might not have met Iris.

The restaurant was in full swing when we got there. In addition to Chris and the twins, there was Ron, Karen, Cleo, Demetrios, Helen, Iris, and me. Though Cleo did not know Helen and Iris, they were soon chatting away like old friends.

In the car, on the way over, I had wanted to hold Iris's hand, but it had not been possible. It irritated me that I had to pretend; though under the circumstances, it was probably the wiser thing to do.

With Big D.'s past, perhaps it was best not to test the strength of our renewed friendship—not yet anyway. Besides, I was leaving the next morning, so maybe it was all for the better. Yet a sense of morbidity crawled over me.

Finally, I decided to let the chips fall where they may. Iris had made me a gift of love and affection, and the least I could do was to accept it with grace. Grace! So much has been said about that.

It was a raucous evening filled with gaiety and laughter. With plenty of charm, Cleo presided over the table like the ultimate matriarch of times gone by, surrounded by people much younger to whom she was acting like a mother, and she thoroughly enjoyed it.

At one moment, I found myself sitting alone with her at the table while the others were dancing. She took my hand and held it for a long time.

"Be careful," she said, while looking in Iris's direction. She knew! But how? Had Iris or Helen said anything to her? Is it women's intuition? Or is there a particular look or scent that gives it away?

"Why do you say that?" I was surprised by her words, not clear why she was saying them, but also playing for time.

"I'm an old woman, I know how some things start, but I also know how they finish," she said a bit darkly.

"Cleo, you sound like an oracle."

"I don't know you," she said. "I know what I see in your eyes and in your hand." She let go of my hand.

"Tell me what you see."

"Sadness, turmoil, confusion, longing. I see fear. I also see strength, loyalty, affection, and tenderness. All is up to you."

"What is?"

"Your life."

"Do you see love and happiness in there?"

"It's all up to you," she answered avoiding my question.

Her look was very serious. I was not sure if I should continue with the conversation. She took my hand again and looked at it as if trying to read my destiny in its lines. Then she turned and looked in Iris's direction again. Cleo seemed troubled. "It could be good or bad," she added, softly.

I looked at my hand and saw nothing.

"Cleo, I need to know more."

"It cannot be known. It is not the time!"

What the hell did she mean? The time for what? I looked at her face, still serious, though I also glimpsed the beginning of a smile. It reassured me, somewhat, but I could sense she would not tell me anything else.

"Cleo, I swear to you I will never do anything to hurt her. Believe me."

"I believe you. Demetrios knows."

The news was surprising and made me uneasy. How could he know unless he had talked to Iris? Would she have said anything? Was I in some kind of danger? I mean, I had not gone to her room. She had come to mine out of her own free will, and twice!

Was I such a monster to accept what had been offered? On the other hand, what was I supposed to do, tell her to go away? There is so much that one can be guilty of, really.

"Is it his business?"

"You need to learn more about Greek people." She paused, a long pause, and never took her eyes off me.

"Should I move back to your house?"

"Do you want to move back?" Her answer sounded like a challenge.

"No," I said, convinced it was the answer she wanted from me.

"Then don't." She smiled, which gave me a bit of comfort.

"Should I talk to him?"

"Only if he talks to you."

Oh, boy, that was just great. Would he talk to me before he cut my throat while I was sleeping? Her next question was sudden, curt.

"What are you looking for?"

"What everybody else is looking for, I suppose."

The question seemed so simple but impossible to answer. As impossible as it was to answer why babies die in their sleep without any apparent reason. What did I want? I did not know; I honestly did not know.

Our human frailty never seemed so clear, as when we confront that question. How in the hell do we know what we want out of life? Is there a drink, a magic potion, that we could ingest the night before and wake up the next morning knowing the specific needs of our hearts and souls and how to fulfill them?

"The truth is that I don't know the answer. Do you know the answer?"

"The answer is always within you!" She asserted with conviction.

"Everybody says that."

"Because it's true. It's like a clear, beautiful sound of a bell within you."

"Why do I have such a tough time finding it?"

"You must listen for it. Yes, Mr. Big Shot American Person, she can help you but it may not be easy." Cleo smiled an enigmatic smile. She let go of my hand.

I was not sure what to make of her words or her demeanor. Was she making fun of me? She had not answered my questions directly. Perhaps there was no answer. Her eyes were burning with a certainty that made me uneasy. Yet her face was restful, pensive, and even a bit distant.

She was not looking directly at me but at something beyond, and she seemed in some sort of trance. I thought she might be looking at someone behind me, but it was not so. The music ended, and all of the dancers came back to the table.

Iris was slightly out of breath. She came and sat right next to me. I had to admit she was cool, a lot cooler than I was. After a short pause, the music started again and Big D. grabbed Cleo, Karen, and the twins, and off they moved to the dance floor. Chris and Ron joined them. Helen, Iris, and I were the only ones left at the table.

I soon felt a sweaty hand grab mine and hold it firmly. I looked at Iris and she was not looking directly at me, but I could sense she was teasing me. I began to get a hard-on. I shifted in my seat.

"How long will you stay in Hydra?" Helen asked me.

"I don't know. I've never met this guy. I don't know how we're supposed to work this thing out."

"Have you been to Crete?" As Helen asked the question, she stole a tiny glance in Iris's direction. It was so subtle, so imperceptible, that had I not been looking directly at her I would have missed it. I felt a slight pressure on my hand.

"No."

"It is very beautiful. Very different," Iris said.

"Maybe I can come one day, and you can show me around," I said.

"I'm going back very soon," she said, and squeezed my hand. I was not sure if this was a yes or a no signal.

That is what this thing is about, I thought. Helen is very much part of this little game we are playing. Now it was beginning to be clear.

"When?"

"I don't know, it depends," Iris answered, softly.

"It depends on what?"

"It depends on many things." Iris gave me a long, hard look filled with mystery before answering my question. Her dark eyes hid many secrets.

I looked at Helen. She sat there taking it all in and not offering anything in return. Another Sphinx, I thought.

"Yes, I think I'll go and visit Crete."

Another squeeze. Again, was it a yes or a no? Their faces, though, were savoring a victory of sorts. It felt as if I had been a participant in a preplanned game. I started to laugh, and soon we were all laughing. I had not felt this good for a long time, a very long time.

Her pleasure came in waves. Her body arched toward me with such ferocity and intensity, such joyousness, such freedom, as if wanting to swallow me forever more.

I knew of no other thought or pleasure that was as complete and final, as when the day ends with the night but it was not darkness; it was bright, clear.

My life ebbing away into her womb to run into that river of eternity whose origin no one doubts and whose final destiny one can only guess, all mixed up in the mystery of love and sex that have lived on and on long before we got here, and will remain behind after we have turned into dust.

Afterward, we were silent for a long time. I was on top of her not wanting to move, very still.

"I can feel your heart," she eventually whispered, softly.

"I can feel yours; I can't feel mine."

"It doesn't matter, I can feel it."

We lay motionless, not wanting to move and so close to each other. I began to get hard again. She responded, and soon we were riding the tides of an ageless ocean whose currents bore us to places we had never seen before but whose shores we visited.

Light and darkness we would experience with the intensity of a hot fire whose embers in the end would leave only a pale shadow of its previous existence.

Then it was time to get up and go and meet the producer. Iris had left the room in the early morning. I treasured the fresh memory of her that I had experienced in the last few hours: mysterious, soft, wanting, giving.

In the kitchen, Big D. was already up. He was in a good mood, humming some kind of song, and he greeted me with a bit of fanfare. However, something in his voice put me on my guard.

"*Pusty,* did you sleep well?"

"Yes, soundly," I said, wondering what would come next.

"That's good, that's good. Here's to wake you up," he said, handing me a cup of steaming coffee.

"Thanks."

"So, you're finally going to get some writing done."

"I hope so."

"Where do you get your inspiration?"

"I don't know. Most of the time it is not there. You have to work hard and hope the gods aren't pissed at you."

"You Americans!" And he laughed. "Always wanting to write the Great American Novel."

"I would be happy just to be able to write a simple novel."

"Do you think you'll ever do it?"

"I don't know."

"Don't you think you should know before you start?"

"Yeah, you're right."

"I envy you."

"Why?"

"To imagine things out of nothing and then write them on a blank piece of paper. It scares me to think about it. I would never do that. I'm not that brave," he said, with a look that was very frank and honest.

"Or that foolish."

"Yeah, writers *are* crazy," he said, laughing.

"It's all about the muses and how disposed they are to grant you favors."

"Yes, the muses."

"When you're in Greece do like the *malakas* do."

"Yes, of course." He gave me a cynical smile. "That's what you're *doing,* ha *pusty*?"

The bastard had me cold. The sound of his voice told me he knew what the score was. OK, I thought. You know what your cousin-in-law and I have been doing and, so far, you have not confronted me with it.

I sure as hell did not ask her or force her to come into my room and screw my brains out. What was I supposed to do?

"I wanted to tell you something—" I started to say.

44

Waving his hand, he cut me off and, for an instant, I saw a murderous look in his eyes. His body was taut, rigid, and almost ready to spring into action but he did not move.

His self-control was incredible. The hand holding the cup of coffee was steady. I was not sure how this thing was going to turn out.

"I don't want to know. A man's house is his castle. No one can abuse it. Yes, things happen," he said.

His voice was soft, a whisper. He looked at me and though the tension was still there, it was now slowly being replaced by a look of mockery in his eyes. It was hard to tell on which side of the fence he was.

"Two things about Greek women: They wait for their men faithfully, and they kill if they're betrayed," he continued, not without an edge to his voice.

I thought it was wiser to keep quiet, and I wondered how close it might have come to my life ending in Big D.'s kitchen.

"We're strange, we Greeks," he added.

To some extent, I was relieved it was no longer a secret. Of course, Helen had to have told him or maybe it was Iris—or he simply guessed. In any event, the cat was out of the bag.

"Anyway, not my business or as you Americans say: 'She's old enough to . . . vote?'"

I started to laugh at his attempt to use an off-color joke in the tense situation, though I did not explain to him the exact meaning of the expression he used as he might take it the wrong way. I had better leave well enough alone.

I did not see Iris before we left the apartment. Later that morning, he drove me to Piraeus from where I would take the ferry to Hydra.

It was a gorgeous morning: blue skies with a few white clouds that made it seem bluer. I sat on a bench, and watched the crowds made up of all kinds of people coming and going, all talking excitedly using broad gestures and motions.

On the way over, Big D. had said little; each of us kept to his own thoughts. As we shook hands, he pulled me over to him and gave me a hug, which was surprising.

"Let me know how your movie turns out."

"I will."

"*Malaka,* come to Crete. Maybe we can meet you there."

"I'd like that." I meant it.

"Well, keep in touch," were his last words.

He had a big frown on his face as he walked back to his car.

The night before, after a long silence, I could tell Iris wanted to say something but she seemed apprehensive. I preferred not to ask anything. Finally, she came to a decision.

"Will I see you again?" She asked.

"Only if you want to."

"I want to. Will you come to Crete?"

Her words were soft with what I thought was a bit of longing and fear. It was hard to tell.

"You know I will."

"You may not like it there."

45

"Why do you say that?"

"There are complications. I need to explain."

"You don't have to."

"Thank you," she said. "I'm confused."

"Who isn't?"

"I don't want to be."

Her voice had trailed off, and I felt her hand reach for me and tenderly start to stroke me. I got hard. Slowly she kissed me, and moved down until she took me in her mouth, softly, shyly at first, and then her tongue was all over me trying to find out what gave me pleasure.

Her warm mouth swallowed me and when the explosion came, it left me limp and spent.

"Strange," she said afterward, and smiled.

I did not know quite how to respond to her comment. She went to the bathroom and came out a few minutes later.

"I'm hungry," she said.

"You're hungry?"

"I didn't eat very much tonight."

I started to laugh and, for an instant, she did not understand why. Her face got red and she seemed embarrassed by my puerile humor, then she started to laugh.

"Lamb chop sandwiches," I said.

"Lamb chop sandwiches?"

I jumped out of bed.

"Yes, the best in the world. Come on, get dressed."

We managed to sneak out of the apartment without waking up the others even though we were giggling. We raced through the empty streets in Helen's Mini Cooper.

I did not exactly know where she was taking me. While getting dressed, I told her what the taxi driver had said, and she thought she knew what he was talking about.

It was a street in Athens, where no self-respecting woman would be caught during the day let alone in the middle of the night. I was able to convince her she had nothing to fear. We would pretend to be tourists who had stumbled upon it by accident.

The street was alive at that time of the night, not only with hookers and their patrons but probably with people who could not or would not sleep. This was more than a place where insomniacs gathered to pass the night.

For some reason, I thought that as much as people were hungry and had to have a place to eat in the middle of the night; it also represented a ritual of some kind.

Some mysterious rite that perhaps had originated with the ancient Greeks and whose tradition was continuing, though, back then, instead of lambs they may have sacrificed young maidens.

We parked the car and walked into the throng. The rich smell of the lamb being cooked told you everything you wanted to know. There were several vendors with groups of people gathered around them and, from the looks of it they were doing a brisk business.

The women looked at Iris and decided she was either a high-priced hooker or an innocent young maiden being led astray. In any event, soon we were able to buy some sandwiches and sat down to eat them. Iris was getting a kick out of the whole scene, and I must admit the food tasted delicious.

I do not know much about food and certainly a hell of a lot less about Greek food, but there was no question I tasted something very special that night.

Only later, did I find out that what might have made this place unique and certainly the food taste delicious: There were rumors of vendors sprinkling the meat with opium, enough to give you a nice glow and make you think you were eating something out of this world, which might have been the case.

"*Pusty,* you found it!"

It was Manos, the taxi driver. He gave me one hell of a dirty look. He stood eyeing Iris. It was not a nice look. The look was so long she got uncomfortable.

"You remember Iris?" I said, trying to ease things out.

He tried to smile at her, and it came out like a shallow grin. Then he looked at me again but in a different way. I thought I detected some respect, but it was probably my imagination, as his voice was not friendly.

"Yes, how are you?"

"Fine," she answered dryly.

Iris was not comfortable at all. Then he said something to her in Greek. She started to laugh, and soon they were both laughing.

"It's not fair, let me in on the secret," I said.

"I've just told her I thought I was a fast operator. Now I understand why Demetrios says you're a 'masterpiece'," he said with a forced smile. I was not sure how I was supposed to react to these words—or his attitude.

"Is that what he said?"

"Yes, something like that," she answered.

Manos did not know what to do or say next. He seemed a bit lost. He excused himself and left us alone.

"What was that all about?"

"He's jealous." Her tone was flat.

"He did say when he first saw you that a man could kill for you."

"He said that?" She was surprised.

"Yes."

She shook her head and continued eating in silence for a bit.

"Men, they are such a mystery to me," she finally said.

We finished eating the sandwiches and walked back to the car.

"Let's go by the Acropolis," I said.

"Right now?"

"Yes."

"Why?"

She was surprised at my request. I do not know why going to the Acropolis seemed like a good idea to me at that time of night.

"Why? I've never seen it at night."

"It is closed," she said, stating the obvious.

"Good, then we'll have the whole place to ourselves. Come on."

The moon was partially hidden by clouds, but there was enough moonlight we could see the Parthenon hidden in the semi-darkness. There was a fence around the Acropolis and it was easy to climb.

At first, Iris did not want to do it, and then she asked a bit apprehensively, "What if the police come?"

"We tell them we're lost."

"Yes, and like Chris we'll get arrested."

"Demetrios will bail us out," I said, laughing. She looked at me and she started to laugh.

She finally relented, and I helped her climb the fence. We walked up toward the Parthenon. The building loomed larger than when I first saw it just a couple of days ago. Only two days ago, and it already seemed like a lifetime had come and gone. Our footsteps echoed in the stillness of the place.

There were several large and smaller pieces of the temple strewn about on the ground. We stood with our backs to one of the columns. I touched it and felt the smooth surface and the coldness of the marble.

"Do you think guards may be here?" She took my hand, whispering as she looked around a bit anxiously.

"They're probably sleeping."

"What if they aren't and find us here and want to know why we're here?"

"Do you think they'll accuse us of wanting to steal the Parthenon?"

She laughed, and I held her close to me. It did occur to me that maybe we were pushing our luck a bit after all.

"You're funny," she said.

It was hard to image this place had been designed and built by people who did not have any of the modern tools or machines to help them. Their degree of artistry, ingenuity, and sophistication was quite remarkable and remains unsurpassed to this day.

The Parthenon bathed in moonlight was ephemeral and magical. The marble holding remnants of time long passed and yet still present and living. For some strange reason, the whole effect made me think of Helen's breast as she was nursing her baby.

Though the Parthenon is man-made and a woman's breast is not, the soft moonlight reflecting as it hit the Parthenon also displayed the everlasting truths of beauty, harmony, the magic of creation, of life and of love.

The Parthenon and a woman's breast were subtle images, remnants that spoke of a mysterious and ancient echo that went back so many eons ago, to the beginning of time, confirming the inner beauty of the human spirit, evolution, and emotion in an eternal and timeless message.

It is said the Parthenon is the perfect building design because it is really imperfect. To give it the sense of perfect symmetry, the columns bulge slightly at the center.

This so-called curvature is meant to correct the optical illusion of columns with straight sides, which seem thinner and give the impression of flimsy support when seen against the light.

In order to get rid of this visual problem, the builders of the Parthenon designed the columns to bulge around the middle, which causes the eye to move up and down along the shaft and not look upward continually.

This imperfection, designed to achieve visual perfection, does not seem strange when you think that the ancient Greeks were very much concerned with balance and harmony.

I held Iris in my arms and kissed her. Her response was immediate and passionate. I put my hand under her dress and started to pull down her panties.

"Tu es fou," she said, giggling, as she tried to step out of them.

Of course, I was crazy. I was crazy about her. It was not the best position but, somehow, we managed to connect. And with the moon smiling down on us on this warm night, I made love to Iris in the middle of the ruins of the Parthenon.

THREE

I had dozed off before the boat entered Hydra's port. There was much animated talk and lots of commotion from the other people as we approached the pier.

I had no idea what the producer looked like. I even considered making a sign to put on my forehead, but then reflected the guy might not have a sense of humor.

As we were docking, the island appeared to be nothing more than hills rising from the water's edge and spreading out in tentacle-like patterns. I knew there were no cars on the island.

It appeared as if only donkeys could navigate the narrow alleys. The houses dotting the island were all whitewashed and spread upward in symmetrical patterns.

I was the last one off the boat. I stood by the gangplank, waiting, trying to make myself as conspicuous as possible. No one came to meet me, so I walked to the nearest café and sat at a table. Vittorio had said if he could not meet me, I was to go to any café and ask them to call him for me.

I ordered a beer and looked around the port. I was not in any hurry. There were lots of foreign tourists as I could tell by the several languages being spoken.

Iris and I had made no plans. We understood that I would go to Crete, though I really did not want to go. There was an uneasy feeling in my guts. Helen had talked about a fiancé. Iris had said something about being confused, and I guessed that is what she meant.

I really did not want any explanations from her. The only hope I had was that she knew what she was doing. The waiter brought the beer. I gave him Vittorio's number and asked him to please call.

Suddenly, my life was getting back into the same, complicated, convoluted, nobody-knows-what-in-the-hell-is-going-on kind of routine I had wanted to get away.

I felt anxious and weary. I had not had much sleep lately, and it was catching up with me. Now I wished I had talked to Iris about what was happening, because I really did not know which way was up.

After a while, a man in his fifties walked up to me and introduced himself. His stylish business card read: Vittorio Cinelli. He looked like he had been out in the sun most of his life. I was not sure what to make of him.

His body language suggested a man who measured what he did carefully and, with the dark glasses he was wearing, he gave the impression he wanted to keep the world at bay. He sat and ordered mineral water.

"Call me Vito. Milo told me you've never been to Greece."

"That's right."

"He also said you had written some material based on the ideas I gave him."

Vito had given Milo some ideas to share with me. They were without humor. Milo had said not to laugh at this guy since he was paying the bills. Besides, we did not have too many producers knocking on the door.

Vito wanted some light, adventure-oriented material. I had written several pages of a treatment based on his ideas.

Milo had also told me Vito wanted his present mistress, Adriana, a Romanian actress, to star in his next film. I reached into my bag and handed Vito some papers, which he started to read. I tried to watch his eyes through the dark glasses, but it was hard.

Not a muscle moved on his face. He put the papers down, looked past me, took off his glasses and wearily rubbed his eyes.

"It's fine," he said.

His words were matter of fact, flat. He could have been saying. "I hate it," and it would have had the same effect. "However, it's not right for our leading lady."

"Why is that?" I was taken aback by his words.

"She's a beauty, she's my mistress, but she can't act," he said without emotion.

Suddenly, I had a different impression of Vito.

"I'm sure we can lighten it up."

"She has to be comfortable with the whole thing."

"Does she have the final say on this?"

My question was accusatory. He saw my reaction and his face softened a bit. I even detected a shadow of a smile.

"No, but—" his voice trailed off and shrugged his shoulders in that unmistakable sign of *ennui* that comes over people who prefer to avoid conflict.

Adriana came and joined us. She was petite and blonde, but for some reason I had imagined her to be a tall, dark-haired woman. Her short haircut gave her a bit of a mannish look.

But she was very striking, with her oval face and fiercely burning, almond-shaped, slightly Oriental eyes. Siamese would be a good description. Her beauty was exotic and quite remarkable. I do not remember much of the conversation.

They were staying high above the hills, were combining business and pleasure, and spoke to each other in Italian most of the time. Adriana would answer him quietly whenever he said something to her.

"*Parla italiano?*" she asked me.

"*Si, parlo un po' d'italiano,*" I answered.

She smiled, and her smile changed her looks considerably. It was as if my presence dictated that she should act seriously. I had the strange impression that without Vito around she would have been more relaxed.

I suspected he wanted her to be quiet and not say anything to embarrass either of them, which might have been the reason why she had asked if I spoke Italian.

I do not know why I felt that way, though, her next words sort of clarified my sentiment.

"Vito tells me that my Italian is sometimes—how do you say it?" she turned to him giving him a teasing and slightly icy smile.

"Adriana, *tesoro,* it was just a silly joke," he said, leaning over to kiss her.

What attracts a man and a woman to each other? A furtive exchange of looks? A word said? A faint fleeting scent of perfume? Sharing a taxi? A vision of the possible? A moment of weakness while shopping for groceries? A warm smile? Is it because we hate the same things, the same people?

Is it fate? Or is it that, in this particular case, Vito was a film producer, and Adriana was the starlet seeking fame and fortune? The sun would burn up the earth before one could understand or hope to find the answer.

The weather was beautiful, and it did not give anyone the right to be depressed; but, nonetheless, I was. Though to be fair, Vito was not really being snooty or smart, and Adriana did not seem a bad sort. I guess I was looking for glamour, and got a businessman instead.

During the couple of days I spent on the island, we did very little work on the script. Vito was a man of great charm and knowledge. I came to like him a lot more, but he was never clear in what he wanted me to do. I understand movie producing can be pretty nebulous.

You start off with nothing and work on that for a while. Then you move on, still working on nothing, eventually ending back where you started with a lot more of nothing while a great deal of money, energy, and time have been spent producing a house of cards. Smoke and mirrors seem to be the *modus operandi.*

I hardly ever saw Adriana. She spent most of the time in their room or exploring the island by herself, and whenever she would join us, she seemed detached, bemused, and somewhat bored by our conversations. I attributed this to the fact she had heard Vito's stories before.

Vito and I talked mostly about stars—the celestial ones. He was an amateur astronomer with a great deal of knowledge about the workings of the universe.

In fact, he had written a book about the sun. He had wanted to be an astronomer but because his mother was from an old Venetian family, she had pushed him to go into the import and export business where he had made a great deal of money.

He never really got back to his first love, and had eventually drifted into film producing. Over the years, he had also acquired an extensive collection of antique telescopes and rare stamps.

He took his stamp collection everywhere he went. In fact, he had it in a bank's safe back in Athens. Every few days he called to make sure everything was in order.

Milo had told me that Vito was known throughout all of the famous watering holes in the Mediterranean for lugging his stamp collection with him.

Maybe that was what the swells normally did with their stamp collections. Vito showed me photos of the stamps. Some were quite beautiful and rare.

Very little substance regarding the film was discussed. When I left, he asked me to give him a longer treatment from the notes and few ideas we had managed to air out, asking the material be sent care of his bank in Rome, which would forward it to him.

He also told me he would instruct his banker to wire Milo more money, a great deal of money I thought, for my time and the future effort.

I was grateful for his expansive gesture. I was also frustrated, as we had not made real progress. I might have been a bit too anxious.

He said he was not in a great hurry that things would work out, that he did have much pleasure talking with me, and he would keep me informed as to the direction he wanted the story to go—I guess that is show biz.

"*Arriverderci, e bon viaggio,*" Adriana said.

"*Grazie.*"

"And perhaps we'll meet in Rome, soon."

"I'm looking forward to it." I did wonder if the next time I met Vito she would still be around.

Back in Athens, Cleo was happy to see me again. Chris had gone to Crete for a few days. She called Demetrios's house, and the person who answered said that everyone had gone to Crete.

"What is it about Crete that people want to go there?"

"It's beautiful and old," Cleo said.

"Lots of places are beautiful and old."

"Not like Crete," she said, with conviction and passion.

Going to Crete made me uneasy. I decided to phone Cécile in Paris. I had expected her to be upset but she was not. She was curious to find out how everything was going. She thanked me for the money I had sent, and asked how long I would be away.

When I told her I did not know, she asked if I wanted her to join me. I was not sure how to respond to her question. When I thought about it, the truth was simple—our relationship was over.

"I'm probably going to be busy with this movie thing. The problem is they don't really know what they want to do," I said, feeling defensive.

"Will you have any free time?"

"Yes and no. It's hard to say when I'm going to be free."

"Promise to call me when you get some free time."

"You know I will."

"I just wish we were together again like in the old days, that's all." Her voice was soft, pained, and resigned.

"Look, I promise the moment I see clearly what's going to happen I'll call you." I knew I sounded false, but it was the best I could do.

"*Je t'aime,*" she whispered.

"*Moi aussi, je t'aime.*"

The line went dead.

Yes, I still loved her after a fashion. The bad that had taken place between us was not anybody's fault. It was just the way it was. For a brief moment, I wished I were back with her in Paris.

The next evening, I took an overnight ferry to Crete. It dropped me off at Iraklion, Crete's main port. As the boat entered the harbor, the morning sun was just below the horizon. I saw this beautiful, blinding yellow disk slowly emerging from the other side of the world.

I was transfixed by the awesome spectacle—magical! The ancient Greeks believed the sun was a golden chariot traveling across the vault of the sky every day. There is no more mystical description.

I had sent Chris a telegram so he met me at the dock. We drove to the beach area where he was staying with the twins. Since we had met, we had not had much of a chance to talk.

It seemed like we never had a moment to ourselves when we could kick back and chew the fat. Chris told me the story of his incarceration.

It was his first visit to Greece. His father's family came from northern Greece, but he preferred Athens. That particular evening, he had gone out drinking with friends.

Before they knew it, it was time to head back to Cleo's because of the curfew the junta had imposed on the citizens of Athens.

On the way back, he had taken a Greek flag from someone's door and, being a patriot and a bit drunk, he started marching down the middle of the street singing a Greek song.

Two unfortunate things happened. One, the song was by Theodorakis, a composer beloved of the greater Greek public, but the man whom the colonels loved to hate as he was against them. His songs were banned.

The other was that when Chris got back to Cleo's place, he wanted to take the flag inside with him, but the flagpole was too long so he broke it in two—an act of rebellion according to the junta.

Someone saw him and reported it to the police. When the cops came to Cleo's, they found Chris sleeping over the flag. They started to beat him up right off the bat. In his drunken half-sleep, half-stunned state he fought back. The cops worked him over pretty well.

By the time they figured out what really happened, Chris was in no mood to be nice to anybody. Even after the cops apologized for beating him up, Chris kept on insulting the head of the junta calling him a *pusty*, a eunuch, and several other choice words, ultimately making it difficult for the cops to let him go.

"My dad was always pushing me to learn proper Greek. I don't know if he would have approved of the language I was using, but the bastards had done a number on me," Chris said.

The fact that he wore his hair long, and had a peace symbol hanging around his neck did not help matters. So, they threw him in the slammer.

"They stole that peace symbol from me, the pricks. It was a gift from my ex-girlfriend. I hated to lose it. When I asked them about it, they said they didn't know where it was. One of them is probably wearing it now. I don't trust these *malakas,* man!"

Chris found himself in a tough spot. He had insulted the head of the military, in essence, the head of the government and the state. Since there was martial law in the country, it was not possible to get him out without sending in the U.S. Marines.

The American embassy was not interested in offending the junta, so Chris was pretty much left on his own. The cops told him he was Greek because his father was Greek.

Thus, he was going to be drafted into the Greek Army for five years, and there was nothing anybody could do to prevent it.

That the American Army had rejected him because he was colorblind would not have made any difference to the Greeks.

"Can you imagine me in the fucking Greek Army?"

"Maybe the Greek Army could have made a man out of you."

"No way, it would have made me a *pusty*," he said, laughing.

"How did you find out about Cleo?"

"Through this guy I met. I came by. She liked me. I've been staying there ever since."

"Love at first sight."

"She says, I remind her of her errant grandson."

"She's really looked after you."

"Yeah, she has. What about you?"

"What about me?"

"What's your game?"

"Just trying to keep body and soul together man, that's all."

"Karen told me you were an international slime ball pimp."

We both laughed.

"Did she say that?"

"That's what you told her."

"I never said I was a 'slime ball pimp.'"

"She really thinks you're a pimp."

"You know, it wouldn't be a bad life: free sex, letting others work for you, plenty of money to spend. No taxes. Those are the ultimate benefits in a perfect capitalistic society." We laughed. "Whatever happened to Karen and Ron?"

"She's here," he said, a bit hesitantly.

"Shit, don't tell me."

"Yeah . . ."

Manos, the taxi driver, had scored!

"She dumped Ron like a wet rag, and without hesitation ran off with Manos."

"You're kidding," I was surprised but not shocked.

"Nope."

"She and Ron seemed so keen on each other."

"Times are changing, man."

"Relationships aren't supposed to be so fucked up."

"I know," Chris said.

"What do we really know about people?"

"Not a damn thing," he said, rather somberly.

"We go through life feeling we've got a fix on things, that we can control our lives. Then wham! Right between the eyes."

"We don't seem to learn anything."

"So where is Ron?"

"He went off to Turkey."

"It's my fault," I said, and at that moment, it felt like it.

"Why?"

"If I hadn't taken that damn taxi, I would not have met Manos."

"If you want to get technical about it, I'm to blame. If I hadn't gotten drunk that evening, I wouldn't have gone to jail."

"Or, maybe if I hadn't come to Greece," I said.

The peaceful countryside under blue skies was lovely. Over in the distance the ocean was still, its mirror-like surface with hardly any ripple. It was a glorious and picture-perfect day, and certainly not a day to reflect on the madness of the human race, on its follies.

"How far do you think we can go back to place the blame?" Chris asked.

"Hell, if I know."

When you think about how things in life happen, Chris and I could have gone back to the beginning of time and believed we had no control. We are merely puppets in this mad show called life, and all we are doing is mouthing off the words.

Man has nothing; the gods have the rest. They rule and our fates are sealed. No matter what one does, the outcome is never in doubt—maybe.

Was that the lesson of the kid back in Africa when he went off to get himself killed? What about the fling between Manos and Karen? Would it have happened whether or not I was there? If yes, I am blameless.

If, on the other hand, reflecting on my own situation at that moment, I am the master of my own fate, what was happening between Iris and I could not be laid at someone's doorstep. It all begins and ends with me. So, which one is it?

"Life's a bitch—make sure you don't marry her," Chris finally said, and we laughed because I knew he did not really believe that.

"How's it going with the twins?"

"OK."

"Getting any action?"

"Well, things are beginning to line up," he said, a smug look on his face.

"I thought you said you weren't going to screw up a good friendship."

"I'm trying not to."

"So, you *are* getting into their knickers."

"Not yet, but I'm working my angles."

"I figured. OK, who's going to be the lucky one?"

For a moment, he seemed troubled by my question. "Lisa," he finally answered.

"How do you know it's Lisa?"

"Well, I just know." But he did not sound very convinced.

"OK, how?"

"I can tell . . . by the smell," he finally said. We both laughed.

"Are you now like a dog sniffing these two women? You sniff them before or afterward?"

"Get off my case."

"Man, how lucky can you get? What if they want to play a game with you? Can you honestly tell who is who?"

"No, but it sure would be interesting," he said. "Hey, maybe I can have my cake and eat it, too," he added, cheerfully. He had obviously been contemplating the situation for a while.

"You're a sly one aren't you?"

"It takes one to know one," he said, laughing.

Chris and the twins had found a villa a couple hundred yards from the ocean. Cozy and warm, it was large enough for everyone to have privacy. The twins were sun bathing when we got there. Both came out to greet us. They were beautiful women.

I saw Chris looking at me and looking at them differently. We laughed. The twins did not ask why we were laughing. Chris did have a problem: There was no way to tell them apart. I would have liked to have had that problem at another time in my life.

I wanted to do some work, so I found myself alone that afternoon while Chris and the twins explored the island. Earlier, Chris said Demetrios had invited everyone to join him and Helen for dinner.

Then he added that Iris would be there as well. It had been several days since I had seen her and, even though the prospect of seeing her brought me wonderful emotions, it also filled me with anxiety.

The place was crowded when we got there later that evening. An open-air café that seemed to be hosting the entire island. The music was loud, and the crowd boisterous and happy.

People were dancing and Big D. was among them. Helen greeted me with a warm embrace. Everyone looked tanned and relaxed.

Then Iris walked in. Her skin was golden. She wore a typical native Greek dress that made her more alluring, but it was her companion who caught my immediate attention. He was a good-looking man in an unfinished sort of way whose attitude seemed bored, distant.

I thought, man, this guy could get any girl he wants. In fact, the proof was he probably had one of the prettiest hanging from his arm. The two of them made a perfect couple.

Suddenly, I wanted to understand more than ever: Why me? There is no way this girl did what she did without some other reason. Again, I reflected on how little I knew about women.

Something was going on here and probably had nothing to do with me, but the idea also depressed the hell out of me.

Helen stood and waved at them. Iris looked in my direction. I thought I detected a moment of panic in her eyes. Maybe panic was too strong a word—discomfort would be better.

As they made their way toward the table, I felt Helen's hand touching my own surreptitiously. They greeted Helen in Greek. Iris turned to me.

"Bon soir, Alex, c'est un plaisir de vous revoir."

The voice gave away nothing. Why was she greeting me in French—formal French—saying it was a pleasure to see me again? Maybe her boyfriend spoke French. Was this some kind of message? I took the hand and shook it.

Did I feel a slight tremble, a slight pressure? I could not tell. Iris's perfume was the same she wore the first night we had spent together, adding to my turmoil and to my sense of isolation.

"Thank you. For me also." I figured it was safer to speak English. There was a long awkward moment. She was looking directly at me, but I could not guess what she might have been thinking.

"May I present you . . . Costas," she finally said, in English.

"My pleasure," I said. I did not mean it.

"Welcome to Crete," he said, as we shook hands.

He spoke English with a heavy accent in a deep baritone. His demeanor was difficult to read. I thought I had better play it cool here. Iris sat between Helen and Costas. Her beauty, her presence were a source of pleasure and pain. The waiter came by and Costas ordered food and wine.

The music stopped. Big D. came back to the table. He greeted everyone in his usual fashion, and as the music started again, he half-dragged Chris, the twins, and Costas to the dance floor. It never ceased to amaze me how nimble he was. He winked at me, conspiratorially.

I turned to Iris. I wanted her in the most desperate way. She looked at me. She was turning red. She knew what I was thinking. Helen started to talk to the girl right next to her.

It left Iris and me pretty much to ourselves. Then, under the table, I felt her foot touching my leg, and it jolted me. She saw my reaction and smiled.

In a nonchalant way, I reached under the table and ran my hand over her leg. The next thing I knew she had her foot right on my crotch. Risky I thought. I pushed her foot away.

"How was Hydra?"

"Fine."

"Are you staying for a while?"

For some reason her question did not seem sincere.

"I don't know. It depends."

"There are many things to see here."

"Yes, I imagine there are."

"I missed you," she whispered.

All of a sudden, I got pissed. It burst out in such a way I could not tell where my anger came from or why. It shook me up. She missed me, man that was bullshit!

She saw my reaction and seemed kind of lost. I hated to admit that Iris just confused the hell out of me. What was she looking for? How did I fit into this whole situation?

"So, how's your life?" My voice was not friendly; in fact, it was a bit hostile. We both knew it.

"Fine, how's yours?"

"Just dandy, hunky-dory. It couldn't be better . . . yeah."

Her eyes were sad in a way that made me angrier and reckless. I was screwing things up, but I could not help it. She was so near, and yet I could not reach for her.

The idea that Costas may have been making love to her was enough to make me go ballistic. I did not want to be nice to her.

Jealousy was never my bag but, at that moment, I was jealous and I hated myself. I blamed her for putting me in this situation. Was this her last fling? Is that what this thing was about?

What did she want from me? Was I just serving a function here, you know, like another roll in the hay before . . . before what?

"So, why did you come into my room?" I could not believe I had asked the question. I sounded bitter, pathetic, and full of recrimination. Had my life really come to this?

"I don't know," she answered. I could see she was afraid.

"You don't know?"

"Yes," she whispered.

Merde. I had been imagining all these crazy ideas that had to do with me, with us. Now she is telling me that she did not really know, which probably meant it had nothing to do with me or with us. Was she misleading me? Was it a game with her? Talk about getting confusing messages.

"That's an easy answer."

"It's the truth."

"Maybe you should lie."

"Isn't that what you wanted? Why are you acting this way?"

Her voice was sad. From the corner of my eye, I saw Helen glancing at me with a firm look that was none too friendly. It brought me back to my senses.

I had an incredible pain in my heart and in my gut. Man, how I wanted Iris. I wanted to take her in my arms, hold her there—fuck the world—but I did not do it. Why was I afraid? She seemed close to tears.

"What do you wish of me?"

"I'm sorry," I said. "I'm behaving like a jerk. I have no right."

Sadness encircled me because I really did not know what I was doing there. I wanted to go. I wanted to stay. I did not feel like I belonged there, though I had no idea where or to whom I belonged. I was behaving like a puppy, all crazy about someone, anyone, giving him affection.

Had the sum of my life come to this? The whole episode had caught me unprepared, out in the open, and I could not hide anywhere. I hated to admit I was hurting.

I wanted to say I needed her in the worst possible way. But I was afraid she would laugh at me. I wanted to ask her again why she had done what she did.

Yet the fear that she might tell me it had been a simple whim on her part was just too damn risky and hard for me to accept at that strange moment in my life. I also feared she would tell me to be an adult and not act so foolishly.

Perhaps, I had held the idea for too long that only men want to have casual affairs, when in fact both women and men seek out changes in their lives—sexual and emotional. I should be adult enough to accept that.

I guess I was living with notions of purity and correctness, which in the final analysis deny we are animals with primitive instincts. My feelings were raw. I could not hide them. I did not want to hide them. I wanted to be truthful—even if it hurt like hell.

But that meant going into territory fraught with emotional vulnerability. Adults are supposed to try to pretend, be polite, or even fear our own sensibilities because showing what we feel or saying what we really think could be tricky and treacherous. It is so often misunderstood, even disastrous to the idea of who we are.

If I was ever to make sense of what my life was about, perhaps now was the time, but how? I did not know. I was still missing the key. The plain truth was that I had no right to make demands on her, and that was why I felt naked. I had to get away from this place.

The situation was untenable. I was so frustrated that we had to observe decorum and protocol because of the others. We had to play this fucked-up game, this self-imposed delusion, and I did not like to pretend. I hated it.

"Nothing has happened," she said, obviously guessing what was partially behind my stupid behavior.

"You don't owe me any explanation," I said, feeling sorry for myself.

"I know, but that's the truth."

I believed her, yet I did not want to believe her because I wanted to go on feeling lousy—the only thing that had any real appeal to my crazy state of mind at that moment. I was feeling sorry for myself—nobody was going to talk me out of it.

"Try to understand," she added.

"You've no idea how hard I'm trying."

"Are you staying with Chris?"

"Yes."

"I'll come by later."

"If you come, I'll never let you go."

"That would be lovely."

Her words were soft, and sad. This had to be one of the craziest moments in my life. I had such conflicting images in my head, all of them floating around in great turmoil. Sitting there and pretending was going to make me explode. I did not want to do that.

The impression I had was of my life being a gigantic charade to which I had been more than happy to contribute my share of nothingness. I wanted some changes. I needed to make some changes. But what kind? That was the crux of the matter.

I wanted to become like everyone else. I wanted to understand what I was. Where I was in the scheme of things? Who I was? I did not want to continue yearning and feeling lousy, lost.

I felt removed from what people did with their lives. This sentiment of strangeness brought me angst, isolation.

People met, fell in love, got married, had kids, went to work, came home, played with the kids and the dog, went to bed, and made love once a week—hell, once a month. The routine continued day in and day out. So, what was wrong with that?

Did they lead desperate lives? Was my life worse than theirs? What was missing here? What was the alternative? Was that all there was to anything? I was looking for something, a glimpse, a sentiment, an insight that would make things clear, neat. No nagging questions.

All tied up and ready to be put away in the vault of life only to be looked at when you wanted to show your kids what they had coming to them after you died, like some kind of coin or stamp collection.

Was that what Vito had meant? He went everywhere carrying his stamp collection because that seemed to define him. He talked about that collection as if he had in his possession Dead Sea scrolls explaining what his life was all about with no ambiguities.

Here I was, panting after a young and lovely woman, in the middle of an island in the Mediterranean Sea, with just one small hitch: an Adonis was hovering over her with whom I could not compete.

She, for some unknown reason, liked me though not enough to tell him she would rather be with me. She might even love both of us or she may not even have known for sure what she was looking for, which made the whole thing a bit sticky, and I felt like I was left holding the bag and blowing smoke.

I did not know how to react. I had never been in such a fix before. What is the nature of love anyway? How is it mixed in the final product?

It was late in the evening. Chris and I were sitting by the beach.

"I think it's all in the way you dance," good old Chris.

"What is?"

"How you find out about the nature of things."

"Right, that and a dime will get you a cup of coffee."

"I don't know about the dime anymore," he said, laughing.

"Explain a bunch of weirdos out there: guys dancing with guys, what kind of shit is that?" I just was giving him a hard time.

"When I first met you," he said. "Greek men had sex with their mothers. Now we're weirdos. I wish you'd make up your mind."

"Oedipus screwed his mother, didn't he?"

"That's mythology, man."

"Maybe it isn't. Maybe it was based on a true story."

"Who knows? In any event, I've zero desire to have sex with mine."

"You guys are just weird *malakas*—like the master weirdo, himself."

"Who?"

"Old Socrates."

"Maybe, but then maybe not."

"Did you ever wonder why they killed him, really?"

"It's hard to say. Socrates was a strange character. A war hero, but he was also a dilettante. He always claimed all he knew was that he didn't know shit. Very clever. He wasn't really a supporter of democracy. He believed in kings, rulers, probably tyrants. But you've got to hand it to him: He had some balls."

The sea was calm, shimmering under a brilliant moon high in the sky. Mysterious. I wanted to believe Iris would come by, but I knew better. There were too many other interests, too many obvious inconveniences around us.

To act out the simple and ancient ritual of love seemed to demand a kind of protocol I did not understand. Another night of fruitless waiting.

The previous night, I had left the restaurant before anyone else because I wanted to be alone, to think, which made things even worse. Iris had said she would come by, and I literally sat all night waiting. She never showed up.

When Chris and the twins asked me the next evening to join them, I told them I had some work to do. After they came back, the twins went to their rooms, and Chris and I sat by the beach with the full moon shining.

I had done some work on the script while they were gone so the evening had not been a total loss.

"You're saying I ain't got no balls?" I asked.

"Never said that."

"What would you have me do?"

"You're asking the wrong man."

"She said she'd come."

"Maybe she tried but couldn't make it."

"Whose side are you on, anyway?"

"Mine," he said, laughing.

"Why would I expect any sympathy from you?"

"First, I have to find it," he said. "Secondly, you need to merit it."
He laughed, but I knew he was better than that.

I had gained something and lost something. Why could I not settle
for that? And Cécile, where did she fit in all of that? The irony of the roles
was not lost on me. In the legend, it was Penelope who waited.

Now a wonderful French woman was waiting and I was no Ulysses.
Ah, these crazy Greeks. I had to get away from all of this. I would take the
ferry back to Athens the next morning.

"Let's go to her house," I said.

"Now?"

"Yeah, why not?"

"It's kind of late."

"Late for what?"

"To pay a visit, don't you think?"

"Do you want to go with me or what?" I sounded pathetic.

"I don't think I have much of a choice."

"All *malakas* have a choice."

He laughed. As we got into the car, I was not sure why I wanted to
go. Though, as we got near the house I felt better about my decision. The
house was nestled on a small hill surrounded by trees. In the darkness, I
could tell that it must have a great view of the sea.

Chris turned off the motor. Only the ticks of the engine broke the
silence. Then even those subsided. The silence was deafening.

"Aren't you coming?"

I knew he would not come. He had a shit-eating grin on his face,
obviously making fun of me.

"No, it's your show. Do you want me to wait for you?"

"That's OK. The walk might do me some good. I'll see you back at
the house."

"I'll leave the light on for you," he said, laughing as he drove off.

After my eyes got used to the darkness I started to walk toward the
house. For an instant, it occurred to me that someone could mistake me for
a burglar, and shoot my ass. It would serve me right.

As I walked around to the front of the house, I found Iris sitting on
a bench with her arms around her knees, staring at the sea.

Even though I had come looking for her I was so startled to find
her there that I thought about skedaddling. A small light filtered out of the
partially opened front door.

"Iris?"

She did not seem surprised by my voice. She turned around and
looked in my direction. I walked up and sat right next to her. Her eyes were
clear but her look seemed far away.

"I knew you would come."

"How did you know?"

"I just knew."

The setting was peaceful and silent with the moonlight reflecting
on the sea, resembling a magical, endless road inviting one to take it and

just disappear into the sky. I had wanted to say so many things and now that I was here, I could not think of anything.

My confusion and my desire for her were driven by her earthiness and physical attractiveness. Her dark eyes and looks, her classic profile and slim body—all seemed like the fulfillment of a fantasy, inscrutable and timeless.

I was right next to her, and yet she might as well have been on the other side of the galaxy. I had no idea who she was. A crazy thought suddenly came to me: Was she a fury sent by the gods to test me and put me in my place, a messenger and not the real thing?

But what message? She was so near and yet unreachable. I wanted to understand her, and perhaps through her understand myself. I was not used to such mysteries.

What was I looking for? My destiny? I did not believe that another person—a woman in this case—could possibly be my destiny. I had always been skeptical that there was one single person in the universe who could make your life gain so much significance.

I was still not clear about such things. Cécile was always criticizing me about this attitude. She thought it was just too cynical.

I could see that this reality, though strange and mysterious, demanded something from me. At that moment, I just was not sure what that was. It felt like I was thrashing around in a sea of conflicting feelings with no spiritual lifeboat I could climb onto and save myself from a possible emotional drowning.

I had slept with a nymph and if Zeus, the supreme deity of the gods, did not approve there would be hell to pay later. You screws up and you pays the price . . . Chris would say. That is how life was.

"Last night I waited for you." So banal, but was the best I could do.

"Yes, I know."

"Look, I don't know what's going on. I had no business behaving the way I did. I'm sorry—" I stopped. What did I want from her, anyway?

"Are you always this impatient?"

"Patience is not one of my virtues."

"Tell me about Hydra."

What the hell, I thought. Why does she want to talk about Hydra?

"I've never been there," she added.

"It's a nice place. No cars. Beautiful port. Lots of tourists."

"Just like any other Greek island."

"I guess so."

"Do you know the story of Hydra?"

"It has to do with some kind of monster?"

"Mythology says it was a nine-headed serpent, and when one of its heads was cut off it was replaced by two others. Many people interpret the metaphor to mean an ever-increasing evil with many sources and causes."

"The island is beautiful. I didn't see anything evil about it."

"Well, it's because you're not Greek," she said, and smiled.

"Maybe you're right. Why are you asking me about Hydra?"

"I don't know how to start talking about us." For a second, I thought she was making fun of me.

"Are you alone here?" She saw me looking back over my shoulder at the silent and darkened house.

"Yes and no. My aunt lives here and she sleeps like a baby." She smiled.

"And your parents?"

"They live on the other side of the island."

I could now hear the faintly the waves crashing in the distance. The muffled sound was soothing and pleasant.

"What about your parents?" she asked suddenly.

"They're divorced. I have very little contact with them."

"I'm sorry to hear about it."

"That's the way the cookie crumbles."

"The what?" She was not sure what I had said.

"It's just American slang. It means in life things like this happen."

"The cookie crumbles . . . I have to remember that."

Why did things with my parents turn out the way they did? The family bond that should have kept us united, even with all the troubles, seemed to have vanished long ago. I often wondered if we ever had this bond.

Over the years, I tried to analyze just what it was that my mother gave me, and other than her fears and the obvious physical attributes, I came up empty. With my father, I was much closer—until the divorce screwed everything up.

Now on this moonlit night, Iris's question had brought back the strange and mixed emotions I had about my parents. Family relationships can be so chaotic that sometimes just going from one day to the next seemed fruitless, impossible.

We were led to expect a lot from our families. Are families necessary other than to bring us into the world? We should not have to owe anyone anything.

"Do you miss them?" Iris asked after a long silence.

"I don't know. Sometimes I think I do then . . . I don't know really."

"I want to show you something."

"What?"

"Come with me."

She took my hand and we walked down the hill and came upon a small car. We got in and she drove down the road. The car was noisy but comfortable. We drove through the darkened countryside. As we came around a bend, she stopped by the side of the road.

The headlights showed a large, ancient site with what appeared to be some kind of construction or excavation taking place. I could see some broken down steps and stonewalls.

The setting was vast, as I could tell by looking at the shadows of buildings looming in the distance. She turned off the lights, and we got out of the car. It took me a few moments to get used to the darkness. The silence was complete.

We walked toward what appeared to be an entrance with steps that led to a building I could barely distinguish in the dark. I touched the stones: cold, immutable, holding eternal secrets.

"Where are we?"

"This is what's left of the palace of Knossos built for king Minos thousands of years ago."

"Were your ancestors living here in this part of Greece?"

64

"I think so. Why do you ask?"

"Just curious. How big is this place?"

"It's very big. To appreciate it you have to come during the day. There is so much to see here. This place is as famous as the Acropolis."

"Why did you bring me here?"

She did not answer me right away. In the dark, I could not see her face.

"I don't know," she said, after a long silence. "I felt like I wanted you to see it, but I don't know—"

She stopped. I waited for her to continue, but her sudden silence seemed to indicate she was struggling, though I was lost as to what exactly she needed to explain. More than anything else, I was looking for clarity, but I must admit Iris seemed to be in uncharted emotional territory.

We were both in uncharted emotional territory, truly. The moonlight falling on the ruins gave the place a haunting quality and a sense of restfulness and mystery.

"Sometimes, I come here at night when there is nobody around and I sit and—" she fell silent, again.

"There is a legend about this place, isn't there?"

"Yes," she said. "It tells the story that thousands of years ago a famous warrior was held prisoner here and a young maiden helped him escape."

I remembered. It was the story of Ariadne and Theseus. Ariadne was King Minos's daughter who gave Theseus the thread by which he found his way out of the Minotaur's labyrinth. She escaped with Theseus, and later he abandoned her.

I did not know all of the details of the story. How did this myth relate to me, to us? I was trying to remember what it was about the story that made it magical yet tragic. I came up empty.

Iris would free me from my labyrinth but was afraid to come with me because one day I would abandon her? Was that Cleo's message to me back in Athens? Cleo had said that Iris could help me, but it would be hard.

I sure as hell was not looking for a riddle; life itself was plenty complicated already. The moon came out from behind some clouds, its light shining down on the ruins. The peacefulness of the setting made me think that perhaps we should not be here.

"Do you think the story of Ariadne and Theseus really happened?"

"Why not?"

"I mean in real life?"

"In real life. Though Theseus didn't really have a fine reputation in ancient times," she said.

"What did he do?"

"He wasn't what we would call a 'nice gentleman'. He wasn't honest and some versions of it have that he took advantage of Helen of Troy when she was just a young girl. A lot of these stories are so strange even to me."

"Your ancestors seemed to have explanations for everything."

"Yes, we're famous for that, though not for everything."

"Well, most things."

"Yes, most things."

"You're right. Not everything. Look at us. What do we explain?"

"There is nothing to explain," she said quietly. "That's how life happens."

"So, we have nothing to say?"

"Our destiny is never in our hands."

"Do you believe that?"

She looked away from me, and her silence was a most direct response to my question. It was as if she had accepted some kind of truth, or fate, she also wanted me to accept.

I could also sense she was withdrawing into a world of immense distance from me. I did not know what to think. I was lost.

Suddenly, an incredible feeling of loneliness and longing washed over me. I thought about my mother. This confused me even more as I had not thought about her for a long time, and Iris had brought those memories back when she had asked about my parents.

What were those sentiments I was trying to decipher? The sense of being abandoned? The guilt it was my fault they had not stayed together. When you are a kid and your parents divorce, it really screws you up for a long time.

I was never privy to why their relationship had not worked out. I only saw anger, tears, sorrow, and separation. All I had left were sad memories, and pain that explained nothing.

My father once told me he and my mother had met long after their divorce and had squared away what was broken between them.

It had allowed them to live their own separate lives. Yet some parts of my life were still broken, and would remain so because my parents had never squared away anything between them and me.

Why was I feeling anguished? Had I been able to resolve that problem, it would perhaps become clear why Iris and I were standing in the middle of ruins dating back nearly three thousand years, trying to figure out the unexplainable.

Was this the beginning of finding a way out of my own labyrinth? Memories always play tricks on you, especially painful memories. They push you to imagine the way things should have been instead of the way they were.

"I don't know what happened. I had this strange desire to be with you. I could tell you wanted me. I have never felt such a strong and direct desire from a man for me before," she said.

"Do you regret it?"

She did not answer right away. It seemed like she wanted to give me an answer and was not sure.

"No," she said, finally.

Her face was turned away from me. I turned her and looked at her. There were no tears. Even with only the moon's light falling on her face, I could tell.

"There are so many things dancing around in my head," she said in a half-whisper.

"Are you afraid maybe of what Costas might do?"

"I don't know." Her voice was heavy and distant.

I realized what a burden I must have been for her. All along, I had thought only of my fears, my confusion. What about her? What had struck her? Had I not come along could she have gotten into this mess?

"Can one still get lost in here?"

"You don't need a labyrinth to get lost," she said after a long silence.

"How true."

"What do you want?"

That was the question, and I was no more prepared to answer her than I was to answer it for myself.

"If only I knew."

"Do you want us to be together?" her voice was clear and direct.

"Yes."

In a way, she was putting my feet to the fire. If I really wanted her, all I had to do was to take her hand, walk down the road, and never look back. In her voice, I even detected a tone of defiance.

I was being pushed to finally make a decision regarding my own place in life, where I was—where I stood in relationship to the universe. The more I thought, the more obvious it got: Whatever decision I made was no longer part of a simple game. The sentiment was suffocating.

My own confusion was now pushing me to decide, and I could not do it. I was afraid to make the wrong decision. It was a longing to have a personal say by living life—and not by reading about it from other men's books—that had ruled my life. I always prided myself that was exactly how it had been so far, but it did not seem so obvious anymore.

Something had changed. I was not sure how to handle it. Cécile's face came into my mind. I did not want to lose her, either. Yes, things had changed; we would probably never go back to the way we were. It was not her fault or my fault.

The idea, however, troubled me because accepting one's own responsibility is also part of who we are. At that moment, I was not sure who in the hell I was or what place I was supposed to occupy.

The moon was now high above the horizon. Not one cloud was visible in the sky. Iris had been silent.

"Make love to me." She whispered, softly, almost begging.

"Here, now?"

"Yes, just like you did at the Parthenon."

The Parthenon! That was eons ago. It happened in another time dimension when all was harmony, sweetness, and innocence. For everything came from us and nothing came from the outside to interfere and make us sad. A whole universe had burst and disappeared since then.

Her request took me by surprise. There was a sense of urgency in her words. I, who never doubted my own virility, now found myself searching for reasons to want to make love to her—there were none.

Her request was sad, and my lack of response was pathetic. I was unable to have any erotic feelings. It was disconcerting and humiliating as hell. She kissed me hard on the lips, but my efforts to respond only made the situation worse, and slowly her own efforts petered out.

We stood facing each other, spent, without hope. The earth, sure as hell, was not about to move for us tonight.

I had wanted some changes in my life, but every instinct seemed to want the exact opposite. Everything had to stay the same because the unknown was just too terrifying. One never knew what was in store. I was torn by a desire of wanting changes but not believing in them.

A sentiment that probably also led me to a life of wandering from one kind of relationship to another. Wishing to find *la raison d'étre,* but not really looking for it.

Afraid of finding it because once the truth is revealed one cannot hide behind veils of deceit. One has to accept the inevitable consequences. It is difficult to face one's own peculiar failures.

Perhaps for me it had to do with my mother's legacy. She was always terrified of life. There was never a good reason to expect it could get any better. In her desperation to deal with her own emotions and uncertainties, she did the only thing available to her: self-protect while ignoring the fears of others.

Fear is primitive. All human beings are afraid of something: the unknown, darkness, death. The trick is to face those fears and not let them paralyze you.

Slowly Iris walked back to the car. I followed her, and we got in. We drove back in silence. I had gone looking for answers and found none. The result was that I had gotten her more confused than could possibly be healthy for either of us.

Yet I could not help it. Faced with these conflicting emotions, I did not know how to make sense of them. Was it possible to make sense of your own fears?

Maybe Cécile was right when she said that I was always hiding from love, from life, and from myself. I was confused and weary, and I was also desperate. My guts told me that I would lose this battle, and there was not a damn thing I could do about it.

I was locked inside this vault. There was no way to get out. Somebody else had the key. She drove back to the place Chris, the twins, and I were staying.

"I came to see you because I need you. It is hard to put into words how I feel. Come away with me."

"I can't, not just now."

"Are you afraid?"

"Yes."

"Don't be afraid. I know it's crazy, but we can do it."

"Alex, if life could only be that simple."

"I know it isn't. We can try. We could make it work. You can help me make it work."

"So many things are hidden from us."

"We can try to find them. Look, you've come into my life and it scares me, and I know that. I want to stay and I want to run. Help me understand it."

"I wish you'd take what is brought to you, accept it, and enjoy it."

"You have no idea how hard I'm trying to do that."

"It's so simple, really."

"Maybe to you it is, Iris come with me, please."

"Oh, Alex . . ." softly she touched my left cheek.

"Please, I need you so damn much."

I was being a coward, and I hated myself for it. I should have been making the decisions for both of us, but something was holding me back, and I was trying like crazy to understand it.

"I know," she said. She looked at me with a sad smile.

"Then come, please, I beg you. OK, maybe not tonight. Promise that you will come to Paris. We can make it work. I know it!"

I was so desperate that it made me afraid and crazy. She put her hands on the steering wheel and kept looking straight ahead.

"I'm tired," her voice sounded very far away and pained.

I got out of the car. I did not know what else to do or say. Everything seemed unclear and complicated. I felt so emotionally drained. Eventually the car started moving away from the house and down the road.

I stood looking at it until it disappeared around the bend and into the night. The moon was beautiful, full, hanging in midair, but she was not about to smile on us tonight. Man, why could life not be as simple, sweet, and innocent as a baby's smile?

I walked into the house. It was quiet. I went to my room, and when I opened the door, I almost fell over for sleeping peacefully in my bed was one of the twins! It was so unexpected that for a moment I feared I had walked into the wrong room.

Quietly I started to back out, embarrassed, trying not to make any noise, but as I looked around there was no mistake: This was my room. My belongings were where I had left them earlier in the day.

There was a small lamp on right next to the bed. Partially covered by the sheets, she was sleeping on her stomach with her head away from the light. I could see she was only wearing her panties.

I tiptoed right next to the bed and looked at her, then drew the sheet over her half-naked body. Her nightgown was on the floor. What in the hell was going on here? This was too crazy.

Was it a joke from Chris and the twins because of what I had said to him earlier? I sat on the chair and looked at this sleeping beauty. How irrational and strange life is.

I did not know what to make of what I was seeing. Finding her in my bed was as unlikely as anything I could have imagined happening to me. It felt like I was an intruder in my *own* life!

She was sleeping with no apparent worries about where she was. Her sleep was peaceful and quiet. It was the sleep of the innocent. A sense of comfort washed over me as I sat there watching this strange girl in my bed.

It felt like she was allowing me to share some intimate moments that went beyond her nakedness and revealing secrets, which perhaps, I had no right to know. She seemed so vulnerable.

After experiencing so much emotional upheaval earlier in the evening, I now began to feel rested and at peace. I do not know how long I sat there silently watching her. I thought of going to find Chris to see if he knew anything about this, and as I was trying to resolve it in my head, she stirred, turned around, and started to wake up.

Now I was not sure what I was supposed to do. She opened her eyes, looked at me, and gave me a warm smile. She raised herself covering her breasts with the sheet. She did not seem surprised to find me there watching her.

"Hi," she said.

"Hi?"

"I fell asleep."

"I can see that."

"I'm sorry."

I did not know whether I should accept her apology or perhaps I should have been the one apologizing. The whole situation was just a little bizarre.

"I know this is nutty," she added, smiling as if reading my thoughts.

"I guess so." I really did not know what else to say.

"I wanted to talk to you. I waited, but I got sleepy."

"They say that sleep sometimes helps resolve many problems."

"I like to sleep a lot."

"So, you have many problems?"

"No," she said, and smiled.

"Then it's OK."

"What's OK?"

"That you fell asleep in my bed. I'm sorry I woke you up."

"You didn't."

"What did you want to talk to me about?"

"Just silly stuff about my sister and Chris."

"Are you jealous?" I was not sure if that was an acceptable question.

"Of course not," she said, smiling as if the joke was on me while making me feel silly for asking the question. With women, things are never easy.

There was a certain sense of *déjà vu* in her attitude. It felt as if I were going to find something that I did not care to find out. I also felt stupid because I had no idea whom I was talking to: Was it Lisa or Robin? Should I ask?

"It's not what you think it is," she said.

"I don't know what I think it is, but it's not often that I unexpectedly find a beautiful woman asleep in my bed," I said, though that was not quite true.

For a moment, I thought that maybe I should tell her about the visit by Iris to my room, but I dismissed the idea immediately. I started to laugh.

"Why are you laughing?"

"About the weird stuff that happens in my life on top of which I can't even guess who you are. You and your sister look so much alike." I did feel foolish.

"Try," she said, smiling a wonderful smile.

"This has to be the craziest thing. You must be Robin?"

"How can you tell?"

"I can't. It's just that Chris told me about Lisa."

"That's where the problem is. I'm Lisa and he and Robin went out to walk on the beach because I'm not interested in what he wants, I guess."

"Maybe he's complaining and trying to convince her to put in a good word on his behalf?"

"Won't do him any good," she said, laughing. I started to laugh with her.

"Crazy, isn't it?" She added, as if the whole thing had no serious significance other than just another topic of conversation at this time of the night between two strangers.

"Look, I can't comment or advise anybody. I have enough problems of my own."

"It's about Iris, right?"

"How do you know?" I was surprised.

"It's easy to guess."

"It shows?"

"Kind of."

"I must be very transparent."

"Not really, Anyway, Chris told us."

"That bum. What else did he say?"

"That's all."

"Sometimes life does get a little too crazy and the heart gets sad."

"Just like tonight?" She asked.

"Yes, just like tonight."

I stood in the middle of the room unable to make a decision about what to do next. She saw that. Her next words were completely unexpected. They threw me for a loop.

"Would you like me to stay?"

"You don't have to do that."

"I know," she said. "But do you want me to?"

"I couldn't ask you to do that."

"Why not?"

"I just couldn't. I wouldn't be good company tonight, anyway."

"Sometimes a sad heart needs to have a happy heart around," she said, and gave me a beautiful smile that really made me feel good.

"It's lovely of you to say that, it really is, but this situation is way out of my range."

"Let it be my decision, then."

She looked at me not teasingly but more like I should have made the suggestion. I was not afraid. It was just that she seemed quite pleased to be inviting me to join her in the bed and like a dummy, I stood there, lost.

She moved over to make room for me, I thought, what the hell! I am an adult; she is an adult. I undressed and got in the bed with her.

No sooner was I in the bed than she put her hand on me. I got hard, very hard. I threw off the covers and there in its entire splendor was my rod stretching as far as it would go.

It was surprising to see how tall and erect it seemed to be considering that not too long ago, barely a few minutes, it resembled a wet noodle.

What ensued was the most physically demanding night I have ever spent in the company of a woman. Even making love to Iris paled by comparison. All my sadness and frustration seemed to evaporate, to be replaced by an incredible energy and physical hunger for Lisa.

She matched and reciprocated my madness and lust for physical intimacy in a way that knew no limits. I do not know how many times we made love. It went on until early in the morning.

We were like two people who had suddenly discovered sex for the first time. We had this incredible and inexhaustible supply of sheer physical stamina and a great need for each other, for whatever each of us represented to the other—without being clear exactly what that was.

Somehow, we had liberated ourselves from whatever holds strangers back from each other. That night we touched, explored, and tasted our bodies—no, drained our bodies—with our hunger for each other.

It was lust, madness, fused into an explosion of pure physical pleasure. There is no other way to describe it. Yes, there were moments of tenderness and softness, but they could not be confused with love.

Men always boast and joke about how many times they can make love to a woman in a single night.

I leave others to set records. We hardly spoke. When we finally went to sleep, I was so tired a cannon going off right next to my head would not have sufficed to wake me up.

The sun was high in the sky when I woke up. I was alone. There were sounds of laughter at the other end of the house. The night with Lisa had left my spirits less troubled by what had happened with Iris and, I found myself physically satiated. I felt less pressed for answers.

A lovely gift from a beautiful girl had been given to me, and this time I did not go crazy trying to figure out what it all meant. After taking a shower, I went out to join the others in the garden—to yet another surprise.

Karen and Manos were sitting there holding hands and seemingly very devoted to each other.

Chris was sitting between the twins and did not show signs that he knew what had happened. Now I was not sure which girl had spent the night with me, as both looked so much alike. It was scary and intriguing as hell.

"Hey, *pusty*," Manos got up, came over and embraced me as if we had been friends from the beginning of time. I went over to greet Karen. She did not seem concerned or surprised to see me. The twins and I kissed each other on the cheeks.

"It's me," the twin sitting on Chris's left, whispered.

I started to laugh because Lisa obviously wanted to make sure I knew it was she. The others seemed curious as to why I was laughing but did not ask any questions. Chris served me some coffee, and I sat.

"Are you the same?" Manos asked Lisa.

"Yes," Lisa answered.

"How are you the same?"

"Well, we look the same," Robin said.

"You look the same, but you're the same inside?"

"Sometimes we are, "Lisa said.

"You're not half of the other?"

"No," Robin answered.

"We're the same and we're different." Lisa said.

"How can people tell you apart?" asked Chris.

"It's simple," Robin said.

"OK, how?" Chris asked.

"I'm Lisa."

"That's what you say," Manos said. "But how can we tell?"

"Well, there's a birthmark that can tell." Robin said.

I remembered what Lisa had told me about her sister the night before. She said that Robin had a tiny birthmark inside her right thigh, which made it interesting if not awkward to verify by asking the girl to disrobe. Of course, there were benefits to this as well.

"You expect people to ask you to show them to make sure?" Chris asked.

I could not tell if he had resolved the problem. Maybe the bastard knew—or maybe his comment was one way of finally seeing if it was true.

"It depends," Robin said, smiling.

"OK, show us," Chris said.

"You know it's there," Robin answered. She was teasing him.

"You told me it's there, but you didn't show it to me," he said.

"OK, show us. We're all adults here," said Manos.

Robin stood, opened her bathrobe—she was wearing a bikini—and then pointed to her right thigh. I did not see anything.

"It's right here," she said. "Look closely."

The men stood to get a better look. It was tiny, but it did exist.

"It's there all right," Manos said. "What about you?" He asked Lisa.

"I have one also."

Manos looked lost for a moment. Lisa started to laugh. Then he understood the joke was on him. He laughed as the rest of us joined in.

"I'm kidding, I don't have one, I'm not that lucky," Lisa continued, and she glanced in my direction as if expecting me to agree with her.

Robin closed the robe her face displaying satisfaction and vanity. It was all quite innocent. Lisa and Robin had probably been asked the same question *ad infinitum*. It was children playing a game of hide and seek.

They had invented the game and its rules to survive people's natural and intrusive curiosity. The thought had occurred to me that it would not be unlikely that from that day on Chris, Manos, and I would wonder about the location of that birthmark.

There was a difference between the twins not physically but in character. Lisa seemed more spontaneous. The night before she had told me that she never took herself seriously only what she did. It was always better to laugh at oneself. It was not a bad idea when you thought about it.

Robin's seriousness may have been due to the fact she was born a couple of minutes ahead of Lisa. Perhaps she felt that as the first-born she needed to have some *gravitas*.

Lisa kept looking in my direction, her clear eyes questioning me as if trying to guess what I was thinking. I did not know what I was supposed to think.

What about Iris? Was I supposed to feel guilty because I had been unable to make love to her? Yet I had engaged in a night of lovemaking with Lisa, and because of the last few hours, she was no longer a stranger but someone with feelings, nice, warm and very human.

My life was really getting crazy, because now I found myself thinking about three women at the same time. Yet sex is not love; love is not marriage; marriage is not sex.

So how should I have looked at this? Maybe it was the old French axiom, *"Dans la nuit tous les chats sont gris."*—at night, all cats look gray.

In French, men use the feminine of the word cat (*chatte*) to indicate a woman's sex. Cécile always hated that expression.

"It's offensive and degrading to women and only idiots resort to using such expressions. It is as if they are still schoolboys. They need to grow up."

"Why are you getting upset about such an innocent expression?" I would say just to bug her.

"It's not innocent, and you know it! I don't want you using it. You tell me not to use your word *fuck*, because you say it's a very vulgar word."

"Actually, it's your beautiful French accent when you say that word that sort of gives it its earthiness."

"You're silly." She said, but she laughed.

"Well, it's true."

"Don't change the subject. The expression about the *chatte* is very vulgar."

I always told Cécile she had no sense of humor.

What happened with Iris was different, though. I was not interested in treating it as just another meaningless encounter. But the night with Lisa had brought home to me, once again, the fragility of the human spirit: How the primitive fear of the darkness, the unknown, can drive us to do anything just to get through the night.

I was under no illusion that for Lisa I probably served the usual male role no more and no less. Greek legend has it once an Amazon was pregnant, she threw the male over the cliff. Had I served the same role for Iris? Was that a fair question?

Was Karen's bedding Manos the same as Iris bedding me? Or was it more like Lisa? Was there a difference between the two? Perhaps, I was back to harsh judgments of others and myself.

Casual sexual encounters sometimes have a significance that goes beyond their duration. On the other hand, making love to a woman for one single night is but a brief moment in the cycle of life—a whole universe is born and dies in such encounter.

The truth was I could love Iris, Lisa, or Cécile, deeply and with honesty. Time had no significance because love was all about giving and receiving and not about keeping a schedule or keeping score. Giving was easy for most of us especially when it was self-serving.

Receiving from the other person and not feeling obligated or pushed into some corner took all the courage we could muster, demanding an incredible leap of faith. Were we humans capable of such grace?

So, Iris, did I betray us last night? What prompted me to accept the passing favors of someone who may be just as worthy of my love as you? Would it have broken your heart if I had told you what happened? I had been jealous Iris might have made love to Costas.

Yet I had made love to Lisa, which made me rather dishonest. Were we capable of any honesty at all? Nothing seemed to make much sense.

Let us take Karen and Ron. Their truthfulness toward each other seemed real. They had plans for a lifetime of happiness when suddenly everything went to hell. Did life get in the way? It seemed like they imagined each other without really knowing who they really were.

Perhaps it is our human conceit that always blinds us to the deep, dark secrets of our own hearts and souls, and we ignore the warnings and the price we will pay if we fuck up. The ancient Greeks understood this arrogance calling it: *hubris.*

Now that Karen had replaced Ron with Manos, were they in better control of their lives? Who were they kidding? I got up and went into the kitchen to get more coffee. Manos followed me.

"*Malaka,* how long you stay here?"

His question took me by surprise. I do not know why but standing close to him bothered me. It was a stupid feeling, really.

"I'm about ready to go back."

"Why, you just got here. What about Iris?" he asked, a kind of slide in his voice as if we were sharing a secret. I had the feeling he really wanted me to stay around, but I resented his asking about Iris. I did not answer him.

"Karen wants to stay in Greece," he added.

"Oh, she does?" Why was I not surprised?

"Yeah, then maybe I go with her stateside if she changes her mind."

"What about Ron?"

He dismissed my question with a shrug of his shoulders. My question was not fair, had no relevance, but I had no desire to be polite. I really did not want him around. He was a leech, and I hated that. On the other hand, who was I to make such judgment in view of what was happening in my own life?

I had to smile at his brazenness. He did not seem particularly bothered by what had taken place between Karen and Ron. At that moment, I really envied the son of a bitch. Chris came into the kitchen. Manos looked at him, then at me, and with a dismissive attitude, he went back to the others.

"So how did it go?" Chris asked.

"It didn't."

"No wedding bells or getting rice thrown at you or empty cans bouncing on the pavement as they trail your wedding limousine?" he asked, making fun of me.

"What the hell are you talking about?" I asked, feigning surprise and annoyance.

"Man, I'm just jiving. So, what's next?"

"Do you have any ideas?"

"I think you should come with me to Athos," he said.

FOUR

Mount Athos is located in one of the most remote areas of Greece. It has a number of monasteries that have been built over hundreds of years. No women are allowed in Athos, only monks with their daily prayers, contemplation, silence, obedience, and poverty.

It was always tricky to go and hope to be allowed to stay—especially as we had not done the proper paper work needed to visit the mountain. The monks did not welcome unannounced visitors with open arms.

"I have some connections," Chris said, smiling.

"What, you have a direct line to *Da* mighty Zeus?"

"Get out of here. Just sit back, and let me handle it."

Though the peninsula is attached to the land, the only way to get to Mount Athos is to take a ferry across the channel. We were taking it. It was early morning, and the sea was tranquil and smooth.

At Ouranapoulis, the port where one takes the ferry, we ran into the problem. We went to the Pilgrims' Office, but we did not have the proper permit, or *diamonitirion*, allowing visitors to go to the mountain—on top of which only a limited number of non-orthodox visitors are permitted.

I was one of them. The people at the office were not amused. Nothing doing they said. They were looking at us impatiently.

"I guess I have to call in my chits," Chris said. He talked to the man he was dealing with who looked at Chris in amazement. You could tell that whatever Chris told him he did not believe or trust.

"What's going on?" I asked Chris.

"Let's see what happens."

"Are these guys monks or priests?"

"I don't know. I call them monks."

Chris shrugged his shoulders, and we stepped out of the office. We sat and waited. Finally, an old monk came out. Chris and he had a quiet conversation.

From the sound of the monk's voice, I could tell Chris was having difficulty selling our desire to visit the mountain. He was one tough old monk.

"Do you want to go back?" Chris asked me.

"What's the problem?"

"He doesn't want us here. He probably thinks we're a couple of flakes."

"Is he the head man?"

"No, but apparently he makes the decision."

"Tell him that we mean no disrespect but that we want to stay."

"He doesn't seem much impressed by what I'm saying." I could tell Chris was disappointed.

"Tell him we'll swim across if we have to, and if we drown it's going to be his damn fault. Does he want to have that on his conscience?" I was just trying to make light of the whole episode.

"Do you want me to use those words?" Chris hesitated, not sure if he should listen to me.

"Yes."

"I don't know if I can say that to a holy man."

"Why not? He pees the same way we do."

"Maybe he doesn't."

"Ask him."

"Ask him what?"

"How he pees?"

"Are you crazy?"

Chris started to laugh. The old monk had merry, dark eyes, and they were shifting back and forth between Chris and me as we talked. Chris said something to the monk who laughed a good belly laugh. I laughed at seeing his reaction.

I do not know whether it was Chris's words, my laughter, or Chris's embarrassment; in any event, we seemed to have touched some earthy nerve with the monk.

He finally relented when we convinced him we were serious about staying—we were not about to turn back. He went back into the office and came out a few minutes later, handing us the permits.

"What did you say to him?"

"What you asked me to say."

"About the way he pees?"

"Isn't that what you said to ask him?" and Chris busted out laughing. I did not believe him.

"Come on, what did you tell him really?"

"It's a long story. One of my grandfather's uncles was a beloved monk here. Our family comes from Northern Greece. I didn't want to pull rank but seeing that they didn't trust us, I gently reminded him about my relative. I told him I was making a pilgrimage to honor my ancestor."

"And he believed you?"

"It's the damn truth."

We landed at Daphne, and waited for another ferry to take us around the southern part where Simonopetra the monastery we wanted to visit was located.

We had a fleeting view of the monastery. It was an impressive sight seeming to emerge from the water, hugging the top of a rock falling over the sides of a cliff.

The size and sheer beauty of the setting were breathtaking. We got off at the next port where we could also see the Greghoriou monastery, but that was not our destination.

From where we stood, Simonopetra seemed a good distance away. There was a bus service to the monastery but I challenged Chris. "Are you game for the hike?"

"Might as well, we can't dance."

The sun was now warm, and we started on our hike. What became immediately obvious was the silence—we were surrounded by it. We were right smack in the middle of a vast shroud of silence.

"I don't want to stay in the monastery," Chris said.

"So where do you want to stay?"

"We'll find something."

We got to the monastery after a long and sweaty hike. The silence was broken only by the wind—a sweet whisper—rushing through the clean, crisp morning. The smell of fresh pine was comforting.

The monastery was amazing, sitting on a rock looking large from the outside. Once inside, most of the space was taken up by the rock it sat on.

We were welcomed with smiles. From what I could tell, what Chris was saying to the monks seemed to please them. For some reason I felt no need to ask Chris for any explanation as to what he was saying.

In fact, we hardly talked to each other while we were there. It was as if there had been some kind of muted understanding between the two of us about what to say—or not to say.

An old monk took us to a charming old farmhouse on the grounds of the monastery. He called it *kellion,* which means cell. But it was not a cell but a building with three floors.

He led us to the top floor. It had high ceilings and the narrow hallways were immaculate and austere. I looked at the well-scrubbed floors, the white walls, and felt a sense of restfulness and timelessness.

He directed us to two small rooms, and left after telling us we were to follow the rules. The rooms were functional. There was a makeshift bed with a straw mattress on it and a very rough blanket, a stool with a small table right next to it, and on the table a candleholder with a small candle in it.

It occurred to me that the candle would last no more than one hour. I later found out that was the idea. The whole set up gave me feelings of asceticism.

The monk also pointed out where the outhouse was, plus a well for fresh water. The monks who lived in that *kellion* worked on agriculture and handicrafts. They were extremely courteous, and the fact that Chris spoke Greek did make things easier.

Perhaps, it did give us a false sense we could get away with not following some rules. However, neither Chris nor I abused their open welcome. I think the monks were amused by our juvenile behavior.

On that first day, the old monk reappeared very late in the afternoon and brought fruits, cheese, olives, bread and wine. Normally you had to go to the dining room, but Chris asked to be excused and the monk agreed.

I found it both interesting and strange that Chris seemed intent in not following the disciplinary practices of the place, yet at the same time, he was very respectful.

I guess due to his family's history he may have felt he could overlook some rules. When I asked him about it, he just shrugged his shoulders and told me to enjoy the privileges, though he did attend church services while there.

Time in Athos seemed strange, measured from when sunset began. I learned that most monasteries reset their clocks every couple of days because sunset time changes, which means that church services take place in the middle of the night— literally. As I had not come for religious reasons, I felt I did not have to attend, though I did attend a middle of the night service.

Later on, the day after we arrived, I was not hungry as much as tired of the long day's journey. Eventually, the sun disappeared below the mountainside, and we were left in darkness.

Neither Chris nor I wanted to light the candles, so we sat in the dark. We did not say very much. After a while, he excused himself, walked to his room across the narrow hall and, after saying good night, he went to sleep. I soon heard a soft snoring.

I was not sleepy. I had gotten used to the darkness so I did not light the candle. I took the blanket, some bread and cheese, the wine, walked downstairs and outside the building to sit on the steps. It was cold.

I covered myself with the rough blanket, ate the bread, the cheese, and drank the wine. Much to my surprise the blanket held the heat inside and insulated me from the cold. Soon, I was warm and comfortable.

The Milky Way was gloriously beautiful, and it felt that all I had to do to touch the stars was to reach out. The wind had died down. It was peaceful, dreamlike.

The deep silence of the night sometimes brought me a sentiment of harmony, as it did tonight, though it is such an overwhelming task to find and to maintain harmony in everyday life.

I could make out some constellations. I could see Mars with its reddish color, and Sirius the brightest star in the visible sky. I was even treated to a falling star.

The vastness of the sky and the millions of years that pass before the light of a distant star reaches us, humble me and make me focus on the fragility of our human existence.

I do not think there is a greater truth of our insignificance than when viewed in the context of the infiniteness of the universe, the unresolved mysteries of space and time—we are irrelevant.

How simple and peaceful everything was on that night. It made sense that people want to withdraw from the world, seeking physical isolation to reflect and perhaps find a direction.

The ancient Greeks believed that one's own life had to be examined, as it was a key to gaining some understanding about who we were and our position in the cosmos.

I had always liked the relationship those ancient Greeks had with their deities, not passive acceptance but a reciprocal involvement between gods and men. Mortals and deities, however, had to obey a much higher order.

There could never be abuses—*hubris*—for once that line was crossed *Nemesis,* the payback goddess, stood by ready to claim her pound of flesh—the retribution would be dire and final.

While the gods were all-powerful and could exercise a high degree of control over the affairs of men, the Fates—*Clotho, Lachesis, and Atropos*—in turn, had their say.

One could never escape nor even hope to escape them, as the Fates were there to insure life's balance—controlling human destiny. Yet within these confines there was also freedom to act, to be, to become.

We are all Greeks. Know thyself! What an idea. Was it a futile search leading nowhere? Does knowing one's own self mean accepting the inevitable outcome—death? That is the second truth. It is said an unexamined life is not worth living. When should such examination begin? At what stage of consciousness?

Does one begin to examine one's own life as one examines his own navel looking for lint? Is this a kind of post-script appended to our reckless and wrecked souls?

Sir, Madame, we are examining your life and we find it wanting. Yes, we are examining your life and it sucks; in fact, it is dead!

What is this life we so desperately need to examine, anyway?

Yes, I examine my life also and I do solemnly declare it sucks, though I have some choices. They are not the best, but it is the hand that has been dealt to me. Have no idea who did it, and how I got stuck here. I can try to make this fiasco suck less, and maybe help others, but I cannot promise anything.

Before going on a hike, Chris introduced me to another monk. I did not ask him how he found him. While in Athos, Chris and I spent a lot of time by ourselves. This was the first time that someone, other than the old monk who brought our daily food, had come to visit us.

We could see the monks carrying out their daily routines, but no one ever approached us. It turned out this monk spoke impeccable English and French, and we would mix both languages as we spoke. We were sitting by a small pine tree up the hill from the monastery.

"Do you have a journal?" the monk asked me.

"What kind of journal?"

"A record that shows you where you've been and where you might go."

"No, I do not."

"A pity."

Right off the bat the conversation with the monk felt like it had been going on for years. He did most of the talking. The conversation was interesting because one of the things one hears about Mount Athos is the vow of silence.

I did not know if we were breaking the rules or if the old monk had not had a chance to speak French with anybody for a long time. In any event, it gave me a great pleasure to sit and talk with him—rules or no rules. Apparently, he got a kick out of it, too.

"I used to have one when I was a kid." I said, about having a diary.

"Do you know why you came here?"

"It seemed like a good idea."

"That's the most honest answer," he said, and started to laugh.

"It's the truth."

"Of course." He paused, and looked at me. His piercing gaze was clear and steady.

"You know," I said, "I must confess to you that my great attraction to Greece is for those ancient Greeks and those ancient times. I don't wish to offend you, but I feel much closer to them—mentally, philosophically, spiritually—than to the modern Greeks. Does that make sense to you? Can we talk about those things? Are you permitted to talk?"

"*Absolument!* If you question me, I must answer you. Let's talk about those ancient times, then. I don't know why you came here. Life has a way of putting us in places not of our own choosing, but it also demands your involvement, you cannot ignore it. We are surrounded by life: the sun to sustain us; the moon to guide us in the darkness; those buildings down the road; the people by the seashore toiling the land; the sweet whispers of the wind; the fresh scent of the pines filling our lungs; the singing of the birds. Life is everywhere!"

"It seems so simple. But it isn't."

"No, it isn't."

"So how have we survived?"

"Because we must. For thousands of years people lived in these surroundings, maybe even sat on the same spot where we are now sitting and contemplated the same questions."

"But are there any answers?"

"What kind of answers?"

"To help you clarify your life, understand it?"

"Very few."

"It seems to me if there are no answers, or few answers, then this whole exercise is for nothing. Aren't answers what we look for? Isn't that the goal—the only goal?"

"No, the only goal, as those ancient people argued, is to know yourself."

"But isn't that then the answer: To know thyself?"

"Yes, that hasn't changed, but it's only the start—*c'est le commencement de votre trajet*—the launching of your search, if you like. What you will then possess is the highest manifestation of the rules of the universe.

"Your self-awareness is the guiding light toward achieving the harmony you seek. Those ancient teachers said, 'Know thyself;' they did not say: '*Voilà la vérité!*' or as we vulgarly say: 'Here's the deal'." He laughed.

"Can we still learn something from them?"

"Absolutely! Their memory is our legacy to honor or destroy."

"Sometimes it seems that what happened to them has no relation to what may happen to me. I know they were afraid, at least I think I know. But their existence seemed basic, reflecting their own realities. I don't know if they were in fact running around in circles the way I find myself doing."

"Of course, they were. There is nothing wrong with being confused about who you are and how you fit into the scheme of things. Or your fear of failure about not having a clear understanding of your own existence.

"Confusion means looking for light, clarification. In some instances, we're lucky and we might get a glimpse of some profound truth, but it doesn't end there."

"Does that bring us closer to the essence of our individual existence?"

"Yes. Experiences await you and may even point to some direction that may make sense to you. But there are no guarantees. Life does not operate that way. You must search, *vous n'avez pas d'autre choix.*—you have no other choice."

"It's about choices, then?"

"*Oui et non.* Human emotions are complex and beyond anyone's capacity to understand—no quick fix formula. At the end of the day, when it comes to adding up our account, we are very much alone and in the dark—though that does not negate our always trying our best, looking for what is finest within us no matter how hard. This is a never-ending voyage."

"But what if at the end of the day we only discover there isn't a way out? That we're stuck."

"There is no elixir for the illness of the human spirit to cure it in a flash. Those wise ancestors of ours wrestled with this problem. It led them to invent philosophy, logic, and drama, but those were tools not answers. You must seek and reflect.

'You cannot abandon your quest. Be brutally honest with yourself. You can't hide behind platitudes, excuses, or faked ignorance."

He was looking at me knowing he was pushing me. I smiled. No matter what I said, the monk had an answer to it. He was not about to let me get away with anything, but there was nothing condescending about the way he was treating me. I liked that.

"I see you're smiling. Good. It shows my words aren't falling into a sack with no bottom. Something will stick in there, I'm certain," he pointed to my head and laughed. "It may not be what you want to take from our talk, but I'm not going to worry about it."

He got up and walked toward a pine tree and touched it. I did not know why his action struck me as odd. He looked at the tree as if wanting to hug it. He continued talking without turning around.

"We must always maintain our spirits open because there is so much beauty to life."

"What about its ugliness?"

"Yes, it is a mystery and at times a very frightening one, I'll grant you that." He turned around. "However, you cannot be shocked by the level to which human beings can descend. I am not disheartened by this. I fight every day to rectify it as I must, as you must."

"I'll let more daring ones deal with that. I don't think my involvement can make any difference."

"That's a most ridiculous idea. I'm surprised by your cynicism. You're much too young to be so cynical."

"My father says it's the arrogance of youth."

"And he's right. But, young, old, there is no age limit to the search for self and what an adventure! You must taste and swallow its richness. Spit out its bitterness. Cradle that which is precious. Nurture it. Have a vision. Insist on giving it your best. Do not settle for less. Work for that vision."

"It's too complicated. Life should be simpler and not so inhuman."

"*Au contraire, mon cher.* Aristotle once said that to change the nature of our political institutions we must change the nature of those belonging to them. He could easily have been talking about the institutions of the human soul, the heart, the human condition, the psyche."

"Do we really learn anything? How do I find the one single thing that will allow me to see life and how I'm part of it, but one that won't swallow me in the process? How do I engage with life?"

"That's the question isn't it: How to engage life? You have missed the point here. You have been engaged and didn't see it. Your presence here tells me so. You're trying to reconcile your nature to the world, to become part of life.

"The beauty is to be able to arrange all the elements and create your own music—then hear it—hear that symphony because that symphony in its purest form is the love you have in your heart to give to a human being, and be worthy of love in return."

"Only one? What about three women?"

"Ah, yes, the affairs of the heart," he smiled. "You may wish to do that if that's your preference, though I would advise it isn't a wise or a brave thing to do."

"There isn't a law that says I cannot try."

"No, there isn't."

"You approve of it?"

"You're very clever, and it's to the good." He broke out in a loud laugh. "Whether I approve or not is inconsequential. One hopes that you'll gain insight into the nature of love and of life from whatever endeavors you engage in."

"Can one love humanity? Do you love humanity?"

"Yes."

"You make it sound so easy."

"It isn't, but we're talking here about your nature. You're the way you are because you're impudent, afraid, but also capable of love, honor, and deeds that surpass the imaginable. Some will say it's all in the intricacies of the human heart: good and bad, light and darkness. The Chinese have a saying for that, though at the moment it escapes me."

I laughed. It seemed that in the isolation of the monastery talking about something Chinese was somewhat strange. He saw my reaction and laughed also.

"Oh, I see that I'm surprising you with this one. We have withdrawn from the world but not from life. Do you think that because we live here, we have forsaken our fellow man? That we're so cloistered and immune to temptations of the flesh, for example? We're men. However, our religious conviction teaches us otherwise, and that's that.

"Anything in excess is, of course, not a sound idea. The danger comes when the activity involves others. You must always be aware of the resulting consequences.

"You will soon know, if you don't already, that the pleasures of the flesh won't last. They'll diminish with time. You must also know our physical presence in the world is timed; it won't go past the deadline or speed itself up."

"What about people who have cheated death, who didn't die or survived some horrendous situation that killed others around them?"

"Yes, that's a nice and neat argument we make to satisfy our penchant for overdramatizing. The truth is rather simple: We are entities with a timing device that cannot be altered. There is no Swiss watchmaker who can advance or delay the final hour. As much as I like the Swiss, and they make fine watches, it's not possible."

"What about the others in our lives?"

"Good question but a technical one. We are linked. We do not unlink ourselves from ourselves or from others. The ultimate truth is that we all come from the same source. Are we the same? No. Siblings are not the same, yet they come from the same set of parents. Yes, knaves and saints spring from the same source."

"If we are knaves, where is the nobility of the human spirit you talked about a moment ago?"

"That's the quest: To decipher that which makes us human yet different. To see how we can understand this code, its inner workings, clarify it. Get the pungency out of it. But you must also commit to seeking the nobility of the human spirit. Learn to love its simplicity, its sweetness and innocence."

"Do we have time to do all that?"

"That's the *only* thing we have time for," he laughed. "But be careful here. Don't think for a moment that it will be easy! The inner workings of who we are as complex as the inner workings of the physical universe we inhabit. Any man worth his salt knows that. There is no way man will ever find just how this mortal universe, this complicated and strange spiritual cosmos inside our souls, was put together.

"It isn't that I'm opposed to its final discovery. On the contrary, I'm rooting for those smarter ones to find it, reduce it to its simplest level so that someone as silly and ignorant as I am can understand—so that a child understands. I pray for it to be found so man can go to bed when the night falls, sleep in peace, and not worry about what the next day brings."

"So, you're admitting that we may never come to the end of this quest and find something we can hang onto before we die, something we can keep with us which will make us free, make us know ourselves. If we cannot find it, the entire effort is meaningless."

"*Pas du tout, mon cher Alexandre.* I disagree. Your quest for understanding who you are is all encompassing, and will never be finished. You are your own quest and you can't change that. The sooner you can see that your quest is unending, the sooner you will accept it. But even more importantly, that truth will bring you the harmony you seek."

"*Pourquoi vous étés ici?*"

When I asked the question: why he was here, it surprised him. Not because he could not answer the question or had never considered it. But because the answer seemed so obvious that only some ignoramus like me would even ask it.

"*Pourquoi pas?*"

He slowly turned around in a 360 degrees circle, his arms extended, taking it all in while smiling and letting me know that his response was all encompassing. Boy, talk about someone calling your bluff and making you feel like a regular idiot. I was there. But he also pissed me off.

"I think you're engaging in some kind of sophistry here."

Though what he said made sense, it also felt like we had been going in circles and were back to where we had started. He laughed and did not seem offended by my words or my immature behavior.

"Not at all. You started with the notion of knowing thyself. You gave me all kinds of arguments, sound arguments at that, regarding this idea. You argued that in some instances, we may know who we are, and in many other instances, we remain lost. How the notion of self-knowledge is not possible. That there has to be an end and the only end according to you is death.

"*Je n'en suis pas d'accord avec vous.* I couldn't disagree with you more. My point is rather simple: The ultimate result is that in the process we discover the hidden mystery of that which is best in us. There is no end of the line for such a quest. It is eternal—"

He stopped and looked at me with a great deal of patience, and then he continued, "If there is no nobility, or love in your heart you will not find them in the outside world. Thus, your choice is clear: Search within yourself. Those attributes are within your soul. You must learn to accept and depend on them. Seek. Through such a journey you will become whole—not an easy journey I grant, but one that will enlighten you. You will not fear life or darkness any longer."

"You make this quest sound as if it's some kind of spiritual labyrinth in which we're all condemned to remain no matter what we do, no matter how we feel."

"*Pas du tout!* Not at all. Yes, life is riddled with angst and anxiety, but it's not a prison. To want to understand isn't to be condemned to some gallows. On the contrary, to reach beyond the obvious is truly a most spiritual undertaking. Don't give up on life and your search for enlightenment and understanding. You have nothing else working for you."

He stopped again and looked toward the valley below us that bordered the sea. The small, well-planted plots of land in the distance with their well-designed symmetrical lines spoke of order, not chaos.

Order. Harmony. Sense.

There was pride in the landscape we contemplated. I could imagine that at the end of the day those responsible for guarding such order would sleep soundly and with great confidence.

They had used what was best in them. They looked up to the heavens and felt at peace—worthy of themselves.

Looking at the landscape from where we sat made me think of Van Gogh's painting *The Harvest* in which colors, textures, angles, were vivid, and strong.

I did not know if in my life I could create such harmonious results—a simple reflection on what I was searching to become. I was not trying to romanticize the people in the distance.

They understood the true nature of who they were and their relationship to their surroundings. They had put something together that made sense. It was creation. It was life. Out of chaos, they had extracted coherence and order.

Michelangelo's *David* also came to mind. The first time I saw it in Florence my notion of time simply disappeared. It jolted me, but in a most uplifting and mystical way. From every angle, it is breathtaking.

The *David* overwhelms us because it demonstrates our purest and most innocent state. It forces us to stop pretending and to concentrate on our hearts and souls—on our human beauty. There is no greater experience. No greater joy.

The *Pietà,* his earlier creation now at the Vatican, has the same effect, except it is also scary to reflect Michelangelo was only twenty-four years old when he finished it.

I have no recollection of how much time I spent in front of those great works when I first saw them. It was like being at a temple worshiping the best of man and understanding the common source uniting us despite what we do to separate us.

It is at such moments that the kinship we have with others makes sense. We encounter clarity and harmony. In life, there is only one matrix, and art is one of its purest elements.

Michelangelo is just one among the many artists and creators who have struggled to make us see the beauty and nobility of the human spirit. They see clearly. They teach us and fill our hearts with emotions transcending our pettiness.

We have a need for a well-defined sense of order, and art lifts us to a higher plane. It makes us aware and less afraid of our mortality, and it helps us deal with our constant fear of failure.

Human artistic creation has been around since time immemorial. The cave drawings at Lascaux, France, were a testimony to that. The artist discovers, absorbs, clarifies, and makes the rest of us his accomplices.

I was envious of people with special talents who do create beauty, who look at chaos and extract order. Who showed us what it was to be in harmony with the cosmos. Michelangelo had done it with the *Pietà*, the *David* and his other works.

He had converted the marble into invisible matter. What we see is the ideal beauty of maternal love and of youth and not the material he used to sculpt it. He touched us because he longed for the purest expression in art.

Other artists, throughout human existence, had strived to do the same. The monk had said all men are creators. The task is to look for what is already there and use it to bring out what is noble, and truthful in the human spirit.

"Is it possible for me to do that? What I have is mundane, mediocre, and vulgar. What could I teach others? I have no gift from the gods."

"*Je n'en suis pas de votre avis,*" he said. "Yes, I could not disagree with you more. There is a lot in you that others could benefit from—if you let them." He smiled.

We had now been talking for a long time. He looked tired. His earlier physical energy was gone, and he now moved with less certainty. I was also tired and sleepy and my back hurt from sitting on the hard ground.

As the sun was no longer high in the sky, the shadows loomed larger and longer in the valley below and on the sea surrounding us. The light had the quality of the day coming to its end.

The talk with the monk had brought back to me, again, the fact that no matter how one reflects on life it can still scare the hell out of you. The monk had ruddy cheeks, lots of white hair, and a long beard.

His hazel eyes twinkled, sparkled, and when he spoke and laughed his ample girth would shake inside the loose tunic he wore. His overall demeanor seemed to radiate freshness and well-being.

He seemed whole and complete at ease with the universe and with himself. He had doubted but such doubting had made him strong and not dependent on the whims of life.

His words were challenging, and were also the words of one hell of a rebel who made his protest known, but had not stopped there.

I thought of Cécile back in Paris, and I had trouble remembering the reasons for our big fights. They no longer seemed consequential. I missed Paris. I missed the madness of the city.

The friends I had, their conversations and cynicism attempting to disguise their sensitivity. I missed my old neighborhood around Montparnasse.

At one time, I lived on rue Vavin in a small hotel—hôtel de Blois—just a stone's throw away from those two famous Parisian watering holes: La Coupole and Le Select. There was a kind of gentleness about being able to walk down to your favorite café, sit at a table to read a book, or just watch the world go by.

My friend Gary had also told me there was the American Center for Students and Artists located on Boulevard Raspail, where people placed ads for apartments and rooms for rent.

It was at the Center that I stumbled upon Ella Fitzgerald's afternoon rehearsal session. The Center was a beehive of Americans and other students. It was not unlike Cleo's, back in Athens, except on a bigger scale. I soon found a room at the hôtel de Blois.

Thinking about Cécile and of Paris made me want to go back, pick up where I had left off, and continue as if nothing had taken place. I wanted to believe one could go back and do just that, but I also knew that nothing was ever the same.

Nevertheless, I held on to the notion that in spite of all the changes within me, Paris the city I loved so much would always remain the same, the way I discovered it. The thought was reassuring.

The conversation had also drained me emotionally, and I no longer wanted to speak or listen to the monk. We both waited for the appropriate time to bid our *adieu*. Nothing was said about meeting again. I went back to my room. Soon Chris came back from his hike.

Since we had been in Athos, we had not spoken to each other at length. We had come here for our own private reasons. It seemed better we keep them to ourselves. Chris and I had not known each other long.

Thinking about how we had met and that I was not too crazy about him at first, our friendship now was as good as it was going to get. What we had been through together for the past few days made it feel as if I had known him for a long time.

He had the sense to talk when you wanted him to talk, and he always seemed to know just when it was better to be silent—especially when it was futile to express a banal opinion.

It is not easy to find friendship in this upside-down world and even less obvious to find the kind of affinity and friendship Chris and I had developed in such a short time.

I was grateful we had met, though too embarrassed to tell him so. He, of course, knew the turmoil with Iris and Lisa's visit to my room.

"You're some lucky bastard," he said.

"Why?"

"I couldn't get to first base with Lisa or Robin."

"Maybe you should consult with Manos."

"Women find you attractive and charming because of that hangdog attitude of yours," he said. I was not sure how serious he was as this was the first time someone had said that to me.

"I don't have a hangdog attitude!"

"Yes, you do! Come on."

"I don't know what that means."

"Yes, you do. You can't lie to me. I've got your number."

"So, you think that women find me charming?" I said, after a few moments of silence.

"Boy, I didn't mean to create a monster." He laughed.

"Come on, maybe it's just my dumb luck."

"Whatever it is, it works," he said, not without a bit of envy in his voice.

"Man, you're making me out to be an expert on women, and I sure as hell don't feel it. Even if I did, it would be the ultimate *hubris*, and the gods don't look favorably on abuse. Besides, admitting it to you would be pretty foolish because I would never hear the end of it."

"Don't let it go to your head. So *pusty*, what do you want to do?"

It was nearly dark now, and though the landscape still had some edges to it, the coming shadows tended to soften it and made it look there— yet not there.

"No idea."

"How's your monk?"

"Where did you find him?"

"I didn't. He found me. This is a small village. I'm sure they think we're just a couple of dummies stumbling around. Maybe they took pity on us." He laughed.

"This guy's something else."

"That's what people at the monastery say. During the war, he was a partisan leader who was once captured and tortured by the Gestapo. He never talked. They couldn't break him."

"That tough?"

"They don't make them any tougher."

"It's kind of interesting he didn't seem bothered by all of my questions, and he responded to them."

"Did you ask him about it?"

"Yes, and he said if I questioned him, he had to respond."

"You know, silence doesn't mean mute."

"I guess not. I wonder how he ended up here and why? He never told me his name."

"They change their names. Usually to the name of the monastery they live in. From what I heard he's originally from Russia."

"Russia? You're kidding? Boy, his French and his English were just flawless."

"So is his Greek."

"Man, this guy knows so damn much. He talked about ancient Greeks as if he himself was one of them. And he's from Russia, you say? Wow."

"Orthodox monks from Russia have come to Athos throughout history, a tradition going back hundreds and hundreds of years. Apparently, one day he just showed up. He's been here ever since. Of course, these guys make vows of silence, celibacy, obedience, and loyalty— they stay here until they die of old age."

"Could you do that?"

He looked at me but did not answer right away. I was surprised. For some reason, I thought Chris would have answered immediately: in the negative.

"Could you?"

"Wait a second, I asked you first. You're Greek, a *malaka.*"

"Yeah, I could," he laughed. "I don't see a set of circumstances where this would be possible, but the idea doesn't scare me."

"Can you imagine never looking at a woman with the same lusty thoughts?"

"That would be tough. I don't know how these guys do it."

"Maybe there is some truth about the rumors one hears, like the story of Achilles and Patroclus in the Trojan War."

"Oh, yes, the old Greek traditions you seem very fond of reminding me," he said.

"Do you think these monks around here are eunuchs?"

"What? Are you crazy?" He busted out in raucous laughter.

Chris could laugh at me because one's friends are supposed to tolerate one's excesses and silliness.

"Hey, it wouldn't surprise me. You *malakas* are all weird, anyway."

"Not that weird. I suppose if I were a monk and made vows of celibacy; it wouldn't be hard to keep that commitment. I mean these guys are special; they have something others don't have."

"Yeah. No balls."

"You know, I keep telling you no balls doesn't mean lack of manhood."

"I know. I'm just—" I started to say.

"Yes, busting my balls again."

"Have you noticed all those cats around?"

"Yeah, why?"

"Where do they come from? Since only male species are allowed here, how do these cats reproduce?"

"In the usual way."

"What the hell does that mean?"

"Cats breed other cats."

"You're not answering my question."

"OK, I'll let you in on a secret. A long time ago, all of the people here recognized that cats keep the rats out. But if there were no female cats there would be no new generations to replace the ones that died. So big meetings—all hush, hush of the muck-a-mucks—took place, and a special exception was made allowing female cats to live here."

"How convenient."

"Especially for the male cats, but don't be so cynical. Got to be practical in life, man. Just don't tell anybody about it, OK?"

"Why did you want to come here in the first place?"

Chris took a while before answering. It was as if he had not thought about the question before.

"I look at it like those people who go to some kind of health spa, you know, like for the waters."

"Come on. You can do better than that."

"Well, it's not that much different," he said. "Some people need to get their bodies buried in hot mud. I need to go and bury my soul in other things. It's no big deal."

I liked Chris because he was not complicated in how he saw his place in life. There was a lot going on, but he seemed detached and amused by much of what he saw. How do things come about, anyway? How do we explain events, people, my meeting Chris, for example?

I had come to Athens to write a film-script for an Italian producer who had read an amusing story I had written for some Italian rag of a magazine. I did not think anybody was awake late or bored enough to read it. In fact, I always thought it would end up on the bottom of a birdcage, which was probably where it belonged.

Somehow, through this alchemical process—and that is really the only term I can use—the article led to Milo, then to Cleo, which led to Chris, Demetrios, Iris, Vito, Lisa, and now to the monks.

A process that seems to come out of nowhere and drifts with the current being bumped here and there with no particular direction or destination—sort of like an eddy in the middle of the river as the water runs into it and around it. Though I suspect it is not quite that way.

Take Karen and Ron. They seemed well suited for each other. Their future had been planned to the last detail. Then did love or life derail all of that? Yes, life got into the picture and the whole enchilada went to hell. It did not seem nice and sweet anymore.

Ron was in Turkey, probably, with his head full of bad thoughts and jealousy. Karen was with Manos and did not seem at all concerned with Ron's fate. Maybe she was.

Manos had said that he and Karen might go back to the States together. Were they going to ask Ron to take the same flight and have all three of them meet the parents back home and explain what happened?

Would the parents ask Manos to reimburse them for the money they had spent on the pre-nuptial trip? Or would the whole episode simply be shrugged off and dismissed as "just one of those things"?

What was the connection? Where did the line begin—the question demanded an answer and there was none.

It is no secret where the river Nile begins and how it eventually meanders down to Egypt and into the Mediterranean Sea. Its path can be traced without ambiguity. But the flow of one's life: How do you keep your head above life's torrent?

If man's suffering just another exercise more or less? Then the encounter with Iris meant what? Or the night I spent with Lisa, or the situation with Cécile? Do these events mean anything?

What about morality? Was the moral judgment we make of our own actions and the actions of others the reason life gets out of balance? Morality, some have argued, was invented to keep man from turning into a total beast.

Hell. The results have not been a great credit to mankind. In fact, when measured by what morality was supposed to do, it has been a monumental failure.

Nothing has changed. But could we replace our values with something new, maybe a second-generation morality with lots of improvements as if it were a brand-new gadget? Use the same ingredients or perhaps change them—or at least change the mixture.

Not a bad idea. But this time around we would have the old blueprints and we could enjoy a modicum of freedom from the previously tried and failed system precisely by not following the same recipe.

Now we would be more experienced, old hands, who could build the new order from old recipes because it had been done before. All we had to do, to be sure of the outcome, was to look at the record and not repeat the mistakes.

The conclusion would be so basic anyone could understand it, resulting in the perfect world filled with what was finest. A system that would not fall short of its intended goal, which was to procure for mankind the best of all worlds—a new dawn.

The new design had to be radically different from the first one. The old one had failed, but there were very important lessons to be reviewed and digested. This was not going to be a situation in which everything had been thrown together in just seven days hoping for the best outcome. This time the experiment was going to be a noble one. Everything was for keeps. There could not be any screwups.

I liked that idea.

For man, liberated from the bondage of his first try, would now have the tools to try again for the last time. He truly could say that nothing depended on chance. Man would then be free, the master of his own fate.

If the second chance turned out to be a bust, man could take whatever consequences the act brought as there would be no excuses: either he would fail or he would succeed. In any event, he would be true to himself.

"I think I'll turn in early," I said to Chris. I felt tired.

"When do you want to leave?"

I did not know what to answer. My thoughts about Paris returned because Iris and I were probably never going to be there together. It was as though I was missing it in the future—hard to explain that.

Then I thought about my father; I do not know the reason. Why had we never enjoyed a normal relationship?

I was sorry we never shared a closeness that would have made a difference. The absence of such a relationship had always followed me everywhere I went. If the day ever arrived when I would become a father, would I end up just like him?

At the end of the day, the ultimate cosmic experience is the love for another human being; the monk had made that very clear. A father's love for his child is one of life's highest manifestations.

Nothing can replace that. Yet another question assailed me: How can we be good parents if we cannot be good sons or daughters?

But it was more than father and child questions that mystified me. And that was the question of my own mortality. I had never been a person to indulge in the idea of death. I was never morbid about it. I had argued with the monk that no matter how one lived, death was inescapable.

What I experienced in Vietnam, of course, was terrifying. I knew I would never be able to forget or understand. One moment you are complaining about not receiving any letters from back home, and next someone is stuffing whatever is left of you into a body bag, a small tag tied to your big toe, ready to be shipped to your final resting place where letters will no longer matter because there is no one to write them to or to receive them.

The truth has now been reduced to a couple of military guys showing up at your family's doorstep bearing their banal gift—news of your demise. Writers have it wrong: There ain't no poetry in death.

The reality of such a gratuitous and violent death slams you into another imponderable dimension, reducing you to a whimpering idiot and to a state of nothingness. It ain't a Hollywood movie.

But in some bizarre way, after seeing body bags thrown on the back of trucks like pieces of cordwood, I had mentally managed to endure that fact because I had also come to realize how arbitrary death was. The kid I saw in prison back in Africa proved that.

While in Vietnam, I thought: Fuck it! If it happens, I hope I am dead before I hit the ground. Like Demetrios had said: When your time is up there is not a fucking thing you can do to prevent it from happening. The monk had said much the same, though in less brutal terms. Being morbid was not a good idea.

That is what I admired in Demetrios: For him it was a very straightforward proposition. There were no secrets, but the fear of death makes us damn vulnerable. It controls our lives. There is no escape—no exit.

While I had not been morbid about death, admitting that I had been afraid of dying made it OK to concentrate on living. Was my father afraid of dying once he became a father? I wished I could have asked him that. The image of Helen as she was breastfeeding her baby came to mind.

There was an incredible sense of oneness between her and her baby, having to do with being alive and wholly committed to another human being.

In the past, I had paid no more attention to this than to the colors of spring flowers. I had taken them to be just stuff around which I needed to navigate every day.

Now I had a glimpse of the significance of my encounter with Helen and why I had marveled at watching her and the baby that afternoon back in Athens. Mother and baby were safe. There was love, innocence, and trust in such a direct connection between mother and child. Michelangelo's "Pietà" made so much sense.

I did not want to stay in Athos any longer. I really had not come looking for anything specific, yet I had found a tiny sense my life was worth examining and the discovery was not so bad. I was no fool to imagine this feeling would last forever.

We never saw the two olds monks again, for Chris and I left the next day. The early morning was cool and fresh. We said farewell to the monks at the *kellion* and thanked them for their kindness, hospitality, and joviality.

I did not feel any sadness or regret upon leaving. We walked down the hill toward the port and took the ferry across the channel. Then we drove back to Athens. Chris was going back to Crete. I was returning to Paris.

From Athens, I contacted Vito and told him that perhaps he should get someone else to work on his idea. He did not seem surprised, but he also said he was postponing any further work. I had the impression I had relieved him of a burden.

When I told him I would send his money back, he said he wanted to work with me in the future so I could keep it as a retainer. He insisted. I really did not care, though I very much appreciated his trust in me.

Then I wrote a short letter to Iris telling her I was going back to Paris, that I was no longer confused about us. What I felt for her was as strong as any feeling a man can have for a woman.

I would have given anything if she came to Paris to join me, but it was up to her. If she did not, it would break my heart, but I would understand. I was not being brave or noble; I was just stating my truth. Chris promised to deliver the letter to her.

"So, it's back to Paris," he said.

We were standing in front of the Acropolis. Chris had wanted to see it at night. The place was quiet and forlorn.

"Yes."

"What is it about Paris that everyone wants to go there?"

"I don't know. Ask the French."

"Shit. They would probably lie. You know they never tell the truth," he said, laughing.

"Sometimes they do, but you really have to pay attention or you'll miss it."

"What do I tell the twins?"

"I'm sure you'll figure something out."

"It's too bad you're leaving. I was beginning to like you."

"Come and visit me in Paris."

"Maybe I will. But for now, I want to stay here for a while. The east is calling and I want to check it out."

"I thought it was: Go west young man."

"Not for me."

"Did you find anything at Athos?"

"Yes, I think so, and you?"

"Yeah, I think I did, though I'm not yet sure what it is," I said. "Well, I can't say I didn't enjoy meeting you. Thanks for everything."

"You're welcome and thank *you* for the other stuff."

We were both trying to appear tough about having to say goodbye. It strikes me as sad and strange American men, unlike European men, are too prudish and too embarrassed to hug or touch in moments of friendship and closeness.

"You want to know something funny?" he suddenly asked.

"What?"

"I'm thinking about Lisa. I wasn't able to impress her, and I don't know if she likes me. But she's a nice person, and a lot of what she does is probably out of fear."

"Sometimes I think life is all about fear."

"No, it is not about fear but about conquering that fear."

"Yeah, that's what the old monk said," I said.

"Can you blame Lisa when the world can be such a hostile place?"

"No."

"She's far more complex. That makes her more interesting than Robin."

"She's no fool. I think she's genuine. She's the true article. My guts tell me that she's a pretty solid broad."

"I guess what you see is what you get. The man she will love will be a very lucky bastard," he said, convinced of his idea.

"Do you think so?"

"I'm telling you."

"Yeah, maybe you're right."

"I know I'm right," he said. "I think she's one of those broads who once she loves a guy, that's it!"

"Come on, no such women exist."

"Yes, they do. You just have to find them."

"Where?"

"They're everywhere!"

"Well, I've not found one under any of the rocks I've turned over so far."

"You haven't found the right rock. I'm telling you they exist; otherwise, this business of love just simply doesn't make sense." He was very formal in his sentiment.

"If you find a woman who will say 'I love you' and more, who will hold your hand and take you places you've never been before. Who will share her innocence, honesty, and the richness of the incredible feelings she has in her heart for you for at that moment you would be complete.

"Even if you're lucky enough to find such a woman, and even if the gods permitted such a state of beauty and harmony, something always screws it up. Let's face it, life is filled with so much uncertainty and pain, so much dishonesty, I don't know if anybody really believes in the purity of feelings anymore."

"I don't buy that," he said.

"It's the damn truth."

"No, it isn't."

"You're a dreamer, aren't you?"

"I'm a Greek remember?"

"You and that nameless monk. Are you sure you didn't talk to him behind my back?"

"What are you talking about? I only talked to him for a couple of minutes. I figured you needed him more than I did," he said.

"Yeah, you're just a couple of *malakas*."

"I'm still intrigued by Lisa's visit to your room that night."

I had briefly told him what had happened without going into details.

"Ask her about it. She might tell you," I said.

"I doubt it. Anyway, it's none of my business. Women, I don't know if I'll ever figure out what to make of them."

"I gave up trying. It's safer."

"You don't think Iris is trying to figure out who she is?"

"She knows," I said, and I knew it was true.

"What about Karen?"

"I don't have much empathy for Karen."

"You think she betrayed Ron." The sense of his words appeared to be more a statement than a question.

"Who knows?"

"I think that's what it is."

"We all betray someone at one time or other."

"True, but that doesn't make it right," he said.

"No, but that's the beast in us."

"I guess that has to do with the fact they made a commitment to each other and she broke it," he said. "On the other hand, her tryst with Manos is not likely to last past this summer."

"Another typical summer romance on a Greek island," I said.

"Just like you and Iris," he said, and I knew he was just giving me a hard time.

"I hope not," and meant it.

"What about the heart? If Karen acted on what her heart felt, how could we judge her? What about you? What about Iris?"

Questions without answers.

Iris! I went back to the feeling I had when I first saw her. She was unattainable. Iris is the name for the goddess of the rainbow in Greek mythology. I had been chasing a rainbow. Was she playing with my feelings?

I remember thinking when I first saw her that getting snared in her web would be like being sucked into a black hole. It was no coincidence Manos had said that here was a woman "a man would kill for."

I desperately wanted Iris to come to Paris, but nothing had been settled. Such a decision seemed beyond my capacity to influence. Though I clung to the desperate hope she would come, I suspected she would never do it.

The gods did not appear to favor that outcome. This made me angry, resentful, and sad, but left intact the reality of our moments together, the truthfulness of my feelings. I also hoped I would not become a slave to such memories—a vain hope. But, then, life ain't fair.

So, the question was: Could I find love again? Was I free to find love again? Would the gods allow that? Would it be the same? I was not rid of Iris, but I also hoped that if it turned out that she would not be part of my life at all, I could be free of sad memories.

That was the best way to explain the sentiments of a hard lesson learned. The passage of time would eventually settle the matter.

I had no answer to give Chris regarding his question about Iris. I went to Greece, met this girl, and slept with her. She went back to her boyfriend. I met another girl and slept with her, too. I do not know who she is going back to. And me, I went back to what . . . me?

"I don't know, maybe for Iris the whole experience was just the flavor of the moment or something."

"That sounds pretty cynical, too glib. Are you saying that's all there was, that it didn't mean more?" I could see that he was bothered by my attitude.

"Sometimes that's how life turns out. Pretty shitty if you want to know the truth."

"Karen could argue the same thing about her and Manos, too."

"True, though she left Ron holding the bag, and that's why I say life sometimes gets pretty shitty."

"You still haven't answered my question: What about the heart?" he insisted.

"Who knows? If I had the answer I would bottle it, and I'm sure I would make a mint selling it to *malakas* like you."

"Well, thanks for your trust in me. Anyway, I don't think the heart ever betrays."

"Maybe you're right."

"I know I'm right."

"Boy, I wish I were as convinced as you are."

"What about Cécile?"

"What about her?"

"Did you betray her?"

Another question to which I had no answer. I had told Chris a bit about my life with Cécile, and he was amused I was now dealing with three women. Cécile and I had been true to each other, and now we were facing the end of our relationship. We were trying to act responsibly and not hurt each other gratuitously.

We had talked about finding a solution, but we both knew that hanging on to each other would not resolve anything. Our time together had been good, but now we had to try to live our own individual destinies.

"Let me get through this life first. I may be able to answer your questions in my next one" I said. "Also, when you see Demetrios and Helen, please give them my regards. Tell them I have appreciated their friendship and hospitality."

The next day, after bidding farewell to Cleo who wished me luck and did not appear surprised that I was leaving, I sold my car to Chris—a car that had sat in a parking lot for most of the time and which I did not relish driving back—and took a plane to return to Paris.

FIVE

I had been back in Paris for about five months when late one afternoon, in early September, there was a knock on my door. When I opened it, there was a willowy girl standing outside. At first, I did not recognize her because of the dark shades she was wearing. It took me a moment to realize who she was.

"It's me," she said, removing her shades and giving me that dazzling smile of hers tinged with certain shyness. She was unsure of my reaction.

"Lisa!"

"Yes, one and the same."

I was completely taken aback by seeing her again. Since my return from Athens, other than a couple of postcards I had gotten from Chris, I had no other news. Lisa had cut her hair. She looked superb with a golden summer tan accentuating her looks.

"You cut your hair!"

"Yes, do you like it?"

I hesitated a moment because I was trying to get over my surprise at seeing her again.

"You don't like it?"

"Yes, I do! It's just that I haven't seen . . . it's a great haircut. I mean it."

"I like it."

"You should because it looks good on you."

"Really?"

"Lisa, I love your haircut. It fits you so well. *C'est très chic.*"

"Thank you," she said, as I stood by the door not quite knowing what to do or say.

"Aren't you going to invite me in?"

"I'm sorry, please come in. I'm forgetting my manners here," I managed to blurt.

We hugged, but it was somewhat awkward. We knew each other, yet we did not know who we really were, what we represented to each other.

She stood in the middle of the living room looking carefully around as if to make sure why she had come to see me. I was glad the room was not as messy as I usually kept it.

"I thought this is how you'd live," she finally said.

"Please, sit down. This is so unexpected," I said, still trying to get over the shock of seeing her here. She gave me a wonderful smile.

"You don't have much faith in humanity, do you?"

I did not know what to answer. To say I was very surprised would be poorly put. In my wildest dreams running into Lisa had never occurred to me or that she would come pay me a visit.

She had suddenly come out of my past right smack into my present. What kind of games were the gods playing now? It was truly an apparition.

"How are you? Where's Robin?"

"I'm fine. Robin went back to the States to her old boyfriend."

"You look great."

"Thank you. I feel great."

"Do you have any news from Chris?"

"I think he may be on his way to India."

"India! I got a postcard a few weeks ago. He wrote he would keep in touch, but he didn't mention anything about India. Good for him."

"He's a recent convert," she said.

"Convert to what?"

"Well, he's not really converting to anything. That's what I call trekking to India."

"What about Karen, Manos, Ron?"

"We never saw them again."

"And Demetrios?"

"Chris told us he had gone away on some business. Chris also said Demetrios is a mercenary."

She said it in a way not sure whether I knew about it or perhaps she should not be saying anything.

"Yes, he is."

"Oh, you knew?"

"Yes, a few years ago I met him in Bangkok when I was in the Army. That's when he told me what he did for a living.

"He seemed like a good guy."

"He got Chris out of jail."

"That's true. I often wondered how he did that."

"I guess being a mercenary sometimes has its good side."

"I always thought mercenaries were not nice people."

"He's the good kind, you know, getting paid to get rid of the bad guys. Given the present state of the world he's probably making lots of money."

"When Chris told us we didn't believe him."

"Well, that's Big D.'s business. How did you find me?"

"I got your address from Chris. I thought I should stop by and say hello."

She seemed to hesitate and looked as if she were expecting me to disapprove of what she had said or done.

"This is such a wonderful surprise. I'm overwhelmed. When did you see Chris last?

"My sister and I went to Rhodes just before he came back from Athos. We didn't get to see him until we went back to Athens where we ran into him at Cleo's. He was with some English girl, and I think she's with him now because they talked about going to India together."

"When did you get here?"

"A couple of days ago. It's taken me this long to work up the courage to come see you."

She gave me a wonderful smile. She seemed very shy and a bit lost. I understood how she felt. Not easy to act normally given what had taken place between us. It seemed casual; *was casual*. Actually, I had not thought much about the encounter.

"Why?"

"I didn't want to intrude. I wasn't sure if you would welcome my visit."

"Lisa, I do. You have no idea how great it is to see you again."

"Really?" She sounded relieved.

"Yes, absolutely. I hope you weren't afraid."

"Sometimes life can be confusing," she said.

"Yeah, tell me about it. Anyway, it's lovely that you came by."

"I'm happy I finally decided to do it."

"Me too. Are you staying long?"

"Actually, I'm working my way back to the States. This is the longest I've been away from home. Also, my father isn't well." She bit her lip. A troubled look appeared on her face making her look like a lost kid.

"I'm sorry to hear about that. I hope it's not serious."

"I talked to him the other day, and he said he's just getting old. It seems so strange to think my father is getting old."

"The inescapable truth."

"I know." Then in a lighter tone, "But what about you? This is a wonderful place you have. Do you live alone?"

There did not seem to be a hidden agenda behind her question. Her words and demeanor were simply the result of the natural curiosity we have about people we have not seen for a while.

"Yes."

"Paris is a beautiful city. It's the first time I've been here."

"I love Paris."

"That's what Chris told us."

"Look, you can come and stay here if you like until you leave. I've got a couple of extra rooms. You're welcome to use one of them."

In my enthusiasm to see her again, I may have gotten ahead of myself. I did not mean anything else. I was happy to be of some help. Though I could tell the idea intrigued her, she did not seem sure.

"Maybe I'll take you up on it."

"Of course, if you want to. Where are you staying?"

"At a small hotel on rue Delambre in Montparnasse."

I started to laugh.

"What's so funny?" She was curious and not sure why I was laughing.

"I've got a theory that Americans who come to visit Paris eventually end up in Montparnasse during their stay here," I said.

"Like we all end up at Cleo's back in Athens."

"Yes, something like that."

"What a great view," she said, as she walked to the window and stood looking at the Eiffel Tower in the distance.

"Yes."

There was a subtle change in Lisa. Maybe it was her new haircut or just my own reaction at seeing her again. No, it was more than that. I had the impression she had made peace with some of her demons.

Although her present shyness was understandable, she did not seem insecure. It was an awkward moment for both of us.

She was a beautiful girl, but not in a perfect way. The combination of her loveliness, a golden summer tan, and the stylish clothes she wore made her look elegant, classy. *Très chic.*

Some women can look like a million bucks without trying, and Lisa did. Since I had last seen her, she seemed to have grown sure of herself as if she had decided that this was her time.

"It's funny, you see photos of the Eiffel Tower, but to see it up close like this is something else," she said.

"I know what you mean."

She was very quiet. She had a wonderful, inward smile as if reflecting on some private memory.

"Remember what you said about not taking yourself too seriously?" I asked.

"Yes."

"These past few months I've had plenty of occasions to put it to the test."

"Did it work?"

"Yes, for the most part."

"My mother lives by it."

"Then it must be OK. What happened after I left Crete?"

"Not much. As I said, Robin and I went to Rhodes. Then we took a trip to the Middle East to visit all those historical places: Cairo, Alexandria, Baghdad, Damascus, and Beirut. We missed Jerusalem due to the fear of an impending war. Then back to Greece where we toured some islands. Then on to Crete and to Rhodes. We stayed there the rest of the summer with some old friends of the family."

"You've been pretty busy."

"Yeah. The trip was fun and interesting. Robin was pleased because she majored in history and got to see all those ancient places she read about in college. We had both read *The Alexandria Quartet,* so it was a lot of fun to try to imagine ourselves in Egypt during the time that Lawrence Durrell wrote about."

"Oh, that must have been great. I love the *Quartet.*"

"Me, too. My parents wanted us to take the trip. It was all civilized and dignified, which gave me lots of time to think, work on my tan, and make plans for the future."

"That sounds serious."

"Not that serious."

"Anyway, I hope your thoughts were good."

"Absolutely. What about you?"

"I came back here and took care of some personal business. I haven't done much of anything, really. Been toying with the idea of writing a book."

"Your memoirs already?"

"Not really. Just some ideas I want to explore, but I don't know if I can do it."

"Well, there's only one way of finding out, isn't there?"

"Demetrios said the same thing."

"It's true."

"You're right. Sometimes I want to do it. Then other things come up. One of these days I'll buckle down and get something going, I guess."

"What about the movie project?"

"Still in the works. Actually, Vito, that's the producer, is looking for a different story. A 'new concept.' I think that's what producers say when they have no idea what they want to do."

"You've been here all these months?"

"Yeah, I have. Actually, this summer I was planning on going to Spain to hook up with some friends and at the last moment, I changed my mind. It's been a couple of years since I've stayed in Paris during the summer, so I decided to remain, enjoy it when the Parisians abandon it."

"I hear that parking in the summer is great."

"That's what the Parisians claim."

"It's a nice place you have here."

"Yes, it is. I like it. It belongs to this guy, Bernard, who lives in Africa. He gives me a break on the rent because he prefers to live over there rather than here. I guess as long as I take care of the place and pay the rent I can stay here."

"Can I use your bathroom?"

"Sure. It's at the end of the hallway."

While she was in the bathroom, I went out to the balcony and looked at the Eiffel Tower. From where I stood, I could see it in its entire splendor. At night, it always gave me a great pleasure just to stand gazing at this magnificent symbol of Paris from my bedroom window.

I was always complaining about my lousy luck, but I was very lucky to have found this place. It is next to impossible to find anything affordable to rent in Paris—especially in the area where I was living. Lisa returned.

"Your visit is a great surprise. It calls for a glass of champagne to celebrate."

We walked into the kitchen. The one thing I had learned about living in France was that one must always have a cold bottle of champagne ready for special moments.

"Here's to you."

"Here's to your happiness and to your book," she said. "Do you know what my mother says about champagne?"

"What does she say?"

"That it never puts a woman to shame."

"That's a nice way to put it. Drink up and have no fear, then. You know, I've heard it said that here in France there are only two reasons to drink champagne: When you're happy and when you're sad. And I'm very happy you're here."

"Me, too. I'm very happy to be here with you."

"*Donc, la vie est belle ?*"

"*Oui, la vie est belle !*" And she gave me a big smile.

We walked out to the balcony and stood silently watching the tower and drinking champagne. The early dusk of September was descending on Paris. Some trees still had golden leaves.

During September, the weather can be wonderful but as it gets further into October, the implacable beginning of the cold winter can invade your soul and the city without remorse.

For me, the beginning of the fall is always the best time of the year to be in Paris. Some people prefer Paris in the spring. I love Paris in the spring, but I prefer Paris in the fall.

Maybe it has to do with the fact that it was in September, a long time ago, when I first arrived in Paris. We walked back into the living room.

"It's strange to see you here," I said.

I was really in the dark about her visit. I was not sure if I should ask her. In the end, I decided it would not make any difference. Whatever her reasons they probably had nothing to do with me. Maybe it was a case of wanting to see a friendly face in a strange city.

"Why?"

"Well, it just is."

"I hope I'm not bothering you," she said, and seemed less sure.

"Don't be silly."

"I guess it does seem weird."

"Yeah, that's what I mean," I said. "It's not often my past suddenly catches up with me."

"Are you afraid of your past?"

"Sometimes. It seems I don't learn very much from it. I keep making the same mistakes."

"The story of our lives," she smiled.

"I wonder if that will ever change."

"It does. It's happened to me."

"I keep waiting for that to happen to me," I said.

"Have some faith, and it will."

"Yeah, maybe you're right."

"You can learn from your past," she said, after a moment of silence.

"Have you?"

"Yes, though I do wish I had done things a little differently from the beginning. Perhaps be more honest with myself."

"Yeah, I know what you mean."

"I think you preserve your sanity just by letting your past fade out of your thoughts, concentrating on today's stuff instead of rewriting yesterday in your head."

"Yes, it's true I do that, but I don't want to rewrite it, really. I just want to admit it, maybe even gain some insight, some truth from it. I want to say I made a mistake and not feel guilty," I said.

"Well, you have to keep working on it. Anyway, I hope I'm not intruding."

"Not at all."

"I'm glad."

"Have you seen any of Paris yet?"

"Not really," she said. "I've been in my hotel room most of the time. Paris is a city to be shared with someone special."

"Yes, that's true. So, you're here, you're special, let's go."

"Thank you. It's lovely of you to say that." I could see how surprised she was by my words. "OK, let's take a walk," she continued, giving me the wonderful smile that I remembered so well from the past.

Lisa and I spent a great part of the evening talking and walking around the Latin Quarter. I discovered someone who was bright, curious, well read, with a bit of classical dancing and musical training, plus a good sense of humor.

I commented on the fact that during the night we had spent together, in Crete, we had hardly talked about who we were. We were preoccupied with *other* things.

It felt good to laugh about those memories, and not be embarrassed. I also remembered what Chris had said about being intrigued by her visit to my room.

However, I was not about to ask her that. There are some things better off sealed in our hearts. It was probably in her mind, however, because she brought it up.

"I wanted to talk to you about Chris and that night in Crete."

"You don't have to say anything. I have wonderful memories of Crete."

"Me, too, and with Chris I was just being snotty. He's a sweet guy, no hard feelings. It was a game, really. It didn't mean anything."

After walking around the Latin Quarter, we were now having dinner at my favorite brasserie, l'Île Saint Louis, which bears the same name as the island on which it is located. The place was lively and she liked the *ambiance*.

There was a sense of vulnerability in what she said about Chris that seemed to go beyond trying to explain herself. I was not sure if this was some oblique reference to what had taken place between us.

"Why are you telling me this?"

"I wanted to tell you the truth. You may think that I'm some kind of floozy."

"Come on. Do you think you're a floozy?"

"No—" she stopped. It seemed the memories of the night back in Crete troubled her. It was not clear what part of that night bothered her; however, she did not seem willing to share any more.

"Actually, Chris and I had a discussion about you. We decided you were a nice person."

"I know, he told me of your conversation," she said.

"He told you?"

"Are you surprised?"

"Not really."

"I just wanted to hear it from you."

"To be honest with you, I don't exactly remember all that Chris and I talked about that evening. It was so long ago. But I do remember we agreed you were a nice person, and we were glad we had met you."

"That's nice."

"Can I ask you a question?"

"What?"

"Remember that bottle of French cognac Demetrios gave the cops in Athens?"

"Yes." She smiled.

"He told me the idea came from you and your sister."

"I'd like to take credit for it, but it was Robin's idea."

"What made her think to do that?"

"I don't know. Except Demetrios thought that was a great idea. And it worked!"

"It sure did." We both laughed now at the memory.

"I never slept with Chris. He was like a brother," she said, after a moment of silence.

"You don't have to explain. You didn't come all the way out here to tell me that did you?" I asked, teasing her.

"Well, one never knows about these things." Now it was her turn to tease me. "I just wanted to set the record straight."

"Things happen for reasons which very often we can't even begin to guess. I have no regrets about Greece. I learned a lot. Most of it was wonderful—and you were a large part of that." And it was true. This seemed to please her. "Life goes on, and it's a good thing."

Yes, somehow, I had managed to survive. It had not been easy. Occasionally, I had these incredible feelings of guilt and sadness about what had happened with Iris.

My life had continued and, yes, I was hurting when I came back to Paris. Thoughts of what might have been were never far from my mind.

But the truth was that things had not happened the way I wanted them to. I was sure there was a reason, and for a long time I looked for that reason. I needed to know. Now, it did not seem important.

"Did you ever hear from Iris?"

"No."

Suddenly, all of those memories of Greece and Iris I had been trying for months to suppress came back to me, but they did not make me sad or angry. Now I recalled them with a sense of dullness. I had made my peace. Iris would never come to Paris.

She had not responded to my letter after Chris had written he had given it to her. Iris. I wished her the best. I wished her happiness. That is the search, is it not?

The ideal that drives us desperately to reach out and grab a little bit of it even if it is only for a short time, and even when the risk of getting hurt is so obvious.

Like a comet, Iris had streaked into my life leaving my heart singed. I often wondered why she and I had met. The whole episode seemed like an illusion, a game the gods had decided to play at my expense.

I was not as desperate now as I had once been. Time had dulled my senses, my anger. With time, everything goes and only souvenirs remain. I had not talked about Iris since I arrived back in Paris.

When Cécile and I were finally able to get together, she knew something had changed but she did not ask me what it was. We both understood that everything was over between us, so we let it go with no tears. We were sad, of course, because it is always sad to part from someone one has loved.

Cécile also said that no matter what the future might bring, she would always reserve a small corner of her heart for me. We saw each other after that, usually for a cup of coffee and small talk, but soon after, she got a job in Brussels.

The only connection we now had were brief conversations on the phone. Lisa's visit and questions about Iris had touched a raw nerve. Some memories cannot be erased.

"You'd rather not talk about it?" Lisa asked.

"If you don't mind."

"OK, I understand. You know, I've always dreamed of living in Paris," she said, her voice thick with longing as she surveyed the room we were in.

"That happens to lots of people."

"You're lucky."

"Yes, I think so."

"My father tells me I should stay. I would like to go to the Sorbonne and do some graduate work. I've even applied."

"It's a great university. I have fond memories of the time I spent there."

"You went to the Sorbonne?"

"Yes."

"I'm impressed. What was that like?"

"Great! One of the best things I've done."

"Yeah, I think I might be ready to suffer the French." She smiled.

"The French can be a pain in the ass, but once you get to know them, they're not so bad."

After dinner, we walked from l'Île Saint Louis, past Notre Dame, then Place St-Michel, up Boulevard St-Michel and toward the Luxembourg Gardens. It had been a very nice evening.

I had forgotten the simple pleasures like walking in Paris, seeing the street life, hearing animated talk—and sharing all of that with a friend.

Then looking at the shops with their tastefully decorated window displays, where the French always managed to present to the buying public what they have to sell with such attractive charm and flair.

Everything you see—the pastries, the clothes, the shoes, the books, the flowers, the galleries, you name it—is always presented with a great deal of taste and style. Understated elegance comes to mind. Sharing Paris with Lisa was great.

As we walked, she took my hand, which surprised me, and I glanced at her and saw a wonderful and happy look on her face as she surveyed the city, taking in the sights and sounds surrounding us. It was like being in a candy store. I knew the feeling.

I felt good she was really getting a kick out of our promenade and that I was exposing her to the vibrant and unique *ambiance* of Parisian street life. I did not let go of her hand.

"I can understand why you love living here."

"I have no regrets about that."

We were sitting in a small café by the Luxembourg Gardens.

"I see it in your eyes and the way you talk about Paris."

"It's a great city. It's a civilized city. It's in the middle of Europe. I've made some wonderful friends. My life is here, and I intend to remain here for as long as the fates will allow. There is no other place I'd rather be."

"It must be wonderful to live here."

"To me it is, though there are lots of other people who hate it."

"The fools!" She laughed.

"That they are."

"Do people ever sleep here?"

"Sure. Why?"

"It seems that everyone is in the cafés."

"It's tradition."

"It's a civilized tradition."

"Yes, it's something that takes time getting used to but once you see how much fun and how much sense it makes, it's hard to imagine not being able to do it."

She was silent. She seemed about to come to some decision. The feeling of closeness she evoked in me surprised me. It was not sex or love. I was trying to figure out just what kind of bond existed between us.

It was true we had shared a long and intimate evening together. It had come about during a strange set of circumstances. I did not know what she was looking for.

One is always looking for something, so she was not any different from me. On the other hand, I did not think she was interested in something that did not exist. I knew I was not.

Before I left for Athos, we had talked briefly, and my impression was that our night together had been an incident, a wonderful incident, but nothing more. We had simply taken advantage of the circumstances, and it had been lovely.

Then without any warning, I was suddenly confronted with my past intruding on my present life. I was grateful that lovely Lisa had bestowed upon me her maiden favors in what now seemed another life.

But I was not interested in pursuing it further, and I sure as hell was not looking for complications. Things were fine now, and I wanted to keep it that way.

"I should turn in," she finally said.

"Yeah, it's getting kind of late."

We walked toward Boulevard Montparnasse and back to her hotel on rue Delambre.

"I can't stay with you tonight because I have my period," she said, suddenly.

It came out of nowhere, without any warning. Her words left me speechless. This was a new one on me.

"Lisa, I never even considered it. I suggested your coming to stay at my place because I thought it might please you. Being alone in Paris can be difficult. You don't owe me anything," I finally managed to say because I did not think she would take my invitation any other way.

"I'm sorry. I hope I didn't offend you."

"You didn't. Look, you can come anytime. In fact, if you don't want to come that's fine."

"It's very sweet of you to offer it. I don't know if I'll stay in Paris or go back to the States, but if I stay, I'll need a place to live. Can I rent a room from you? I'm a quiet person. I'm also neat and orderly, and I would be delighted to take the dog out for his walk."

"I don't have a dog," I said, and laughed at her words.

"A man needs a dog."

"Why does a man need a dog?"

"Man's best friend." She said it with a rich, wonderful laugh.

I loved her sense of humor. We got to her hotel, kissed goodnight on the cheeks. She said she would call me. It occurred to me—and not without feelings of nostalgia and regret which took me by surprise as I walked toward Boulevard Montparnasse—that Lisa would probably go back to the States, and I would not see or hear from her again.

I was happy she had taken the time to visit me, though. It had been a while since I had talked to a woman in such a way. I realized how much I had missed it. Living alone in Paris had its downside. These past few months, I had been preoccupied with trying to put my life back together.

Montparnasse! Among the many unique quarters in Paris, Montparnasse stands out. There are five cafés located at the corner of Boulevards Raspail and Montparnasse—Le Cosmos, Le Dôme, La Rotonde, La Coupole, and Le Select. La Coupole seems to stand out more than the others do. This is not to take anything away from the other cafés.

After its doors first opened in 1927, La Coupole soon became a landmark in Paris's rich historical and social scene: The place to meet. Some say that it is *the* place to be seen and where the table you sit at and by which pillar—whether in the restaurant section or the brasserie section— seems in many instances to accord and define whether you were "in" or not. As the waiters got to know you, they served your customary drink without your having to ask for it.

Ben, an American guy I had met at La Coupole, knew about all of this. I have no idea how he found it out. Asking him how would have met with his usual pretentiousness. It was best to accept it and let it go at that. Maybe he had talked to the waiters.

I had not been in Montparnasse for a while. Tonight, I decided to go and sit at Le Cosmos and order a cognac. I had a great view of La Coupole just across the street.

After I got back from Greece, I kept pretty much to myself. I felt wounded and sorry for myself and did not want to share the misery with my friends.

I tried to keep busy and toyed with several ideas among them writing a book, or doing more translations—that is how I used to earn a few bucks in the past. I liked it, but it did not pay much money.

Then a couple of months ago, Milo had approached me about doing a new translation of some of Albert Camus's writings. I had put him off. Then in a kind of dare that often changes a person's life forever, he called back and challenged me to do an English translation of *L'Étranger.*

"It'll help you to think like a Frenchman," he had said.

"I don't want to think like a Frenchman."

"Why not?"

"I would make a very poor one."

I thought it rather cheeky of him to dare me and even more preposterous of me to accept his crazy idea. It seemed about as practical as jumping off the Eiffel Tower to see if you could survive the fall.

"Look, I know we can publish it. I also know there won't be a lot of money in it, but you didn't do too badly with the film project," he insisted.

"That's true, but this is different."

"No, it isn't. Anyway, you have to do it for your own sake and the sake of your children."

"What children? I don't have any children. I don't *want* any children."

"For the sake of art, then. Besides, it'll keep you busy and less concerned about yourself," he said, probably suspecting that part of my funk since coming back from Greece had to do with women.

Milo was an interesting guy who lived in a big apartment surrounded by stuffed animals. He had a thing for stuffed animals. A bit flamboyant, he came from an old family in Normandy. His first name was Modeste, but he hated it so he used Milo instead.

I met him not long after I arrived in Paris, when I read an ad in the *International Herald Tribune* that he was looking for someone to help him translate a book about birds from French into English.

I knew nothing about birds. I thought translating the book would not be difficult. Well, it was difficult. He did not hire me. I was kind of happy he had not. If truth were told, I could not have translated the book without a great struggle. He said to keep in touch, but I never called him.

Then one day, unexpectedly, he called me. At first, I did not remember who he was. He was now looking for someone to help him translate an American play: *The Sandbox* by Edward Albee, into French. When I read it, I was not too keen on translating it and told him so.

My words had the exact opposite effect because he insisted, I take a crack at it, which I reluctantly did. I was in the middle of doing the translation when he called back and told me to stop.

Apparently, the people who had commissioned the translation were no longer interested in it. He felt bad but insisted on paying my fee.

We kept in touch and got together a few times for dinner. He knew Alain, the owner of a press agency—Alpha—that in turn had led Alain, in the past, to hire me to do some freelance pieces for some of his clients. That was how I ended up going to Africa.

Milo also owned an art gallery with his ex-wife, and I had helped them put together several catalogues in English on the paintings and other works of art they sold.

There was one particular incident, which probably led Milo to consider me a special friend. He called one day saying there was a group of Japanese businessmen who had come to Paris to purchase some paintings from the gallery.

He had invited them for dinner that weekend, and asked me to help him with the translation, as the Japanese did not speak French, only English, and Milo's English was not very good. The dinner was taking place at his summerhouse near Versailles.

It was a warm day in the middle of August. When the group arrived, it turned out that a young Japanese student was with them who would do the translation. He insisted on speaking French with Milo even though the student's English was much better than his French.

Maybe the translator was just trying to earn his fee. Anyway, the group arrived in the early evening. There were five of them with the translator.

As is usual with the Japanese, they were very polite, smiling and bowing a lot. Milo wanted his visitors to have a favorable impression of what he had to sell and had selected a series of paintings for them to consider after the dinner. He also wanted them to enjoy typical French hospitality.

While he prepared the dinner, the five Japanese men went out to the garden to admire the flowers now in full bloom. I stayed to help Milo in the kitchen. As is typical of the French, he was very meticulous about what he was going to serve his guests.

He asked me to go down to the basement and bring back the special wine from his private reserve, which he had chosen for the occasion.

When I walked back into the kitchen, Milo signaled for me to be quiet and to come over and look out to the garden through the window. He had a strange and worried frown on his face.

I looked out, and saw the Japanese guys looking at the flowers—all of them in their underwear. They had taken their clothes off! No wonder Milo was worried.

"What in the hell is going on?" I whispered.

"I wish I knew. Here I was getting this damn dinner ready, and I happened to look outside and saw five half-naked men in the garden admiring my flowers!"

I started to laugh, but he gave me such a stern look that I stopped.

"Oh, you find it funny?"

"It is. How often do you see five Japanese guys wearing only their socks and underwear in the middle of Versailles?"

"This is most annoying."

"What are you going to do?"

"I don't know." He did not sound happy.

"I wonder what prompted them to take their clothes off."

"I have no idea," he said. He was truly perplexed. "It's the middle of August, and it's hot, but this is ridiculous," he added, after a long silence.

I started to laugh again. This time he joined me. Through the open window we could see the men and hear their conversation, but since we did not understand Japanese, it did not help us at all.

We really had no clue as to why these guys were all standing in the garden in their skivvies.

"What should we do?" From the sound of his voice, I could tell he was getting worried.

"Did you say anything? Did Chantal,"—his ex-wife—"say anything?"

"I just can't imagine what she could have told them. These are important people. They may be doing this because they think it's—"

"La coutume française!" . . . French custom. I finished the sentence, trying to humor him. He was not too pleased with my levity.

"Call Chantal and ask her. Maybe she knows something."

"She's out with friends and I haven't the foggiest where she is. We've got to do something."

There was now panic in his voice. The situation was baffling.

"We'll have to do like they did and take our clothes off," I said, after a moment of reflection.

"That must be your great American sense of humor." He was clearly irritated.

"What choice do we have?"

"Are you mad?"

In a sense I was. I argued that if those five half-naked men came back in the house and saw us with our clothes on, there would be loss of face and total embarrassment.

On the other hand, if we were all in our underwear, we would be accepting everyone's behavior as normal. Maybe then, we could figure out what happened, and bring them back to their senses. We had to take the chance.

"Otherwise, just go out there and ask them why they took their clothes off."

"You *are* crazy," he said, horrified.

"Do you see any other solution?"

He shook his head. He was clearly lost. I thought, what the hell, the worst that can happen is that we will put our clothes back on. So, I started to take my clothes off. Milo resisted until the last moment.

When he saw the five men turning around and walking back to the house, he had no other choice. He undressed in a big hurry—and I mean big hurry, making me think of those old movies with Charlie Chaplin.

I was laughing my head off, and Milo did not know whether to laugh or to strangle me. The men came back, saw us in our underwear, and took it to mean everything was normal.

Milo prepared a wonderful dinner. After the coffee, the cognac, and the cigars, I very casually started to put my clothes back on. Four Japanese men looked in the direction of the guy I took to be their leader; he smiled, and started getting dressed.

Soon we were all dressed. They studied the paintings, talked to each other and bowed some more.

When they left, the translator said they had been most pleased with the dinner and the warm welcome. They wanted to meet at the gallery first thing on Monday to complete the purchase of two expensive paintings by Corot and one by Dali.

The evening had been a resounding success! After they left, Milo and I fell to the floor laughing.

"Did you see the guy with the hernia scar? Nasty looking!" Milo said.

"Yes, and the guy with those shorts,"—one of them was wearing a pair of shorts that must have been dated from World War II.

"Nobody, but absolutely nobody, will ever believe this."

"I don't know. Just think: These guys will go back to Japan and say everything they've heard about the French is true."

"Yes, we do have a reputation, but this is extreme."

"Anyway, I think they had a good time," I said.

"Yes, it seemed that way."

"They certainly seemed to have enjoyed your dinner."

"I don't know if they enjoyed my dinner or the fact they sat half-ass naked while eating it," he said, shaking his head.

"Maybe it was both. Well, you can't complain. They will buy the paintings."

"Thank God for that. What do you think happened?"

"I don't know. What did you say when they walked in?"

"I just told them to make themselves at home," he said, still mystified about the event.

It was back in my apartment later that evening when it finally occurred to me what might have triggered the whole episode. I called Milo.

"I think I know what happened."

"First, let me tell you that Chantal did not believe me when I told her what happened. She called a few minutes ago. She thinks I'm making this whole thing up."

"Maybe she put them up to it," I said, just to bug him.

"If she did that, I would murder her. No, she couldn't possibly have done it. It's too amateurish. *Non, c'est trop vulgaire.*" Vulgar is the one thing the French do not want to be under any circumstance.

I had gone over all the details of the evening's events, especially what Milo had said to the Japanese when they arrived. He told them to make themselves at home. In French, the word *nous* is very close to *nu* in sound, which in French means naked.

The translator probably misunderstood *nous* for *nu;* thus, the greeting in French may have sounded to him like, *fait nu chez nous* or something like that. In other words, make yourselves naked and at home.

Though in French the sentence makes no sense, it would not have been impossible for someone with limited French to misinterpret and end up understanding something entirely different. That, plus the fact that it was a hot day, and the Japanese are very polite.

"*Génial!* Only someone raised on Mickey Mouse, Coca Cola, and the *Reader's Digest* would ever come up with such an explanation. We owe you Americans for giving us back Normandy, but this is cosmic," he said, laughing.

The reference to Normandy was very personal to Milo. One of the great battles of World War II, at the beginning of the invasion of France, had been fought on the property Milo's family owned.

A couple hundred American Rangers had to scale sheer sea cliffs to capture some big guns the Germans had placed on the property.

Very few American soldiers survived the bloody battle. But in the end, they captured the guns emplacement saving thousands of other lives. For Milo, this historical fact and where it took place had become sacred.

He had once showed me one of the harpoons the Americans had used to propel themselves up the cliff; it was one of Milo's most precious war relics.

After that dinner, I knew I made a friend for life. The other references he made about Coca Cola, Mickey Mouse, and *Reader's Digest* were just a way for Milo to make fun of Americans.

Later, he told me that when he went to Japan he never had as much success as an art dealer as he had after our famous "*Le Naked Dîner,*" as he called it, on that hot summer evening in Versailles.

Sitting at the Le Cosmos now, I thought about my need for some form of therapy, something to occupy my mind; however, translating *L'Étranger* would be anything but therapeutic, which was why I kept putting it off.

What I really wanted to do was write a novel as I had told Lisa. "The Great American Novel" Demetrios had once said in jest. It was not "The Great American Novel,"—it was not the great anything.

It was for nobody's benefit but my own. I wanted to use my experiences in Vietnam as background, but I was not sure just how to do it.

I had made lots of notes, and I was having a tough time putting them in some cohesive narrative form.

The whole thing was just a whimsical idea in my head. Big D. had also said I had to know if I were going to do it. I had not yet reached that point, I guess.

The few bucks I had in the bank could carry me for a while if I watched how I spent them. I was free and liking it a lot. Now here was Lisa—what the hell did it mean? Complications were not what I needed.

I wanted my life to be simple and quiet with no romantic entanglements of any kind, Lisa or no Lisa. I had learned my lesson with Iris, and it had not been very pleasant. Not to worry, I thought, Lisa was leaving.

There was no reason to doubt she was on her way back to the States. Her telling me she had her period was surprising, though. Her honesty was refreshing, and intriguing.

She was a beautiful girl, but I had no romantic feelings for her. I just liked her because I thought she was a nice person. Her comment about the dog was funny.

It had been tough to come back to Paris without Iris, to find myself dreaming about her and seeing the emptiness of my reality. Weeks went by and spring eventually dissolved into a glorious Parisian summer, but that did not bring me any solace.

Those were long weeks of feeling like a caged animal, going around in circles before I regained some control over my feelings. Days and nights had melted into each other leaving a trail of empty memories, despair, and anger.

For a while, I was certain she would come. Then I was less sure and eventually understood she would never do so.

Why had it not worked out? Cleo's words back in Athens about Iris came back to me many times, and they did not make any more sense now than when she said them.

Many long nights when sleep would not come that question was the only thing occupying my mind and my heart—and there was no answer. I blamed myself.

Ultimately, just out of sheer necessity to survive, the question became less pressing, and now I had learned to live without an answer. The gods had, indeed, taught me a hard lesson about life and love.

Eventually, I got in touch with Cécile, but we did not get together because she was going with her parents to Cambodia for several weeks.

She was happy to hear from me and invited me to come join them, but I declined. I was not in the mood to be sociable, preferring to keep to myself.

It became obvious to her that something had happened in Greece that had affected me a great deal. She asked me in a roundabout way, but eventually dropped the subject.

Cécile was curious about the movie script I was supposed to be working on. I had managed to get in touch with Vito and, much to my surprise, he said he was now looking at another story for his film. He wanted me to work on the new concept, and he would let me know when his ideas were clear.

Milo told me that when Vito was ready, he would call me, not to worry. I was enjoying much-needed emotional equilibrium feeling I was now back in control of my life.

Then Lisa showed up!

It did not seem to have anything to do with me and I was glad, as it appeared to be a case of two not-so-total strangers meeting in Paris. But was it? I was surprised she had told me about her period.

Would she have volunteered to come and pass the night with me if she had not, had it? Good question. Old buddy, better take it one day at a time, I thought. With women, sometimes, life was not what it appears to be.

I liked sitting at Le Cosmos by myself. As I have already mentioned, there are five cafés in this part of Boulevard Montparnasse made famous not by American expatriates writing about them, but by the fact that most of the men starting them came from parts of France that seem to produce lots of café owners, who somehow know what Parisians want in a café. Some people argue that La Coupole is better than Le Select. It is really all a matter of personal choice.

I liked all of them, though Le Cosmos always seemed to be less crowded than the other cafés. A couple of weeks after arriving in Paris for the first time, I started living in Montparnasse, at the hôtel de Blois on rue Vavin.

Living in a hotel was a new experience that I soon found enjoyable. It was small, clean, and very convenient, just a stone's throw away from all the cafés. The hotel catered to couples for short rendezvous sometimes in the afternoon, but mostly at night.

The first three floors of the hotel were used for these short visits, and the other three floors were rented out monthly. The women who used the hotel were not young, maybe in their forties, and neither were their clients. The women wore heavy makeup, and their dresses were skimpy even in winter.

Sometimes I saw them standing outside the café shivering in the cold while waiting for their regular customers. At other times, when they were in between clients, they would go into Le Cosmos to get some warmth before going back out to the street. I never saw any of those women at the other cafés.

I had a nice room on the top floor of the hotel. Madame Richard, the owner who also ran the place during the day, was very formal, always impeccably dressed, and devoid of any kind of levity.

It was all a very serious business. Didier, the night clerk, seemed more open, and sometimes he and I would talk a little about life in Paris.

One evening, I came in late and found Madame Richard behind the counter. She told me Didier had married one of the women, and that they had bought a small farm in Brittany, where they had gone to live.

Madam Richard had been upset but not about the marriage. "*Très romantique*," she had said, and was very happy for the newlyweds. However, there were a couple of small problems to be resolved.

One was that *Madame*—meaning the woman whom Didier married—was someone who had "*une clientèle considerable et fidèle*," which had been good for the hotel business.

"*Elle est très fort dans son métier,*" Madame Richard said. "*Mais, c'est la vie. Contre l'amour on ne peut rien faire, Monsieur,*" she added, in a tone of voice that was obviously resigned to the inevitable.

I did not know whether to laugh at Madame Richard's words regarding the other woman having a "rather large and faithful customer base" or the fact that she was also "gifted," I guess, in her profession.

But when it came to love, Madame Richard bowed to the inescapable. When I asked Milo what he thought of Madame Richard's words, his response was that one of the beauties of the French language was it had developed expressive and lovely romantic expressions.

He called it: "*superbe étiquette et belles expressions,*" when it came to explaining certain life situations, especially when confronted with two people who were in love.

The second problem for Madame Richard, and a far more serious one, was that Didier had been the night clerk for a long while, and she was very much concerned about who she was going to hire to replace him.

"*Il me faut quelqu'un honnête, sérieux, discret et respectable. Un homme, toujours un homme,*" she said.

Madame Richard did not appear too eager to hire a female to replace Didier for this most important of positions in her hotel operations. She needed an honest, serious, discreet, and respectable male for her business. Always a male. Women need not apply.

After moving into the hotel, La Coupole became my home café. I used to go have breakfast there or just linger over a coffee and watch Parisian life go by.

I liked it in the morning because it was quiet and empty. They served the best croissants and had the morning newspaper—in English—I could read to my heart's content.

I also met the owner, René Lafon. Mr. La Coupole was what some of my friends and I called him. He was a tall, very distinguished old gentleman, who wore a suit and a tie and was always tidying up the place.

He was there from very early in the morning until after the tea hour, when lots of old ladies would come to La Coupole to have their afternoon tea. Whenever he was not so busy, we would chat for a few moments.

He told once that he was going to have to sell the place. There was no one to take it over. Apparently, his son did not want to continue being a slave to La Coupole; instead, he wanted to go and live in California. Mr. Lafon seemed amused by what his son had told him.

My friend Gary had told me about the American Center for Students and Artists. It so happened that the center was on Boulevard Raspail, about two blocks from the intersection of Boulevard Montparnasse and Boulevard Raspail at which location, quite literally, sat all five cafés.

From day one of my living in Paris, Montparnasse became my *quartier*. One could receive mail at La Coupole, and it seemed that everyone I met in Montparnasse would eventually end up there.

In Paris, the *quartier* where one lives tends in the end to define one's idea of who one is. There are the *quartiers populaires,* filled with the working poor and the newly arrived immigrants mostly from Africa and the Arab countries. Then there were the other *quartiers* where the bourgeoisie lives.

I was not sure what Montparnasse represented, perhaps it was a combination of lower and middle class. The reason I ended up living there was that it was closer to the American Center, which was a nice place to visit when you did not know anyone in Paris, and you could also take a free shower there.

Since moving to Trocadéro, about a year ago, I had not come back as often to visit Montparnasse, though, I was still faithful to my old and favorite *quartier*.

I was remembering those days when a couple of friends, John and Pete, walked into Le Cosmos.

"Well, the prodigal son is back to his old haunts," John said.

They gave me a warm embrace. I was happy to see them.

"Where have you been?" Pete asked.

"Around. I went to Greece."

"Ah, yes, the myths and all that junk," John said.

"So how was it?" Pete asked.

"It was OK."

"No, nothing is 'OK.' You didn't like it?" John asked.

"Yes, I did," I said, a bit defensively.

"You didn't like it," Pete said, convinced it was so.

"Yes, I did. I mean, I got to Hydra. I even managed to make it to Crete."

"Did you stay in the caves in Crete?" John asked, with what I took to be a suspicious look.

"No."

"Alex, do you mean to say that you went to Crete and did not stay in the caves?"

"No, was I supposed to?"

John pretended to be shocked at my lack of *savoir vivre*. In other words, I had not measured up to the highest standards of adventures they held so dear. They looked at each other silently. I had obviously made a ghastly *faux pas*.

"Nobody, but absolutely nobody worth knowing goes to Crete and ends up staying in some dumpy hotel while the caves are there for the taking. I don't know what's come over you. Haven't we taught you anything?" John finally said, after a long and embarrassing silence.

"I'm not sure I want to sit at the same table with his kind," said Pete.

"What's so special about the caves?" I protested.

"Boy, oh boy, we're in trouble," John said.

"He's been hanging around Cécile too long." Pete said.

"She didn't go with me."

John and Pete exchanged silent looks.

"Wait a second, she didn't?" John said, after a while.

"No."

Both looked at me slyly. For some reason, it felt like they knew about my recent breakup with Cécile.

"Things are OK with you two?" Pete asked.

"Sure," I said, trying to hide what was going on.

"So, she split," said Peter, more an affirmation than a question.

"No, I mean, we just kind of called it quits."

"You had a 'Tracy' with you in Greece?" John asked.

"No."

"Tracy" was the word we used for girlfriends, wives, and female companions. I do not know who had picked the name. It seemed from the beginning of our friendship we used the name when we talked about women. It was always a "Tracy." I kind of liked it. It was classier than the word "broad."

"Did you find one over there?" Pete asked.

It was always interesting to reflect on the way people view you. In the circle of friends I had, we might not see each other for weeks or even months, yet we knew each other's secrets without really knowing much about each other.

Pete was a painter from New York, and John was from Wales. I had met them in a very strange set of circumstances. *Strange* may be the wrong word really, fortuitous would probably be better.

One evening, shortly after my arrival in Paris, I was sitting in the terrace at La Coupole minding my own business and reading the *International Herald Tribune,* when this guy came over, introduced himself—his name was Ben—sat at my table, and started talking.

He told me he was a painter living in Paris and he came from Nebraska. I saw nothing really unusual about this except that Ben was not a painter in the sense everyone took him to be: He painted houses!

Everyone assumed when he said he was a painter he meant an artist, but he was not trying to fool anybody. I always argued with him that there was art in house painting.

"Do you know why I like La Coupole? He asked.

"I don't know."

"*Les grands cerveux*—all of the heavyweights—have been here: Joyce, Hemingway, Fitzgerald, Picasso, Cocteau, Buñuel, Dos Passos, Man Ray, Dali, Gershwin, Gide, Miller, de Beauvoir, Calder, Malraux, Pound, Brancusi, Sartre, Beckett, Aragon—you name them, they've all passed through these doors."

"How do you know all that?"

"I read, man, I read, come on. And now it's me and you, the last survivors!" He let out a proud laugh.

"So, we're keeping up the tradition, like in *The Last of the Mohicans?*"

"You bet. Ever notice the columns inside with all them paintings?"

"Briefly."

"Masterpieces!" He looked toward the inside of La Coupole with a beatific smile on his face. It was as if he were looking at his children and proud of them.

"So how did you end up here?" he asked.

"I was at the American Center looking for a room to rent. I walked down to Boulevard Raspail, turned left, saw this place, and liked it."

"You couldn't have chosen a better place to get a feel for Paris. This is it!" Suddenly, he stopped and glanced at the door. "Oh, boy, things are going to get hot in here," he said.

I looked toward the door and saw Peter walk in. He looked angry. Pete was probably in his early sixties, a heavyset man but with strong traces of a ruggedness and handsomeness that must have done him no harm with women in his younger days. He stood by the door looking around, then someone waved at him and Peter strode toward that table.

Ben got up and walked toward the same table A few minutes later, he came back and asked me if I wanted to join them. It seemed like a good idea, and I followed him.

Besides Peter and John there were other people sitting around the table. Ben made the introductions. They were having dinner.

I was sitting right next to Pete when, suddenly, he reached across the table, took some food with his fingers from someone else's plate, and ate it. I was taken aback and looked around the table, but nobody seemed to mind.

Everyone sat there as if nothing out of the ordinary had taken place. He once did it to Cécile. Later, she made me swear that under no circumstance was I ever to invite her when Pete was around.

"I don't mind Americans, but I will not accept American pigs," she said.

I always kidded her that she had no sense of humor, that she was a little too harsh on Peter.

"Vulgar people are disgusting!" she added. As I have said before, vulgarity is the one sin the French do not forgive.

Anyway, on that evening when I first met Pete at La Coupole, he kept on taking food from other people's plates with his fingers and eating it.

Then there was a lull in the conversation when, suddenly, Pete grabbed a bottle of wine, stood, and—without as much as a by your leave— threw it with considerable force toward a large window across from him.

The bottle and the window shattered into many pieces of broken glass with a loud bang. It was something else, and it happened so fast! The immediate commotion was incredible. People were yelling in panic and shock.

Pete just stood there glaring at everyone with a defiant and angry attitude, daring anyone to say anything.

The *maître d'hôtel* and some other waiters came running by and stood around talking excitedly and wondering what to do next.

Fortunately, no one had been injured. People just could not believe it. Soon after that, we heard the famous sound of the Paris police siren as the gendarmes came to investigate what had taken place. Pete sat, and continued eating as if nothing unusual had occurred.

Another thing that stuck in my mind was the reaction of the officer in charge. When he saw Peter, he seemed to recognize him.

"Bon soir, monsieur l'artiste, vous allez bien?"

The policeman calling Pete an artist and asking if things were "OK" after what he had done came as a surprise. The way he said it immediately told me he was not going to arrest Pete. Apparently, it was not the first time Pete had been in trouble.

The gendarme gave Pete a lecture on responsibility and honor. To him, Pete obviously represented someone special, a creative person, an artist, thus a certain degree of respect and tolerance were permitted. These cops are cool, I thought.

It was my introduction to the attitude the French have toward artists, the sense of freedom they give the artist. Intelligence, artistic creativity, and sensibility are so treasured in France that I do not know of any other people who revere them like the French do.

It is part of who they are. Without these qualities, the French would be boring. With them, they are very wise, arrogant, and unbearable!

The respect the policeman displayed toward Pete the artist was quite remarkable. Can anyone imagine what would have been the attitude of the cops back in the States?

Of course, Pete had done something very reprehensible and dangerous, the gendarme said. Pete sat, very contrite, and did not say a word. This also surprised me because I thought he would get up and say or do something.

The police did not take Pete away. Soon the incident seemed to have been forgotten. A *garçon* came by and swept away the broken glass. Occasionally, people would glance in our direction but the looks were not accusatory.

I left shortly after that still wondering what madness had possessed Pete to do what he had done.

A few days later, I saw Ben and he told me what followed the incident. Pete came back to La Coupole the next morning carrying one of his paintings, which he handed over to Mr. La Coupole. Both men shook hands and the incident was put away.

Ben said it was not the first time Pete had caused trouble there. In fact, there were a couple of Pete's paintings hanging on the walls in Mr. La Coupole's office, and sometimes the paintings sold for $10,000 apiece.

Mr. La Coupole had seen all kinds of people over the years at his restaurant. Mad behavior from artists was to be expected and he would be the last person to press charges; however, he did get Pete to promise to behave from then on.

Ben also told me Pete now sold his paintings for $200 each. He woke up one day and decided that was the price he wanted for his paintings.

You had to offer him $200, not a penny less or a penny more, otherwise he would be offended and would not sell you the painting. It did not make sense to me because Ben said the paintings were selling for a lot of money.

Ben said that was just simply how it was. Pete was a maniac but his paintings, especially his landscapes were captivating, filled with wonderful soft images, rich colors, expressive, poetic, and full of fantasy. Nothing about them showed violence or meanness.

Ben had also told me it was not a good idea to discuss with Pete anything about his paintings, though one day I did manage to ask him about them. He looked at me and shrugged his shoulders.

I bought two landscapes from Pete—for $200 each—and took special delight in them for they were very unusual. Cécile did not like them because they came from him.

I did not want to go into any details about what had happened in Greece, so regarding Pete's question about a "Tracy," the night I met him and John, at Le Cosmos, I answered no.

"So, Cécile is now of the past." The way John said it sounded like he had just read her epitaph.

"She never liked my paintings anyway," Pete said.

"Of course, she did," I protested.

"Very decent of you to defend your ex," Pete said.

I guess the fact that Cécile and I were no longer together brought them relief—as if they did not have to worry about me anymore. I did not know why they felt that way.

"I did not expect less," Pete continued, "but we both know she tolerated my presence because you have taken a shine to me."

"Pete, the problem was you took her too seriously."

"One cannot be too careful about French women," he said, sounding a little pretentious. John and I laughed.

Pete was older than John was. Often, I would see them together. Then I found out that John had been a very successful businessman selling women's clothing. His wife designed, and John did all the rest.

He was so damn busy making sure her stuff sold he did not have time for her anymore.

When he finally awoke to that fact, she had found some other guy, and John was left holding the bag. Thus, he ended up with no wife, no business, and no money.

John had bought several of Pete's paintings at the time when nobody was buying them and paid him top dollar. Pete always remembered that.

Pete and his girlfriend, Roxanne, took John in and gave him back some of the money that John had paid for the paintings. Since his divorce, John had found a new girlfriend—Juliette—whom he had met at a communist party rally.

John was now working and going to school to become a chef. He wanted to open up a restaurant for the proletariat, Ben said. He also told me that John was really a good chef.

Pete kidded John that he had gone from being a capitalist pig to being a communist skirt-chaser, but both men remained very close. Pete believed that friendship was better than love. It does not become tabescent—the word he was fond of using.

"Hey, Leon is back," John said.

"He is? What about Thea?" I asked.

"She's back with him. This time he doesn't want to take any chances."

Leon was another of La Coupole's regulars when he was in town. Leon's family had emigrated from Germany to the U.S. just after Hitler had come to power. His father had wisely guessed that being Jewish was too dangerous.

Leon had been attending boarding school in Switzerland at the time. His father had come one day and, under the pretext of spending a weekend in the mountains, took him out of school, and then fled with the whole family to England and eventually to America.

Leon once told me that he never even had time to say goodbye to his best friend, another German kid, who was at the same boarding school. Leon's father forbade him to get in touch with this kid, and Leon had always resented his father for it.

In America, Leon's father continued working in the same business he had lost in Germany, the clothing business, and had flourished manufacturing and selling military uniforms to the U.S. government.

Leon hated living in the U.S. He loved Germany with the passion of an exile, and Germany had rejected him. He also did not get along with some of the Jewish people he met in the U.S.

He found them crass and crude. I argued with him that it was all a matter of culture. He agreed, but still preferred living in Europe.

Leon had drifted from one job to another back in the States and eventually came back to Europe after the war. He had gone to Germany to look for his friend and found him.

The friend had lost his legs to an American land mine and did not want anything to do with Leon. The friend's rejection was the ultimate blow to Leon's spirit.

It made him hate the U.S. even more. Leon, a bit of a showman—on a dare perhaps wanting to show his father or to prove to himself that he could—started a clothing business of his own.

He hated it but became very successful. That is where the connection between Leon and John had been made. John used to sell his ex-wife's stuff to Leon.

Over the years, Leon had tried to be a business failure, and it never seemed to work. On the contrary, everything he touched made money.

"Once a Jew always a Jew," Leon was fond of saying to excuse his success.

I always thought it was a great gift to be able to make money, but Leon insisted it was a curse. I kidded him about my wanting to be so accursed. One day, Leon needed to get a loan and went to a bank in Frankfurt.

The banker knew who Leon's father was and had been very eager to lend him the money. Leon told me he hated the banker because he found out that this man had been a member of Hitler's Youth.

Then he accidentally ran into the banker at a restaurant and the banker was with Thea. Leon fell in love! Theodora was a gentle, Teutonic looking girl, a Valkyrie, a bit taller than he was.

He used to say that had she lived during Hitler's time, she would have been the best example of the Aryan type—a poster child for the Nazis.

Leon had not only fallen in love, he also wanted revenge. He chased Thea with a passion only love or hate is capable of producing. Eventually, she left the banker and was now living with Leon.

He never failed to introduce her as having been the one he had "rescued" form a "Nazi" banker. For Leon, Thea was the prized possession. She seemed to find the whole affair amusing, was good-natured about it, and never complained.

The last time he had been to Paris, Thea had stayed back in Germany, and she and the banker had a rendezvous—all very proper and innocent she told Leon—though he had his doubts.

I always thought he was afraid she would leave him and go back to her banker. He denied it, but the rest of us suspected it was true.

"He's back at this thing with the Renoir statues," John said.

"Is he still trying to put it together?" I asked.

"You know he won't give up." John answered.

It appeared Leon had gotten a hold of some statues attributed to Renoir. Lots of people were keen on them, as Renoir did not have the reputation of being a sculptor. If the statues were genuine, it would be a great breakthrough in the art world.

However, very few people believed the statues were Renoirs except Leon, who was doggedly pursuing every lead to determine and prove they were authentic—a project that seemed to take a great deal of his time.

He was constantly shuttling between Germany, France, England, and the U.S. His life was now spent in airport terminals and hotel rooms. Thea, very dutifully, accompanied him in his travels. I always thought she loved him. Leon was never sure.

Leon's father had returned to Europe—Paris—after the war but only to visit. He never went back to Germany. The old man had bought an incredible townhouse in Paris, filling it with all kinds of art. Leon had always talked about his father's collection, and for a long time nobody really believed him.

He was not allowed to go to the house.

It had to do, Leon said, with the fact that one day in one of his darkest moods he had "borrowed" an original Monet and then decided to sell it, and was able to find a buyer. His father was pissed, and the incident had led him to forbid Leon to come to the house when the old man was not around.

Leon said it really was not the taking of the painting that had gotten his father upset. After all, he had promised Leon the painting was going to be his one day. It was that Thea was not of the Jewish faith.

He had taken the Monet to show her, and his father claimed she had talked him into selling it, which Leon swore was not true. You could tell Leon derived no great pleasure from finding himself estranged from his father.

It was by accident that I ended up being one of two people—Ben was the other—from our little group who got to see the inside of the house.

Ben's French was atrocious, but he made up the deficiency with an incredible knack for meeting all kinds of people. It seemed he knew everyone around Montparnasse.

He was full of wild stories. The most outlandish was when he claimed to have flown from New York to Paris without a passport!

The French police wanted to send him back to the U.S. but, somehow, he talked them into calling the American embassy, which eventually issued him an American passport.

Nobody had believed his tale, but he did have a brand-new passport that he would show to anyone who doubted him.

All the regulars at La Coupole knew Ben, and they all liked him. It was also through him that I met Beauford Delaney, another American painter---a real painter and not a painter of houses, Ben would say. I would see Delaney around La Coupole.

He was a very quiet man, and I never really had a chance to get to know him. Peter and Beauford were good friends, and Pete always talked about Beauford with a great deal of affection and admiration for his talent as a painter.

"He's a fucking saint," Pete used to say. "This guy's a major talent and Americans don't know shit about how to honor and respect his talents.

Fucking bigots and racists." Beauford was black and, apparently, a homosexual.

"Amen," Ben would say to Pete's words.

Another story that Ben was fond of telling happened while he was visiting Budapest, Hungary. Ben had arrived there with very little money, maybe about three hundred dollars. Though it was not a lot by American standards, it was substantial by Hungarian standards.

The three hundred dollars were all in Kennedy half-dollar coins that he claimed weighed nearly a ton. Ben sold all those half-dollar coins to anyone on the street for three dollars apiece. People loved Kennedy! He sold all of them and with the money he made he lived like a king in Budapest for several weeks.

He had brought a bit of America to them, making everyone happy, the people because it was a wonderful souvenir, and Ben because he got to make money to live very well which he "invested" back into the country, he said.

He kept a list of the names and addresses of all the people who had bought the Kennedy coins, as he promised to mail each of them a postcard when he got back to America. I did not doubt he would do that.

At another time, I saw Ben in a very intense and intimate conversation with a man at La Coupole. I was with Cécile and, for some reason, the manner in which both men were so engrossed in their conversation made me hesitant to go to their table to say hello. They left La Coupole shortly after that. I ran into Ben a few days later.

"Do you know the guy I was talking to the other day?"

"No, who was he?"

"His name is Wilhelm Van Derhurscht, he's a forger."

"A what?"

"He forges paintings, masterpieces. I'm telling you: he does the most unbelievable forgeries you ever saw."

Ben was awed by him. The guy had mastered the techniques and signature of famous masters, Picasso and Monet, among others. He also had an underground following around Paris of all kinds of people to whom he sold his forgeries.

Ben said people just ordered which painting they wanted reproduced and the guy painted it.

I was very curious about how Van Derhurscht had learned to master the styles and techniques of such different painters, but Ben did not want to give me any details when I told him I was interested in doing an article on this forger.

He said he was afraid I would do a hatchet job, discrediting the guy and making life harder for him. Ben argued that Van Derhurscht was bringing pleasure to people who simply could not afford the real thing.

He had a point. I did not press Ben for more details as I saw that he would not share them with me. He even refused to introduce me to Van Derhurscht. Ben showed me one of the guy's forgeries. It was of an early Picasso: *Motherhood*.

Ben had bought the painting from Van Derhurscht, and he was making monthly payments on it because he did not have enough cash to pay for it all at one time.

I am not an art expert, and perhaps with a trained eye the painting would not have passed inspection. Ben had a large photo of the original that was in some gallery in Chicago, and you could not tell the difference. Like Ben had said, unbelievable!

Ben also told me many people in the art world knew what this guy did, but he was so good they did not care often buying and selling the paintings as legitimate.

"The Monet Leon took from his father's house, is it real or fake?" I asked Ben.

"I've asked Van Derhurscht."

"What did he say?"

"He just smiled."

"Come on! Don't tell me it's a fake."

"Actually, he just said that he hadn't done it."

"What does that mean?"

"He said he hadn't painted it. You draw your own conclusions."

"So, it's the real thing," I said, figuring that I had trapped Ben into admitting it.

"Since Van Derhurscht didn't claim it as his own," he said, shrugging his shoulders not answering the question directly.

"When he says he didn't paint it, it means it's the real thing?"

"I don't know. He's very cautious. He doesn't want stuff he didn't do attributed to him."

"That's very big of him."

"You have to be so cynical."

"I'm not," I said, amused at Ben's wanting to protect the forger's reputation.

"Hey, you've got to admit it's much nicer to bring pleasure to people than to ruin their days."

"Yeah, this guy's a real prince."

"You're just upset because I won't introduce you to him."

I had to laugh. Van Derhurscht would not authenticate the paintings he did not do, and his denials went a long way toward intimating they were probably the real things. It was not so stupid when you thought about it.

Ben always refused to let me meet him. I think it was more out of some wicked pleasure just to bug me. Since the guy appeared to be a recluse, I never had the chance. I always thought his would have been an interesting story to write.

Ben went back to the States a couple of months before I left for Greece. He sold his *Motherhood* painting before he left, and got a great deal of money for it.

He paid Van Derhurscht off, and invited everyone to an elaborate and fancy dinner at La Tour d'Argent, a very famous restaurant in Paris. Van Derhurscht did not come to the dinner, and Cécile refused to go because Pete was going to be there.

"What if he starts to take food from other people's plates with his fingers?"

"Come on, he won't" I said, knowing how she felt about Pete's behavior.

"You know he will, and you will defend him because you find the whole matter *très amusant*."

I did not find what Pete did amusing, really. And Pete did not take food from other people's plates that evening. Later, when I told that to Cécile, she did not believe me.

Leon and Thea, who happened to be in town, joined the rest of us. We all thought it was a wonderful dinner.

At the restaurant, Ben went around to all the tables, gave the women roses he had ordered, kissed them on both cheeks, and wished them a happy and long life. All of the women were surprised and delighted, calling him: "*un charmant américain.*"

One day, Ben found himself short of cash so he went to the American embassy to see if he could hustle a job. I have no idea what prompted him to think he could do that. If you came from Nebraska that is what you did, he said.

As he was trying to wrangle a date with the receptionist, she remembered a phone call that had come in inquiring if the embassy knew of a house painter, someone who could speak English, to do a small paint job.

To get rid of him she gave him the phone number. Ben called and sealed the deal with the butler over a couple glasses of wine.

A couple of rooms in the house needed painting. Ben knew what to do and he was going to be paid under the table. He must have done a great job because when the owner saw the finished product, he was delighted.

He then, asked Ben to do several other rooms. Ben and the butler had another couple of glasses of wine and made another deal.

Ben had not made any connection between the house and Leon until one day the butler told Ben a little about the owners of the house. Presto! Ben knew who that was.

Ben and I had not seen each other for a while until the evening he showed up at my hotel, and we went out to grab one of our special dinners at a small Polish restaurant—Chez Wadja—catering mostly to students and workers.

It was just a couple of blocks from the hotel, on rue Grande Chaumière, and for a couple dollars, you could have a proper meal.

Ben was friendly with the owners and was allowed credit when he had no money. He had also been given his own napkin—a special privilege offered only to those the owners like best. Ben was in high spirits that night and wanted to splurge.

He chose Chez Wadja instead of Mille Colonne, on rue de la Gaité, my usual favorite-easy-on-the-pocket-restaurant to go grab something to eat, where they served an honest *coq au vin* for less than a dollar. That evening Ben looked like the cat that ate the canary.

"You're gonna shit your pants when you hear this," he said.

"What?"

"You know how everybody makes fun of Leon about this supposedly great house that belongs to his father that no one has ever seen."

"Yeah."

"I've seen it. I've been inside!"

"Get out of here."

"It's true," he said, a little miffed I did not believe him.

"Come on."

"I'm telling you. It's the damnest thing. I didn't make the connection until today."

"What in the hell are you talking about?"

"I told you about the job I got painting this house." Ben had described the place as a small replica of the Louvre.

"Yeah, I remember you telling me about it."

"Well, the house is choice. I mean, really, heavy bucks. Beaucoodles dollars," Ben said laughing. "Tonight, I was talking to François, the guy who hired me. He told me a little bit about the people who own the house. It belongs to a rich American who's not really an American but a German who had gone to the U.S. and made lots of money."

It was not until François said something about the old man not wanting to have his son come over to the house because he was afraid he would steal something that the whole thing clicked with Ben. He was giddy about having found this out.

"Are you kidding?"

"No."

"Come on, you're making that up."

"I'm not. I'll take you there if you don't believe me."

"Tonight?"

"I don't think François would let us in. Come by tomorrow," he said, and in his eyes there was a look of triumph.

The next day, we took the Métro and went to visit the house. Ben was not kidding. The French call this kind of house, an *hôtel particulier*. It was at the end of a dead-end street in the 16th *arrondissement,* surrounded by high walls enclosing a well-kept garden. Like Ben said: choice.

Ben told François I was a good friend of his, and he wanted to show me how "rich" Americans lived in Paris. François did not suspect anything and we never told him what we knew about Leon.

He gave us a tour of the place. The tapestries were exquisite, the statues were gorgeous, and the paintings were absolutely stunning. François told us it was a shame the house was empty for most of the time. It resembled a museum, but as François would say, gloom, indifferent, never open for people to come and enjoy what it had to offer.

"I wouldn't mind having a museum like this one," Ben said.

"*Oui, Monsieur, mais vous étés gai, ici c'est trop noir, trop triste,*" François said, with a great deal of regret in his voice contrasting Ben's happy guy attitude with the darkness and sadness of the house.

He then showed us the Monet Leon had taken from the house, the one his father had accused him of trying to sell. It was behind a glass case, and there was an elaborate alarm system throughout the place.

The house had three floors, and there was an elevator we took up to the third floor. Sitting on top of the grand piano, there was a photo of Leon and his father in happier days.

"This Renoir business sounds strange," John said, the night I ran into them at Le Cosmos after dropping off Lisa at her hotel.

"You guys never believed him when he told you about the house and the Monet," I said.

This was a sore point with them because we never told them where the house was. When Leon found out we had been to the house he was pleased. We told him Ben had a connection. Leon did not ask for any details, he felt vindicated.

"It's unfair to keep us from learning where the house is," John said.

"I made a promise not to tell."

"You and your promises," Pete said.

"Come on. That's water under the bridge," I said.

"I think Leon was crazy when he gave the Monet back to his father," Pete said.

"He stole it," John said.

"How could he steal it when his father told him the painting was his? The painting was *liberated!* A Monet belongs to us all. Anyway, I think he was crazy, probably crazier than I am," Pete said.

"So, you do agree *you're* crazy?" John asked.

"No, I was just using Cartesian logic," Pete said, laughing his head off.

Looking at these guys, looking at all of us, one could say we were all mad. We all came from different places carrying our personal baggage. Yet in this loveliest and craziest of cities, somehow, we had managed to connect.

In spite of our own loneliness and despair, we had all plugged into some strange and mysterious source that gave us hope and made us dream. Paris has that effect on many.

"Are you free next weekend?" Peter asked me.

"Yes. Why?"

"Roxanne and I want to celebrate our having lived together for the last eleven years without boring or insulting each other."

"That's a record," I said.

"One devoutly to be wished," John said quietly, quoting Shakespeare.

On that note, we left the Cosmos.

SIX

Lisa did not call the next day. In fact, I did not hear from her for the next four days. Deep down, I felt a sense of loss and regret—somewhat surprising.

Perhaps she had indeed gone back to the States, and I would not see her again. I thought of going to her hotel but at the last minute decided against it. I thought, what the hell that is how life is.

Then she showed up! She was carrying her suitcase, a bunch of flowers, and was in wonderful, high spirits.

"I thought you had gone home!"

"No," she said, taken aback. I could see we were both confused.

"What happened?"

"I'll tell you later," she said. "Is your offer for that room still open?"

"Yes."

"I'll take it. These are for you." She handed me the flowers.

"Nobody has ever given me flowers." I was touched.

"Well, there's always the first time. I was going to get you a puppy, but I liked the flowers better."

"It's so sweet of you. Thank you so much."

"You're welcome. OK, how much?"

"How much what?"

"The room."

"Oh, the room . . . to tell you the truth I don't know."

"I'd better warn you that having lived all over the place I drive a hard bargain," she said, smiling.

Then seeing that I was standing in the middle of the room and did not quite know what to do with the flowers, she took them away from me, walked into the kitchen, looked inside the cabinets, found an old vase, put water in it, put the flowers in, and brought them into the living room—all without missing a beat. Unexpectedly, the room looked transformed, bright and cheerful.

"So, where's the room?" She asked when she saw I was still a bit lost by her surprising return. Her smile was contagious.

We walked down the hallway, and I stood in the doorway while she went about tidying up the room. In no time, at all, she had emptied her suitcase and put her things away, and the room did look better than it had just moments before. I marveled at the way she seemed to have taken over.

We went back into the living room. Suddenly, the idea of her living in the same apartment seemed a bit scary. I was not sure if I had made the right decision, as I did not quite know what I was getting myself into. It was confusing.

"I talked to my mom yesterday, and she said not to worry about dad, that things are looking up, and that I can stay if I want to. I told her I was going to rent a room from you, and she said it was fine. Robin sends her love."

When I did not respond, she looked at me with a questioning look. "Is that OK about renting the room?"

"Yes, of course. I mean, somehow, I knew you would act this way."

"I told you: I'm organized. I even registered at the Sorbonne. My parents are curious to see if all the money they invested in giving me French lessons is going to pay off. You know something?"

"What?"

"I understand a lot of French. I didn't think I would, but I do understand better what people are saying, and I kind of know how to respond to them—well, most of the time."

I started to laugh and shake my head. The whole situation seemed out of joint, not what I could have imagined.

"It's true. You don't believe me?" she said, her eyes questioning.

"I do. It's just seems unreal," I said. "You show up here out of the blue. You tell me you're on your way back to the States. I drop you off at your hotel. I don't hear from you for days, so I figured you left. And now here you are!"

"Does it surprise you?" she asked mischievously.

"Yeah, kind of, but it's great."

"OK, for four days I walked all over the city. I didn't take the Métro, the bus, or a taxi. I just went around and visited. Ask me about Paris. Go ahead."

"You walked for four days?"

"Yes. I was so tired every night, but I wanted to do it."

"Why?"

"I needed to see the city, to sense the city, to make sure I wanted to stay."

"Are you always this possessed?"

"Especially when I'm happy as I am today because I've made the right decision."

"Going to the Sorbonne *is* the right decision."

"I know. Now I won't be so jealous of you."

"Jealous of me?"

"You studied there. It's wonderful to go to such a great university. My parents think it's fantastic to be a student at the Sorbonne."

"So do I."

"Thank you for agreeing with me. Oh, and one more thing: You have to teach me the *argot*—slang—and all of the bad words in French." She was serious.

"The bad words? Why do you want to know the bad words?"

"I want to understand what the taxi drivers are yelling about, that way I'll feel like a true *Parisienne*."

"Don't worry about that. A couple of weeks at the Sorbonne and you'll know those words, and you'll learn them from the original source: *les Parisians*."

"You think?"

"I know so."

"Good," she said, laughing.

Her laugh was infectious, free, without any guile. It was the innocence of the pure at heart. Her energy and enthusiasm were high. Suddenly, I felt good about her being here, and even though the idea of Lisa staying at the apartment had seemed scary and threatening just a moment ago, it now felt natural.

"Do you want to know something else?" she asked a moment later.

"What?"

"I'm a good chef."

"Here in France, you'll have a lot of competition."

"True, but they don't make a mean chili," she declared solemnly.

"Chili in Paris," I laughed. "That's a good one. I don't think the French know much about chili."

"We'll teach them. Where there's a will there's a way."

Where there is a will there is a way! That was Lisa. She never had time to be depressed or moody. Her life was filled with surprises because she looked for the best in others.

In no time, at all, she had met some of my neighbors who always seemed to be frowning, and who had barely acknowledged me in the past as I met them in the hallway, and they would smile and greet her as if they had known her forever.

This was a bit of shock because I always felt my neighbors were just not interested in being friendly to anybody. She rented a piano and had it delivered.

Now the old apartment was often filled with the rich sounds of her playing. Even the neighbors seemed pleased that Lisa was doing this.

In no time, Lisa also knew the butcher, the baker, and the other *commerçants* of the street-market that came to the neighborhood twice a week. In typical French male fashion, the men would steal glances her way. Their attitudes, manners, and words they used with her were those of Latin males responding to a beautiful girl.

When you are a Frenchman, it is part of your being to show how much you appreciate female charm and beauty. It is what always makes women desirable and mysterious to males. Lisa understood the game, and how it was played.

I could see how pleased the men were to face this lovely American girl. Always cheerful, open, friendly, with a charming American accent, and soon I was known as *"Le monsieur avec la très jolie mademoiselle."*

Often, I would catch the sly looks of envy. In their imagination, I was doing things to this beautiful girl they would have loved to do—except that I was not doing anything.

She slept in her bed, and I slept in mine.

Lisa was enrolled at the Sorbonne and faithfully attended her classes. Her parents would have been happy and proud to know the money they invested in French lessons—*argot* and bad words now included—was indeed paying off.

Schoolwork kept her quite busy, but she also found time to enroll in a dance class. Now there was Lisa, always rushing out of the apartment to keep up with her busy schedule.

For her, dancing was a beautiful, personal experience she needed to have. Her father had been the musical influence in her life. He was a wonderful and talented pianist.

It was also through music one could discover much about her. I used to kid Lisa about her philosophy of life.

"Dancing and politics, are you sure you can mix them?"

"Yes. You need stimuli for your brain and your body. I don't see any contradiction. On the contrary, they complement each other. *Mens sana in corpore sano.*"

She made friends at the Sorbonne, and there were phone calls from her classmates. Many of them were males. If truths were told, I was jealous but I reminded myself I had no right: She was young, beautiful, free—and this was Paris.

"I would like to ask your permission to have a small birthday party with some friends from school," she said, one Saturday morning.

It was a few weeks after she had moved in. I had gone out early that morning to get us some fresh croissants, and we were sitting in the kitchen having breakfast.

I was always surprised the apartment was now well kept. She had said she was not going to be picking up after me, but she ended up bringing order to the place because she hated disorder.

"Here?"

"If you don't mind."

"No. Tell me when you want to do it, and I'll get out of your way."

"It's my birthday!" she protested.

"Oh."

"You don't have to leave. You're invited, too."

"Thank you, but I'll probably get in the way."

"Why do you say that?"

"They're your friends. I don't know them."

"They can also become your friends."

I felt a little silly because secretly I wanted to stay for her party. I was very happy she was including me in her personal life. Old fears are so tough to get rid of.

She looked at me as if she were studying me, making me curious about why. I was afraid to ask.

"I'd like you to stay."

Suddenly, I saw desire in her eyes. The way she looked at me was enough. An electric charge went through my body. I began to want her in the worst possible way. It really shook me up. This is crazy, I thought. I do not want to get into this. My head said no, but my heart said yes.

I knew I had been suppressing my feelings about her. I was afraid to show them. What did I have to lose? My pride? My perennial bitterness? My fear of another broken heart?

I could not bear to be a loser again. Yes, I could want her from a distance and that was fine, but was it? On this morning, when the sky over Paris was gray, when the city oppressed me to no end, when the only thing that made sense was to make love to her.

I sat there fighting the fear of not wanting to be hurt again. Not to be disappointed was far more important than the heart.

"Why do we fight it?" she asked, softly.

She stood in front of me, taking my head and pressing it against her. She was wearing a robe with nothing under it. I touched her, and she was flowing. Slowly, she opened her robe, and I buried my face in her. She tasted warm and sweet.

She moaned and swayed. She helped me take off my clothes and we stood naked, trembling, and pressed against each other.

Filled with excitement and desire I kissed her breasts, lovely, hard. There was no rush or false movements. We stood pressed against each other for what seemed like an eternity. I had an erection putting to shame the mighty Eiffel Tower!

Lisa was looking at me with such intensity, with an incredible sense of purpose, beyond her desire to be physically intimate with me one more time.

There was finality about what was taking place between us. Lisa was doing this with everything that she was, with her whole being, not holding anything back. And it scared me. Boy, did it scare me.

Yet I longed to be like her, to act like her, to be honest and giving. I wanted to be hers just like she was mine at this decisive moment. In looking at her eyes, I understood why people say that they are the windows of the soul.

She was not just showing me she was mine: she was living it! There was no other truth. Her kisses were shy, tender—truer than anything I ever remembered receiving from another woman. She held onto me as if afraid I would walk away from her.

I had been celibate by choice since Greece. Now making love to Lisa was like an awakening—a discovery of what was best in her and in me. A hidden universe filled with sweet and wonderful surprises was suddenly revealed.

I did not have to be afraid anymore. I wanted to be pure in my feelings toward her. I did not want to continue making any more excuses about myself, about my life, always feeling like a loser.

I longed to share the sense of innocence she was showing me as if it was the first time—for her, for me. Though I fought not to let myself be taken in by this incredible emotion, I also knew it was out of my control.

Deep down in my heart, my guts, I wanted to match the simple truth Lisa was demonstrating: There are never barriers to love; it exists. *Pointe finale!*

It was a truth I had lost to time, and bitterness. One that I could never dream to be lucky enough to find again for I had convinced myself that love was beyond hoping.

Lisa seemed to sense this and her tenderness was the more touching because she, better than me, instinctively knew and understood my emotional fragility.

Women can be so incredibly decisive at such times. We men have so much to learn from them. The realization that I could have such strong feelings for her was comforting, scary, and disconcerting.

Lisa and I had known each other's bodies before, but this was better, so much better. I wondered if the gods gave mortals a second chance. Would they give me another chance?

"I wanted you for so long I thought I would go crazy," she said, afterward.

"You told me you had your period," I said. This sounded lame, and I knew it.

"That was three weeks ago."

"OK, what was I supposed to do?"

"You could have asked me."

"Oh sure: 'Excuse me Lisa, is your period over?'"

"It was that simple," she said, challenging me.

"Nothing is that simple. Anyway, I wasn't sure."

"Are you sure now?" she asked. Her eyes searched my face.

"I don't know," I answered.

She sat up and laughed that wonderful rich and lovely laugh of hers, making uncertainty bearable.

"The fool says he's not sure. Do you know how many of these horny frogs—*grenouilles excitées*—have been after me?" she said, laughing, but she was not bragging. Many Americans use the word *frog* to refer to the French.

"Is that supposed to make me jealous?" I asked, hiding that I *had* been jealous and afraid to admit it.

"It should. I've been telling them that I was not free, that I belong to you."

"No, you didn't."

"Yes, I did!"

"You didn't."

"Yes, I did." She was serious. "Don't you think I haven't noticed the look in your eyes as other men look at me when we go shopping at the street-market? I know the way you act. I've been observing you. 'Hands off, guys,' was the message." She was right.

"It always pleased me when you did it," she added.

"Really?"

"Yes."

"How come I never saw that?"

"Because you were looking the other way."

"The story of my life."

"Anyway, why didn't you come into my bed?"

"I thought about it, but I was waiting for you to make your move."

"It's a good thing I did," she said. "If I hadn't, I'd have probably ended up sleeping alone for the rest of my life."

"Come on."

"It was *your* turn."

"Yes, but you have more courage than I do."

"You seemed so forbidding. I thought maybe I was doing something wrong, that I didn't please you. I'm yours if you want me, but if you don't—" she stopped. A long silence followed. She did not take her eyes off my face.

"Lisa, I have wanted you for so long. I have wanted you in the worst possible way. I have wanted you when I was awake. I have wanted you when I was sound asleep."

"Is that true?"

"And how! A man loved by you would be the luckiest man," I said, remembering what Chris had said back in Athens.

"Alex, are you that lucky man?"

Her face was serious and expectant. She looked at me with those beautiful eyes of hers. I drew her toward me and held her against me.

132

"Yes, I'm that lucky man," I said, and for the first time in my life an immutable truth spoke, clear, beautiful, and final. I just had to learn to deal with it.

"You know those four days I spent walking around Paris? I thought so much about you. Everything I saw that moved me made me think of you. I felt so lonely. Of course, I wanted to walk around by myself, but I always imagined I would come back and find you waiting for me at the hotel—you didn't even call."

"I thought you didn't want to see me."

"Really?"

"Well, you said you'd call me and you didn't."

"Yes, I said that. But I thought since I had come by your apartment that you would call me instead. And now you don't want to come to my birthday party."

"Oh, come on. It's not true, but I do find birthday parties depressing."

"Why?"

"Maybe it's because I didn't have too many of them when I was a kid. Are you sure it's your birthday?" I asked, trying to humor her.

"Do you want to see my passport?" Before I could answer, she jumped out of bed, went to get it, and brought it back.

"So, you're an October baby, and you were born in Ethiopia!" I said, marveling at finding this out.

"Yes. My father was working there building roads and bridges. After we were born, the people he worked with insisted Robin and I had to be taken to the bush where a very ancient tribe blessed and adopted us.

"Initially, my mother had some difficulty breast-feeding us so this wonderful woman who had also just had a baby fed us for a while. She's my second mother. I have a rather extended family running around in the wilds of Ethiopia," she said, laughingly.

"And you expect me to believe that?"

"It's the truth."

"You're making that up."

"No. You see this?"

She showed me a bracelet she was wearing on her left wrist. It was a rather delicate ivory bracelet with grooves filled with very fine strands of gold.

The gold had been threaded gracefully inside and around the ivory in unique patterns. I had noticed it before, and now looking at it closely I realized it was exquisite.

"This protects me. I never take it off. I belong to my tribe. If you're mean to me, they'll come to find you and punish you."

"I don't want to be punished by Ethiopians."

"Then be kind and love me," she said, placing her head on my shoulder.

"I will."

"You promise?"

"Yes!"

She gave me a wonderful smile and embraced me.

"I liked your long hair better," I said.

"It'll grow back."

"S, what do we do now?" I asked, still feeling insecure, trying to get my bearings.

"Well, until you kick me out of your bed this is where I'm sleeping."

"Do I have any choice?"

"No, besides it'll save me some rent money," she said, and laughed.

"That's what this thing's about. You're just looking to save money on the rent."

"Why not? I believe in bargains."

"I'm not such a bargain, really."

"Oh, no, I've made a big mistake?" She said, feigning disappointment.

"I'm afraid so. I'm really damaged goods."

"I'm a sucker for damaged goods. My mother always warned me about such things."

She pushed me back on the bed and got on top of me. She leaned over, her bright eyes intensely searching my face. I pushed my head forward and kissed her lovely breasts. She closed her eyes, and when she opened them, they had a wonderful, peaceful, shiny look in them.

"You're a fool," she said, after a while with a soft smile.

"That I am. I'll never kick you out of my bed."

"You promise?"

"Yes!"

I was getting hard again. Now it was her turn to ride me into the magnificent plains of ecstasy. It was lovely to have Lisa share her tenderness, and who she was. To show me her pleasure when we made love, giving of herself to me, the total abandon on her part, and what she sought to bring to my otherwise troubled soul and spirit.

For the next three days, we stayed in bed, literally.

Lisa moved in the apartment a few days after I ran into Peter and John at Le Cosmos, and the following weekend Peter and Roxanne were having their party.

I asked Lisa if she wanted to come with me. She was the hit of the party, and to top it all off Peter gave her one of his paintings. Everyone was in shock.

"And you said you didn't have a 'Tracy' with you." John said.

"I didn't," I protested, knowing he would not believe me.

"So off he goes to Greece with this lovely bird and doesn't tell his friends about it," complained John.

"She wasn't with me."

"Like you just found her over there, right? Lisa emerged out of the *foam* like Aphrodite does in Greek mythology?"

"Well, maybe she did."

"And you'd expect us to believe you weren't holding out on us?"

"I wasn't. I met her there. It's the damn truth."

"I like her better than Cécile," Pete said.

"You must. You just gave her one of your paintings," I said, still trying to get over the shock.

"When I love, I give!" He said, and walked away from us.

"Is she a model?" John asked in what I took to be a proletarian tone.

"No, she's here to study philosophy and political science."

"Is this a new fad for you Yanks?"

"She's serious."

"That certainly changes things around, doesn't it? Yes . . . she's nice for an American." This from John the cynic.

Later, Lisa did not mind when Pete took some food from her plate.

"I never thought that old fool would be so taken by a young woman," John said, in a mixture of love and curiosity about his friend Pete.

"It goes to show you how well you know him," said Roxanne.

"OK, OK, maybe he thinks she'll pose for him," John said, still suspicious Lisa had less lofty ideas than serious studying.

"I don't think so." Roxanne thought for a moment and then shook her head. "He finds something in her he understands."

It was the way she said it more than the words she used that caught my attention. There was a deep sense of communion between Roxanne and Pete.

I saw a glimpse of what Pete had meant, of wanting to celebrate eleven years of living together without having insulted each other. It was hard to imagine a man and a woman capable of such grace.

Having seen Pete throw a bottle of wine at a window did not indicate a man easy to live with. On the contrary, it showed a complex character. Yet Roxanne was not pretending.

There was naturalness and serenity about her. She radiated warmth, and thoughtfulness. Around her, Pete behaved differently. There was a symbiotic relationship between the two.

They had found an inner peace that manifested itself in how they treated each other. There was a mutual respect that made me envious. It seemed to have transcended all the grind and pettiness of a couple's domestic living.

Perhaps the demons that always hover around the relationship between a man and a woman had been exposed, and Roxanne and Pete found them to be without any substance.

The final secret in their lives was that there was no secret: It was open. Yet their relationship was intensely personal, loving, but uncluttered—real. To me it was strange and comforting.

Much later, when I made a comment to Lisa, she said successful relationships were the result of people whose destinies had been put to the test—and who had survived. That is how love must be.

Suddenly, Lisa pervaded my whole life. Her energy and openness were contagious. She made me laugh and made me realize happiness is possible; one does not have to sacrifice something else, just be true to oneself. Man, why is it so damn hard to be oneself?

Lisa was so incredibly without hang-ups it was next to impossible to get her upset or to be upset with her. One evening, I woke up and she was bending over me, observing me. I was startled.

"What are you doing?"

"I'm watching you sleep."

"Why?"

"Because you're beautiful when you sleep."

How could I not fall in love with her?

Others fell in love with her, too. It was not that she was trying to make people notice her. She was just a vibrant young woman filled with desire for life, spirited, natural, with lots of fantasy, always looking for the best and never settling for the false or the mediocre, believing it was better and more practical to think of the glass as half-full than half-empty. I had so much to learn from her. I wanted to learn from her.

We spent lots of time just walking around Paris visiting museums, and art galleries, discovering restaurants, little bistros, special places that always seemed like havens for lovers. It was how we discovered *Chez Berthillon,* on l'Île Saint Louis, the best place for ice cream and *marron glacés,* the delicious, glazed chestnuts.

And *La Rhumerie*, on Boulevard St-Germain-des-Prés, where they served wonderful, exotic, and delicious rum-based drinks both hot and cold—so many unforgettable and rich experiences.

Part of falling in love in Paris is exploring the city together, making it yours, letting the city encircle you with this wonderful sentiment of happiness and joy reserved only for people who are in love. The city of lovers made for lovers. I always think Paris was invented to protect lovers.

Lisa wanted to see Place de la Contrescarpe, a place Hemingway had made famous in his writings about Paris, so we spent one entire evening there talking to a couple of *clochards*—tramps.

They were touched we wanted to talk to them. We sat at a sidewalk table and shared a bottle of wonderful wine and some ham sandwiches with them.

We talked about nothing and about everything. Afterward, Lisa and I walked by the Parthenon and marveled at that magnificent monument dedicated to honor and safeguard very famous French citizens' remains.

There are some wonderful apartments around the area, and we wondered about the people who lived in them, whether they were as happy as we were. We decided nobody could be happier than we.

"I'm sure they have more money than we do," she said. "But we have the whole city of Paris and our love for each other, and if they knew about it they would be jealous of us."

"Do you think so?"

"I know so," she said, and kissed me.

Late one evening, we stopped by Shakespeare & Company, the bookstore in the Latin Quarter also made famous by Hemingway in his writings about Paris.

He used to borrow books form Sylvia Beach, the woman who ran the store. There had been other writers, during the twenties that Sylvia helped.

One that comes to mind is James Joyce, the author of *Ulysses*. She became his publisher. After browsing a bit, we left the bookstore. As we came out there was a guy selling paintings of Shakespeare & Company, so Lisa bought a small one and gave it to me.

"There's a lot of history in that place," she said.

"We should have asked the man inside if one can still borrow books."

"Do you want to go back?"

"No, we'll come back some other time."

"Yes, we must."

On another occasion, we went to the Latin Quarter to see Kubrick's latest film: 2001. The film was so overwhelming we spent half of the night talking about it. Then we had dinner at a small Tunisian restaurant. We were the only clients there. The couscous was delicious.

Afterward, she wanted to find a small hotel and stay there for the night and not go home. Unbeknownst to me she had made a reservation at a quaint Parisian hotel.

And we would pretend we were star-crossed lovers and this would be our only night together in Paris. In the morning, we would say goodbye and go back to our dreary lives.

"It will be like in Crete," I said.

"This time we'll never see each other again."

"Oh, no, that's too sad."

"Well, maybe we would run into each other around noontime," she said, laughing.

"OK, that's much better."

The night clerk at the hotel gave us a pretty room on the top floor overlooking the Parisian rooftops. We slept with the curtains open so we could see the rooftops first thing in the morning.

However, the weather in Paris was now turning into its usual damp, wet, cold, and along with the weather, I was also turning damp, wet, and cold.

I found myself looking forward to Christmas, hoping it would help me through the days, even though Christmas is not my favorite time of the year. There were moments when I woke up filled with morbid thoughts about everything; even Lisa's presence was not enough to lift my spirits.

I had asked myself so many times why I was this way. The answer always eludes me and seems to exist in another time, another dimension, out of my reach and understanding.

Lisa, in her artful way, knew better than to question, though I soon learned that for her the things I brooded about were just as important for her as they were for me.

She argued the difference was she did not take them to mean they were there to make her life miserable. One dealt with those imponderables within one's own capabilities. Rome had not been built in one day. People would always be people. Life, more often than not, was not going to change overnight.

One did what one had to do and went on with the things that mattered. As for the rest, one gave it one's own best and that was all that was required. To be brooding about it was not only unhealthy, but also made it worse. The larger picture was what one had to keep in mind.

One evening, toward the end of the year, we were invited to have dinner with José and Ulla. José, born in Puerto Rico, grew up in New York City. He was a flamenco guitar player who had come to Paris and had been living the bohemian life.

He had survived by playing his guitar in the Métro, collecting a few bucks here and there until one day some guy heard him play and asked him to come to this nightclub for an audition. He was hired on the spot.

Ulla, who came from Sweden, had gone to the club one evening and met him. Since Ulla was also in the same class at the Sorbonne with Lisa, the two had become fast friends. José and Ulla came to Lisa's birthday party.

I liked him right off the bat because he was smart, fearless, and a very talented musician. The nightclub where José performed was owned by a group of musicians from Spain. José thought they were gypsies.

They were surprised by the way he played and could not believe he was self-taught. He had never taken a guitar lesson in his life. When José played, the guitar became an extension of him and after a while, it was hard to tell where one ended and other began.

He had arranged, as a complete guitar solo, a well- known concerto by the Spanish composer Joaquin Rodrigo—"*Concierto de Aranjuez*"—and he played it magnificently. The musicians were blown away.

"I wanted to do it like Miles Davis did with his trumpet in his "Sketches of Spain" recording and not like this French guy who had put lyrics to the music, which I hated," José said.

"Oh, it's not so bad," Ulla, said.

"It's terrible. Anyway, the guys at the club hired me, though what I was trying to do was no great shakes. The fools."

We all knew better. The people who hired José were no "fools." Some years earlier, Joaquin Rodrigo had been a visiting professor at the University of Rio Piedras, in Puerto Rico. José read about this and convinced his parents to let him go by himself from New York and attend a couple of Rodrigo's lectures.

That was the easy part. The hardest part was convincing the university to let a non-student—a sixteen-year-old kid still wet behind the ears—attend any of the lectures. Nothing doing, they said.

José went anyway. And one early morning he stood by the front door of the building where the lectures were held. When he saw the composer, he introduced himself without preamble and told him why he was there.

Rodrigo was surprised and impressed by the kid's brashness, plus the fact that José spoke Spanish. Rodrigo agreed to let the kid attend a couple of his lectures. The powers that be did not like it one bit, but they were not about to argue with Rodrigo.

When José came to Europe, he had hitchhiked to Spain to pay a visit to the composer. Rodrigo remembered him and had been surprised and delighted when José had suddenly shown up at the door. He was invited by Rodrigo and his wife to have dinner with them.

They told him they admired his courage and his commitment to the guitar, to the music. He could visit them anytime. For José, this was one of his proudest moments—one of the highlights of his young life.

"Did you play for him?" Lisa asked José.

"No. He didn't ask me. I was ready but with someone like Rodrigo, you wait to be asked. I'm sure I would have been scared, but I would have given it my best shot. Can you imagine having an open invitation to Rodrigo's home?"

"Will you go?" I asked him.

"You bet. And maybe next time I won't be so scared about asking if I can play for him."

He had a photo of him and "Don Joaquin" as José called the composer. Rodrigo's wife had taken the photo and sent it to José. Rodrigo had written: "*Suerte matador.*"

José believed that since that day his luck had indeed improved. The words were a blessing of sorts from the world-famous blind composer.

The people at the nightclub kept telling José that his kind of playing only happens on rare occasions. They kidded him that it was probably one of their gypsy ancestors who went to the New World and carried the seed from which José sprang.

The only problem with that theory was that his father was black and his mother was a Russian Jew who had named him in honor of the doctor who had saved his life in a complicated delivery. The group did not believe José. They preferred their own version.

He was asked to join the ensemble. So, José found himself gainfully employed and part of a newly acquired and extended family made up of a wild, lovable, and talented bunch of musicians. Lisa and I had gone to listen to the group, and it was fantastic.

It was hard to imagine the four guys had been playing together for just a few weeks. They had the place jumping, and Ulla told us that every night they played it was the same story.

The dinner that evening was special because José and Ulla were going to Stockholm to visit her parents. Afterward, they would travel to Spain, where he and the group had been invited to play in a flamenco music festival.

It was a great honor to be invited, and even more so, for a guy like José who was not Spanish. It was just the kind of wonderful news that makes everyone happy. We could not believe it. José could not believe it!

"One day, this guy showed up at the club and told us we had to be at the festival. It was actually more of an order than an invitation. The other guys told me that even if I were dying, I still had to go. This is the ultimate. Manitas de Plata was once honored by them," José said, beaming.

Manitas de Plata was a Spanish flamenco guitar player, one of the best, which is why they called him "Silver Hands." He had a huge following in Paris.

It was said, that whenever Picasso wanted to hear flamenco music, he would ask Manitas to come and play—two old Spanish masters listening and learning from each other.

"How do they select you?" Lisa asked José about being invited to the festival.

"They won't tell you. You know how gypsies are, very secretive."

"Are they really gypsies? Lisa was curious.

"Of course not," Ulla said.

"Of course, they are," José said.

"He's just saying that because now he's a member of the group," Ulla said.

"I know they are gypsies or *Roma* as they call themselves. Or *Gitanos* as they are called in Spain. Just look at the way they live."

"How do they live that makes them gypsies? Lisa asked.

"They've got this big apartment, and there are all kinds of people walking in and out day and night. I don't know how anybody gets any sleep there. The whole building is like that—a big and happy family. All they do is talk, play their guitars, make up these beautiful, haunting songs about lost love and home in the old country.

"It's in their blood. When you ask them where this old country is, they get a misty and faraway look in their eyes, and let me tell you for them it's this mythical, magical land filled with music, love and happiness."

"That doesn't make them gypsies," I said.

"If that doesn't, I don't know what does," he said.

"The only thing I know is that I wish I could play the guitar the way you do," Ulla said wistfully, and I knew just how she felt.

"Only if you are a gypsy," he said.

"You're not a gypsy," Ulla said.

"Yes, I am."

"I've heard of Russian madmen named Boris, Ivan, Sasha, but José for a Black-Russian-Jewish-Puerto Rican gypsy?" Ulla said, shaking her head.

"That's the ticket," José said.

Then we toasted and drank champagne to success, music, love, women, Paris and Black-Russian-Jewish-Puerto Rican gypsies. Ulla looked at me in a funny way.

She had been doing it throughout the night, then looked at Lisa as if wanting to say something but decided against it when she caught Lisa's eye. I did not know what it was all about.

I was feeling a bit tipsy when we left their place. We got off the Métro at the George V stop, as Lisa wanted to walk. Christmas was not too far off, and the decorations were now in full splendor along the avenue of the Champs Elysées. It was cold, but bearable. Lisa seemed in wonderful spirits.

She kept humming "Feeling Groovy," from Simon and Garfunkel. My tipsiness was slowly fading away as the cold weather sobered me. We walked to the top of the avenue and stood watching the *Arc de Triomphe* across from us, and suddenly she wanted to climb it.

"You know, since I lived here, I've never been up there."

"Because you're not a tourist," she said.

"I'm a tourist," I protested. "The problems of the French aren't my problems. The problems back in the U.S. are too damn far away for me to really do anything about them, either. I live in a world that is neither here nor there. In a way, I'm the ultimate tourist."

"Yes, but are you happy?"

"Tonight, I am."

"Just tonight?"

"No, every night and forever. I love you. I love Paris. I don't give a damn about anything else."

We stopped and we kissed. "You're acting more like the natives," she said, a moment later, laughing.

"OK, and how do they act?"

"You know their attitude: *Je m'en fous*—I don't care."

"Can I not care about anything just for tonight?"

"OK, but only for tonight."

"I care about a lot of things. Like, for instance, how many twin girls with beautiful green eyes and high cheekbones exist in this world?"

"You know, I read somewhere that here in France they have a festival celebrating twins."

"OK, let's go and join them."

"Right now?"

"Yes, right now."

"You're crazy," she said, giving me a warm smile.

She took my hand, and we walked in silence for a few moments. Lisa had become part of my life in a way I had never experienced before with another woman. It was hard to imagine she had been around for only a few weeks.

I had this splendid sensation that I had known her all of my life. The wonderful thing about her was that she did not seem bothered by my moods, my restlessness, and my complicated outlook on life.

Lisa had become part of my existence, but she left me alone. I never had the impression she was fearful or insecure about our relationship. She had a sense of security about herself, about me—thus, about us.

She viewed life through straightforward eyes. You did your best today. It was the only thing required.

"Care to climb the Arch tonight?" she asked.

"OK, I'll race you to the top."

Before the words were out of my mouth, there was Lisa madly dashing around cars, negotiating through the heavy traffic going around the circle of *L'Etoile*, laughing and rushing, with me behind her trying to catch up. We laughed all the way up, and when we got to the top, we were out of breath.

The night was clear and from the top, we had a great view of the city. The Christmas lights and decorations on the trees down the Champs Elysées were bright and warm, and I wondered why Christmas had always seemed less than a joyful occasion to me.

"Aren't they beautiful?" she asked.

"Yes, but Christmas always brings me a sad sense of longing. It makes me melancholic, and I want to be alone. It has nothing to do with religion or beliefs. There have been so many of these feelings since I was a kid, I've given up the hope of feeling any different."

"Why do you feel that way?"

"I don't know."

"Do you believe in Santa Claus?"

"Not really."

"That's the problem."

"Do you think so?"

"Yes," she said. "If you believed in Santa Claus, you wouldn't be so melancholic during Christmas."

"It's too late now."

"Too late? It's never too late to believe in love and happiness. OK, I know he doesn't exist, and I don't care. Santa Claus is such a great, magical, and wonderful idea. It's a fantasy, and we need more fantasy in our lives.

"Here's this jolly old guy, bringing gifts, laughter and happiness. Christmas should be the happiest excuse to be surrounded by loved ones," she said, putting her arm around me.

"This time it'll be different."

"Why do you say that?"

"Because you're here."

"Really, that makes a difference?"

"More than you can possibly imagine."

Her eyes suddenly filled with tears.

"Hey, what gives?"

"It saddens me to think you were unhappy, and I wasn't there to cheer you up. A sad heart always needs a happy heart," she said, wiping her tears and laughing at herself. Those were the words she had used in Crete the first evening we had spent together.

"You are beautiful, and I just simply adore you," I said, and kissed her.

"Really?"

"Yes."

"But why?"

"Why what?"

"You feel that way and use those words? What's behind all of that?"

"You don't know?"

"No."

"It's simple: I have nothing more interesting to do with my life at the moment."

"Oh, OK, that makes sense."

She busted out laughing. I picked her up and twirled her around several times. We were both enjoying the moment, acting silly.

"And if you believe that, I've got me some snake oil for sale."

"You do? Does it cure everything?"

"Almost."

"I don't even think you know what snake oil is," she said.

"Oh, so you think I'm lying to you?"

"No, you could never lie to me."

"I would never lie to you, ever!"

"Good." She hugged me and gave me a warm and magnificent smile. I loved her smile.

"So, all of the sadness is in the past?" she asked.

"Absolutely."

"Are you sure?"

"Yes," I said.

"Lovely."

She leaned against me, and we stood close to each other just looking at the bright lights down the long avenue.

"I want to tell you something, and this is a very special place to tell you," she said, after a long silence.

"What is it?"

"Can you guess?"

Her look was intense but affectionate, and her eyes were clear, focused on my face, intent in not missing my reaction to what she was going to tell me. I had seen this look before when we were making love.

Then, for a second, my heart felt a tremor of fear. Was she leaving to go back to the States? Sometimes, we men can be so obtuse.

"No," I answered. I was lost.

"Soon there will be a child in my belly," she said. She was beaming!

"What?

"We're going to have a baby!" Her face and her smile held no secrets. I was completely bowled over. She was looking at me with those wonderful eyes, searching my face to gauge my reaction.

There was a glow about her I had never seen before. She embraced and held me very close. Something was about to change in our lives that would be profound and timeless. I was speechless.

"How, I mean?" I finally managed to blurt out.

"How? In the usual way! If a man and a woman make love, one fine result is that she may get pregnant."

"No, you dummy. What I mean is why you didn't tell me. I can't believe it."

"You had better believe it because you had a lot to do with it."

She laughed, and I loved her in the craziest of ways.

"You're sure you pregnant?"

"Yes! Remember the other day when I told you I was meeting Ulla. I went to see a doctor, and today I've got the results."

"Are you sure?" I said, still trying to wrap my head around what she had said.

"Of course, I'm sure."

It was a bolt of lightning out of the sky. Now, I understood why Ulla had kept looking at me with a questioning look during dinner. It was the look of people sharing a secret, but then I had not been part of their secret.

"Is that why Ulla kept looking at me in a funny way?"

"Yes. I was afraid she was going to say something because she's so happy for us."

"I was wondering if I had done something wrong."

"No. In fact, you have done something right," she said, laughing and with a very happy face.

"You think so?"

"Absolutely!"

"Then I guess I have. OK, let me see your tummy." I knew I was being silly.

"Here? Now?"

"Yes."

"You can't see anything. Besides, it's too cold for me to be taking off my clothes."

"It feels different."

I put my hand over her stomach and rubbed it.

"It doesn't"

"How do you feel?"

"Wonderful!"

Her face said it all. She held my face in her hands, looking at me, searching, wanting to make sure of my reaction.

"And you," she asked, "how do you feel?"

"I'm stunned by the news. I mean, this is something."

"Yes, but are you happy?" She kept looking at me with a serious look.

"Yes."

"Are you sure?"

"Yes!"

She kissed me and I held her close. What she had just told me was so unexpected.

"I have never been as overwhelmed as I am now. I don't really know what to say."

The words were true. It had never crossed my mind that she would get pregnant. How ridiculous was I? All at once, this was no longer a casual affair. The enormity of the news was hard to digest on the spot. I was astonished.

"Just say you love me."

"*Je t'aime. Je t'adore!*" I shouted.

She started to laugh. The other people around us looked in our direction and laughed.

"*Tu es complement dingue,*" she said.

Yes, I was totally and completely crazy in love with her! Instead of walking back to the apartment, we took a taxi—my idea.

"You *are* crazy. I can still walk, you know."

"No, it's too far." Of course, I knew I was being silly.

I told the driver to go up and down the Champs Elysées and around the *rond point* of L'Etoile at least three times. He looked at me like I was nuts, but he did it.

It was a ritual Americans performed when we came to Paris, I explained. We had been doing it since the time of Benjamin Franklin and Thomas Jefferson. Back in the U.S., it was taught in schools.

"*Alors, si Monsieur Franklin et Monsieur Jefferson l'ont fait . . . OK, d'accord . . .*" he said in typical Parisian tolerance of silly American behavior.

He agreed that if Mr. Franklin and Mr. Jefferson had started this tradition then we might as well respect and continue doing it.

Lisa was laughing her head off and having a wonderful time. I could picture the driver going home and telling his wife the story: How he had driven a couple of crazy Americans up and down the Champs Elysées three times because it was an American tradition while they visited Paris.

And his practical wife, probably thinking her husband had been working too hard, would consider he needed a few days off, after all.

I wanted to make love to Lisa that night, but something new had entered our lives and it bothered me.

"Everybody does it," she said.

"It just feels strange, that's all."

"Alex, you're a riot. Just because I'm pregnant doesn't mean we can't make love."

"Maybe it does."

"You have some weird ideas."

"How do you know that we can still do it?"

"Because I do."

"I guess it's the newness of this whole thing," I said, not really understanding my own feelings.

"You had better get over this, fast! Time's wasting," she leaned in and kissed me.

She got up from the bed and went into the bathroom. When she came back, she was completely naked. By now she had lost most of her tan, but Lisa seemed more attractive, different, lovelier, and more mysterious. She held the key to life and I felt like I was really no part of it.

Yet because she was now pregnant, we were as close as a man and a woman can possibly get. Whatever happened from that day on, we would always remain linked to each other through the baby.

I was looking at her with a sense of who she might be, and such mystery was no more clear or closer to me than it had been in the past. I touched her belly, firm and smooth. She had a wonderful smile on her face.

I ran my hand over her lovely, soft mound; she moaned and swayed as I moved my hand. She always told me that when I touched her, she got so wet it was like Niagara Falls—and it was true.

When we made love, Lisa never closed her eyes. She always looked at me like she was also making love to me with her eyes. That night, our lovemaking was furious and passionate. We were so hungry for each other.

Our destinies were now entwined in a way that made them seem less clear, but we could never go back to the way we were. The past had become the present, and the present was about to become the future.

Later, as she slept right next to me, I was alone with my thoughts for the first time since she had told me the news about her pregnancy. Seeing her sleeping so peacefully always brought me pangs of jealousy and longing because I wanted to sleep just that soundly.

I thought of how little I knew about her, of her life before me. Where had she come from, really? Who was this woman who had changed my life so radically?

"All you need to know is that I love you," she had once said.

"That's all?"

"Yes. Why make things complicated? Love is not a mathematical formula. It's the heart acting as it was designed to do. Why go looking for answers when you already carry them in your heart—" she stopped, searching for the exact words that would express what she most deeply felt now.

"The heart is truly a marvelous human component, isn't it?" she continued. "Once it finds love or gives itself to love there's no going back. It rules everything! It's beyond comprehension."

How true and simple the whole thing was if you are smart enough to see it.

Watching Lisa in her peaceful slumber—her all-American looks belonging more to girls on Southern California beaches, tanned, good looking, healthy, great bodies, perfect teeth, and handsome guys hanging around them.

The question was, how in the hell did this lovely girl end up in my bed and, from what I have been able to gather, in love with me? A total mystery, defying everything I was familiar with. Were the gods about to test me again?

When I was about fifteen years old and living in San Francisco, during one weekend, a friend and I went to visit his mother in Newport Beach. His parents were divorced and his mother had moved down to Southern California, but he had stayed with his father.

We took a bus from San Francisco, and we got to Newport in the evening. The next morning, we hit the beach early.

As only fifteen-year-old males can do, we were trying like crazy to score with some of the blonde mermaids we saw frolicking around the beach that day, and whose lives were seemingly filled with laughter and fun—not with divorces, loneliness, and sadness.

We knew we had no chance with the girls who were surrounded by guys we could not possibly compete with in a million years. Life forced us to forfeit the game ahead of time. My buddy was less philosophical than I was about meeting those lovely women. I just assumed it was out of the question.

Now here I was in Paris, some years later, in my own bed, with one of those mermaids who seemed so unattainable then. Yet I did not want to know everything about Lisa. I wanted to keep her and the idea of her as a mystery, to believe she may have been someone who was there that morning, back in Newport Beach, so long ago.

"Perhaps I should tell you about my old boyfriend," Lisa had said one day.

"Only if it's important to you."

"It isn't."

"We all carry stuff with us," I had said. "You, me, everybody. What matters is we're together. That's all."

"Are you sure?"

"Positive."

"You're wonderful," she had said, with a big smile on her face.

"Sometimes."

I wanted to wake up every day and discover her once again. In so many ways, Lisa knew what she wanted. She never seemed to have doubts about her life or about the place she occupied. For her, life meant one day at a time and making the best of that day.

Given that our lives are never completely clear and are prone to getting entangled in extraneous contradictions, Lisa's attitude was sane and healthy.

How I envied and admired her for she was the complete antithesis of who I was. Life's cynicism had not yet touched her, and I hoped never would. She was young, lovely, and still innocent about life's bitterness. Yes, the gods do have favorites.

In the past few days, I had found myself battling my restlessness and bad mood. The more I considered Milo's idea of translating *L'Étranger* the more I feared the project was out of my league. I had never read the original French version.

Milo had put this wild idea in my head, and no matter how much I fought not to think about it the idea kept coming back. Frankly speaking, who in the hell did I think I was?

"The only way you're going to find out if you can do it is by trying. Besides, it may help you get some ideas about the book you're going to write," Lisa said one Sunday afternoon shortly after announcing her pregnancy.

"I don't know if I'm ever going to write a book."

"Of course, you will!" End of conversation.

How is it possible to have such a blind belief about a loved one? The source is so complex and yet so simple. We love people. We believe in them. Period.

We were walking that Sunday by the Seine. It was always a great pleasure to browse through the stalls of the *bouquinistes* of the Seine, the booksellers by the river with their stands mostly filled with wonderful and very often pristine editions of old books. One never knew what literary treasures were going to be found on any given visit.

The sun was shining and though it was cold, people were out in droves. One could almost detect that Parisians had finally gotten into the Christmas spirit, dressed in heavy overcoats that made them look like stuffed penguins, their faces did not seem so frozen in the typical Parisian frown.

There was animated talk and lots of laughter. I found a series of paperbacks I had once read: *Les Thibault* by Roger Martin du Gard, a French writer whom I much admired. I bought the books for Lisa.

"You'll love the story. This guy is a good as Tolstoy and while Tolstoy never won the Nobel Prize for Literature, which I think is a great injustice, Martin du Gard did back in 1937. One of the characters in the story is a great revolutionary. I think you might discover some affinity with him."

"Really. Thank you, I will read it."

"This thing with Camus is crazy. He's the ultimate in modern French writing: original, lucid. Milo not only wants me to suffer, he also wants to laugh at me. He wants me to die of ridicule and shame. What did I ever do to him? I thought he was my friend."

She knew I was protesting in vain because the idea intrigued me. We had often discussed it. The challenge was both exhilarating and terrifying.

"We believe in you."

"I wish I believed in me like you guys do."

"The least you can do is buy the book."

No sooner had she said it than she went straight to one of the *bouquinistes* and asked him if by any chance he had copy of the *L'Étranger*. The man said no. I was relieved.

"I'm sure we'll find a copy around here," she insisted.

"I could no more do a translation of that than to translate the Rosetta stone." I tried one more time to protest.

"You have to know about Camus. You have to study his life, his writings. I don't know how anyone can attempt to do this kind of work without some knowledge of the man, of who he was," I said.

"You discover who he is through his art," she said. "What better way? IIis art will not lie. It stands there in the open. I don't know of a true artist who hides behind his art."

"There have been some."

"They aren't true artists," she said. "They're charlatans. Don't you see? Art is there to show the beauty of our souls. Great works of art prove how wonderful it is to be alive, to feel things so deeply, and to awaken that which is best within us. You listen to Mozart or Beethoven, or read Tolstoy or Camus, or look at a Botticelli painting or a Monet, or see a ballet choreographed by Balanchine—it is all there!

"It's about as basic as you can get. That's why such manifestation of the human spirit touches us deeply. We see the artist's creation, and we know it is true because it is us. We come face to face with what's best in ourselves—we're free!"

"How in the hell do you know all of that, anyway?" I challenged her.

"Come on, Alex, you know it, too. You just have to face it, that's all."

"I can't imagine you just buy the book and start translating it. I don't think I can do it."

"Why not?"

I did not know the answer because I simply had no answer to her question.

"It's your destiny. Do it for your children."

"So now Milo's got you on his side."

"'Do it for your children!' I love that expression!"

She grinned and patted her belly. Milo's idea of me doing the translation was so preposterous, really. Yet not attempting it was really the ultimate failure. I would be dammed if I did it, and dammed if I did not.

"Today mother is dead," she suddenly said. "Aujourd'hui maman est morte."

"What a great sentence to begin a book," I said. "Imagine starting a book by saying your mother is dead. I wonder how long it must have taken him to come up with it."

"Do you think it really took him that long?"

"It had to."

"I don't think so."

"What makes you say that?"

"I don't know," she said. "I have the feeling Camus started writing his book with that simple sentence. It was the first thing he wrote. Then everything fell into place. I believe that."

"Why?"

"There are many things in life that are simple, dispensing with all of the nonsense and going directly to the essence of who we are. The vault of life is open, and we see the treasure inside. Camus understood that. All great artists understand that."

"Anyway, 'Mother died today' is what I prefer, but there is a problem."

"What problem?" she asked.

"The word 'maman', how do you translate that word?

"Mother?"

We walked in silence for a few moments. There are words in French that cannot be translated into English or vice versa. Maman is one of them. Mom would be a poor choice. Either you kept the word "maman" the way it is in the original or you used "mother." There was no other solution.

"You're right about the word 'maman' in English it does not fit," she said.

"I know. Anyway, I think 'mother' is a more practical solution."

"Why?"

"Because his second sentence would flow better."

"What's his second sentence?"

"Something about yesterday," I said, but was not sure.

"You see, you need the book," she said, with an air of finality.

I knew when I was trapped. We found the book at the second *bouquiniste*.

"*Nous cherchions une copie de L'Étranger,*" she said.

"*Oui, vous cherchez un exemplaire de L'Etranger, d'Albert Camus.*"—Yes, you are looking for a copy of The Stranger by Albert Camus.

The French, when they hear a foreign accent speaking their language, always repeat the complete sentence they hear back to you in proper French. Not that Lisa had made a mistake. That is the way they are. It has to do with the immense pride they have in their language.

"*Oui.*"

"*Je crois que j'en ai un exemplaire ici quelque part.*"—I believe I have a copy here, somewhere.

He started looking in a box and after pulling out several other books, he found a rather pristine paperback copy of *L'Étranger*.

"*Voilà.*"

He wrapped the small volume very carefully with colorful tissue paper. He then tied a red ribbon to it and presented it to Lisa as if he were making a special and personal gift to her. He gave Lisa a big and charming smile. I paid him.

"*C'est un cadeau idéal pour une fille jolie et intelligent.*"—It's an ideal gift for a beautiful and intelligent girl.

"*Merci,*" she said, smiling.

I thought the guy was cool and typically French in what he said to her—the wrapping of the book was a nice touch. Afterward, we felt kind of guilty when she unwrapped the book so we could read it.

"OK, let me read the second sentence," she said. "*Ou peut-être hier, je ne sais pas.*"

"I find that sentence very strange."

"Why?"

"How could he not know when his mother died? He says, 'Or maybe yesterday, I don't know.'"

"Well, the telegram only tells him his mother is dead. It doesn't tell him when she died. So, it's normal he's guessing."

We walked in silence for a while. "You know," she continued, "I think that's how he sets up the premise for his book, his own take on the absurd, and the so-called Existential Philosophy. It is individuals who create meaning in their lives and not some other force, like a god or religion. And you're right."

"About what?"

"About translating that first sentence. 'Mother died today.' I think the flow is better to get you to the second sentence, 'Or perhaps yesterday, I don't know.'"

"*Aujourd'hui maman est morte. Ou peut-être hier, je ne sais pas,*" I repeated trying to determine the rhythm and tone.

"Today mother died. Mother died today or perhaps yesterday. I don't know. Today mother is dead. Or maybe yesterday, I don't know."

Since buying the book, I had been wrestling with finding the right pitch for the translation of the text. It was not easy. I despaired over what I felt were my shortcomings. The fact that the writing is strong and clear made the translation exciting and frightening.

The narrative was firm. Nothing was superfluous or irrelevant. And because of that I very often found myself convinced I would never find that which made the story so compelling and capture it in the translation.

But with my own crazy and romantic notions, fueled by Lisa's even crazier support, I plodded on in the vain hope of doing a halfway decent job.

"Look," Milo said when I complained, "nobody is asking you to become Camus's disciple or his critic. His philosophy is complicated and nihilistic. I'm not sure I agree totally with the notion of how absurd life is the way Camus and Sartre argue.

"I'll leave all of that to crazy Americans like you and Lisa to deal with," he said laughing. "All I want is a correct translation of the book. And if you do that, whatever it is Camus has to say will come through because that's the nature of the beast."

"Easy for you to say."

"*Mon cher, Alexandre,* if for one single moment I had doubts about you, and what you're trying to become in your life, I wouldn't have asked you to do it. I'd have simply found some second-rate idiot to translate the damn thing.

"It would have saved me the aggravation, but the result wouldn't have been what I believe you're capable of producing."

Not surprisingly, Lisa agreed with him.

I did not want to just do a common, vulgar, banal translation of the text. Maybe I was making the thing harder than it was. In any event, the choices of how to translate the words were not that many. Nevertheless, only one was correct—finding it was driving me crazy.

Whenever I complained to Lisa about how hard the work was, she would look at me with a tolerant and lovely smile on her face as if to say, *enough of your complaints, old buddy. We have been through all of this already. You have no other choice but get the job done. So, stop wasting my time.*

And, of course, Milo agreed with her.

SEVEN

Again, I glanced at Lisa sleeping so peacefully. I was wide-awake. There was no question that Lisa's news about her pregnancy was not part of any plans I had ever anticipated or contemplated.

I got up, being careful not to disturb her, and went into the room she had used when she first moved into the apartment.

The room was clean, tidy, and smelled of her. I opened the armoire and her clothes were neatly and properly arranged, and right next to them were my clothes all neatly and properly arranged.

I marveled at the difference between Lisa and me. Everything about her was orderly but not in a fanatical way. I found a dried-up flower, what was left of a rose I had bought for her from a gypsy. The letters from her parents were all neatly tied up in a bundle.

A black and white photo of her and Robin when they were babies was taped to the wall. I also found two stubs from the *Cinémathèque* where we had gone to see a Greek movie, *Electra,* and had spent half the night listening to its director discuss the movie afterward.

The *Cinémathèque* became one of our favorite places to go and see films from all kinds of directors. The French have a great reverence for film as an art form.

All her books, school notes, class assignments, music sheets, pencils, pens, maps of the Paris Métro, and notes reminding her of things she had to do were placed so she could find them without trouble.

She always argued that if one used something today it would be desirable, if not practical, to put it back where one found it in the event one would need to use it again. I could never do that.

Before Lisa moved in and took care to make sure that there would be order in the place, the apartment was what the French call "*un veritable bordel.*" Not dirty, just messy, with stuff all over the place.

It was almost as if within me there was a neuron sensor that was not particularly wired to respond in an organized and logical way.

I looked at her notebook; it was well organized in neat handwriting. Anyone reading it would have understood what the lecture had been about.

The whole apartment was now made to look as if normal people lived there, with flowers, photos, paintings, and posters all strategically placed or hanging from the walls, giving the apartment a lived-in look.

It was no longer a pell-mell arrangement where things were left everywhere and would stay there until I could no longer ignore them and had to straighten them out, mostly out of guilt.

I had resisted making the apartment my own. I do not know why that had seemed such a hard thing to do, though, I would justify this lack of order by the fact that I did travel and was absent a lot.

Lisa had dropped a bombshell with the news of her pregnancy earlier that evening. I was stunned by it—afraid. I had been thinking of calling Alain about an assignment, as it seemed more practical and less confusing than translating *L'Étranger* or writing a book.

Now, with the news that Lisa had given me everything had suddenly changed. A baby! What about twins? The very idea was beyond my conception of reality.

Man, that was all I needed. It was not impossible to believe I would become the father of twins given that Lisa was one. How am I going to deal with a baby, or babies? I had always kept away from the notion of having children, or a family. The whole idea was foreign to me.

However, the truth had to be faced: Lisa was pregnant. Now what? The memory of Athos and the thoughts I had about fatherhood came back to me. It might be fine to make an abstraction of what Lisa and I were now facing, but the reality was something else.

I had gone to Greece with the idea that my life needed some changes. I laughed. Children were not part of what I was looking for that is for damn sure. On the other hand, children and what they bring to their parents do not need to be a threat.

The changes could be wonderful—new dimension. Still, based on what had happened in my own life, I was not too crazy about the idea. I did not need a mirror to see that my life as a kid had not been a great adventure.

What would this child, children, look like? Would he, she, or they, resemble Lisa? I could not see a child inheriting my looks. What would my preference be: boys, girls, or maybe one of each?

The truth, however, was that I would simply not have any kids at all. I did not know what kind of father I could possibly be.

I did not have what it took. Besides, I saw no reason to bring a child into this chaotic world. Too damn many problems already. Lisa never said anything about not having a child. Perhaps, that was the key to understanding what was going to happen.

In telling me she was pregnant, she had suddenly opened up another vast universe filled with still more uncertainties. The idea of my own immortality, of passing something as personal as my genetic code to a child had been sort of a clever thought in the past, simply because it was an abstract idea.

Now that this abstraction had become a reality, it was not so clever anymore; in fact, it was confusing and scary. How had this thing come about, anyway? I wondered who was keeping track of the things we humans do and think.

"What are you doing?" she stood in the doorway, rubbing the sleep from her eyes.

"Trying to figure things out about you, us."

"And what did you figure?"

"It's a big mystery. One thing, though, I'll probably have to get rid of my bike."

I had an old, powerful, Norton English motorcycle still in great mechanical shape that I had bought from Bernard, the guy who owned the apartment. Riding the bike around Paris had always been a great pleasure.

Lisa had been afraid of riding it at first, though she had gotten more used to it.

"Why?"

"You're pregnant. Riding a bike wouldn't be a good idea. Besides, you really never liked it."

"You love that bike."

"I know."

"I want you to keep that bike. It's yours. I can't see you without it."

"Neither can I," I said, glumly, and already resigned to losing the bike.

"Oh, Alex, I'm sorry."

"It isn't your fault. Anyway, in the winter it's too damn cold to ride it."

"OK, but don't get rid of it because of me."

"What choice do I have? It's the bike or the baby."

"Oh, so now we have to make a choice?"

"I *do* like my bike."

"That settles it."

"I knew you'd understand."

"I do. A man must have his bike."

"Absolutely," I said.

We started laughing because we both knew that in a contest between a baby and a bike, the bike would not stand a chance. She walked over and sat on my lap. She embraced me and held me against her.

"Oh, well, we might as well kiss-off Italy, too," I said.

"Why?"

"With you pregnant and then with a baby we can't go anywhere."

"What are you talking about? That doesn't sound like the father of my child. Where is your sense of adventure?" she asked, challenging me.

"Look at my mother! She had two and she managed."

"Yeah, but did she run around on motorcycles?"

"She probably did worse things."

"You're not worried about having a baby?"

"No. You know, my mother did pretty well when you think about it. And she traveled and lived in strange places like Ethiopia. Come on, Italians love bambinos."

I put my arms around her.

"Are you scared?" she asked me after a while.

"If I say yes, it would be a lie, and if I say no, it would also be a lie."

"You don't want us to have the baby?"

"What kind of question is that?"

"Just checking."

"This whole shebang's so strange to me," I said.

"There is nothing strange about having a baby. It happens all the time."

"But you're not scared?"

"No." I knew she was not.

"Life is full of beautiful surprises," she continued, "and none is as beautiful as having a child. This is the first time that I've been pregnant. I want to experience it to its fullest—even morning sickness, swollen feet, the baby kicking, and even constipation."

It was that simple. We walked back to the bedroom and got into bed.

"We'll have to get married," I said.

"Why?"

"Because . . ." I could not explain it, really.

"Don't marry me unless you love me."

"I do love you. I want to marry you."

"Are you sure?"

"I just don't believe in kids outside of marriage."

"You don't believe in children outside of marriage, and that's why you want to marry me?"

She was laughing at my silly ineptitude to come straight to the point.

"You don't think I love you?"

"I never said that."

"I love you. I'm crazy about you, and I want to marry you because you're going to be the mother of my child."

"Children!" she said, in a clear, strong voice.

"Children."

Her face got serious and tears swelled up in her eyes.

"Hey, what's wrong?"

"Do you really mean it when you say you love me?"

"Lisa, if you could rip my heart open—" I started to say and I stopped.

The feeling was not something I knew from my past. Now it was different, powerful, and serene. I could not explain why. The lonely moments of other times now felt odd, and without much significance.

Of course, I still had to fight the old demons, but I felt less threatened by them. I wanted this relationship to be normal. I needed it.

"I'm not jealous of Iris anymore," she said, quietly.

"You were jealous?" Another surprise.

The ancient Greeks thought that men and women were pretty much the same, driven by and possessing the same emotions and desires. If there was a difference, it was in the womb, which is where the word *hysterics* had originated.

"Women have it over us. They bear life." Milo was always saying. "Men are condemned to always wonder about this difference. If only wombs could talk."

"I know that love has no time for jealousy, and I was," Lisa said.

"Why?"

"Because you stole my heart, and I wanted yours to be mine but it wasn't."

I thought she might be playing a game but I saw no signs of that. She held my look and never took her eyes off me. Her truth was so simple, and yet so scary. How do we prepare to hear words with such finality?

"Wait a second."

"Alex, I've loved you since that first night. Before I left your room that morning in Crete, I looked at you and you were sleeping like a baby. That had to be the craziest day in my life, but everything seemed so clear and so right. Yes, you didn't know it, but my heart was yours."

"Why didn't you wake me up or tell me afterward?"

"It wouldn't have been the same."

"What do you mean?"

"I don't know. I can't explain it. I've asked myself that question so often."

"Were you afraid?"

"Kind of."

"Why?"

"Because maybe I had made a fool of myself." She was serious.

"I never said that you had."

"No, but . . . couldn't you tell?"

"How could I?"

"Not even afterward."

"No."

"It wasn't obvious?"

Perhaps she was giving me more credit than I deserved.

"Why did I think you would see and understand without my having to explain it?" she asked, laughing at my obtuseness.

"Well, I didn't see it."

"Are you suggesting I made a mistake about your intelligence?" Now she was teasing me.

"I've never suggested anything."

"All right, give us your explanation."

"Sometimes, I'm not as smart as I should be."

"Then I did make a mistake."

"That's not fair."

"You're right." She hugged me.

"You complain that I'm complicated. Boy, you're more than I could ever be."

"I'm not." She had this wonderful smile on her face. Her eyes twinkled. "I've never understood, really," she continued. "I didn't get hit by a thunderbolt. I woke up and everything had changed, as simple and beautiful as the sunrise on a clear summer morning. Yes, there it was. I knew my heart was yours! But I'm no more capable of explaining that than I am of explaining quantum mechanics."

"Quantum mechanics?"

"I read somewhere that there are only a handful of people who understand the theory of relativity, but nobody understands quantum mechanics."

"Is it that complicated?"

"I'll let you know when I understand it. Meanwhile, all I know is what my heart feels, and you own my heart because you make it very happy." Her look was clear and direct. "I knew she was playing with you." She added after a moment of silence.

She was looking at me, challenging me to contradict her, confronting me with a fact I had never wanted to believe. Boy, this was really my night for surprises.

"How do you know that?" I finally blurted out.

"Women know about these things."

I also knew it. What other explanation was there? It was just that I had kidded myself, and Lisa with a few simple words had unveiled the truth

I never wanted to accept. That part of my life was truly over. I started to laugh.

"Why are you laughing?"

"Because you're nuts."

"You're not upset?"

"Why should I be? The truth is the truth."

There followed a long moment of silence. She looked at me, smiled, and held my face in her hands.

"Alex, I'm already married to you. I have belonged to you even before I met you, and I will always belong to you."

The conviction in her voice was unambiguous and deeply humbled me.

"A man could die to hear you say that."

She started to have tears in her eyes. It was one of those silent cries that come from deep within us and when it is over, we are different people. I was at a loss for words.

Lisa jealous? She could not have been. Yet she said she was, and I believed her. Can anyone ever know what the human heart hides?

"I've never held anything back. I don't know what the future holds, and I won't worry about it. This child was conceived in my heart and in my womb out of love. Nothing will ever change that or take it away from me. Nothing and nobody."

"You're just saying that today. What about your dancing? What about being a Rockette? Isn't that one of your dreams?"

Lisa had said she wanted to dance in those spectacular dance numbers Radio City Music Hall and the Rockettes put together in New York City during Christmas.

"I'm too old for that. Besides, I much prefer what I'm doing now."

"Yes, but you still love dancing and you can't dance looking like the rear end of a double-decker London bus."

She laughed, stood on the bed, and looked toward the mirror examining herself. Not in a vain manner, but in an act of curiosity. Her lovely body, firm, young, elegant, and on its way toward fulfilling the most basic of all the rites of passage that belong to women: Giving birth.

"Do you think I'm going to look like that?"

"Lots of pregnant women do."

"I'll blame it on you."

"You love me enough to suffer through that?"

"That and more! As for my dancing, it's a good trade-off don't you think?" she asked as she got under the bedcovers again. What could I say?

She was smiling. What she had said was both scary and wonderful. Lisa did not beat around the bush. Sometimes her directness was disconcerting because so much of my life seemed to have been a constant struggle to put on masks to hide my sentiments and vulnerabilities. Afraid, always afraid.

"You don't believe me?" she asked a moment later.

"I do but time brings changes, cruel, sad changes. People change. Life gets out of tune, the heart and the spirit suffer," I said, still doubting.

"Are you afraid that one day I won't love you?"

"Yes."

"Dear heart, fear not. I'll carry my love for you to the end of time."

"Oh, you're planning on living that long?"

"Yes! Aren't you?"

"Absolutely."

"OK, we're in agreement."

Perhaps for Lisa—as it should be for all people—love and happiness, free of time limits, were the only things that mattered. She was smiling like some grownup trying to explain things to a child who has not understood what was being said. She kissed me. I wanted her. Lisa, tenderly and lovingly, gave herself to me, and we were one.

"I wonder if we'll have twins," she said, afterward before going back to sleep.

Her words and her confession had humbled me. I thought back to what Chris had asked me in Athens, what about the heart? I was not any clearer about it now than I had been when he first asked. Twins!

I did not know anything about children. Children should be the result of stable lives, not of confusion and uncertainty—certainly not the children Lisa deserved to have.

My life was getting complicated again, though this time the complication had a degree of certainty not there before. Some things were true: Lisa was pregnant, and there was no getting around it. She wanted to keep the baby. Not much of a surprise there.

What is the source of love, anyway? This most mysterious and splendid of feelings that stop us from yearning, invading us, conquering us, controlling what we think, what we see, what we do, who we are, who we become.

Does this feeling transform us and make our souls fuse with the purity of the cosmos? Does it make us whole and bring out what is best in all of us and make us dreamers?

When this feeling of love disappears, it leaves us empty by the side of the road of life with our hearts heavy in sadness like some discarded piece of useless spiritual junk.

Love—is that finally accepting the idea of God?

I am not much of a religious person, and I think the idea of God is a human invention that transcends race and gender. Humankind had enough sense to understand that without a force outside ourselves we would be in serious trouble due to the duality of good and evil in us.

I often wonder what we would do without such a contradiction. We had to conceive a "Creator" to help us in our struggle to survive the darkness of our human existence.

He is the father figure who protects us because the evil of man is ready to take over. We have seen evil and it scared us. We could not control it, so we invented God, and everything—all things--came from God.

Our very existence became the realization of God's wishes and grand designs that were already ours to begin with. Within our own schematic, we metamorphosed into God's children! The mystery of our own existence was no longer to be wondered about and feared.

We are born and we die: The ultimate truths. The madness is what happens in between. There is no mystery about the actual mechanics of living. Therefore, God, then, is man's noblest and greatest invention. A work of genius!

This amazing inspiration rules our lives. There is incredible beauty in the idea. It is the best thing we humans will ever invent! We are, indeed, God's children because we have created God to be our Father so that our transgressions can be forgiven.

The beauty of the world around us, the beauty of the universe, is our Father's creation because it is good, lofty, and bigger than we are; thus, we are God's creatures. Yet more often than not, we act more like creatures of the devil—the ultimate paradox—and it is this contradiction that is at the crux of our existence.

We have to have God to define and help us give order to how we live, to put a damper on our worst instincts. We created God for practical and selfish reasons.

Humans are capable of great expressions of love, tenderness, and sorrow, expressions that can stir the soul in ways unfathomable, lifting our souls to be one with the cosmos.

Nobody can explain what happens or why. Is that God? Yet at the other end stands evil, for the same humans can be so debased, cruel and vicious. How can we claim to be the children of God?

Perhaps the ultimate beauty of God is not that He rules, but that He serves. We made God our insurance policy. Man created this Overseer, his own ultimate Policeman who would love us, strong, able and willing to correct us, to keep us from straying by our natural tendencies and to whom we would address our own sense of mortality because death is so final and so unforgiving that we live in fear of it.

Is it God? There is no alternative. God has so willed. The idea of a God makes sense since we agreed to give this Supreme Being all the power we ourselves have but cannot control.

We are not to question His magnificence nor are we to question His design. Similarly, we also want to make sure He can hear us. We want Him to listen to us when we ask for favors, when we pray for miracles.

Miracles . . . memories came back to me of what had happened in Yugoslavia on my way to Athens. I needed a miracle then in the worst possible way. Marty, a friend from San Francisco who was visiting Europe, and I, teamed up to share the expenses of the trip to Greece.

Cécile did not want to come with me, so it was good to have a friend along, a nice long trip through several countries.

Eventually, we drove into Yugoslavia and on down the Dalmatian coast along the Adriatic Sea. The map we were using showed that upon reaching the border of Yugoslavia and Albania there was a road that avoided and skirted the border, and went up about twenty-five miles into the mountains.

Albania did not allow any foreign visitors. The road was supposed to take us to a small town on the other side of the mountain from which we could eventually join the main highway that led to the Greek border.

It was early morning, and we were looking forward to getting into a hotel with running hot water. Suddenly, the road became unpaved, then a dirt road that turned into a trail and just sort of disappeared into the mountains. It was nearly impassable, filled with potholes and big rocks. Somehow, we gathered up our courage and continued.

Finally, we got to the top of a mountain dominating the region and there in the middle of nowhere, this shack, a café! No traffic, no people, just this sad-looking café. We stopped and had some strong Turkish coffee. We were the only customers. The man who served us was correct but not friendly.

As we came out of the café, there was a kid about ten-years old standing by the car. He tried to sell us some oranges. We told him no. He asked us if we were Germans.

It may have been one of the few English words he knew. We told him we were Americans. His face lit up in a big wonderful smile that soon gave way to an incredibly sad face.

Marty and I thought he was unhappy because we had not bought any oranges. Then the kid just handed us the oranges, and kept saying: "Kennedy, Kennedy, Kennedy," several times to himself; turned around, walked down the mountainside, and disappeared. Marty and I were left standing there, speechless.

This incident reminded me of something similar that had happened while I was visiting Japan. I was waiting at a huge train station in Tokyo late one evening. The place was deserted except for two teenagers, a boy and a girl, also waiting for their train.

They kept looking at me and having a discussion, which, by the way they looked in my direction, appeared to have something to do with me. They finally walked over and bowed.

"American?" he asked.

"Yes."

He mimicked putting a cigarette to his mouth.

"I'm sorry, no cigarettes," I said.

He smiled and said something to the girl. She reached into her purse and took out a very small package. It was wrapped in colorful fabric. Slowly and delicately, she started to unwrap it.

It was as if she was performing an ancient ritual. Layer upon layer of tissue she unwrapped, and then I saw it. Sitting on the bottom of the fabric was a Kennedy half-dollar!

She brought it up closer so we could all see it. They both had this lovely, shy smile on their faces. I put my arms around them and hugged them. It made me think of Ben selling those half-dollars in Budapest. It is humbling to reflect on the impact America has on the rest of the world.

We stood looking at the coin until my train arrived. I did not want to move. I did not want this magical moment to end. At the last moment, I embraced them, then, hurried and jumped onto the last wagon.

I saw the two of them smiling happily holding the coin higher and higher as the train sped away. It was as if they were offering a gift to some higher entity. Yes, the human heart is something else.

Now here I was standing with Marty on a desolate mountaintop in the middle of Yugoslavia, moved, once again, by what the human heart is capable of feeling. When we came to our senses, the kid had disappeared so we could not even pay him for the oranges.

We had a hard time eating them later. They seemed to be a very special gift. It took us nearly eight hours to negotiate the twenty-five or so miles into the next town. By the time we got down into the valley, it was dark and raining.

Then we saw another kid trying to thumb a ride. We picked him up, rode into the town, and he showed us where the hotel was. Upon trying to register into the hotel, Marty and I discovered that our traveler's checks were missing.

To this day, I do not know if we lost them somewhere else or if the kid we picked up, who had sat in the back where our bags were, had stolen them. We preferred to think we had lost them.

The hotel clerk, who spoke a little English and French, was very understanding when we explained our predicament. He said the only American Express office was in Belgrade about three hundred miles away. There was a train leaving that night, and it would reach Belgrade sometime the following day.

We decided that Marty would go to Belgrade to get his checks replaced while I waited for him at the hotel. The clerk then lent us money for Marty to take the train. I put up my passport as security.

On the following day, Mohammed, the hotel clerk, came to see me early in the afternoon accompanied by two big beefy guys wearing suits and ties. Talk about not passing the smell test, these two guys flunked it on the spot.

I was driving a VW bug I had bought from Gary in Paris when he went back to the States, and it was in excellent mechanical shape. They wanted to trade their VW for mine, offering also some additional cash, just about what I had paid for the car.

Since the cars were the same color and pretty much the same look, though mine was newer, their idea was to exchange cars and license plates. I would drive their car out of the country with cash in my pocket. They would get a newer car. All of us would gain something from the deal.

If they had bought the same car as mine from a local dealer it would have cost them a fortune with the taxes. It was cheaper for them to make this kind of swap. Everyone would profit from the deal, so they said. There were several problems with this deal, however.

What if these guys were police? What if their car was a piece of junk? What if they were trying to set me up so they could steal my car? I was bothered by the situation because Mohammed had been very kind to lend us the money for Marty to take the train and allow me to stay at the hotel.

After telling them I was honored by their request, I explained that my VW bug was not in good mechanical shape and I did not want them to end up with a lemon. I do not think they believed me. In any event, they did not insist.

Then later that evening, Mohammed called me from downstairs and asked if I could do a favor for him. He said that his wife was about seven months pregnant, and she was having terrible problems. He needed to take her to the hospital, and he did not have any transportation.

His request coming after the visit from him and the other guys made me think they had decided to take the car at any cost. I was torn by doubt and suspicion but Mohammed had helped us. I told him I would help him. It was a pretty risky decision. But I felt I had no other choice.

I went downstairs, and we left to get his wife. We drove out of town over unpaved roads. Pitch black. Eventually, we came to a settlement in the middle of nowhere. He asked me to stop and wait so he could go get her. I thought, well, this is it!

There was a tiny light hanging from a wire in the middle of what appeared to be a street intersection. I left the engine running, just in case, and kept a wary eye in the general direction where Mohammed had disappeared. Then I saw a bulky shape coming out of a building.

I could distinguish a figure carrying someone else and struggling. I got out of the car. It was Mohammed, indeed, carrying his young wife. She was moaning softly in obvious pain.

I helped him carry her, put her in the car, and off we went to the hospital driving back over the same road. Pitch black.

The hospital was a small building. Maybe it had two or three floors. I cannot be sure. The maternity ward was on the top floor and there was no elevator. Mohammed and I carried his wife upstairs.

The place was grimy, depressing, with some people sitting around in need of medical help. The midwife, a rather large woman, took Mohammed's wife from us and carried her to an examining room.

I could not help feeling that when she took Mohammed's wife from us, she appeared to be carrying a small child in her arms. The midwife called the doctor who, after a few minutes, came out of the room and essentially said the baby would most likely be born prematurely.

They took Mohammed and me to wait in another room. My presence seemed to have surprised people in the place because they whispered and pointed at me with shy smiles on their friendly faces.

Much later in the evening, the doctor came to tell Mohammed he was now the father of a premature baby girl. Mohammed went to see his wife. He came back and told me his wife was afraid to see the baby.

"I'm happy and I'm sad." He said a wan smile on his face.

"Do you have an incubator?" I asked the doctor, in English.

He looked at me not understanding the word. When I described what an incubator was to Mohammed who translated to those around us, they all looked at me like I was crazy, especially when I tried to describe how I thought it was supposed to work.

The doctor knew, of course, but the others had no idea. There was no incubator in the area. The closest hospital that would have one was in Belgrade hundreds of miles away! After some conversation between the doctor and Mohammed, we left the hospital.

Mohammed was so grateful for my help he invited me to go and meet the rest of his family, and also insisted I stay the night at his house. When I protested, he said it would save me from having to pay the hotel for another night.

His family was modest, and they did everything to make my visit comfortable and pleasant. I spent half the night talking to his father in my poor Italian.

His father had lived in Italy, as a laborer, and we talked mostly about politics, the world, and how in the U.S. babies can have incubators any time they needed them.

He and his family were convinced that if this incident had taken place in the U.S., there would have been an incubator to protect the baby and everything would have been fine.

I did not have the heart to tell them that there were also problems with babies in America. It was another stark reminder of how America can come back to haunt you.

The choices confronting Mohammed were brutal and stark: Let the baby stay there in the hopes she would make it. Or try to get her to a hospital with an incubator, or better medical facilities, three hundred miles away.

The only mode of transport available to him was the bus or the train, the very same train my friend Marty had taken the night before to go to Belgrade to replace his lost checks.

But even that was not such a practical idea because the train left every night at nine o'clock—if it were on time. Mohammed would have to wait twenty-four hours to take it, plus another twelve hours for the actual train ride.

The entire family was having this discussion and Mohammed translated for me. His father would say something to the other men, Mohammed would quietly agree with his father, and the conversation continued. The women remained silent for the most part.

Mohammed told me his young wife had been happy about her first baby. What struck me very deeply was the incredible sense of peacefulness and dignity they exhibited.

There were no hysterics, no laments. They were just dealing with the facts of a cruel and hard life over which they had no control. That had always been their existence.

I remember sitting on the floor without my shoes, as they were Muslims, listening to the sounds of their language. Yet through those sounds, the voices, their faces, I recognized and felt their anguish. At that instant, we were all connected to the same source.

There were no secrets. I wanted to believe we were all the same, but I knew I was not like them. I came from a different part of the world where premature babies were treated almost routinely.

Yet Mohammed and his family were behaving in this desperate situation with dignity, patience, and love. Their attitudes of resignation and humility were disconcerting and yet touching to me.

This was the barest and the closest to a pure form of existence, where everything has been stripped away and one is left with what is essential. I remember thinking they were far superior to me in so many ways.

There was nothing intellectual or analytical. There was one basic truth and nothing else. How I wished that I could have used magic to create a miracle for them. I hoped that whichever god was on duty that night would not let the baby die.

It was so unfair and ugly, and I wanted to believe that no god was ugly or unfair. I felt like this was my very own family that they belonged to me and I belonged to them.

If the baby died, we were all going to die a little bit with her. Just like other times when I had seen death around me, like that of the young boy in Africa or during my military tour in Vietnam, I thought of the absurdity of our human condition. How do we deal with such absurdity?

It does not take much to become a total cynic when one is confronted with innocent babies dying. This whole business of believing life is hunky dory appears to be nothing but a scam. Who are we kidding?

Later, Mohammed took me to his room and prepared his bed so I could stay for the night. I continued to protest without success. All night I tossed and turned.

The thought that this baby would not make it was terrifying. I wanted to believe she would live and grow up to be a healthy and lovely member of her family. I thought that by believing it, it would be so. What an idiot!

Morning found me bleary-eyed and weary. It had been a rough night. Mohammed and his family had decided that if the baby were still alive that evening, he would take her to Belgrade on the night train.

"I will take you. I have no money, but if you pay for the gas, I'll drive you and the baby to Belgrade now," I said.

He was taken aback by my suggestion and told the others what I had said. They looked at me and I could see they all were completely lost. His father said something to him.

"He said we cannot ask you to do that," Mohammed said.

"You're not asking me. I'm asking you to let me help."

"Please, it is not your responsibility."

"Yes, it is."

"I cannot put you in that position."

"I'm in that position. We can't sit here and wait until tonight for you to take the train. We must go now. We must take a chance. We owe it to the baby."

He translated what I said, and the women started to have tears in their eyes. His father was trying to hide his tears, while his wife held his hand. My heart was beating so fast, and it did occur to me I was attempting something that was completely beyond what I knew and understood.

Yet that sentiment was also liberating, as if for the first time in my life I was doing something that was honest, pure, and as true as I would ever face. Once the decision had been made, I felt much better.

The whole family was crying when I said goodbye. They embraced me and held me very close to them. We went back to the hospital. The baby was still hanging on. Mohammed told his wife what we were going to do. I did not see her. She was still refusing to see the baby.

After an interminable wait, proper documents were prepared. They handed us the tiny baby wrapped in a heavy woolen blanket and they gave us a bottle of sugar water, I believe—the nipple seemed bigger than the baby's mouth.

As we were walking out, I heard this horrible wailing, a cry with so much pain, piercing, and I knew that it came from Mohammed's wife. It was gripping, desperate, wrenching—a cry so intense one can never forget it.

The haunting sound made me think of the loud wailing of elephants in the jungle, mourning the lost members of the herd.

Mohammed was pale and shaking. I put my arm around his shoulder, but I knew that was not enough. He smiled sadly. So off we went with Mohammed and the baby in the back seat and me driving like a maniac.

In Europe, my experience has been that driving that many miles on two-lane roads, poorly kept, and teeming with heavy traffic, is precarious at best and downright dangerous at worst especially at the speed I was driving. In normal times, it takes forever to get to your destination. We made it to Belgrade in just over eight hours. We hardly spoke during the trip.

I remember thinking as I was driving that it was total insanity to be doing this. What if the baby died on us? What would Mohammed and I do? I was cutting in and out of traffic like there was no tomorrow.

And for the three of us there was no tomorrow—no exit. Our reality was simple: We had to get the baby to Belgrade. Everything else was irrelevant.

After getting lost a couple of times in the city, we found the hospital. Mohammed explained to the people there what we had done, and they could hardly believe it. They took the baby with them, and Mohammed and I walked out of the place.

We sat on the steps and he started to cry. All the emotions of the last twenty-four hours just burst out in a flood of tears of hope and elation. I kept saying that the baby was going to be OK to try to comfort him.

"My wife is very afraid. We are Muslims, and she says people here will not take care of our baby because we are not like them."

I did not know what to say.

"I'm not so afraid," he said, but I knew he was.

Nevertheless, leaving the baby behind was an agonizing decision. He wanted to stay with his baby, and he also wanted to go back to his wife. He could not stay; he could not go.

Mohammed's spirits were down, and his state of mind was quite desperate because he knew he was abandoning his baby to her unknown fate.

Yet not being the mother and with the baby now under medical care, the only viable choice for him was to go back and hope for the best. Either way, it was a shitty decision for anyone to make.

How fucked up can life get?

We found a hotel for the night, and the next day we went to the American Express office to see if Marty had been there, but the office was closed because it was a holiday.

Mohammed called the hospital. The baby was still hanging on. I asked him if he wanted to go by the hospital before we headed back, but he said no.

As we drove, he kept asking me if I thought the baby would make it, and I kept saying that after what she had been through, she would survive anything! I hoped for the miracle that would make his baby's life whole and long.

I wanted so damn much, so desperately, for this miracle to take place, but deep down in my guts I also knew that neither Mohammed nor I really believed in miracles.

We got back to the hotel in the evening. When Marty saw me walk into the dining room, he almost fainted. Apparently, when he had gotten back that morning nobody could explain to him what had happened, and the only thing he could vaguely understand was something about a hospital and me.

Naturally, he thought I was ill and had been taken to the hospital back in Belgrade. I brought him up to date on what had taken place; he was very moved by my strange odyssey.

Meanwhile, he had made plans to hook up with a friend in Istanbul. We divided the money he brought back, and I would wire him the loan he gave me the moment I arrived in Athens.

Later that night, I took him to the train station and he left. He told me I had nothing to fear, that when I died, I would go to paradise for what I had done. I did not give a damn about that. I just wanted a miracle for Mohammed's baby.

The next morning, many people from the hotel staff came to wish me a safe trip. Marty paid for the hotel. Mohammed didn't want us to pay, but we insisted

The last image I remember seeing, through my rearview mirror, was Mohammed waving goodbye with a tiny American flag in his hands, tears were running down his cheeks. I thought, son of a bitch, what does it all mean?

I glanced at Lisa sleeping right next to me, and many thoughts about our earlier conversation came to me as I marveled at how peacefully she slept.
Did she dream of babies? She had talked earlier about being jealous of Iris.

I shook my head at the idea. It had been her secret and I would have liked it to remain so, but Lisa was Lisa. That is how she was, and also what made her special. Had she come to Paris to reclaim what she thought should have been hers?

She had said something about making plans for the future. Lisa was not devious; nevertheless, here she was pregnant with my seed and sleeping right next to me seemingly without a care in the world.

There was a thread that tied us together—me, Lisa, Iris, Mohammed, his wife, Chris, Pete, Cleo, John, Ben, Marty—everybody. Were our humanity and our seeking what made us the same?

Was this yet another proof we all come from the same source? If there is a mystery, all we have to do is open our souls and hearts and accept the purity of what is there.

Then there would not be a mystery but the real thing, liberating us and making us rise above all the pettiness of the world, making us the same, worthy of each other, worthy of love.

I loved Lisa. I had also loved other women; however, I was not going to spend my life with them or have a child with them. My reality had changed so much.

Lisa had provided me these past few months with a greater sense of what was still possible. I had resigned myself to the fact that so much around me was meaningless. Yes, there are things we cannot do without— oxygen, the sun . . . love . . . can we do without it?

What about the heart? What about the soul? Why was there so much confusion and darkness about them? Lisa's devotion and loyalty were as mysterious to me as the other side of the moon. She had never asked me for anything.

She had never imposed conditions. One had to wonder how that was possible. Was I making her out to be more than she was? No, I knew I was not. What insights do some people have that liberate them allowing them to soar through the thermals of life like a bird, untroubled, free?

Was my life about to get complicated so much so that it would end just like before with no rudder to guide it? I needed Lisa far more than she needed me. She was that tiny light that would help me see the other side, the brighter side.

Finally, I fell into a troubled sleep. I had a dream in which I saw a face that appeared to be Mohammed's wife. I could not really tell if it was her face, though I could hear a cry.

Then the face was unknown. Then it became more familiar—or at least I thought it was. It appeared to be Lisa's face, then Iris's, but now it blurred into the face of my mother.

Next, I found myself in an open field. Something was chasing me, and I was running like crazy while behind me wild dogs nipped at my heels. I was terrified. Someone was calling me, and I wanted to get away.

As much as I tried, whatever was chasing me was gaining. It felt like my legs were full of lead. I could not run faster. I fell and hurt myself and was in pain.

Someone called my name again, and I woke up. Lisa was leaning over and shaking me. She looked terrified and she was trembling. She hugged me and held me against her. I was sweating.

"I've been trying to wake you up."

"It was this terrible dream." My whole body ached. I felt like someone had just beaten me up. My mouth was dry.

"I was so scared," she said. I could see the trepidation on her face.

"I'm sorry."

"Are you going to be OK? Do you want to talk about it?"

"Maybe later. Go back to sleep now. I'll be fine."

"Are you sure?"

"Yes, I'll be OK."

She was not sure but she kissed me, and a few minutes later she went back to sleep. I could hear her soft breathing shortly thereafter.

Eventually, I received a letter from Mohammed. He had sent it to the American Express office in Athens, which had forwarded it to me in Paris. There had been no miracle. The baby had died a few days after we took her to the hospital. OK, I thought, who went to pick up the baby?

Or was the tiny body shipped to them inside a cardboard box, or a tiny coffin, special delivery? In the Muslim religion, a dead person has to be buried immediately after death.

Did his wife see the baby at all? The experience was just too painful for me to dwell on, so I tried hard to put it out of my head. It sure as hell was not easy.

And Mohammed's wife, I did not even know her name. I tried to imagine her waiting for some news, hoping against hope, then the terrible news that surely left her wondering and desperately searching in her heart for a reason as to why life had dealt her such terrible pain and tragedy.

Their lives would be truncated, always missing something. The scar in their hearts would never heal. There was something brutal, and inhuman about parents burying their children. It was not supposed to be this way. It was ugly.

Yeah, life sucks!

The gods have more power and man has none. Who was to be blamed? If there was a god, which god, whose god; or was it the small town for not having an incubator; or Mohammed and his wife for wanting to have a baby; or my driving the way I did; or Marty and I for having lost the traveler's checks?

How far back do we go to lay the blame or take responsibility? In such situations, it is phony to think that life has good intentions for us or that it is benign. It is better to accept the simple truth that we humans do not count for much. I do not know how one can have faith in anything after such an event.

I did not know how Mohammed and his wife felt their pain. I had tried to imagine and I could not. I thought of Demetrios and Helen. How come they had a child and life brought them so much happiness because of it, but Mohammed's baby was dead.

How simple life is when one looks at it in terms of birth and death. Both events are final, imposing a new order of things. There is no ambiguity. We cannot undo them.

The newly born and the newly dead share an inexplicable bond. How to explain that? How I wished I could have truthfully told Mohammed and his wife that I understood their pain.

Nobody understands such pain. I suppose one could always express inane platitudes, but I did not want to be a phony.

Now my present life was taking me in the same direction as his when he found out that he was going to be a father. Of course, Lisa and I were living in a country where incubators were the norm.

We could believe we were safe. What about Mohammed's wife? It was her baby. So much emptiness in her broken heart. Would she ever get over it?

The haunting sound of her cry was impossible to forget, terrifying. When people have babies, it is all the first of everything. The first cry, the first burp, the first poop, the first smile.

When a baby dies, we count what? The first minute of death? The first day of death? The first night of death? The first insane pain of the heart? The first instance of emptiness—the first of what?

In an ideal world, Lisa and Mohammed's wife would have become the best of friends. I tried so hard to remember his wife's face and the faces of the rest of his family—and I could not. It felt as if I were betraying them because I was unable to remember.

Slowly, I let my mind drift away to places, to people. Lisa was wonderfully happy with the news of her pregnancy. Maybe for a woman that was her ultimate secret. Men cannot claim such a secret.

I was on my way to becoming a father with all that it entailed and I was not sure if I was up to the task. My role models were not so hot.

My parents made so many mistakes and missed so many opportunities to make things right for them and for me. People are always saying history repeats itself, and the monk in Athos had said that we all end up emulating our parents. He was very convinced of that.

I did not want to make the mistakes my parents had made. I did not want that for my child. Should I go and visit José's friends, the gypsies, and ask them about the baby's future, my future?

Maybe take the baby back to Ethiopia and Lisa's tribe, and have them give their blessings just as they had done with her and Robin so our baby would always be protected.

My friend Leon came to my mind. I had not seen him for a while, and I wondered if he had made peace with his father over the Monet he had taken from the house.

I pictured a young Leon who, throughout the war years, had but one yearning and that was to find out what had happened to his boyhood friend.

The two of them had been in boarding school in Switzerland and had dreamed of all the wonderful adventures that life had in store for them. They had a right to have such dreams.

Then Hitler came, and fucked everything up!

The father of Leon's friend had sent his son to France thinking he would be safe there, only for the son to be thrown in prison by the French at the beginning of the war because he was German.

When the German Army invaded Paris and found him behind bars, they were ready to shoot him as a deserter.

He was made to work for the German Army at the Russian front, only to be captured by the Russians who would have shot him had it not been for the fact they needed all able males to help with the war effort, saving him from certain death. He worked as a laborer for the Russian Army until the end of the war.

He managed to escape and walked back to France where there was a warrant for his arrest, *"pour son evasion d'une prison Française!"* Eventually, the Red Cross had straightened it out. He had not escaped from a French prison, but had been taken out and forced to work for the German Army.

He was later able to get in touch with his family, through the Red Cross, and went back to Germany only to have his legs blown off by an American land mine.

Yes, life sucks and then you die.

I wondered if Iris was growing a baby in her womb. Do we grow wiser as we grow older, or are we just too damn tired to care any longer? What are the things that matter? Why is it that we spend a great deal of time searching for some meaning, for the idea of being?

Do we ever have any choice in that search? Is it encoded in our brains—reptile brains according to some people—that we must seek at all costs? And upon finding it, if ever, will everything fall into place?

Does anybody ever figure out what makes him or her so special? Is it accomplishments? What makes a life worth something? Is it to love someone with what the heart is capable of feeling? Is it inventing a cure for cancer?

How are we to measure one's passage through this time dimension? Does it matter? Does it really matter? Who is ahead in this fucking game of life, anyway?

Who's got it made?

I got up again and went into the living room. Lisa had rearranged it and now it made more sense. I was also trying to become more responsible living with her and did not, as a matter of routine, leave my clothes hanging on doorknobs as had been my habit. Was I getting domesticated? I laughed. It was not so bad, after all.

Lisa had put Pete's painting right above the fireplace between the other two paintings I had bought from him. It was a lovely painting. She had also hung the small painting of Shakespeare & Company she had bought for me. We had talked about going back to that store.

I had been touched by Pete's patience with all her questions. He had been quite taken by her. This brooding man whose life seemed so complex and yet who somehow found a way to deal with his creative madness.

I envied him. Pete seemed to have a mission in life, and he was not afraid to accomplish it. He would spend long hours in front of his canvas and something interesting always seemed to come out of that.

It was true he brooded, but even in his darkest moods, Pete seemed to move beyond that. He had never given away any of his paintings unless one counts the ones he gave to Mr. La Coupole, but that was paying off a debt. When he gave Lisa the painting she had been deeply touched, and so had been the rest of us.

The weekend after Lisa moved in, I took her to meet Roxanne, Pete and the others, which culminated in Pete giving her the painting.

"Who are these people I'm going to meet?"

"You'll see."

"Are they nice people?"

"Yes. Are you worried?"

"No, just curious."

"They're good people, and they're my friends."

Pete and Roxanne's apartment was near Place des Vosges, one of those charming and unique urban settings for which Paris is so famous. Lisa had just moved into my place.

The arrangement was awkward, as I was still trying to deal with my feelings about having her living there.

Though we had been intimate in Crete, and the circumstances of the encounter had been strange, now it belonged to another time, another life.

It seemed both of us were intent on not advancing toward each other. I do not know if it was fear or shyness—more fear on my part. Lisa also seemed to want to respect my privacy.

"Who is she?" Pete asked.

"Just a friend," I answered. I did not want to go into explanations about Lisa renting a room from me. I would never hear the end of it; anyway, they would find out soon enough.

"A friend, right?" John, of course, did not believe me.

"His taste in women has improved remarkably," said Pete.

"Maybe there is hope for him, after all, though I don't see what she sees in him," said, John the cynic.

Peter and Roxanne lived in an elegant loft that made you jealous because if you had a choice that would be the place you would want to live. It was large, airy, and open, with plenty of sunlight filtering through the skylights.

Roxanne and Lisa hit it off as I knew they would. I had not mentioned to Lisa that Roxanne was a wonderful dancer. Pete had, a few months earlier, invited the whole group to a dance recital Roxanne had put together set to the music of Erik Satie.

Roxanne had done the recital with lights, shadows, and costumes. One could have sworn she was dancing in the nude in this ephemeral, magical setting, with plenty of artistic imagination and sensibility.

She was like a beautiful, delicate butterfly that had just freed herself from her cocoon and had extended her multicolored wings quivering softly in midair as the rays of the sun caught her flying away.

As the light shone through her wings, creating an incredible harmony of pure vivid colors, we were transported into a mythical land of feelings, overpowering beauty, joy, and freedom.

Enchanting was the English word that came to mind, though, I much prefer to use the French word to describe it: *Féerique!*

Roxanne had been touched that Lisa had brought her a lovely bouquet of roses the first day they met. That seemed to please Pete, too. I saw the three of them talking excitedly. I loved Roxanne. She was just a wonderful human being, and a creative and talented dancer.

After living alone for the last few months, having Lisa share the apartment had not been without apprehension. Lisa, on the other hand, took it all in stride and seemed quite comfortable with her new life. I marveled at how easy it was for her to make the transition.

She was excited, looking forward to going to the Sorbonne, and becoming part of Parisian life. Lisa did not seem to be losing sleep over what had taken place between us back in Greece. If it had bothered her, it was not bothering her anymore. We had a wonderful time that evening at Roxanne and Pete's place.

A man's needs in life are really simple: a few close friends, a good woman to love and support him, great food and fine wine, interesting conversations, curiosity about the world, and a willingness and a desire to be true to himself and let the rest take care of itself. I often wonder why living has to be so damn complicated and corrupt in the first place.

After a long and wonderful dinner, capped off by Pete giving Lisa one of his paintings, life could not be any better. Lisa had been stunned when Pete gave her the painting. Roxanne then invited Lisa to see Pete's work in the studio without the normal protests from Pete.

"When I love, I give! He had said.

There are moments in our lives when we can capture events and situations that touch us deeply, that freeze in time, allowing them to remain embedded in our psyches forever. They give us pause and also a glimpse of the good, of the possible.

It was such when Peter announced he was giving his painting to Lisa. To say that the rest of us were shocked does not convey the truth. The gift was overwhelming, honest, and pure. Lisa had stood in front of us nailed to the floor, unable to speak.

Peter, the old fox, stood in one corner of the room beaming, a beatific look on his face. How I envied the bastard for allowing himself such pleasure, such spiritual freedom. He was lucky.

When we got home late that evening, Lisa sat in the living room clutching the painting to her as if afraid it might fly away. Her face was flushed with excitement and happiness.

"Aren't you going to bed?"

"No."

"Do you plan on sitting there all night holding that painting?"

"I might," she said, laughing like a giddy schoolgirl.

The painting was of a girl, about ten-years-old standing by a window. We only see her profile so we do not really know what she looks like. Her long hair is shining from the sunlight streaming into her bedroom.

In the foreground we see some furniture, but by the way she is looking through the window to the outside immediately draws our attention away from her and toward the outdoors.

In the distance, we can see a small river, and the girl seems to be listening to the river flow because her head is cocked to one side as if she is, indeed, trying to hear its sound. The effect is that we immediately strain to listen for the river also. The painting was lyrical, magical, and musical. It was the music of the river. Pete had titled it: Mozart!

"That's me," Lisa said, quietly, almost in a whisper.

"Really?"

"When I was a little girl, we lived in upstate New York and there was a creek that ran behind the house. I remember the sound of the water, and I also remember that from my window I would strain to hear the water running downstream."

"Did you tell this to Pete?"

"I started to. He stopped me, walked over, took the painting down, and handed it to me. He said, 'It was just waiting for you!' I was so overwhelmed."

"It was a lovely gesture, and it's a beautiful painting."

"I know. The whole thing just took my breath away—" she stopped. "Close your eyes and imagine that you hear the sound of the water," she said, a moment later.

I closed my eyes and for a moment I was not sure I heard anything, but as I got into it there was no doubt the sound of the river was running through my head. It was uncanny. "You're right."

At first, I did not think that the little girl resembled Lisa, though the closer I looked the more it seemed that she did.

"I've never heard of Peter giving away one of his paintings to a total stranger."

"There's always the first time."

She was not boastful with an oversized ego. It was the statement of someone who lived in a world of harmony and truth where what was best in us showed, and others reacted accordingly.

"True. I wonder what prompted him to do it."

"It's all in the cosmos."

"Do you believe in that?"

"I wouldn't be here if I didn't," she said, with finality.

Somehow, through whatever secrets the universe had, Lisa and Peter had connected. No one but absolutely no one could have foreseen it.

In a sudden twist life takes us through, Peter had bestowed upon her a single gift from his soul, one that transcended everything and everybody.

It had come about as purely and as innocently as the gift of life itself before we corrupt it in our fantasies by thinking that we can do better. I envied Peter for making such a personal gift to a total stranger. And I envied Lisa more because she received it with grace and nobility.

The incident had touched their hearts and souls in a way the rest of us could only guess at—no, envy. I was happy for both of them. I often wonder if that was not the beginning of my falling in love with her. I do not know.

She did not hang the painting until after we had become intimate again. One day I came home, and the painting was hanging above the fireplace between the other two paintings by Peter.

"It now belongs to us," she had simply said.

As I now stood contemplating the painting, its beauty and simplicity reflected in the mirror of my own existence how much my life had been enriched by Lisa's presence. It also seemed fitting that, like the painting hanging between the other two also by Pete, Lisa had now come to occupy a central part in my life.

In the past, I had argued against the notion that one single person could become one's own destiny. It had never seemed possible given the complexity of the human psyche. Seeing the consequence of Lisa's impact on my life left me no choice but to accept that the reality of what I was now experiencing could no longer be doubted.

Lisa had become my destiny. The circle had closed; the gods had spoken. Earlier on this cold day of December 1967, Lisa had told me she was pregnant. She was now sound asleep in the next room, and this was Paris.

I walked to the window and saw the Eiffel Tower in the distance, most of it hidden by the night fog. The New Year would bring our baby into this mad world. I wondered what other surprises life had in store for us.

EIGHT

Then Paris finally awoke from its long winter slumber, and the beginning of spring smiled upon the city. Overnight the trees and their naked branches appearing to pray to the heavens for some relief, from the harsh cold weather, had now metamorphosed into a dense, bright mantle of green.

One day, as if by a miracle or like a magician working his wizardry, spring suddenly burst out into shapes, colors, sounds, laughter, smells. Paris's face in the spring would now be shiny and happy—unlike the world around us that was getting darker, sinister, and more frightening.

Lisa and I had pulled down the shades of our spiritual windows to try to keep the depressing events that were taking place from overwhelming us.

It was a desperate attempt to remain sane. We both knew we were not being responsible citizens, but we chose to concentrate on what was positive and immediate in our lives.

Toward the end of March, I came home one day and found Lisa and Ulla talking to a young guy who seemed vaguely familiar until I remembered he was one of their classmates who had come to Lisa's birthday party.

He came from Prague, Czechoslovakia. He was very formal and appeared under a great deal of strain. When I came in, he found an excuse to leave and left with Ulla.

There had been lots of incidents at the schools in France lately. The newspapers were reporting the unhappiness of the students, though in France unhappy students is routine during the regular school year.

"What was that all about?" I asked Lisa.

"You mean with Adam?"

"Yes, I hope I wasn't the cause of their leaving so abruptly."

"You weren't. They had to go someplace. They were late."

She came and put her arms around me, and gave me a wonderful hug and held me against her.

"What's going on?"

"Can't I kiss and hug you just because I want to?"

"You don't need permission for that."

"Adam's one of the smartest guys in the class, and he's also involved in student protests. Under pressure from the French, the Czechoslovakian government canceled his scholarship.

"He doesn't want to go back, but the French tell him that without his scholarship there's no reason for him to stay—on top of which he has no money. He doesn't know what he's going to do."

"Did he hit you up for some dough?"

"No, and he wouldn't take it even if I offered it to him."

"What did you promise him?"

"You know me too well," she laughed. She looked at me with those innocent yet not so innocent eyes of hers.

"You offered him the room?" The words were out of my mouth without thinking.

"It's only for a few days."

I held her close to me.

"He needs friends," she continued softly, "he's the one who knows how to organize things. I don't know where he finds the time to do the things he does. The powers that be don't like him because they think he's a rabble-rouser, which of course he is, but he's doing it for a good cause. Ulla and I want to help him."

"A Human Rights Committee for the Protection of Adam."

"I knew you wouldn't mind."

"Adam, that's not a Czechoslovakian name, is it? How did he get a name like that?"

"His mother went to England as an *au pair* when she was a young woman, and the little boy she took care of was named Adam. Apparently, he was a sick little boy and died after she went back home. In his memory, she named her own baby, Adam. I thought it was very sweet."

Adam adored Lisa and Ulla. He was the revolutionary one reads about in history books. For him the cause of the French students was a sacred cause. He argued passionately that the educational system was out of touch with reality.

He wanted to change it and was impatient with the slow process. So it was that Lisa and Ulla became involved in student politics at the Sorbonne.

Yet student unrest at the Sorbonne was not that much in the news, this was taking place at another university, Nanterre, located outside of Paris. The students there had occupied the administration buildings, insisting the system was archaic and no longer responding to their needs.

The newspapers labeled the students "anarchists," which, in the French tradition and depending on who was doing the labeling, could be good or bad.

Lisa did not seem particularly concerned when I asked her if the unrest would spread to the Sorbonne. The political protests of the French students were not my personal concern, but because Lisa was part of that student body the risk that it would somehow touch her was not very far from my mind.

In addition to the fact that Adam was one of the students directly involved with this issue and he was Lisa's friend. I was uneasy, but she kept telling me there was no reason to worry.

"French students are a bunch of romantics and a bit impractical, really," Lisa said.

As a student, she had to be in solidarity with her classmates in their demands and in the need for changes, she saw as necessary for the benefit of everyone.

"I just want you to be careful, that's all. Is that too much to ask?"

"I'll be careful."

"You promise?"

"Yes, I promise," after which she walked out of the door to go and join another student demonstration!

It was amusing to some and intriguing to others that Lisa—a product of a different culture with no backbone, as the French were fond of saying about American society—was now supporting leftist student demonstrations, with no traditional anti-government attitude or protests as part of her personality.

She was still uncertain about her own political convictions and certainly not someone you would call a revolutionary or even a rebel, and pregnant to boot.

So here was Lisa getting personally involved in the politics of not only a student movement, but also in the politics of a country that was not her own.

"She can do that because essentially Americans have no cultural definition," Milo said. "Anything new appeals to you because history has no meaning for you. Your history is always in front of you, never behind."

"Come on, as much as the French want to believe it, you're not the only people who care about history or politics."

"Well, most Americans are reactionaries."

"You've got some horrible people in this country, too."

"That's true, but we're a little more sophisticated when it comes to political awareness."

"Are you saying Lisa has no political or personal convictions?"

"She's probably among the few Americans who do. I might even include you among those few." He laughed. "The rest of your fellow Americans I don't have much faith in. They're very superficial when it comes to political awareness. Americans would be a lot wiser if they understood sex better."

"Sex? What the hell does that have to do with politics?"

"Look at it this way. Americans engage in sex, but it doesn't seem to occur to them that this very act causes a woman to get pregnant. Politics is the same. You do something, and there is always a final result. You can't escape it. In politics, as in sex, there are serious consequences that follow such acts."

"You think they're similar in nature?"

"In both instances, they demand more than just a casual involvement. They're both very powerful human acts having dramatic results for the people involved. Americans don't accept that politics has an impact on who they are.

"They've convinced themselves that government *is* the enemy. It's so idiotic. They don't understand citizens *are* the government. That notion's just too abstract, too dangerous for their simple minds. In fact, they refuse to admit it."

"You don't give us much credit, do you?

"It's the truth. They'd rather watch TV. Just look at the numbers of people who vote in your country. And when they vote, as they will this coming presidential election in November, they'll most likely vote to elect Nixon—a man who merits nothing but contempt and disgust from any half-intelligent person.

"Politics is one of the most profound and significant human acts we can participate in. Americans don't really see it that way, and they are wrong."

"I still don't see the connection between sex and politics."

"No, you wouldn't. The truth is that everything we do in life has a political consequence, whether it is having sex or reading a book. Americans ignore the political conviction they must develop to make themselves a better people. The Vietnam War is a typical example of such obtuseness."

"I disagree. Those demonstrations against the war back home are real. They're not just for the TV cameras."

"Yes, I guess I have to grant you that much," he said, without conviction.

The war in Vietnam had polarized not only American students, but also students around the world in a way no recent world event had done resulting in Americans, in general, not openly welcome in some places. The war left many people questioning the basic nature of the American political system.

The French, in general, showed the usual hostility toward the U.S government. Individually, though, I found them to be no more anti-American than they are anti-anything.

Since I was against the war, I stole their thunder. Still, Milo was not optimistic about American culture becoming a viable choice. He always saw us as shallow and immature.

We were a society only interested in making money because we idiotically believed money would resolve all of our problems—on top of buying handguns, instant gratification.

Stealing other people's natural resources, amassing large personal debts, spreading fast food joints so everybody would get fat, selling underarm deodorants, and making credit cards available to the whole population, even children.

"Come on."

"Don't get me wrong," he said, "my complaint is that you've the potential to do much better, not to make the same mistakes Europeans have made over the years.

"You can lift us from our baseness; you can show us how not to muck things up; you can help us by giving us the best that's in you; you can teach us to embrace your American democratic ideals.

"You don't have to be mean or a bully or shove it down our throats. I suppose you'll rule the world one day with your jeans, T-shirts, sneakers, soap operas, and fast food. How banal."

In spite of his complaints about American culture, however, he adored Lisa. He was always reminding me how jealous he was of me because love like hers happens only once in a lifetime.

You had to be French to understand such sentiments. He kept repeating that I was damn lucky and too dumb to know and appreciate it anyway—and probably did not deserve it.

He was constantly asking me about her and how she was doing, marveling at the fact that Lisa's pregnancy did not seem to slow her down. He admired her lack of cynicism, her openness, her daring, her "Americanness," as he often said, plus her enthusiasm for what he perceived to be a quixotic quest as far as the student revolt was concerned.

"Sometimes," Milo said, "I think Americans really believe that politics is like a Hollywood movie. You know, images without substance and a wonderful happy ending. And if the whole thing can be presented to

176

you as a new gadget, wrapped in a colorful plastic container with a nice, shiny label on it, you guys are willing to buy it with no questions asked.

"An American writer, I cannot think of his name, didn't he say something about not losing any money underestimating the taste or intelligence of the American public? Isn't that what he said?"

"Yeah, but that's not fair."

"You're right. But that's also why I like Americans. You don't know any better," he said, and he laughed.

Lisa's friends at the Sorbonne also joked that it might be the first time an American baby would be born at the "barricades." I was definitely less, a hell of a lot less, liberal about this.

The doctor was pleased with the way the pregnancy was progressing and had put no restrictions on Lisa. Eat well; get lots of sleep, proper exercise, and no dancing.

We will let nature do what she does best. In the final count, that was all that mattered. Yet I worried a lot. The memories of Mohammed and his wife were never far from my mind.

"But that was back in Yugoslavia," Lisa said.

"I know, but problems with babies aren't exclusive to the Yugoslavs."

"I'm fine. I exercise. I eat well. I sleep fine. Well, only when you're not waking me up so we can make love."

"Are you complaining?"

"Who's complaining?"

It was true. Lately, I had been waking her up to talk to her, to make love to her, to see the sun come up. She knew about my life and all of its quirks. My heart was filled with wonderful emotions about her, about the baby, our destiny, about everything. She had once said to me that men also get "pregnant."

I could almost see how that came about. But I also felt displaced; I had no more roles to play. That did not seem fair. If a woman is fulfilled by her pregnancy, a man, by definition, must feel empty—no double meaning intended. I wondered why nature had not made men and women equal so that each could take turns carrying the baby.

"Here, unplug it. I'll carry it for the next three months." That would have been a fair and equal deal.

Men were always saying both sexes were equal except that when it came to having babies, women were more equal. Hell, they dominated that universe.

It was like being at a baseball game. It is the bottom of the ninth inning, your team is seven runs behind, your pitcher is batting with a full count on, and you are two outs. Man, you know how that is going to turn out. Yeah, one strike, and I was out!

"Of course, you're not out of the game. It's all in your head. I don't know how I could have become pregnant without you."

One day, Lisa's pregnancy and the need to tell her parents came up while we were sitting at a café by Place du Tertre, in Montmartre. We had gone up looking for Pete because sometimes that was where he exhibited his paintings, but he was not there.

I did not want to press the point about her parents and preferred to let her make the decision. She did not seem too concerned about it, though timing was always delicate.

Is there a right time to call up your parents, a continent away, to announce that you were pregnant by someone they have never seen or met?

"When are you going to tell them?"

"I don't know."

"Are you afraid of what they'll say?"

She was silent for a moment. "Well, my father's the one I fear will be most affected. He's a shy, sensitive man, and has been so traditional about everything. My mother is less traditional. I'm sure all parents prefer the usual, you know: engagement, ring, marriage, kids, and whatever."

"Yeah, followed by divorce."

"Even that," she said, smiling.

"So, you think it'll be OK?"

"Yes." Then she added in a conspiratorial and playful manner, "I want to tell you something, and you must promise never to talk to anybody about it."

"Who would I tell?"

"I don't know, but you must promise."

"What is it?"

"First, you have to promise."

"I can't promise to keep a secret when I don't even know what it is," I said, wondering what her secret was about.

"Yes, you can," she said, firmly.

"OK, I promise."

"I once talked to my mom, and she told me that she and my father had made love before they were married."

"She told you that?"

"Yes."

"Why did she tell you that?"

"I wanted to know," she said, and seemed surprised at my reaction.

"There are some things children aren't supposed to ask their parents about," I said.

"Why not?"

"I don't know. I don't know, really."

"You're right, but she trusts me. Besides, my mother's a cool lady, and I knew she wouldn't get embarrassed or hide the truth from me."

"She has to be cool. For example, if I had ever asked my mother how I came to be? She probably would have had a heart attack or she would have argued Immaculate Conception or something."

Lisa started to laugh.

"Yeah, my mother would have argued another Virgin Mary story," I said.

"She can't be that bad."

"Well, I don't know what she would have said. How old were you when you sprang this thing on your mother, anyway?"

"About thirteen. It was when my first period came. She was telling me how important this event is in a girl's life and, somehow, I ended up asking her about my father."

"She must have been surprised."

"She was, and she wasn't."

I could picture Lisa asking her mother about this. I have always envied kids who had a normal relationship with their parents. Not even in my wildest dreams, could I have envisioned the rapport I had with my own parents would have been as close and as loving as the one Lisa had with her parents.

"My mother said I could tell Robin, though she did ask me not to tell my father she had told me. I thought it was lovely. I mean they loved each other! My mother was seventeen when she married my father."

"How old was your father?"

"He was much older. He was twenty."

"Your mother married a dirty old man." She laughed and hugged me.

"I thought it was cute and innocent."

"We're so different," I said.

"No, we're not."

"Yes, we are. You've told me so many wonderful things about your parents. And I can't bring up some small incident that would tell you, show you, my parents are fine folks. I'm sure they are in their own way, but I'm ashamed to say I don't have too many wonderful memories of my parents."

"I'm sorry."

"*C'est la vie.*"

"We don't bargain for the kind of parents we get."

"I wish we could."

"I've had problems with my parents, too. You know the usual stuff. But they've been wonderful. I wouldn't want to change them for anybody else."

"You're lucky."

"I know."

"With all of the moving around your parents did, were you ever lonely as a kid?"

"My refuge was in dancing. Robin was less interested."

"Why dancing?"

"I don't know. Maybe it was because I didn't have to carry a piano around to do it. It was just my records, my old record player, and me in some corner of the house."

"What did it bring you?"

"All kinds of things," she, said softly and wistfully.

"You told me one day that you don't daydream, and dancing is all about daydreaming."

"Of course I daydream," she said, categorically.

"That's not what you said."

"Everybody daydreams, but some of us would rather not talk about it."

"I talk about it. When I was a kid that was the only thing that kept me going."

"What did you daydream about?"

"I'm not telling you until you tell me what you daydreamed about when you were a kid."

"I daydreamed about a kind world, with respect and civility. A world in which young men don't have to go to war and young women can get to be presidents of their nations if they want to. I daydreamed that one day I would find this wonderful man who would love me like crazy, and would ask me to live in Paris with him."

"And have you?"

"Have I what?"

"Found this man?"

"The jury's still out," she said, laughing.

"Thanks a lot. Now you're making fun of me."

"I'm not," she said, and she leaned over and hugged me. "Of course, I've found that man!"

Her look was serious and tender. There was no ambiguity. At that moment, the world around us did not exist. It was just the two of us.

"So, what did you daydream about?" She asked after a while.

"About faraway places. Other kids had thoughts about being cowboys or firemen. Me, I wanted to go and walk in the desert. For some reason, the desert was always a place of magic and mystery to me."

"I also daydreamed about dancing," she said. "Actually, I'm not very good at daydreaming. I'm better at doing practical things. When I was a kid, very often I got up in the middle of the night, when I had a tough time trying to get to sleep, and went to dance by myself. My parents thought I was a little nutty, though they never kept me from doing it."

"They never called the guys in the white coats to come and cart you off to the funny farm?"

"Come on, music is my father's world," she laughed, "I got that from him. He taught me how to play the piano. He's an amazing musician, very introspective, with lots of sensibility. He doesn't talk much, but I understand how he feels."

"Were you ever afraid of the dark?"

"Sometimes, when it rained and there were thunderstorms I would crawl in bed with my parents and it made me feel safe. Even today, whenever I hear thunder, I call them. My mom always asks me if by any chance there are thunderstorms around," she said, laughing.

"She knows."

"Yeah, she knows. I love my parents."

"That's wonderful. You're a little too big to crawl into bed with them though."

"Yes, but now I have you, and you'll protect me from thunderstorms, right?"

She threw her arms around me. Yes, I would protect her from all harm in spite of her magic bracelet and her Ethiopian tribe of warriors ready to pounce on anybody who threatened her.

"But will your parents love our baby?"

"Do you know grandparents who don't love their grandchildren?"

"It happens," I said, and not without some trepidation.

"My parents aren't monsters. They'll be crazy about her and so will Robin."

"What do you mean *her*?"

This was the first time she had talked about the sex of the baby. For me, it was strange because I had never really thought about it.

180

"We'll have a girl," she stated without hesitation.

"How do you know that?"

"I just do," she said. And perhaps destiny was on her side after all.

"One question: What did you say to your parents about renting a room from me?"

"That's all. Why?"

"Just curious."

"My parents trust me. My mother has always told me that as an adult I'm free to make my own decisions, but to understand I have to live with the consequences."

"So, no regrets?"

"None!" Then she gave me a lovely smile and kissed me.

Lisa was growing more beautiful with her pregnancy. Still slender, her abdomen was beginning to become more prominent. Her beautiful breasts were more rounded. I derived a great deal of secret pleasure watching the physical changes taking place in her body.

Such a mystery. Many women glow when they get pregnant and nature did not fail Lisa. The doctor had said that everything was coming along fine, that Lisa should have a normal pregnancy.

"It'll be a girl, then?"

"It's the fathers who determine the sex of the baby."

"I get it, now it's my fault we won't have a boy."

"It's not, but we'll have a girl." End of conversation.

Yet my attitude toward the whole situation remained a bit muddled. Motherhood was something males are not privileged to know firsthand. We can only observe it and not feel it. In the past, I often thought that nature, in general, tends not to favor females.

I was beginning to question if my reasoning had been correct. Lisa, like countless other pregnant women before her, occupied a unique position in this universe. There was no ambiguity about that. The physical changes in her body were obvious.

But the changes taking place inside her, her soul, her psyche, in those hidden and private worlds that the rest of us can only guess at, that was something else; a law mysterious and powerful now ruled her.

She had become whole. She was no longer a single entity. On the surface, she appeared the same but was not. There were subtle changes—permanent.

There were moments when I caught her with a faraway look in her eyes, daydreaming, lost in a world belonging only to her and to her baby—a world I was not part of. It was not that she left me out.

On the contrary, I found her more loving, tender, and gentler with me. Very often, in the middle of the night, I would feel her hand reaching and touching me as if to make sure I was still there, but more so to reassure me.

In a very primitive way, she understood my feelings, my need for reassurances. I had, she had once said, "something to do with this," but I did not feel it. I knew that because of what—my utility, Lisa was pregnant?

Not much of a mystery there. Once the deed had been done, however, something had taken over, and now Lisa was in the driver's seat, and I had to content myself with merely going along for the ride.

My presence counted for very little, really. Of course, I had given this child my own genetic code, but that was all. The rest was up to Lisa and how her oven was going to bake the goodies.

Women needed men for a moment. Lisa did not agree. She thought it amusing that I was tormented by these sentiments. In her life, without me, she would not be pregnant, she argued.

"Wait a second, any guy can make you pregnant. Why do you need him afterward?"

"Because you keep forgetting we're not talking about horses here. Somewhere in the cosmos, all of the elements were fused and *voilà* we're here: You, me, and our baby. I told you if I didn't believe in this, I wouldn't be here. It's so simple, really."

I was always asking her about everything that had to do with her pregnancy. She found it touching and from her responses, I knew she was just as intrigued by my questions as she was about her own answers.

But a baby needs nine months, and no matter how one wants to rush such reality, it is not going to cook before its time.

The attitude of other people when they found out Lisa was pregnant also told me a great deal about them. Take the concierge in our building. She had been a bit distant since I first moved into the apartment. I have no idea why she had remained so. Then, when Cécile more or less camped there with me she was a little more tolerant.

Milo said that one had to be French to understand the mentality that had created the concierge. I should not try to figure it out because it was really beyond the comprehension of the most intelligent human beings, and that included some American types.

When our concierge found out that Lisa was pregnant, everything changed. Everything! Suddenly, there was Madame Commère taking care of the apartment. She argued that given Lisa's state, she could no longer be expected to do it.

"*Il est hors de question.*" It was out of the question.

Besides, I was not much help around the apartment. This is how Madame Commère had ruled: What could I say?

"How did that come about?" I asked Lisa, a bit irritated.

"What?"

"That she's now invaded the place."

Lisa laughed at my pretend anger.

"I didn't have the heart to tell her no. Besides, she can use the money. Now I won't have to worry about picking up after you. She'll do it."

"So, she's bribed herself into the household."

"She didn't," Lisa said, laughing, too innocently I thought.

Madame Commère had, and of course, she was right. Lisa was also being practical. It is just that I had never really liked the concierge. Before Lisa, she never even bothered bringing my mail up to the apartment as she was doing for the other tenants.

Now, she made it a point to bring it up just so she could chat with Lisa about babies and motherhood. One would have thought she was going to be a grandmother—in a larger sense, maybe she was.

Madam Commère now treated me with a little more respect. Not *much* more, but there had definitely been a change in her attitude. The news of the baby had somehow created an intimacy between us, and she meant to keep it that way.

She would now give me a big smile and greet me as if we were sharing a secret that belonged to both of us.

"Bon jour, Monsieur. Tout le monde va bien ?"

Oui, Madame, merci."

"C'est bon."

I was always wary of her, but it did not seem to make any difference. It made me think of the legend of the Amazons back in ancient Greece. It was probably concierges, just like Madame Commère, who started the practice of getting rid of the males once the deed was done.

Now I could be gotten rid of or, at a minimum, simply be tolerated. After all, I was just the father but what really mattered were the mother and her baby. Yeah, I suspect French female concierges probably still do rule France.

"I think she likes you a little better," Lisa said.

"That's very big of her."

"Come on, she isn't that bad."

'I think she's more than that. She's terrible. Anyway, like Milo says, only the French understand this business of the concierge, I sure as hell don't."

I had run into Peter at La Coupole one day, and I had told him Lisa was now pregnant, and we were very happy about the news.

"The gods have smiled upon you," Peter said.

His face was saddened and distant. I was surprised to see him react this way. It was funny, for the more changes the times brought the more detached he seemed to be.

I always thought that Pete would be the one who would champion the need for changes, that he would go with the times, with the revolutions, movements, and the new generation's attitudes, but he did not seem to be much interested. His attitude about the madness taking place was somewhat detached, benign.

"It's the only thing that I deeply regret. I know Roxanne would have loved to have gotten pregnant, but—" he stopped. Pete's comments about Roxanne seemed to add another dimension to the couple.

"What happened?"

"It was an accident of nature."

"I'm sorry to hear that."

"There's nothing to be sorry about. It's nobody's fault."

"Did you see a doctor?"

"Yes."

His face was serious but not troubled. There was a sense of nostalgia in his voice and his words came out softly and directly. The feeling I got was that Peter had never talked about it to anyone before. He was not making a confession just ruefully reflecting on what life brings you.

"I had asked the doctor to tell me first no matter how painful. I wanted to be sure Roxanne wouldn't get the news except from me. Also, this doctor was one of her best friends. He told me I was fine, and that she wasn't. Nature works that way. To this day Roxanne believes it is me. I see no reason to tell her otherwise."

He looked at me with a soft smile on his face. It was not painful, depressing or dramatic. I have never forgotten the poignancy of the moment. It was the way it was. Again, dealing with one's own destiny was not like getting hit by a thunderbolt but was comprised of everyday stuff: banal and without poetry.

In the silence that followed his words, I could hear other conversations around us, though I could not understand what they were saying.

"You're one hell of a man," I said.

"I did what I had to do. There's no hero here."

"She's never found out?"

"No, and she never will!"

The conviction in his voice was not meant as a warning to me. Peter was above that, way above that. His words were more than a simple and banal truth. In their most immediate and truest sense, this was the code he had chosen to live by.

The secret—his secret—he would take to his grave. He was not being a hero or brave. The choice he had faced had not been easy, but that is how our lives are made up. Every day one gets up and faces one's own destiny. It did not require a Ph.D. in living. Was it not what the monk in Athos was trying to tell me?

Simple stuff, but must be done every day. I thought back to Big D. who said getting killed in the line of the work he did was part of the deal. There was nothing dramatic about it.

For some reason, I saw a parallel between him and Pete. Both men had made their choices and that was that. Birth and death; Death and birth. It is all the same. What counts is what is in between—rather basic and simple when you thought about it.

Then in April, I got a call from Alain. He was Milo's friend, the guy who owned the press agency. When I came back from Greece, I had contacted him but nothing came out of our conversations.

Lisa and I had met him for dinner a couple times. In fact, we had spent a rather sad evening together when we learned that Martin Luther King, Jr. had been assassinated.

"Why do the good guys always get killed?" Lisa asked that night.

"Americans are wonderful people," Alain said. "But America is such an illusion . . . a dream. One has to wonder if you will not end up destroying it. Like in so many large societies there are plenty of outcasts, outlaws, fanatics, racists—just bad people. It isn't a perfect world we live in mes amis."

"Events like this make me not want to go back to the States," I said.

There had been all kinds of riots in several cities in the aftermath of King's murder. All these events were ugly and sad.

"Yeah, but you can't stay exiled for the rest of your life," Lisa said.

"I know."

"Do you think we're doing any better here in Europe?" Alain asked. "Where do you go to find the perfect place, the perfect society? Does it exist?"

The questions had no answer.

"How's Lisa?" Alain asked me that day when he called. He was happy for us to learn Lisa was pregnant.

"She's fine. The doctor says she'll have a normal pregnancy and a healthy baby."

"*Parfait*. Give her my regards. Listen, I wonder if when you have some free time you can drop by the office. I've got a couple of ideas I want to talk to you about."

So it was that one fine day, in the middle of April, I went to Alain's office in the old quarter of Les Halles on Rue du Louvre. It was an old building with a rickety elevator that took forever to go up.

Alain was a guy who loved the newspaper business. He had not been successful working for a newspaper so he started his own press agency.

Though it was small, he had managed to establish a solid clientele not only in France but also around Europe and in the U.S. In fact, it was because of him I had gone to New York the time I had not taken Cécile with me. After the usual greetings, he got down to the reason for asking me to come by.

"Things are getting crazy in Prague I was wondering if you wouldn't mind going over there to have a look around."

The people in Czechoslovakia were in the middle of a peaceful revolt against the Russians and their communists flunkies who controlled the country. There had been all kinds of dramatic reports on what was happening in Prague.

"What about here? Things don't look so good."

Things in Paris were fluid now. Since the time the students at Nanterre had decided to go on strike, the unrest had found supporters at the Sorbonne and the situation, in a larger sense, was getting closer to home: Lisa was at the Sorbonne.

There is an area in Paris called Cité Universitaire. In a campus-like setting, it has buildings representing many nations where students can rent a room while they study in Paris. A few days prior to Alain calling me, there had been an incident involving some female students who had decided to go visit a male's dorm.

The aftermath of that incident was that the authorities called in the riot police. A couple hundred of them showed up and the women were locked out of their dorms. This had caused lots of anger in the student population.

Other students had protested against such tactics. Now the troubles were far more serious than many people wanted to believe. The newspapers, however, seemed to treat these events as just another student prank—it was spring after all.

The editorials took the smug attitude that the unrest in other countries—namely the U.S.—would not find an echo in France because France was dealing with such things in a proper and civilized way. The canon was: "We've got things under control here. We know what we're doing. Our students know better than to waste their time with such idiotic behavior."

"You're right," Alain said, responding to my question, "but here I can handle it. Prague, on the other hand, may be up your alley."

I had visited Prague just for a couple days some time ago. I found it to be an old city, gray and sad, whose charm and history were nowhere in sight, with her courageous people now cruelly suppressed through fear and intimidation by the Russians and their Czechoslovakian flunkies.

"The Russians aren't going to stand by and let Czechoslovakia walk away from them," he added.

"With Lisa and the baby, I don't know."

"I understand, but you also told me she's doing fine. Anyway, it wouldn't be for long. If I thought it would be risking too much I wouldn't ask."

The idea had great appeal. However, with Lisa back in my life and now pregnant my reasons for wanting to go were almost nonexistent. Besides, I was beginning to work on *L'Étranger* translation and I was feeling that I could find the right frame of mind to do a decent job.

I was also secretly hoping my work on the translation would spur me, somehow, to finally sit down and start working on my own book.

"When would you want me to go?"

"As soon as you can manage it."

In coded language, he would not have minded if I left that very night.

"OK, let me talk to Lisa about it."

"Absolutely. You have your passport with you?" I always carried it with me. I handed it to him.

"I'll get going on your visa approval to avoid any unnecessary delays if you decide to do it. I would prefer that you go in as a tourist to avoid all of the bureaucratic nonsense."

"OK."

We had done it in the past. We both knew it was risky, but under the circumstances obtaining accreditation as a journalist and as an American, especially with what was going on in Prague, was iffy at best. Getting stuck in bureaucratic limbo was not an option. A tourist visa would have to do.

I came out of his office, and decided to take a stroll down by the Seine. A walk along the river might help clear up my thoughts. I went past Le Louvre and took the long walk toward the bridge Alexandre III.

It is a beautiful bridge among the many standing over the Seine and one of my favorites. Paris is such a lovely city, the city for lovers and of lovers.

Other cities I have visited evoked in me certain feelings about them, about their mystery, magic, and charm; Istanbul, Hong Kong, New York, Venice, Moscow, and Rome, to name a few.

But there is no city that evokes the feeling of love, the way Paris does. At least once, in our lifetime, we must come to Paris and fall in love while we are here. We owe it to our hearts and souls.

I stood on the bridge watching loaded barges float down the river. Among the things I have always liked about Paris is that the French use names for their streets instead of numbers.

You look in any direction and you find its history, its style, and its destiny. Often Lisa and I had taken this walk and many other walks around the city.

"My mother wonders how the French are treating me, us," Lisa had said one day as we were out walking in the Tuileries Garden, one of the parks that give Paris its charm, and a great joy and pleasure to visit.

Lisa was finding out the French can be and are, in fact, a pain in the ass—*constipated* was the word Milo used to describe his fellow citizens.

They can also be painfully modest, wonderfully excited about America—jealous of our attitude, of our sense of adventure, in awe of our open ways, that we are not stuck in our history.

Intrigued by our fast ways: willing to accept that Americans, in general, are like a bunch of rich adolescents a bit spoiled by life but still good at heart.

The French also believe Americans are naïve about the world—they are right. We *are* naïve about the world. We spend so much time, money and energy wanting people to like us, and often the effort is misunderstood and backfires.

Of the protests against the Vietnam War taking place in Paris and throughout other cities in Europe, for example, the one common denominator was that Americans in our naiveté and stupidity we were essentially destroying the very ideals that made America great.

Equality, compassion, fairness, justice, freedom, dignity, respect for the individual—these were principals that made us different. Yet we appeared bent on destroying our own convictions, which to a lot of our friends made absolutely no sense.

What the protestors were doing then was simply throwing the damn thing back in our faces, compelling us to see how ignoble and cruel we were becoming.

"How can you be so indifferent to all this madness and suffering you're causing?" Milo was always asking, "Why are you behaving like a bully when the world looks up to you with so much hope? You're the beacon of hope. You're turning so many people of good will against you. How can you be blind to this?" The sad truth was we *were* blind.

It was such a contradiction about America. In their criticism of us, other countries hoped that she would wake up to find her people, through her elected government, were doing unspeakable things not worthy of a nation, of great people; they, however grudgingly, much admired.

Perhaps, our innocence was finally coming to terms with itself and we had no choice but to confront we were not any better than the other guys. For many Americans, that was a shocking realization.

The emperor had no clothes except, in our case, the whole people had no clothes. Not a pretty picture of us, but it was the damn truth. We did not have the monopoly on innocence, no matter how we claimed, otherwise.

Innocence! I was in Bangkok on leave—Rest and Recuperation or R&R as the Army calls it—in November of 1963, when the news came that President Kennedy had been assassinated!

After two years of military life, half of it spent in the Far East, I was looking forward to going back to the States to become a civilian again, to pick up where two years earlier, as a recent twenty-one-year old university graduate I had been drafted into the Army.

The horrible news and the realization we would never be the same were beyond what our generation had ever experienced. I, like everybody else, remembered exactly where I was when it happened.

And when I heard it had happened in Texas my first thought had been: What the hell was he doing in Dallas?

I was sitting at a bar in Bangkok, the Suzy Wong Café, getting drunk and thinking that I had to get some action going with one of the barmaids when the news was announced.

"Kennedy shot; President killed!" That is all the bartender could say.

Everything changed for all of us that day!

Neither drink nor sex had any importance at that moment. When we finally learned he was indeed dead, the sick feeling in my stomach was overwhelming. We would never go back to being innocent, never! That period of our lives was over. Kennedy was dead and so was our innocence as a people, as a country.

It was impossible to imagine, to accept, such immense tragedy in our lives. Dead, just a cold corpse no different from the dead bodies I had seen in the jungles not too far from where I was sitting.

I did not have much recollection of what I did that night. At one point, I found myself walking around the empty streets, strictly against the rules but I did not give a damn.

A few nights before, I had stumbled upon the bar by accident. I had met Manuel, a Filipino guy with an open and friendly manner, who was working for some foreign mission in Bangkok, and I had also met Demetrios, who was with him.

The three of us had hit it off pretty well and we got a little drunk. That is when Big D. said he was a mercenary. When I told him, I was going to be a journalist he wanted me to write an article about him, which I promised to do.

The night after Kennedy's death, I went back to the bar. I needed friendly faces around me. Demetrios and Manuel were there along with a guy from Australia, also a mercenary, plus a couple of barmaids. They were solemnly drinking whiskey chased with hot sake. One girl seemed quite drunk.

"I'm stinko," she said, when I sat at the table. There were a couple of half empty bottles of Jack Daniels on the table surrounded by little empty bottles of sake. There was a conversation going on that would start and stop, start and stop.

It was like a confession, yet what each said seemed not to have any relationship to what the others were saying, each of them was having a disjointed, private monologue aloud. The atmosphere was bizarre and funereal.

Apparently, the hotel where Demetrios and the others were staying also lodged American military personnel. Demetrios was saying that on the night of Kennedy's death, the guy who occupied the room above him, some bird Colonel in the U.S. Army, had spent the night having sex with some girl. He said, he could hear them giggling and carrying on.

"I wanted to go and blow up his fucking brains," Demetrios said.
"Why?"

I asked him more out of curiosity than because I really cared. I was so numb with what had taken place the day before that nothing was going to surprise me.

"Can you imagine? Here was his commander-in-chief, dead, killed by some crazy guy . . . and this chicken Colonel is upstairs banging this girl on the night his commander-in-chief was killed. No respect. You're a fucking American, you explain it," he said, angrily.

What could I explain?

"I don't understand it either!" The Australian guy seemed just as outraged. "You should have gone up and cut his balls off," he added in his beautifully clipped Australian accent.

"Yeah, teach him to have respect," said Manuel, his friendly demeanor nowhere in sight.

The conversation stopped. Silently we contemplated the magnitude of what this chicken Colonel had done at a most terrible time. It did not make any sense to the three of them. I was not sure how I felt.

The girl, who had said she was "stinko", reached over and poured herself a rather strong drink. If I drank that much, they would have to carry me out of here feet first, I thought.

She kept staring at the glass and turning it in her hand. When she spoke, her words were gentle, poignant, soft, and childlike in her broken English. We did not need correct syntax to understand her anguish.

"You know, GI Joe come home with me last night, and he cry. I know he feel like shit. I need money, but no can do. He don't try nothing. I hold him and we cry. I don't know him, and I love him with my heart!

"I don't want to do business. My girlfriend come home and asks: 'Hey, what's wrong, girl? Come have party.' I get pissed and yell and call her all kind of names. I say to GI, 'Hey, Joe, can make you happy, catch short time.' He no interested . . ."

She stopped, reached for her glass, twirled it, and looked at the alcohol as if seeking in the liquid the answers to her sadness. It was a while before she continued.

"He say, 'Just hold me, honey.' I hold him for long time. He cry and me, too. I so very sad. Him very sad more than me. He break my heart, big. I say, 'Honey, can make you happy. I give blowjob, can make you happy,' but he only look at me with very sad eyes, like puppy, then he go. I don't want him to go, but he go.

"He want to give me money and I say, 'no.' I honor president, you know. I put candle. I'm Christian, you know. I make no money. It's hard. Have old father and old mother, business not important, money not important, it's OK. GI Joe sad heart, very important."

She reached over and took a long drink from the glass before Demetrios gently took the glass away from her. Tears were cascading down her cheeks. She put her head down on the table. I thought she had passed out. The girlfriend got up and left.

After a long silence, Big D. stood, picked up the girl like a rag doll, put her over his shoulder, and started to walk out of the bar followed by the Australian guy. The other patrons either did not notice or just did not care.

"I better get her home before she gets sick," Demetrios said.

Manuel sat there moodily staring into space. Neither one of us wanted to talk so a few minutes later I left. Yes, America, wake up America.

You lost your innocence, America. I and everybody else with our broken hearts weep tears of sorrow and despair. I wished it had not happened.

For the chicken Colonel, nothing changes for death was secondary to sex. For GI Joe, the president was dead. Long live his president! For the girl, there was no business done. She lit a candle and made no money.

Who was right? The girl, GI Joe, the chicken Colonel? Who the fuck knows? Could anyone please tell me so I could sleep peacefully and not be so afraid of the dark?

Right on, America! Where did your fucking innocence go?

So, Lisa's mother asking about how the French were treating us that day at the *Tuileries* made so much sense in that we, all of us at one time or another, have been driven crazy by French behavior.

For the French are good at finding someone else to blame for their problems, a system they invented and have developed to a fine degree. Their attitude is what counts. They are masters of it.

We Americans think the world should love us because, well, because we are Americans. We take it hard when we are criticized and not liked—especially by people who are supposed to be our friends.

The secret to understanding the French is simple: They dislike everybody, either collectively or individually, who is not they!

"You have to understand," Cécile had always made it clear to me; "we must be the only people at the top without forgetting, of course, to behave nobly toward lesser individuals. *Noblesse oblige*, you know." She laughed.

"*Noblesse oblige*, how kind and gracious of you."

"I don't know why you have problems with that, really," she said. She was damn serious.

"Because it's not nice."

"What does that have to do with anything? You Americans are always making things so complicated."

"Is that your idea of a sense of humor?"

"It's rather simple," she said, and she laughed again.

The attitude was very French. It's almost genetic. That was the way it was. There was no mystery about it. In a curious and perverse way, I kind of understood what Cécile was trying to say.

To look for another reason because Americans cannot accept the notion that the French believed everyone was beneath them was really an exercise in total futility.

Once you understood dislike for others was rather democratic, that the French are not singling us out because we are American, it is easier to see such an attitude has nothing to do with us personally.

You then find the French to be a nice, warm, and caring bunch of people—you can actually begin to like them. If one can understand that, I think the problem pretty much disappears.

Le Jardin des Tuileries is very popular with children, and on that day, I saw how Lisa looked at the kids. I could picture Lisa walking our baby to the park to play. I saw her quietly recording, in her mind, the little scenes of other children at play with their parents or other kids.

We saw one little boy, his clothes all disheveled, dirty pants, shirt hanging out, knees in pretty bad shape, scuffed shoes, but he was having the time of his life being pursued by his father around a tree shrieking with delight. Lisa marveled at how much fun the little boy was having.

"Little boys are so adorable," she said.

The way she said it, it was with a sense of wonder and yet somewhat melancholic, as if wanting to have a girl denied wanting to have a boy.

"It's hard isn't it," I said, after watching the little boy.

"Yes, I wish we could have one of each," she said, wistfully.

"Maybe we will."

"No, Dr. Brisson said she only hears one little heart."

"Well whether it's a boy or a girl, the important thing is to have a healthy baby."

"Will you still love me after I have the baby?"

"More!"

She smiled, put her arm through mine, and we walked for a few moments.

"Do you like living in Paris now, I mean more than before?" she asked after a long silence.

Her question surprised me, yet it made sense. I always assumed that because I love Paris others had the same feeling. Often that was not the case for lots of Americans were often flummoxed when dealing with the French.

"Why do you ask?"

"Because I was thinking that if I wasn't here where would you be?"

"I don't know, maybe here, maybe someplace else, I don't know. There's one thing I do know: I'm here with you, and the other stuff doesn't matter."

I could feel her shivering.

"I want to understand life. Do you understand the rhythms of life? How to find them and use them?" Her voice was soft and longing. "I don't want to lose my innocence about the world, become cynical. Perhaps my fear is just the proof that I'm not wise."

"What brought that on?"

"I don't know. Alex, I want to say to you the things that are deep in my heart. I want to make you happy. I want to become a good woman for you."

"You are a good woman. You make me happy. I have never felt what I feel now."

"Are you sure?"

"How can you doubt it? I'm more than sure. I'm totally convinced of it."

We stopped, I kissed her, and she held me close. She gave me a wonderful smile.

"Sometimes things get all confused," she said. "It's like trying to grasp water with your hand. You know you have touched it, but you still have nothing in your hand."

"Welcome to the club."

"I don't want to miss life. I don't want to wake up later and find that I missed it. I want the whole thing: the good, the bad, and the worst. The question I'm trying to answer is: Which category do you fall into?"

"The worst."

"Yeah, I think you're right."

"Really?"

"No, dear heart. You're the best!"

"Are you sure?"

"Yes!" and she embraced me.

"There are so few answers that we can hang on to. The truths we perceive are so few and far in between, and they seem so illusory that we end up distrusting not only what we see but also what we feel," I said.

"I know that," she said, "and it's not easy to figure out where one fits. So many things are changing. They seem to come at you so fast. I fear the world my parents knew, that I grew up in, won't be there for our baby. I wonder what that world will be like twenty, thirty years from now.

"Will we still find innocence in it? Will our baby be safe? I want everything to be simple, honest, not so cynical and corrupt. It scares me, but I also want to remain an optimist—" she stopped.

Her voice was soft and distant. Lisa was not one to go around brooding over life the way I did. She believed you did your best, and that was what was expected of you.

There were moments in life when the simple truth about what we feared, about the fact that we did not understand, could make us see the futility of living; yet at the same time, it could also make us see it was wonderful to be alive because to try to understand who you are, where you are, was to love life. What a contradiction.

I did not know if Lisa was simply reflecting on it now that her own life was taking her in an unknown direction, that such a state of affairs would prompt her to tell me she was afraid and confused.

I wished I had not complicated her life so she would not risk losing that which made her so different from me.

I should be more careful not to contaminate her with my own ambiguous and often morbid attitude of what life was about. I hoped she would never change, that she would always remain the way she was. It was not a rational thought, but I clung to the idea that if I fervently wished it, it would come about.

"I thought you believed in the cosmos," I said.

"I do, but that doesn't mean I understand it. Do you understand it?"

"If I understood it, I would write a book, make millions, and we would go live in the most wonderful castle. We would fill it with kids, our own and others, we would have incredibly magical things to play with, and nobody would bother us.

"We would do what we wanted whenever we wanted. There would be love and peace and nobody would hate one another or have fights, and we wouldn't even have to go see a dentist even if she were kind."

"But would we be allowed to go to bed late and have chocolate ice cream for breakfast?" She asked.

"Not only that, but any time we wanted to eat all of the wonderful candies we could do that, too."

"If we ate all the candy that would mean we'd have to go see a dentist."

When love strikes and you are among the lucky ones, the silliest things become pleasurable, affectionate and tender.

"No, because in the candy there would be a magic formula that would keep your teeth clean and healthy any time you ate it. Dentists would be totally obsolete. If somebody wanted to be a dentist, she would be banished from ever eating candy again."

"Would chocolate ice cream for breakfast still be OK? She asked.

"Yes, she would be allowed that. Of course!"

"That wouldn't be so bad," she said, pleased at the thought, "but you know what my biggest dream is?"

"What?"

"To own a Stradivarius violin."

"Are you serious?"

"Yes."

"For that you would need all of the gold in Fort Knox."

"Yes, but it would be worth every penny."

"But you play the piano not the violin."

"True, but it would be cool to own one."

"Yup, it sure would."

That afternoon, Lisa and I stood by the obelisk of the Place de La Concorde and looked up the long avenue of the Champs Elysées rising gracefully as it reaches into the Arc de Triumph. I told her the story of how a French tank gunner had knocked out a German tank during the liberation of Paris, in World War II, at about where we were now standing.

The French gunner remembered how many meters there were between La Concorde and the Arch because the distance between the two monuments is precise. So, he set his sight accordingly and blew the other tank away.

"I read somewhere that if you pay a fee to the city, you can actually get them to light up any monument in Paris after they go dark," I said.

"Really? Would you do that for me?"

"I would light up the whole city for you."

She gave me a lovely smile, and embraced me.

Paris is such a beautiful city. From where I stood at the Alexandre III bridge, after my earlier discussion with Alain about asking me to go to Prague, I looked around and marveled at how well laid out the city is with plenty of green spaces logically designed—with abundant charm—and built for people to walk and enjoy their surroundings.

One would think that this logic would apply to how the French generally behave, though that is not the case. They are a pain, not always the easiest people to get along with, but they are by far the most interesting of all Europeans.

Their idiosyncrasies are legendary. Take the human liver, for example. The French believe there is an illness of the liver that has nothing to do with alcohol drinking. To get sick from this illness is very French because no one else in the world suffers from it. To have a "*crise de foie*," as they often refer to it, is indeed, to be French.

Milo was always arguing about it, totally convinced he was right and wanting me to agree with him.

'Come on, everybody gets it."

"I never heard of it until I got to France. It isn't medical."

"It doesn't have to be for it to exist," he protested.

"How can you have an illness your own doctors admit doesn't exist?"

"I've suffered from it. I don't know anyone in this country who hasn't, from time to time, been its victim."

"Right, it's all in your heads."

"OK, show me where you have read it's all in our heads? I mean, a whole people, an entire nation can't be wrong," he said, truly puzzled nobody else in the world seemed to suffer from such an illness.

"Let's say you French are a bit peculiar. Such peculiarity appears to give you the right to suffer from an illness other humans aren't privileged to enjoy," I said, trying to make fun of him.

"You Americans think we're silly. If you stay long enough in this country, you'll get it." He was very formal about this sentiment.

"I hope not. That's one thing I don't want to catch."

"I bet you deny its existence because you don't want us to get credit for its discovery," he said, defensively.

"There's only one reason people get a '*crise de foie*' in this country. It's just so they can get off work and go spend a couple of weeks at those wonderful spas for their annual cure, courtesy of their fellow taxpayers."

"Do you think so?"

Milo was just being French.

I was thinking about Milo and his crazy idiosyncrasies as I stood watching Paris's splendid river, La Seine, as it meandered through the city. They built an expressway on both sides of the river for the thousands of foul-smelling-spewing-pollution-automobiles that crawl into the mad traffic of the city every day.

Then the signs. Everywhere you turn, there are signs telling you: *Défense* this, *Défense* that. In other words, you are forbidden from doing anything.

In typical Latin logic, the French developed what they call: "*Système D*" which was impossible for the Anglo-Saxon mind to comprehend let alone practice. Behind it all was the verb: *Débrouiller:* To be resourceful in all circumstances, and ignore what others say or do.

Though many people argued the expression: "*Système D*" actually stood for another verb: *Demerder,* which could be translated as getting your act—or your shit—together, depending upon just how crude you wanted to be.

The French, in their everyday language vocabulary, used the word: *merde,* or shit, quite extensively. In fact, often times one heard it on the radio when people were expressing a strong or rude opinion about something they did not like or did not approve.

In a land where just about everything was prohibited, thus the ubiquitous signs: *Défense,* all around you, where the individual could not do much there was always a way to get around, to manage, thus "*Système D*". It was almost like a religion. Everybody in France practiced it.

The notion to wait patiently in line at the bank or at the post office, for example, quite often appeared unthinkable to most of them. They just went straight to the head of the line and looked nonplused when you told them it was not polite or right.

There was never an apology and they took you for a fool not only for bringing it to their attention, but also for the fact that you were not doing it yourself!

It seemed that French workers were always on strike or supporting someone's strike against the phone company, the Métro, the airline company, the electric company, the gas company, the railroad company, or any of the government monopolies or large companies in the private sector. Maybe it was because the right to strike is written in the French constitution.

Thus, from day one, the French grew up with this right. It allowed them to participate and organize themselves to bring attention to the powers that be that things needed to be changed, that getting elected was not the end of the process.

On the contrary, it was the beginning of the social contract between the government and those who elected them. The strikes were powerful tools used by citizens to force the government to respect its part of the bargain.

The public sector in France employed a large number of citizens, and the unions were very powerful, so there was a constant battle going on between them and the government. The workers were on the political left and the government was on the political right.

As Milo, in his cynical way had once said: Since everything in French life was political, it was not surprising that everybody was trying to screw everybody else.

Take parking. People parked their cars everywhere. On the sidewalks, blocking driveways, right next to fire hydrants, in the middle of the street, you name it.

They got parking tickets, of course, which they never paid for the simple reason they knew that whenever there was a change in government it also came with an official decree forgiving all *citoyens Français* their parking fines!

They drove like lunatics. Ben used to tell me he never felt entirely safe when crossing the street even when inside the pedestrian zone.

"These frogs are nuts!" he used to say.

When an ambulance or police car or a fire truck needed to get through traffic, nobody moved out of the way or stopped like we did in the States.

On the contrary, they shrugged their shoulders and waited for the other guys to do it. That was what Lisa had meant about the native's attitude: *Je m'en fous*—I don't care!

They smoked like chimneys everywhere. The ministry in charge of selling tobacco made millions of francs for the government, while the health ministry spent millions of francs trying to get people to stop smoking.

In both cases, the two ministries administered a kind of monopoly and competed against each other to save *La Grande France* from each other.

It was Napoleon who nationalized the tobacco industry. He was giving a *soirée,* when a woman walked in bejeweled from head to toe with the most exquisite and expensive precious stones money could buy.

Naturally, old Nap was curious and intrigued as this woman had more jewels on her than his beloved Josephine. He asked the woman what kind of business her husband was in, "Tobacco, sire," she answered proudly. The next morning, he nationalized the industry.

To this day, the tobacco business in France still remained a state monopoly. Milo was the one who told me the story about the bejeweled woman. I did not know how true it really was. Milo swore that it was.

It was also Napoleon who came up with the idea of not only using numbers for house addresses but also using the odd and even numbers for opposite sides of the street. He probably did it just so his troops could find the enemies they were looking for.

"You've heard of the empty suitcases?" Milo asked me one day.

"No, what is that?"

"Every month each ministry sends some guy with an empty suitcase to the Bank of France where they fill it up with cash. The money is then distributed by each ministry to people they like or who have done favors for them."

"Just like that?"

"Yes."

"Come on," I said.

"It's true."

He was mystified to find I did not believe him.

"How could that be? It's unethical. It should be illegal. It's a swindle."

"Mon cher Alexandre, you're much too naïve. *C'est fabuleux, ça!* It's the French way!"

There was nothing "fabulous" about defrauding the public's coffers. I did not trust what he was telling me, anyway.

At our meeting in his office earlier in the day when Alain had asked me to go to Prague, he had said, "The Czechoslovakian people know what the Russians did to the East Germans and to the Hungarians. Those are events one never forgets."

There had been all kinds of news about what the Czechoslovakian people were calling Prague Spring. They were pushing for and apparently enjoying more freedom since the mid-forties just after World War II, before they were taken over by the communists and their Russian masters.

However, the situation was fraught with danger. Nobody trusted the Russians due to their historical brutality. They demanded order not chaos within their empire.

But here in Paris things were also moving in the direction of an outcome that did not bode well for the country. There were rumors that some young workers around France were beginning to get restless, too— bad sign. Once the workers start protesting the outcome of such social unrest was anybody's guess.

The French had a history and tradition of violence in their protests. People were getting very angry. I was not sure what Lisa would say to Alain asking me to go to Prague, though I suspected that she would say, go!

196

We had been living together now for several months, and had not been separated since the day she came back, ostensibly, to rent the room.

"Rent the room, my eye!" I had said, making fun of her.

A couple of weeks earlier we had been standing on the deck of a *Bateau Mouche*—one of the river-cruising pleasure boats that go up and down the Seine—eating crêpes and enjoying the scenery. It was a sunny day in the early spring, and Lisa looked striking.

Her pregnancy was showing more. Her cheeks were filled with that healthy look of girls who have drunk milk all of their lives in preparation for the day when it would be time to pass the good genes on to the next generation. She was becoming a very beautiful soon-to-be-mother.

We had gone to see Dr. Brisson earlier that day, and afterward Lisa said she wanted to take a boat ride down the Seine. The doctor was happy with the progress and had told Lisa to keep doing what she was doing.

At the doctor's office, I heard the baby's heartbeat for the very first time. I sat there completely enthralled and fascinated listening to the sound of this tiny heartbeat as regular as nature had designed.

What a miracle! Hopefully that heart would not stop beating until it had completed its programmed cycle.

I wondered what spiritual expanse this tiny heart would travel in its lifetime, seeking its own path. Of course, it would find love just like its progenitors did. It would also have its share of disappointments and, if my own life were any indication, it would also get confused but survive.

I had tears in my eyes when I listened to *the* symphony of life for the first time! The doctor told me it was not the typical reaction of French men abo

ut to become fathers. They were much "*trop pudique*"—too reserved—she said.

From where we stood on the boat's deck, we could see both sides of the river as it meanders through the Parisian landscape. Lisa had said teasingly that all she had ever wanted to do was to come to Paris and go to the Sorbonne, that was why she had come back to rent the room from me.

"It's true," she said, smiling and blushing.

"Liar."

"I'm not. I am going to the Sorbonne."

"Yeah, you got the Sorbonne while I'm still longing for Italy." I said. She laughed.

"OK. I promise you we'll go to Italy next year."

"Yes, but it won't be the same."

"It'll be better. Imagine the three of us. We'll take her to all the museums. We'll go to Venice and ride gondolas in the moonlight."

"They probably won't let us."

"Of course, they will," she said. "I keep telling you that Italians love babies. The gondoliers will be crazy about her. I guarantee it."

"Do you think she'll be as beautiful as in a Botticelli?"

"Botticelli's paintings will have nothing over her," she said, and embraced me.

"Anyway, you ended up with more than just the Sorbonne," I said, touching her belly.

"Hum, well, at least you have to agree your child will be better off with parents who went to the Sorbonne."

"Boy, that's a great line."

"OK, maybe I did have some tiny part of me that was more interested in other things," she said, giving me that wonderful smile of hers.

"I want to ask you something."

"What?"

"You once told me when you were in Greece you had done some planning for the future. Is this big belly of yours part of those plans?"

"I'll never tell," she said, laughing. "Though now that's happened you won't find me regretting it."

I leaned over and kissed her. In Paris, lovers kiss over everything, even over *les crêpes*.

"Do you have any regrets?" she asked.

"None."

"Good."

When we got home from our boat ride, Lisa called her parents in the States to tell them the news about the baby. From what I understood of the conversation, they were shocked at first, then surprised and eventually delighted.

I am always a bit cynical about such matters, but I could tell by looking at Lisa's face that what her parents said came from the heart.

"They would like to hear what you sound like."

"They do? I sound normal." I was apprehensive.

"Fine, then talk to them."

She handed me the phone. I swallowed hard. It was a crazy conversation in which we kept interrupting each other, across vast distances, wanting to convey so much in such a stilted fashion.

We had to show the very essence of who we were immediately, because once the phone conversation was over, we would all be left with a lingering and frustrating doubt that we had not expressed what was deep in our hearts.

I told them I loved Lisa; she loved me; she was very happy; she made me happy. I wanted their permission and their blessings because I wished to marry her. We hoped to give them lots of grandchildren.

Lisa later told me her mother had said Lisa's father had tears in his eyes upon learning he was going to be a grandfather.

"You see, it wasn't so bad," Lisa said.

"It's easy for you to say. You didn't see my knees shaking, did you? I was terrified."

"How do you think they felt?"

"I don't know."

"Imagine getting a phone call in the middle of the night with the news that your daughter is pregnant. Then you, a total stranger, asking for their permission to marry her? It's a good training for us when our turn comes don't you think?"

There was a lovely smile and clear gleam in her eyes.

"No way. I will insist on meeting all of her beaux," I said, laughing.

I was already picturing myself like a worried father, sitting on the front porch, probably with a shotgun, waiting for some snotty kid to bring my baby back from a date at the precise time I had ordered him to do so.

"Poor baby. I feel sorry for her already," Lisa said, smiling.

After my visit with Alain and standing on the Alexandre III Bridge for a while, I went home and told Lisa he wanted me to go to Prague. I did not tell her that I would be going with a tourist visa.

That would have been very touchy, and I did not want her to start worrying about it. I felt dishonest, but I thought it was better not to say anything.

"OK, you have to go," she said.

"I don't have to go. He would understand."

I was torn between going to Prague and staying with Lisa and also aware of my fear that something may happen, and I would not be there for her, that I would be in a place where I could sit for days at some airport trying to get out. I knew what that was like.

In the old days, I really did not care. I just sat at some bar and proceeded to get drunk while waiting for the people in charge to get their act together. I could not do that anymore.

I went through the list of things that might go wrong: A miscarriage, an accident, an illness? Paris is a big city. Life seemed kind of crazy at the moment. So many things could go wrong.

How in the hell did I know? She came close to me as if seeking protection and reassurance. I was not sure just how to act.

I was really not afraid for her safety for I knew people she could count on would surround her. It was just the separation seemed to come so damn fast without a warning. Life never gives you time to prepare for what it has in store. It just dumps on you and good luck.

We had not lived with each other long enough to have developed the necessary mechanisms and codes couples use to deal with this kind of situation.

Her reaction had been happy and sad. She did not want me to see it, but I knew better. She had once told me that we had been together since the beginning of time and that night it felt that way. We were sharing so much.

I could no more think of leaving her than going to the moon. I held her in my arms, my heart heavy and uneasy. It was disconcerting to her that suddenly we would be separated.

"Will you remember me when you're over there?"

"Maybe, maybe not."

"Please, don't joke with me. I don't want you to be away from me. It seems so unfair. Alain is unfair." She sounded dejected.

"You don't mean that. I thought you liked him."

"I do. It's just that I don't know how long you're going to be gone. What if I want to hold your hand, or kiss you and make love to you and—" her voice trailed off, soft and sad.

It's only for a few days," I said, trying to hide my own anxiety.

"I don't know why I love you so much," she said, looking at me with her wonderful smile and sad eyes.

I was torn between my love for her and the guilt that I was also the cause of her pain.

"Why don't you come with me?" I blurted out.

The moment I said it I knew it was a bad idea. I saw her face light up, but then I also saw she knew it was a terrible idea. The memory of

Mohammed, his wife and the problems with their baby, suddenly came to me. I did not want that for Lisa.

"Do you know where I would like to go" she said.

"Where?"

"Normandy, where the Americans landed when they came to liberate France."

"Why?"

"I just want to see it."

This was a strange request that seemed to come out of nowhere.

"OK, let's go and spend a few days there. Then I'll leave for Prague when we come back."

"Will Alain get upset because you're not leaving right away?"

"He's French. He knows that in life nothing is more important than love."

"Can we ask Milo if he would let us use his house?"

"Absolutely, he owes me one." I kissed her. "OK, no more sad faces."

She smiled wanly, got up and went to the piano. Lisa had said that playing the piano was much safer than dancing now that she was pregnant. Thus, dancing would have to wait until after the baby. I knew it was a great sacrifice on her part.

Getting the piano in the apartment was not easy. Fortunately, it was not a grand piano. A truck with a crane had come and the guys who did it, seemed happy to do it. In fact, even Madame Commère was happy. I was not surprised knowing how much the French support the arts.

When she first got the piano, I would ask her to play for me. One of my favorite pieces was *"Clair de Lune"* by Debussy. One evening, she surprised me when she danced to the music. She had choreographed it. When she finished dancing, I was stunned by what she had done.

"I love you and this was for you," she said. By such moments, life could be made bearable.

The haunting melody of *"Clair de Lune"* always moved me. It evoked a sense of longing, a kind of forlorn, bittersweet sentiment. She had learned to play it, and now she could do it with a great deal of feeling and technique.

I loved to hear her play the piano. It made me think how much I had missed when I was growing up. My childhood seemed to have passed without much music.

She started to play *"Clair de Lune"*. I sat and listened during the twilight of an early evening in spring as Lisa played the lovely notes. The music washed over us, and I became aware she was suddenly in another world, by herself, alone but not lonely, where only she knew where she was.

Where nobody was allowed unless invited, but I did not feel removed from her. On the contrary, she was talking to me, and what she played only my heart could understand because it also came from her heart.

Falling in love was so unfathomable, so mysterious. There was no set pattern. No formula. It was there or it was not. Afterward, our lovemaking was just like the music she had played.

Our hearts and our bodies were talking in a language that was ours, which only we could understand. No other truth could be as powerful as the one we were both clinging to.

NINE

Then a couple of days later Lisa and I took the train from Paris to Normandy. Milo had given us the use of his family's old farmhouse. There was a caretaker and his wife on the property and when we got off the train in St. Lô, he was waiting to take us back to the house.

His name was Pierre, and his wife's name was Monique. When they started to call me *Monsieur*, I told them my name was Alex and the beautiful pregnant lady with me was Lisa, and we wanted them to call us by our first names.

You could see they were not comfortable by being too familiar—the French can be very formal. They finally agreed, though occasionally they would forget and call Lisa *Madame*. Pierre and his wife were very solicitous of us and did everything to make sure our stay was memorable—and it was.

"Here in Normandy Americans are like our family," he said.

We borrowed their car the following day so we could tour the countryside. Normandy is where the famous Camembert cheese comes from. Lisa liked the cheese. It was always a great treat to your taste buds to discover the variety of cheeses from all parts of France.

We went to visit the famous American military cemetery in Colleville-sur-Mer that sits on a bluff overlooking the sea. We appeared to be the only two visitors that day. The cemetery has about nine thousand U.S. soldiers' remains buried there.

It is one of the most dramatic sites I have ever visited. Very moving. Hard to forget. It engulfs your senses when you realize the people buried there were most likely killed on that early cold and miserable morning of June 6, 1944.

As you stand there, closing your eyes and thinking back, it is possible to imagine still hearing cries for help—from the wounded and dying—among the crushing sounds of steel tearing living flesh to shreds.

In the haunting silence of the place, a forlorn voice for reason still echoes across the long years of painful memories to which no one pays attention anymore.

It tries to talk to the living. Its lonely cry rises like a wounded bird flying toward nowhere as it begs us to listen, searching for our dignity and tolerance.

Yearning for our so-called humanism and we are unable to hear it because we are deaf. We are all fucking deaf! So, the lonely voice falls, weeping, and dies crushed by man's ignoble self and his total rejection of lessons learned.

Looking at the headstones and toward the sea, there is a distinct impression that row after row of headstones they are either coming out of the sea or marching toward the sea. Because the land rises slightly then dips down toward the sea, the effect is quite stunning.

We walked around the well-kept grounds. At the entrance of the cemetery, there is a monument with tall walls where the battle of Normandy is depicted.

I stood looking at them while Lisa was looking at the graves. I glanced in her direction and saw that she would kneel from time to time and wipe a grave's old leaves away.

I had visited Normandy once before and it was with crazy Ben. He had talked me into going with him on a hitchhiking trip. We were thumbing our way through a lot of countryside. When people found out we were Americans, they were very open and friendly.

We eventually got to a small village late one evening. There was a quaint café open, so Ben and I walked in. We did not have French money with us, so we asked the man behind the bar if he could exchange some of our dollars to pay for food and lodgings.

He said he could not exchange our greenbacks, but that he would try to help us. He got on the phone, and sometime later, a guy walked into the café wearing his bathrobe and his bedroom slippers.

I had the impression he had been roused out of bed. I was not sure if this was good or bad. He greeted the other customers, and the man behind the bar pointed at us.

My first thought was the man in the bathrobe was a cop. He seemed so serious. It turned out he was the town's banker, and he would exchange the dollars for us. Ben and I were really bowled over.

The three of us walked over to the small branch of the bank, where he opened his office and exchanged our dollars for French francs. We walked back to the café, and we wanted to thank him for his kindness and asked him to join us for a drink.

Anyway, one thing led to another and before we knew it everyone at the café had joined us and the rounds of Calvados—the strong local drink called *Eau-de-vie-de-cidre*—were going down the hatch, as if there was not going to be a tomorrow, celebrating the warm friendship of Americans and the people of Normandy.

"If you drink enough of this stuff, it will knock your socks off, and make hair grow overnight on your chest," Ben said, laughing.

The people at the café refused to let us pay for anything.

It was sometime in the early morning, when Ben and I walked— *crawled* would be *le mot juste*—over to the small hotel where the owner was waiting for us. Ben and I crashed and slept through the morning, awakening with monstrous hangovers—humongous!

Just before we left, the banker came by and told us about an old hermit who was always claiming he was friendly with some famous American general back in the U.S., and he had a letter to prove it, though no one had ever seen the letter.

Everyone seemed to think the old hermit was dimwitted and nobody paid much attention to what he said. The banker thought that if we went—being Americans—and talked to the old man, perhaps he would show us the letter, help solve the mystery, and people in the village would stop making fun of him.

Thus, we went to see the old hermit—hair of the dog and all. It turned out that he *did* have a letter from the Pentagon! After offering us some of his homemade brew, which was probably the cruelest thing anybody can drink while nursing a hangover, he produced the letter.

"Between veterans, we trust," he said, in his French-accented English with a twinkle in his eyes. I had told him I was also a U.S. Army veteran, so between veterans we could trust.

Apparently, the old hermit had immigrated to the States as a young man. He had been drafted into the U.S. Army. He served for some time and talked about Panama and the Philippines, which meant years ago.

What the letter said was that the Pentagon had been looking for him because they wanted to send him some money—a pension of some kind. During his military service, he had been injured and for many years the Army had been trying to find him.

When I told the banker the letter was genuine, he was amazed, which led to another round of Calvados. The old man was not surprised. I had confirmed what he had been saying to his neighbors for god knows how long.

"It's true," he said in English without hesitation. He had no doubts the American Army had sent him the letter, which is why he had said: "It's true." We saw the great pleasure he had in speaking a few English words.

This time, however, the couple of drinks Ben and I had were good enough to give us a glow, and help us with the hangover, and we left before things got out of hand.

I wrote a letter to the Pentagon, explaining who Ben and I were and that from what we had been able to determine the old man was the person they were looking for. To please forward his pension care of the banker, who would do all of the necessary official paper work needed to verify the old man's identity.

The old hermit was laughing because he knew he had the whole village over the barrel. The banker was now looking at him differently and scratching his head.

Clearly in the banker's eyes, this was no longer a case of some crazy old coot, in the middle of nowhere, babbling nonsense. That night the café, hell, the entire village would be buzzing about with the news. The old guy shook our hands strongly and profusely.

"Vive l'Amérique," he shouted when we left.

I stood watching Lisa as she kneeled over to wipe the leaves off a few graves. In the last few weeks, as she had said not too long ago, I had been waking her up at strange hours of the night to talk, share ideas, feelings, to make love.

We were not being very practical but, what the hell, when you are in love lack of sleep is the least of your worries.

She had told me a lot about herself and Robin. It seemed being a twin had its advantages. Many things that happened to her in the past were almost identical to what had happened to Robin. Sometimes, they lived each other's lives vicariously.

Though she and Robin were identical twins, in many ways they were different. She said her parents, from the beginning, had made sure each girl developed her own personality.

"My mother is very practical. She insisted that my sister and I have a normal upbringing, as she did not want to complicate our lives more than necessary. She dressed us differently. She even sent us to different schools. Our respective classmates were always surprised when they eventually discovered that each of us had an identical twin."

At times, it had been hard on both the girls; however, now that they were adults everything had turned out fine. They were the same but also different. Listening to Lisa's stories was like listening to Robin's stories. To understand how that happened one had to be a twin.

"How did your mom know who was who when you were babies?"

"She painted Robin's right big toenail with red polish from day one."

"It wasn't the birthmark Robin showed us back in Crete?"

"No, it was too tiny then."

"She painted your sister's toenail?"

"Yes. We grew up with that. My father used to paint it, in fact. Then when we were about five years old, it occurred to my sister to paint my right toenail red, also."

"What happened?"

"We went to see mom and we wanted to show her how clever we were."

"What did she say?"

"She was so upset she started to cry. We didn't know what we had done wrong. It was so terrible for my sister and me. Robin said she had done it because she thought it would be nice. The three of us were crying. Robin and I were so afraid. We promised, we would never do it again.

"My mom agreed that I could have my left big toenail painted red if I wanted to. But Robin's right big toenail would always be painted red. I know you didn't pay attention to Robin's toes, but you'll find that even today she always puts a touch of red on her right big toe."

"And you?"

"No, I don't do it. Later, my parents said they could tell who was who just by listening to our voices. I have a lower tone in my voice. Robin has a higher tone. I can't imitate her no matter how hard I try. She can't imitate my voice, either.

"My mother never told us that until we were grown up. That little escapade with the toenails has become part of our personal history that we share only with those whom we really love."

"Well, I must be doing pretty good."

"You are." She gave me a big embrace.

"Was there a time when you felt your mom loved Robin more than you?"

"Never! Though the one thing that seemed strange was that on our birthday, my mother would bake only one cake and put all the candles on that one cake. One day, Robin asked her about it and my poor mother had no answer. After that, she always baked two cakes and put a different set of candles on each cake."

"Do you think Robin is also pregnant?"

"No. She would have told me."

"How much of your life do you share with her?"

"Just about everything. She's my other half. My family's your family now. Alex, you belong to us," Lisa said, with conviction. It was a wonderful feeling to have.

I walked up to where Lisa was standing by the graves. She gave me a wan smile.

"Do you notice anything?" she asked, looking pensively around her.

"About this grave?"

"Well, about all of them?"

I looked around. All of the graves with their headstones of crosses, and a few scattered stars of David among them resembled each other. It was what gave the place its incredible haunting quality.

"Check their ages," she said.

Engraved on the stones were the names and the dates of birth and death. I read: Nineteen, twenty, nineteen, twenty-one, eighteen, nineteen, twenty-one, twenty-three, eighteen—all of the graves contained remains of young guys! It took me, momentarily, back to Vietnam, to the painful memories about other young guys who were no longer.

Something that I had read by an American poet—John P. Bishop who had served in the U.S. Army in Europe during World War I—and which had stuck in my head came to me as I stood looking at the graves.

Bishop had written, "The most tragic thing about the war was not that it made so many dead men, but that it destroyed the tragedy of death. For not only did the young suffer in the war, but so did every abstraction that would have sustained and given dignity to their suffering."

It is impossible to make sense of the cruelty of humans toward other humans. Animals do not kill for the pleasure of killing. But we humans are constantly trying to improve the means of not only inflicting pain and humiliation on others who are not like us, but also in perfecting the tools we use to kill.

We never seem to reach the point of having had enough. We are always looking to make such tools pitiless, faster, and more insidious. Our cruelty has no bounds. Nothing justifies such terrible behavior.

Are we ever going to stop the tragedy represented in the graves we saw around us? Lisa must have seen something in my face because she came and put her arms around me and held me close to her.

"I'm sorry I asked you to come here."

"It's OK."

"Are you sure? Do you want to leave?"

"No, I'll be fine."

She took my hand and we walked silently among the graves. The only sound came from our steps crunching the gravel. It is such a contradiction the reverence humans have for war cemeteries.

We conveniently forget and ignore that we also create the need for war cemeteries, such as the one we were visiting, to happen in the first place. We humans are so incredibly stupid. When are we going to wise up? When?

"They are so young," Lisa said.

She had said, "*are*" as if they were still alive.

"In my mind, they will always be young. I will get old and senile, but they will always remain young. It's something," she said, as if answering my thoughts. "My father was here, and he never wants to talk about it. I've tried to get him to tell me about it, but he would rather not. I'm doing this for him."

She seemed to gain some strength from walking among the graves. We stopped, and stood silently for a long time looking at the graves and toward the sea, quiet and smooth in the distance.

It was hard to imagine, that here thousands and more thousands of young guys—all terrified of what awaited them—had landed, fought, lived, laughed, dreamed, hoped, cried, prayed, and died . . . all within a short time.

Though my own Vietnam experiences had been unbearable, I could not imagine how it must have been to go through the Normandy landing.

"What if something bad happens to you in Prague?"

"What could possibly happen to me?"

"I don't know. Maybe they'll throw you in jail."

"For what?"

"For being American. They'll think you're a spy . . . I don't know."

I took her in my arms and held her close to me. I felt better now about the fact I had not told her about the visa situation. I just have to be careful, that was all.

"I'm afraid. I know it's silly," she said.

"No, it isn't. I'm more worried about leaving you here by yourself."

"We'll be fine."

"As long as you don't go to those crazy demonstrations."

"If I go, at the first sign of trouble I'll leave."

"It's a deal. I'll be careful and you don't go to too many demonstrations."

"OK. Promise you'll be careful."

"Lisa, come on."

"You *have* to promise me."

"I promise!"

"If you don't come back when you say you will, I'll come and get you," she said, fiercely.

"You would do that?"

"Yes!"

We walked down the beach as the waves softly lapped the rocky shore. She picked up some small pebbles, held them in her hand, and looked toward the sea.

"I'm sure they were here on that day. I'll give them to my dad."

She put the pebbles in her pocket.

"Do you think Adam and his mother will ever be free like we are?"

Her voice was soft, and the words came out in a whisper.

"I wish I knew."

"He's such a dreamer, and so full of courage."

"I know."

"I look at those graves, and I see thousands of Adams buried here. What happened to their dreams?"

"They are still alive. I don't believe their dreams died with them."

"That's what my father says. You know, I feel like an idiot talking about my worries in a place like this."

I did not know how long we stayed there. Lisa was right. It was hard to talk for in such a setting words and personal anxieties are irrelevant.

Later that evening, Monique shared her memories of the invasion of Normandy with us. They were vivid.

"Suddenly, we heard planes. We had heard them before, but this time they seemed to come from inland and not from the sea. The Germans started shooting at the sky. They had large lights pointed upwards and soon we saw soldiers coming down from above.

"The Germans killed many of them while they were in the air. I remember one of the parachutists when he landed. He was so young, so dashing with his large scarf around his neck; but he looked scared, very scared."

We were sitting around the fireplace. I was drinking an exceptional twenty-five-year-old cognac—*Bisquit*—that Milo had introduced me to. He had told me to tell Pierre, I had his permission to go into his cave and help myself while I was there.

Lisa was happily sipping hot chocolate. Pierre had gone to bed early, as he needed to get up at the crack of dawn to milk the cows.

"What did you do?" Lisa asked Monique.

"I was very scared, of course, but I ran to the garden and was looking up at the sky. I knew they were Americans! I knew it . . ."

She stopped. Her face was serious and sad. The powerful memories of that night still seemed to linger fresh in her mind, as when she first saw the Americans falling from the sky many years ago.

"There were many of them. Many were killed. It was so terrible," she added, after a moment of silence.

"We saw the graves. They were very young," Lisa said.

"Yes, young boys . . . innocent," Monique agreed.

She shook her head at the memory. She then got up and walked to an old armoire standing on the other side of the room. After opening it, she got busy searching for something.

"*Ah, voilà.*" She brought us an old, thick, and dusty photo album. On the inside of the cover page, she had glued a small American flag. There were all kinds of photos in the album that needed to be glued. The photos were all in black and white and small.

She showed us a photo of her and some GIs—so young—smiling, with their helmets cocked to one side, daring the photographer to record their mockery of the world in which they were most probably now condemned to die.

In the photos, Monique seemed shy, embarrassed to be surrounded by boys as she had said. She then showed us other photos of herself, her family, and her friends.

Of Pierre when they got married. He looked very formal and serious in his ill-fitting suit and tie, and Monique wearing a hat, looking happy, and smiling like any new bride should look.

"I was very *coquette* in those days. I almost married a young GI, you know."

Her eyes were smiling. I prefer the French word *coquette* to the English word: flirtatious. It seems more feminine, though the French often use the word flirt as well.

For a moment, I detected a tiny hint of regret in her voice, and then it was gone. It was not a regret that keeps one from living and loving others, but rather what we feel about a missed opportunity that keeps us wondering how it would have turned out—all without sadness or bitterness.

"What happened?" Lisa asked.

"It was the war, *Madame*. Young soldiers were not expected to live long. Billy, the American boy, wrote that if I didn't hear from him . . ." she hesitated. Then continued softly, "he had kind eyes *et quelle sourire*"—a wonderful smile.

What were memories for? Especially bittersweet memories like the ones Monique was sharing with us? To keep us human? To keep us away from despair and sadness? She was quiet. Her face was peaceful, serene.

There was no sense of betrayal that life had taken something away from her. It was the way it was. It made me think of Mohammed, Pete, Manos; all accepting what fate had brought them.

Monique reached inside the album and pulled out a piece of paper that had obviously been folded over many times. She opened it slowly. It was a letter written on an old, yellowish, fading paper.

You could see her lips were moving as she looked at the paper like she was reading it. But she was not actually reading the letter as much as reciting what in her heart she knew was a lost, youthful, and most probably a sweet dream.

Lisa looked at me, and we were without words. We waited. Monique finished looking at the letter and handed it to Lisa. I could tell Lisa did not want to take the letter because it was so precious to Monique. The letter belonged only to her and Lisa did not want to intrude. Monique understood. She gave Lisa a warm smile.

"Please read it. It is very nice letter."

Carefully, Lisa took the paper and with a steady voice, she read the letter aloud.

Dear Monique,

> *I cannot tell you where I am now. I'm not allowed to do that. It seems I haven't slept for days, always marching, always the bullets flying, and always people dying.*

> *We're moving forward and what pleases me is the look of so many civilians when they find out we're Americans. I see kids' faces and think of my kid brothers back home. I pray they never get to see what I have seen.*

> *We hear all of the time that this war will be over soon. I hope so. But every day we still have to march and still my buddies die.*

> *I think so much about you and I have your photo taped to the inside of my helmet for good luck. I surely need it.*

> *I was thinking and I know this will make you sad, but please don't be. If you don't hear from me for a long while . . . you will know . . .*

> *I hope you can translate this letter. Maybe you can ask your English teacher to do it for you. I didn't say anything bad. So, it's OK.*

> *You'll always be in my heart. I pray you and your family are safe.*

With love and very truly yours.

Billy.

p.s. I'm now sergeant William K. Lockhart. I got promoted! They tell me I will make more money. Boy, I surely hope I get to live long enough to spend it.

Lisa's voice was soft. I was watching Monique's face. She had closed her eyes and seemed as if she had never heard an American voice read the letter in English to her before; obviously, I did not know that.

But from seeing Monique's reaction, I would have bet that through all of the years she had been imagining the sounds the letter contained, and now for the first time she was hearing Billy's words in a typical American accent. The moment was incredibly amazing and poignant. I was sure Lisa was also feeling the same thing.

The silence that followed Lisa's reading was deafening. She handed the letter to me. The handwriting was strong and without any hesitation. I handed the letter back to Monique. She held it in her hand for a long moment just looking at it.

How many times had she looked at the letter? How many more times would she continue looking at it perhaps trying to remember the sounds she heard when Lisa read the letter?

"I never received another letter," Monique said, quietly. Another moment of silence ensued. "Of course," she continued smiling, "my father had been against this crazy idea. Come to think of it, if I had married Billy, I wouldn't have married Pierre and I wouldn't have met you!"

The way Monique spoke was touching, charming, and very humble. She had given Lisa and me a wonderful compliment. She put the letter back inside the album and gave us a hearty laugh, her eyes sparkling in merriment. Monique did not strike me as someone who would allow this sad event to ruin her life, to wallow in self-pity.

There is a lot about people, about life, that I desperately need to learn, to understand, to accept, I thought. It is always humbling but also reaffirms that it is in the honesty of others that one can find one's own honesty and integrity, if one is willing to search for them and accept them.

"That would have been our loss," Lisa said, in response to what Monique had said. Lisa got up, walked over to Monique and embraced her. Monique was beaming.

"I loved the American movies. I loved the American music, to go to dances." Monique said. "Wait, I may have some 33s."

She went back to the armoire and started searching for the records. It seemed like the stuff had not been touched for years and much to her delight she found several old albums of American popular music.

Lisa and I were just as happy as Monique was for her find. She selected one of the albums, looked at it, and ran her hand over it. It was dusty.

She wiped it down, then walked to an old record player sitting on a small table at the other side of the room, and placed the record on the turntable. She fiddled around with some wires and controls, put the arm down, but nothing happened. We only heard scratchy sounds. For sure, I thought, she would never make this thing work.

"*Zoot, alors*"—a great expression of French frustration.

She went back to checking the wires. Lisa and I were getting a kick out of Monique and her desire to have us listen to music she loved. Having declared herself satisfied with her electrical expertise, she put down the arm again.

This time, the music played through an old set of speakers. A distinct female American voice—Doris Day it turned out—suddenly filled the room with a wonderful rendition of "*Sentimental Journey.*"

Monique sat on an old chair and her head swayed to the music. Lisa walked over and put out her hands, inviting me to dance. I am not much of a dancer, but it was not technique that was needed.

With Monique watching us with a radiant smile, Lisa and I danced a bit. Lisa stopped and with her beautiful eyes sparkling, she looked at me, and I immediately knew what I had to do.

I went up to Monique and put my hand out to her. She was surprised that for a moment she was embarrassed and lost. Shyly she stood, and we started to dance. Again, I am not much of a dancer but, somehow, I found the right steps.

And in this old farmhouse, on this April night, in the middle of Normandy, to the strains of wonderful American music and lyrics, I danced with two charming and lovely ladies.

"That was such a touching letter, wasn't it? It was so sweet of her to show it to us and the manner in which she reacted to my reading it," Lisa said later, as we were getting ready to go to bed.

"I don't think she has ever heard the letter read by an American voice."

"You felt that too?"

"How could I not? You saw it on her face. I didn't know what to say."

"Yeah, it left me speechless too. I'm so lucky," she said. Her face was glowing and happy.

"Why do you say that?"

"Here I'm in this strange and faraway land, where I have experienced such touching moments with Monique. I live in Paris. Paris belongs to us. Nobody will ever take that away from me. I love going to the Sorbonne even with all of the madness now taking place.

"I'm pregnant with your baby. I love you like crazy, though I don't know why. You know, I come from rather simple, peasant stock."

"Is that where you get those beautiful, high cheek bones of yours?"

"Most probably. I look at these people around here, and I'm just like them. Good dependable, solid, peasant stock. My family loves me. I love them. You love me."

"I thought it was supposed to be my secret," I said, teasing her.

"Don't worry, your secret is safe. Then think of the interesting people I know about or met—Milo, Cleo, Roxanne, Peter, Alain, John, Chris, Ulla, Juliette, José and all of his gypsy friends, Dr. Brisson, Demetrios, Helen, and even Iris . . ."

She was looking at me with a bemused look on her face, as if it had been a rather insignificant event in both our lives, not worth worrying about anymore. I had to laugh. I held her closer and kissed her.

"And the taxi driver, what was his name?"

"Manos."

"Yes, Manos. Then Ron, Karen, *Madame* Commère, and the ones that I never met like the boy in Africa, or Gilles the photographer who was upset about those poor people killed in Africa, and who wanted to become a farmer so he could see life grow instead of being trampled upon by man's brutality and evilness.

"Then the forger with the unpronounceable name, and Ben, and Mohammed and his wife and their baby . . . and their family. And the hermit here in Normandy, and the banker who wanted to help him. And the half-naked Japanese guys who bought the paintings from Milo.

"And Mr. La Coupole, and your encounter with Ionesco and his wife, and the guys who wanted to buy your car in Yugoslavia, then Beauford, the American painter. Oh, and the mercenary friend of Demetrios and the Filipino guy.

"Then, Vito, Marty, Gary, *Madame* Richard and Didier the clerk at the hotel de Blois, you know the one who got married to that lady of the night. And the people at the restaurant that gave credit to Ben so he could eat. What was the name of the place?"

"*Chez Wadja.*"

"Yes, *Chez Wadja*. And Leon, Thea, and Leon's father so upset Leon had tried to sell the Monet painting. And the monks in Athos. Oh, and the little boy who gave you the oranges in Yugoslavia and the two Japanese kids in Tokyo. Now there is Adam with all of his revolutionary ideas. And *mes copains*"—and here she used the common French word for buddies— "at the Sorbonne who want to change the world overnight.

"And the kid you gave a ride to who might have stolen your checks. And the Thai girl who cried when President Kennedy got killed and her friend. Even the chicken Colonel that Demetrios wanted to kill. And Thea and her banker friend, and François the butler at Leon's father house.

"And now Pierre, Monique and her memories of Billy, the American boy she wanted to marry. Your parents. And all of the people you knew in the Army, and all of the others you told me about. Hey, those are the characters for your book," and she gave me a smile of complicity.

"I mean how often does a girl like me find herself in Normandy, an ancient place filled with history, and dance to the sounds of wonderful American music in an old farmhouse, the sky above filled with shiny stars, with the man she loves, and carrying his baby?"

She embraced me. She pulled out of her pocket the small pebbles she had earlier picked up at the beach. "Now I can tell my dad I was here in Normandy. Everything's special."

"You *are* special!" I said, because I remembered the first night she had come to Paris, and how pleased she had been when I told her she was. Then I only suspected it. Now I knew!

"You were beautiful tonight," she said, before kissing me goodnight. That night we slept peacefully and I did not wake her up.

I had gotten up early the following morning and went out to the barn where Pierre was milking the cows. His dexterity and technique were something to see: his fingers working the cows' teats, filling bucket after bucket with the rich, creamy liquid without missing a beat or wasting a drop.

The night before, we had talked briefly about the war, the long occupation of France by the Germans, and how it had affected him.

"Here in Normandy, we're grateful for what America sacrificed on our behalf. Americans are like our family."

"How was it really, the war I mean? It's hard for us to imagine," I said.

He stopped milking, stood, then went and poured the milk into a large container.

"I could take the *'boche,'*" he said, using the derogatory word the French apply to the Germans. "As a soldier, I understood the spoils of war. I remember I was only seven years old when World War I started. *La Grande Guerre* it was called. I saw my father go to war. I still remember the day he left and how my mother cried.

"I was the oldest of my brothers. My father told me that I was now the man responsible for the family. Then we had to evacuate Petit Fort Philippe, the small town where we lived, because the Germans were about to invade it. We had no place to go. I remember it so well—" he stopped, his hands shaking.

"But what the French did," he continued, "to other French during World War II—that *was* inexcusable. Nobody can tell you how you will react when your friends or neighbors turn into informers. That was the most difficult part for me. I had been a soldier—" he stopped again.

I could see the painful intensity of the memories he was sharing with me by looking at his face.

"French betraying their own people was not correct," he continued. "Most people who denounced others did it driven by personal hatred and jealousy and not because they were forced by the Gestapo. French people are quite capable of turning against their own neighbors.

"There were thousands of collaborators with the Nazis. I'm still ashamed. The victims were innocent, for the most part, of the crimes the Gestapo arrested them for," he said sadly.

It is true that this sad chapter of the French during World War II is one of the darkest and ugliest in their modern history. A most despicable thing they did to each other: Official government collaboration with the enemy.

The French, in their usual manner, had not really dealt with this part of their past. Not only in terms of the large number of French citizens who volunteered to help the Nazis, but also the brutality that took place after the war was over.

What was also somewhat comic, but sad, was that after the war everybody declared to have been a resistance fighter and not a collaborator with the Germans. Innocent people were killed, in many instances, due to personal vendettas versus being guilty of helping the Germans.

In fact, more often than not, the French tried everything they could to erase that dark chapter out of their lives, out of their history, by pretending that it never happened. It was a sore point with them when one brought it up.

Milo and I had once spent a whole evening arguing about it. He was both tortured and grateful nobody talked about it. In typical French logic, he hated those who tried.

At the same time, he championed the idea that truth had to be told—but not within his own lifetime. His position was: The French public was not ready for it.

"That makes no sense," I had argued. "On the one hand, you admire Americans for being so open about our warts, mistakes, about exposing the skeletons in our closets.

"You think that's how it should be. When we protest the Vietnam War, you cheer. Yet in the same breath, you accept that it's all right for the French to hide one of the ugliest chapters of their otherwise rich history."

"Alexandre, only people who are as old and jaded as we are, and comfortable with it, can hold two opposing views at the same time and manage to make them work."

"That's pretty cynical, not to mention unscrupulous."

"Of course, it is. You Americans are too sentimental. You see, we're an old country. France is in the very heart of Europe so people are either going somewhere or coming from somewhere.

"The hazard is that to get to wherever they are going, they have to enter our land. It's like we're the whore of Europe. When that happens, you develop a certain tolerance for the ambiguities that life presents."

"But don't you risk that such tolerance eventually becomes cynicism? Why not bring out the truth, deal with it, and be done? Wouldn't that be better?"

"You're much too naïve, always going on about moral rectitude . . . it's impractical and much too Quixotic. The world outside the U.S. is different. I'm a realist, *mon ami*. In our history we, French, have conquered and controlled other nations, other people, just like the Brits. I grant you, we haven't been as idealistic as you Americans."

"You think we're too idealistic?"

"Yes. That's why you're going to lose this war in Vietnam. You see, we were there long before you. We ruled the country. We did! Had you helped us when we needed it back in 1954, this war wouldn't be taking place and American boys wouldn't be dying. But you with your notions of freedom, equality, liberty and all of that. Yes, it's fine but . . ."

"I thought you admired us for our idealism?" I interrupted him.

"I do, but a dose of skepticism is healthy. What you don't understand is that you're dealing with human beings—imperfect. In a sense, you've corrupted the world in reverse. Other people just simply can't be like you. It can't happen. *C'est impossible!*"

"I don't agree."

"Of course you wouldn't. There is no way your system of apple pie, motherhood and Fourth of July can be introduced to people who are barely out of their diapers—politically speaking. They say: 'The Americans said it was going to be easy. How come it isn't? They sold us a bill of goods. So, fuck them! Let's burn their embassies down and throw the bums out of our country.

"Thus, you have to rely on the likes of Papa Doc, Franco, Oliveira Salazar, Somoza, Haile Selassie, Chiang Kai-Shek, Trujillo, Marcos, the Nguyens, and even Nasser—people unworthy of anyone's trust—all because of your maddening fear of communism: the FBI's 'Red Menace.' The greatest danger for the American Way of life! Let's see, there are, and tell me if I'm wrong: 57 varieties of communists in the land of Mickey Mouse, *non?*"

He laughed. He was referring to an American film in which senator McCarthy was portrayed as claiming to have discovered 57 kinds of spies in the State Department.

"That's what McCarthy said, yes," he continued. "The world isn't your oyster, *mon cher*. About the only thing you have going is that your pockets are filled with dollars, and they can buy you just about everything, maybe even democracy. But sometimes, expediency is more practical than the truth. I know it's pretty cynical, but that's the world we live in."

Milo's words seemed simplistic. In another sense, they had a ring of truth that was hard to dismiss. I was thinking about them as I watched Pierre milk the cows.

I went back in the house, and Monique gave me a large bowl of coffee and milk, which was utterly delicious. She had also made some hot chocolate for Lisa, as Monique did not permit Lisa to drink coffee. It was bad for the baby. I took the chocolate upstairs to Lisa.

"Wake up sleepy head. Wake up."

She opened her eyes. She had once said that she looked forward every morning to wake up and see me smiling at her. I told her she was not very difficult to please.

"I need to get up. I promised Monique I would go to the farmer's market with her. I wish our stay here would last forever and ever."

"I thought you liked living in Paris."

"I do, but this is also wonderful. I don't think I would be bored here. What about you?"

"I don't know. I like living in the city. I miss the sounds and madness of big cities. I'm a child of the city. It controls me. I find safety in the city. I find comfort in the city. In the countryside I'm lost."

"When you are rich and famous, let's buy a farm here and come as often as we can," she said, cheerfully.

"What am I going to do to become rich and famous?"

"Aren't you going to write a book and have it become a bestseller?"

I laughed. Lisa never allowed me to forget the book. She never failed to make a connection to it no matter how farfetched the whole idea seemed.

She had told me I was kidding myself if I thought she would let me forget it. She had decided that I had to write it, and that was all there was to it.

Where did women get the notion the men they loved could get to do and be whatever they wanted? I guess it was because sometimes it worked. I did not know of any man who remained immovable in front of a woman who loved him and believed in him.

It did something for your psyche to hear the woman you loved tell you that you were capable of moving mountains. Some men actually did. I wondered how I could become one of them.

When we came back from Normandy, Lisa invited Adam to come and have dinner with us before I left for Prague.

215

"You must go, Alex. You must. It will make a big difference!" He really believed it.

Lisa had cooked some of her famous chili, and Adam was quite taken by it, as he had never tasted chili before.

"Marvelous. I love it! My compliments to the chef. You must give me the formula, no I mean the recipe, so I can make it for my mother when I go home."

That pleased her. Though she had told him he could use the room at any time, he had used it sporadically. Very often, he, Ulla, and Lisa would huddle together and have discreet discussions while quietly poring over a map of Paris, making notes and seemingly keen in making sure they knew and understood the layout of the land.

They seemed secretive about this activity. I never asked her about it. I figured if Lisa wanted me to know she would tell me.

The conviction in Adam's voice that evening about my trip to Prague was strong, passionate, and almost childlike. But it showed a kind of desperation that only comes from the very depths of one's soul when you sense that everything is about go to the shits.

"Why do you say that?" I asked him regarding my trip to Prague.

"Because only you Americans understand and can help us."

"Adam, I'm nobody. I'm only one person. I couldn't help your country even if all of my being were to wish it."

"It doesn't matter. Yes, you're only one person and Lisa's another, and Ulla is another, and José . . . don't you see? That's how we must begin. You must come back and tell the truth. The American public will believe it!"

"I'm not sure the American people are in a position or mood to look at what's going on in your country. Their immediate concerns are in the jungles of Vietnam."

"Yes, that's true, but one must never lose hope. The more other people know about our situation the more they'll help us. I know it!"

His conviction was so touching and so unreal, I could not argue with him. His eyes sparkled and shone with the brilliance of a flame that would not die, however many times others tried to extinguish it. For him, a lone American showing up in Prague and asking questions was enough.

It would be the beginning of others and yet others, until, somehow, the total mass of the idea of a free America would show up in Prague; thus, his country, his people, he himself, would be rid of the Russian yoke.

How simple the gods make the innocent at heart behave. By seeing his face emaciated yet filled with hope, that only one as young as he was can have, it made me think only the pure and blessed believe in miracles. Lisa was also looking at me as, if, somehow, I would be strong enough to save Adam's dreams.

How I wished to be the man who could rise to that pinnacle where both of these lovely and mad people wanted to place me. Not too long ago, back in Yugoslavia, I had needed a miracle and it had not happened.

Adam's baby face made me feel old. Was I ever that young? How long ago was it? Was I ever such a dreamer? Had I lost the incredible innocence of the pure at heart? Did I ever have it? How unreal, silly, and noble their sentiments were.

I felt depressed because, in my cynicism, I was betraying what is noble and honest in all of us. Somehow, I was excusing my lack of valor and courage. I could no more save Adam's dream of his revolution, than I could save the world from annihilating itself. The helplessness this sentiment brought me was painful.

"I would look after Lisa for you. I would protect her with my life," Adam said, forcefully. Lisa gave him a wonderful smile and hugged him.

How sweet and wonderful his sentiments were. Adam's words were so touching, so powerful, yet so desperate. They came from the middle of his guts, which is where most ancient peoples believe our very being exists. I hugged him. If only I could make this world worthy of them, worthy of the child Lisa was carrying.

But, alas, no. Life sucks. It's a game played by imbeciles. Then, you died.

Lisa wanted to come to Orly airport with me, but I asked her not to. There is coldness, harshness about airport terminals—goodbyes make them inhuman, sterile, and devastating. She stood on the balcony, outside our apartment, without moving.

She tried to hide her tears. As the taxi pulled away from the curb, I saw this lovely woman—who had now become so entwined in my life I could not imagine living without her—letting her sad tears roll down her cheeks.

"But absence makes the heart grow fonder," I had said before leaving.

"Yeah, people who say that have no hearts."

"I'll call you every day."

"It's not the same. Besides, I know what it's like trying to phone from cities like Prague." She was right.

The night before I left, Lisa's lovemaking seemed so desperate, so wanting. She could not have enough of me. Her womb was already filled with so much of me but it did not seem enough for her.

"I want you so much. Please don't stop. I want you to fill my heart, my soul, my body with the life that flows out of you. I want all of you. I know I'm already carrying so much of your life, but I want more. I love you so much, oh, God so much! I will never get enough of you.

"I want to feel you everywhere. I want you to own me, to surrender to you. I want to be yours forever and always. I want you never to stop loving me. Come back to me, please, come back to me safe . . ."

Oh, Lisa, mon amour, lovely, beautiful, innocent, and sweet Lisa. I will never be able to thank the gods for your love even if I live until the sun dies. I do not know how it has happened that you came into my life.

By what design you were brought to me. And now you are carrying a baby, our baby. I hope I will be a good father. Oh, gods that rule this universe and the destinies of men, please keep her safe. I do not ask for much.

Please keep her well and protect her. Without her love, I am nothing. I am unworthy. She makes me worthy of living. Please let her love me until the moon falls out of the sky. It is not a lot that I ask. Her love is so sweet, so pure, and so honest. I do not ask anymore why she came to me. All I know is she is here, and for me that is enough. Protect her dear gods, just like Adam said he would protect her. She is so innocent. Do not make her suffer. Make me suffer, instead.

I love her. She is my life. That is all I know!

Such were my prayers.

TEN

Prague, on this beautiful spring day, was going through a festival of sorts, but my spirits, thoughts, my heart, were with Lisa back in Paris. From the airport and as the taxi drove into the city, I could sense an incredible feeling in the air; an over-the-top madness.

The possibility the Czechoslovakian people could actually live their own destinies as opposed to dreaming about them, and having others impose their sick plans—nightmares—on them.

From what I remembered of my first visit here, the dullness of the city had changed and now it was full of optimism. Colorful posters announcing whatever it was—I could not read the language—were everywhere.

"I envy you. I want to be there, and I want to be here. I don't know what to do," Adam said, just before he left the night he came to the apartment for dinner on the eve of my trip to Prague.

Adam was happy that Alain had asked me to go to Prague, but frustrated that he could not come with me.

"Try to finish what you're doing here then go back," Lisa said.

"Yes, but if something bad happens over there, I'm here and go back to nothing," Adams said, darkly.

"One thing at a time. Those are life's contradictions. I don't know how you resolve this, nobody does," I said.

"I want to do both," he said, frustrated.

He had given me several names and addresses of his friends in Prague. He thought they would be willing to meet with me. Though he was afraid I would most likely be searched at the airport, he was confident I could talk my way out of any trouble.

I was touched and fearful I was not up to the task he had imagined I could do. Alain, on the other hand, had said he would telex some names in a coded manner so as not to alert the authorities' suspicions.

In both cases, I thought they were pissing in the wind. If people Adam and Alain wanted me to meet—people free of the lingering fear that always resides in the human spirit even when we are desperately struggling for changes to make our lives better—it would be a miracle.

I did not believe in miracles, especially when it came to political repression. I was not that naïve to ignore the dangers these people were facing, and how wary they were of strangers who often come with the best intentions but with empty hands.

One person I had promised to try to see at all costs was Adam's mother. She was a French teacher, who had managed to survive all the political repression her country had suffered; however, things were very iffy for her as well.

Adam had reassured me she knew what she was doing. The last time he had talked to her on the phone, she had said I was to come to her apartment and she even invited me to stay with her. Alain did not think that was a good idea but he left it up to me. There was a Holiday Inn in Prague, and he had reserved a room.

Here was one of the most repressive countries in the world, run by a cadre of scum—not unlike the scums Big D. told me he would be happy to kill—and my capitalist compatriots were doing business with them. This always drove me crazy. But Alain also saw the practical side of this.

"Who else but Americans would dare go into a communist country and build Holiday Inns?" he said. "Only Americans understand money has no political leanings, no political history, no morality, and no memory. Power comes in one color: dollar green. Besides, the phone at the Inn probably works."

He had a point. I was not searched at the airport to my great relief. I decided to stay at the Inn, as I did not want to press my luck by going to stay with Adam's mother. I called Paris, and the gods were smiling at me because Lisa answered the phone on the second ring.

"No, I haven't forgotten you. Even after I die, I'll remember you," I said.

"I miss you so much," she said. Her voice broke, and my heart cried, too.

"OK, while the line is clear, I just got here. I'm going to try to visit Adam's mother. I'll call you tonight or early in the morning. Let's hope the Holiday Inn has paid the phone bill on time."

I was thankful for the phone not acting up. Lisa said that Madame Commère had come to see her, and had stayed for a while telling her how her own husband had gone on a business trip and had been absent for two full days.

"*Les plus longues journées de ma vie . . . terrible, terrible.*" Madame Commère had said.

Lisa had imitated the concierge, as she had complained that those two days of her husband's absence had been the longest and worse days of her life. I laughed and felt better that Lisa could laugh at herself. My hopes were that her sense of humor could sustain her during our separation.

Adam had called his mother from Paris and told me she was expecting me. The taxi took me to the outskirts of Prague. Adam's mother lived in a small apartment building that somehow had survived the sad and desolate tracts of drab buildings of the communist era construction.

Row after row of ugly looking apartment buildings that disappeared in the horizon. The sameness was crushing. Her building seemed a bit of an oasis in an otherwise manmade and bleak landscape.

His mother was a very cultured, simple, and slight woman. You could immediately tell she was a person of strong convictions and character, who had come to her position in life not by compromise but because others could not measure up to her. She always thought before speaking. Her words were never spoken in vain.

She volunteered to show me the neighborhood. We knew why. Houses in this part of the world have too many ears. She was in the process of writing a long critique about one of Eugène Ionesco's plays: *The Bald Soprano*. She had been to Paris twice, had met Ionesco, and kept a correspondence with him.

I had also met Ionesco in Paris, quite by accident. One day, while I was having breakfast, Mr. La Coupole came by and asked if I could help one of his regular clients translate a couple of paragraphs from the American publication he was reading. It turned out this man was Ionesco, and he was reading the *New Yorker* magazine.

He was there with his wife, a small, charming lady. For about an hour, we sat and talked, mostly about America. He was very familiar with the States. It was really a great treat for me.

His wife addressed me as *"Monsieur,"* and when she referred to Ionesco, she would either say: *"Mon mari,"* or *"Eugène,"* which made an impression on me.

A person of Ionesco's literary status is usually addressed, in French, as *"Maître"* a high form of respect. I do not know why but his wife calling him *"Mon mari,"* or *"Eugène"* struck me in an odd way. I guess, I expected her to call him *"Mon cher Maître."*

When I told Ben that I had met Ionesco, he was impressed and got a kick out of my reaction to how Mrs. Ionesco addressed her husband.

"Come on," Ben said as he laughed. "She's married to *Eugène*. He's her husband, the guy who takes out the garbage or fixes the leaking pipe."

I could not quite picture the author of *Rhinoceros* and the *Lesson*, taking out the garbage or wielding a pipe wrench in his hand trying to stop a leak under the kitchen sink.

Adam's mother was thrilled upon getting her son's letters. He had written two just in case they confiscated one of them. One letter was in the suitcase and the other I carried with me. I had not been searched so she was delighted and grateful both letters had gotten through.

When I handed her the letters, she took them and very lovingly rubbed her hand over them. She smelled them as if searching for traces of Adam's scent.

"Vous me permettez de lire," she asked, shyly.

"Bien sûr."

She looked at me slightly embarrassed and smiling. It was touching to see her reaction. We walked in silence while she read the letters. You could tell how happy she was to receive news directly from Adam. It reminded me of Monique back in Normandy reading the letter she had from Billy, the GI she had almost married.

"It's such a pleasure to read them. Thank you for bringing them," she said, with a shy smile on her face. She put the letters in her pocket. "Do you think America will intervene?"

"No." We both knew there was no reason to pretend.

I had the sad impression the question had been nagging her since I arrived—not because she did not know the answer but because the heart always hopes.

"I have tried to make that clear to Adam, but he's only a boy, an innocent boy full of dreams."

"Yes, but a strong boy."

"Yes, that's what I fear. Strength and innocence."

"Do you think the Russians will invade?"

"One has to be realistic. I try to put myself in their shoes. Yes, I would invade. They cannot just sit there and do nothing. They must hang onto their illusion of power but it will end one day. Maybe not in the near future, but it will end. I know it sounds *farfelu,* but—" she stopped.

The most benign interpretations of the French word *farfelu* are weird, off the wall . . . bizarre. I could tell the thoughts she was sharing with me were painful. Her face looked sad and distant.

It was strange to hear her talk about invasion and in the same breath also talk about the day the Russians would leave. Based on what I knew and had read, Russians walking away from their empire seemed, indeed, *farfelu.*

How many generations of political and social slavery does it take to make people free, for them to seek out their own destiny without an ugly big brother around? We fantasize it in our heads and end up calling it hope.

We cling to this fantasy because there is no alternative. Otherwise, we might as well throw ourselves under the bus. Boy, the world sure as hell ain't a nice place, I thought.

When she resumed talking her voice was soft—down to a whisper— as if afraid she would reveal too much of her most intimate feelings, yet anxious to share her ideas and thoughts.

"Do you speak German?" she asked.

"No."

"It was my second language growing up."

"How many languages do you speak?"

"Slovak and Czech, which are similar. Russian, German, French, English, and a little Hungarian."

"Why did you ask me if I spoke German?"

"It has to do with Einstein and what he said about historical events in Russia. Many people thought he was from the left. What Einstein said was, he respected what Lenin was trying to do in Russia—his commitment to social justice—but not Lenin's political philosophy. It is a clear distinction. Of course, Einstein was totally opposed to the *methods* Lenin used. The Russian character is so contradictory."

"Do you admire the Russians?"

"Admire is a strong word. It's a beautiful country. I respect their history, their traditions, and their rich culture. Think how poor we would be if they had not given the world: Tolstoy, Pushkin, Stravinsky, Chagall, Mandelstam, Akhmatova, Tchaikovsky, Nabokov, Kandinsky, Pasternak. The list is endless. Great people but so troubled and completely enslaved by their leaders.

"They have always been their own worst enemies. They defeated Hitler at such human costs and instead of giving themselves, or us, freedom, we all ended up with Stalin. One kind of fascism was replaced by another.

"When you look at their history, what they have done was because they feared themselves and not because they were powerful or wise. The day they leave my country, they will discover they have gained nothing. They are not free, not any more than we are. We're all losers in this madness."

"Do you think one day they will leave?"

"Yes, it's inevitable. When they do, there will come a time when many of us in our country will long for those days of dreariness, intimidation, silence, and slavery. Was it not the great Shakespeare who said, it is better to deal with the evil we know than the evil we don't know? Freedom is a beast that needs to be managed with a great deal of care. I'm afraid we don't have much experience doing that."

Her words had been uttered with simplicity. She put her arm though mine and now spoke in a more cheerful note.

"But here I'm babbling on like some demented person. We must return to the house so I can make you some tea. And you are going to be a father," she said, with a big smile on her face.

"Yes."

"You must tell me all about your Lisa and the others and, of course, my Adam. What name will you give the baby?"

"I don't know. Lisa will select the name. She's convinced we'll have a girl."

"*C'est beau, ça*"—it's beautiful.

The visit to Adam's mother was unique, and though I saw the depressing lucidity of her ideas, she also managed to make them appear exciting. I got a glimpse as to why Adam seemed to have the strength of character that attracted people to him.

Once, during the conversation, she commented on the silliness of the Czechoslovakian government wanting to bring Adam back by canceling his scholarship to the Sorbonne under pressure from the French.

She had no kind words for the French government either, but she saw what was happening as an exercise for Adam's sake. He had to learn the hard way.

That is how character was forged.

Our view of the world was always filtered through what we knew as citizens of our respective countries. Most of us grew up accepting certain things, attitudes, behaviors, traditions—our own cultural definitions— without ever stepping outside these confines and exposing ourselves to other ideas, other realities.

Yet my own travels—my discoveries of the world outside the U.S. and outside my narrow view—showed me a much different story. The world was varied, exotic, dangerous, often hostile and impossible to get a fix on.

What I knew and believed in could easily be stuffed into a small capsule and that would be the end of it. I knew it was safe. I was safe. My life was not in a "worker's paradise" where there would be a knock on my door, in the middle of the night, and my family would never hear from me again.

That reality existed in Adam's life, in his mother's life, and in the lives of people living under repressive governments. Yet nowhere did I get a sense of foreboding from her, of an impending sense of doom.

On the contrary, she seemed to be rather cheerful about her life— troubled by it, certainly—but also rising above the pettiness of daily living. Perhaps, this was just a result of years and years of fearing the worst that one ends up not taking it seriously anymore.

The heart finally plays the ultimate trick, leading us to take chances by spraying a fine mist on our psyche, and blinding us until it is too late. The knock on the door, in the middle of the night, is the ultimate abstraction of our lives.

Humans are capable of just about everything and can, in fact, get used to everything—even the worst from each other—given enough time. We are both victims and victimizers.

Adam's mother knew all about Ulla and Lisa, and hearing some additional details directly from me gave her an immediate pleasure.

"I know so much about all of you through what Adam has said and written that I think of you; in fact, as being part of my own family. I'm so grateful he has found such wonderful friends."

She embraced me. I noticed that over her small dinner table there was a photo of Ulla, Lisa, and some other people. She had made a circle around Lisa and Ulla's faces maybe to make sure she would recognize them if she ever met them. After we had some tea, she offered to accompany me to find a taxi.

"I'm not a fool who thinks the house may not be bugged. It probably isn't, though I can't speak with absolute certainty."

We were walking down the street. I did not see a taxi or a taxi station anywhere. It did not appear likely I would find a taxi in this part of the city.

"You must be careful with your luggage at the hotel. Make sure you leave no documents around. Always take them with you. I'm sure you understand the need to be very careful."

"I do."

"*Parfait.*" She smiled. A weight had been lifted off her shoulders. "Do you plan on staying long around our city?"

"I don't know. Alain just asked me to come and look around. Talk to a few people if I can find them."

"Yes, Adam also told me that. I know the people he wants you to talk to. He said so in his letters."

I must have made a face because she was soon smiling. "He wrote in code," she continued. "It's our own code. I know what he's looking for."

That was their reality: Trust no one, communicate in code, and never leave compromising documents around for prying eyes. How can one live like that?

"I'll get someone to come and see you at your hotel. Don't worry it will be safe. You may have to contribute some dollars, but it's still for a good cause," she added, smiling.

Her suggestion appeared as if nothing were out of the ordinary—perfectly normal. As we got to the corner of the street, we saw only one car going exactly in the opposite direction from us.

She turned around and put her hand up. The car made a U-turn, came over, and stopped at the curb right next to us.

"It's not a regular taxi, but he'll take you back to your hotel. Pay him in dollars and you'll make a friend."

"Do you know him?"

"No, that's just how people who have cars here try to make extra money. Don't worry. The fare should be around four of your dollars. Don't give him more than five."

With that she embraced me, kissed me on both cheeks, said something to the driver, a man with a huge mustache who smiled, and I was driven back to the Holiday Inn. I gave him ten dollars the smallest bill I had with me. He could not thank me enough.

"Merci, merci."

Ben would have been proud and happy of my contribution to the local economy. There was a message from Alain that he would contact me later. I went up to my room and tried calling Paris, but the operator said the lines were busy so I went out for a walk. Prague seemed to be covered with confetti and posters as if some giant carnival was taking place.

The city that was gray the first time I visited it, had now undergone quite a change. With its traditional European architecture, it did have lots of charm reminding me of Paris. The atmosphere was festive.

There was also a sense of anxiety in the air, however. It was as if people were taking advantage of the last change before the storm. Adam's mother had been very convincing and certain.

I walked by the river and found myself following groups of people onto the St. Charles Bridge that spans the river. Though covered with scaffolding at one end, it had not prevented people from gathering. It was a nice, old bridge, lined up with statues and with a beautiful view of Prague.

The bridge was filled with lots of people. The best way to describe the scene would be that it resembled a giant outdoor rally. The mostly young crowd was singing a mixture of their own folk music, and American peace songs—the whole set up seemed logical but incongruous.

Plenty of guitars and bearded guys with long hair accompanied by lovely women with their striking high cheek boned faces, some dressed in their native costumes, all talking, laughing, and enjoying a beautiful spring day. But there were plenty of sad and worried faces as well.

It was a day to just be, and not a day to fear the storm everyone knew was on its way, like a giant tidal wave, unpredictable, dangerous, merciless, and ready to destroy all of them in its path, along with their dreams.

The conversations I heard were lively and passionate. The human connection was not broken due to my inability to understand what they were saying. One did not need to understand the language because the syntax used was the syntax of the human heart seeking freedom.

There was no need of a Berlitz dictionary or a United Nations voice translating what they were saying—fear was not new but it was there, basic, naked, and raw. Everyone understood. We were all inside the same time capsule.

Those people were deciding—on that bridge, on a beautiful day—what their world was going to be. Yes, invading armies would crush them, and for many that might turn out to be their last spring, but they dared to dream of a better life.

A passing fantasy gripped me for one flashing moment: I wished with all of my heart for the miracle Adam and Lisa wanted. I thought why not? Why in the fuck not?

How easy it is for the heart to be naïve and impractical. The truth of their lives had to be measured by the present reality, just as the sun was now warming us up.

What did they expect? What could they expect? Would their lives turn into . . . what? Yet, I felt that of our different positions, they were free, and I was not—strange feeling.

I was not as free as they were for at that moment they had seen and understood what life had in store for them, and that reality made them freer than I who was not facing such a dire future. I felt out of touch and without roots. Their fears put them in touch with who they were.

My own fears made me feel sorry for myself, for my lack of resolve, and maybe my lack of courage. Again, the memory of the young boy in Africa who had gotten himself killed came back to me. He would have been right at home here. He would have understood.

He was just like those kids I was now hearing sing "We Shall Overcome", sounding preposterous, and it was.

I thought of Adam suffering that he could not be in Paris and here at the same time. True, his country would be invaded but his compatriots' dreams would never die.

His dreams, their dreams, were as alive as the ones that live and continue to live in the cemetery in Normandy. Lisa's father was right; those dreams had not died, and would never die!

But I also felt depressed, and found myself wondering why I had come to Prague in the first place. What was I seeking to accomplish in what Milo would have said to be another Quixotic run at the windmills of oppression?

I started to walk back to the hotel. In another sense, I also felt like just another vulgar invader. I had come here to snoop, to bring back with me, what?

Sad memories of how impotent we all were in the face of brutal, cold, naked force? People often say that life must go on. They leave out the other side of the equation: death most go on, too.

I got a bit lost in the city. I did not feel like playing tourist and eventually found my way back to the Holiday Inn. There were no messages. I tried calling Paris.

I wanted to talk to Lisa just to hear her voice, to tell her what I was feeling; however, the operator said the lines were still busy that I should book the call in advance, which I did without much hope of getting through.

Back in my room, I examined my belongings very closely, and could not detect any displacement, though I had to admit I had not paid much attention before I left the room earlier. Many novels I had read about spying came to mind.

I should have asked Alain about this, I thought. Though, I hoped my notes would not give anybody a reason to suspect anything—vain hope. Nevertheless, the truth was that I had to be very careful. Message received and understood.

I had not worked on the translation of *L'Étranger* in a while, so I took it out. I had now translated most of the first chapter. It had been tough going because I had been so careful to make sure I would not only translate the text, but also make the translation transcend both the culture and the language barriers.

I wanted to get as close to the spirit and intent of Camus as I could. *L'Étranger* is an exciting and complex book. I read and reread the text and all of the references I could find, but that did not make things any easier.

Studying and trying to understand the narrative was like being inside a dangerous, dark, and dense jungle where you were confronted with the reality of defining your own truth.

Camus's contention was that what made his character Mersault a "stranger" to society came about because he did not cry at his mother's funeral; thus, he risked being condemned to die. He also argued, that *L'Étranger* "is not about playing the game."

For the "game," he writes, "is to lie as lying is not only saying that which is not. It is also, above all, saying more than what it is, and when it comes to the human heart saying more than what we feel."

We did this every day to make our lives easier, Camus maintained. Mersault, in *L'Étranger,* did not want to simplify life. He says who he is. He refuses to give a *higher* value to his sentiments and, of course, with his attitude, society immediately feels threatened.

It wants to force him to say that he "regrets" his crime, which according to society is a reasonable thing to do. Mersault refused to do so. His response to such demands was that it was more of an irritant than a true regret.

And he rested his case. It was what condemned him. *L'Étranger,* was the story of a man who without histrionics accepted dying for his truth, which, Camus argued, made Mersault free. Some tough cookie this Mersault character. So was Camus.

Lisa had humored me at how I reflected upon, analyzed, and agonized over each word, each sentence, seeking the nuances of the original. What always brought me a great deal of pleasure was that Camus's writing was so sparse, economical, and lucid.

The hardest part was not in trying to translate the words, but in trying to find what was behind the words.

I had asked Lisa one day not long after I started working on the translation, if she wanted to do something special during the school break.

"Like what?"

"Go to Lourmarin, and afterward go to Morocco and catch some sun."

"What's in Lourmarin?"

"That's where Camus is buried."

"I didn't know the name. Where is it?"

"It's somewhere in the south of France."

So, it was that on the eve of Camus's death anniversary—January 4, 1968—we found ourselves on a night train going to visit Lourmarin. Camus had been killed in a car crash in 1960. The countryside was bleak, but it was also good to get away from Paris if only for a day or so.

We took one of those night trains that offered *couchettes* for sleeping. The train would drop us off in the morning, and then we would take the express back to Paris in the evening. Lisa did not want to go to Morocco.

From the small train station in Lourmarin, a taxi took us on a tour. It was a typical small French town. The church was right next to the office of the tax collector. Very apropos, I thought.

The taxman stands at the door of the church when they wheel you in, and hands you your final tax bill, which he will wait to collect—when they wheel you out feet first—his cut of *les impôts*—taxes, that France collects from every French citizen who dies.

There were a few cars on the road and the local cemetery, whose location was shown by a handmade sign posted near a street intersection, was not far.

I asked the taxi driver if by any chance he knew where Camus's house was. He did. He drove us by it. The house was in good shape, and from what I saw it was a simple house not different from the houses next to it.

You could tell the taxi driver was rather curious about a couple of Americans showing up in the dead of winter to visit a cemetery, though he did not ask any questions.

The weather was cold, but not aggressively so. Camus's tomb was something else.

It looked abandoned. It was abandoned!

It was as if no one had been there for a long while to take care of it, with weeds growing around it. I was shocked. I suppose, I had expected something more dignified. I was disappointed and saddened by what I saw.

It was also disconcerting: Here was the tomb of the writer who had won the Nobel Prize for Literature in 1957, and yet there appeared to be no effort to maintain the tomb properly, to make it presentable.

We had come unannounced, had found no one home with all the closets open, and had perhaps intruded upon an ugly family secret. It felt that way. We stood by the tomb for a long time, while the taxi driver stood at the entrance of the cemetery smoking.

I did not know what I had expected to find. It was painful and depressing that the grave of the one of the most original thinkers and literary figures of his century seemed to have been left to the ravages of time. Maybe we had come in between regular cleaning times.

Lisa was more disappointed for me than for her. I had insisted on coming because I thought it would help me gain some kind of insight into the man, but upon seeing the state of the tomb I had gained nothing and I felt guilty.

I was fighting like crazy not to have this feeling even though it was the truth, and the truth shouted back at me that when a person is dead, that person is dead. End of the story.

The message was clear: Life is never sentimental about death. We humans are. Lisa and I walked back to the taxi driver and I asked him if he knew who took care of the tomb, but he did not. He seemed intrigued I was making a big deal out of the situation.

I asked him if he thought Camus was important in the scheme of things, he said he thought he was but did not give this fact much significance. Perfectly fitting with what Mersault would have said in *L'Étranger*. Camus would probably have appreciated it, too, I thought.

Nevertheless, I gave the taxi driver some money and asked him to please go find a florist, buy some flowers, and bring them while we waited for him. He was kind of surprised at my request. Lisa decided to go with him at the last minute.

Life has a way of making a fool out of all of us. We think we have a fix on it and *wham*! We get it right between the eyes, and off we go to lick our wounds. I was struggling with the idea of defining what was important: Was it Camus the man or was it Camus the writer?

It seemed Camus, the writer, had nothing to do with the man buried here. It was a very strange sensation. I tried to reconcile the idea in my head, and I could not do it. The writer was alive beyond his grave, but the man buried here was turning into dust. Who was I looking for? Was it possible to separate the man from his art?

I always thought the two were tied together, but for some reason it did not seem that way as I stood looking down at the tomb. What made him write the things he wrote about with such passion? The man or his art? Seeing the neglected tomb of Camus was sobering and painful.

I started to pull out some weeds then stopped. It felt like I was doing it for convention's sake. What was forcing me to pull out the weeds, politeness or some vague notion about what one was supposed to do?

I did not feel honest about doing it. It did not come from my guts, and I resented what I was doing because it was dishonest. It was phony. Camus was right. One cannot live a lie! One must live an "authentic" life. One must stop playing the "game." I was truly lost.

Talk about an out-of-body experience. Death was the great equalizer that nobody escapes. You could write one of the greatest novels of all times and end up with weeds growing out of your groin.

How does a man find the strength to focus on a small portion of his life and start reflecting on it with such intensity, honesty, that the result is *L'Étranger*?

How does that happen? By what miracle? Is it the accumulation of what has gone on before since the beginning of time that eventually catches up with him and shows man what he is worth?

Does death end all?

What happens to that which makes a person alive? One day, it is there for the whole world to see, and the next day it is gone. Do we become stardust and join the cosmos, our original point of departure? Or go to paradise or hell, as some religions would have us believe?

I wish I understood. The sun came out while I was waiting for Lisa and the taxi driver. It was not so gray, damp, and cold as it had been early in the morning.

Lisa and the taxi driver finally came back. She walked to where I was standing and put the flowers on the tomb. She took my hand, and we silently walked back to the car.

After having a hot and rather somber lunch at a small family restaurant by the train station, we took the train back to Paris. I was in the dumps. The question that had been nagging me for a long time had not been resolved.

"Do you know what the taxi driver said?" She asked.

"What?"

"Votre bon homme est un mec très chic."

It seems one of the highest compliments a Frenchman can make to another man is to call him *chic*—meaning, he has class. He has *savoir faire*. He is cool. Lisa was pleased by the compliment.

"He said that?"

"Yes. It was so sweet of him. I told him I agreed." Lisa gave me a big hug.

"Why did he say that?"

"He said he's never heard or seen anybody come here in the dead of winter to bring flowers to Camus."

"So, who's buried there? The writer or the man?"

"Both. Why separate them?"

"I don't know," I answered, still troubled by what I had seen and about my feelings.

"Are you disappointed?" She was holding my hand in an attempt to console me.

"Yes, but I don't know why."

"To me they are the same. The artist can't live outside his art. He lives inside it. That's what makes him whole and unique. That's what he shows the rest of us. That's how he teaches us what's important in trying to understand where we're going, who we are—life!"

What she was saying made sense up to a certain point, but did not clarify the question for me. Something was missing. I could not figure out what it was. Was the writer of *L'Étranger* buried there or was the man? Were they the same, as Lisa argued?

The question drove me crazy because I could not get a fix on it. Camus loved the sun of his native Algeria. Mersault loved the sun of his native Algeria—perhaps Lisa was right.

Camus had died and is buried in a cold climate, in some nondescript town, in the middle of France, which was not really his *patrie* or his *pays*. The French make a distinction between *la patrie*, which is the nation or country, and *le pays*, which is a region.

It is Camus's alter ego, Mersault, who lives on, while his progenitor is buried in some frozen ground apparently half-forgotten even by his most immediate folk. Was there an answer to the question of who we are? Where the truth is?

We know when and where we are born. Life is partially designed for us to spend the rest of our days wondering when and where we are going to die.

If I had been expecting some kind of thunder and lightning from the heavens to illuminate Camus the man, it had not happened. I felt let down. Lisa, however, did not think the trip had been a total waste.

At least I saw with my own eyes where Camus was buried. One thing remained, she insisted, and that was Camus, the artist. His writings were alive and doing well, very well. Thus, the writer and the man being one, as she argued, had not disappeared into the dustbin of nihility.

On the contrary, they were complementing each other. I should concentrate on the writing and not on the other stuff. Lisa, as always, managed to get to the heart of the matter without wasting time.

The phone rang in my hotel room. It was my call to France. Lisa sounded less agitated than earlier in the day. I briefly told her of my visit to Adam's mother without going into details and that I had been working on the translation.

She told me her mother had called to see how things were going. Her father was now thinking that when the baby was born, the whole family should come to Paris and meet the new member of the family and, in passing, meet the man Lisa had chosen to spend the rest of her life.

I had thought we should go back to the States. When Lisa suggested it, her mother said it was too much for a baby so young to be traveling. In her view, it was better for the rest of the family to come to Paris. It was the grandmother talking. Grandmothers are usually the wisest.

"I miss you," Lisa said. "I should have gone with you."

"I asked you."

"I know. Anyway, you didn't really want me to go. I know your fear about something going wrong."

Since Lisa had come back into my life, we had not been separated. Other than the daily absences for work or school, we had been as close as any two people can be. I did not remember having been this way with Cécile.

I guess it had to do with the fact Cécile had her own digs, so it was not unusual for her to go back to her place, while I was away, so to be separated seemed normal.

With Lisa that had not been the case. From the moment she came back, we had been together. At the beginning, she counted the days we had been together as she did not want to lose them, as if counting them she would keep them alive, not faded yesterdays.

She had told me, she was faithfully keeping a journal and that one day, when I no longer loved her, she would show it to me to shame me back into loving her.

"How do you know that one day I won't love you?"

"I don't. This is just a warning ahead of time not to stop."

"You think it's possible to fall out of love?"

"Yes."

"So you will fall out of love with me?"

"No!"

"Wait a second; you said it's possible to fall out of love. When I ask you if you will fall out of love with me, you say no."

"I'm talking about other people, *pas de moi.*"

"Of course." I laughed.

We were in the bathtub when she had said this. The apartment had a great old-fashioned bathtub with carved spindly legs, elaborate claw feet, and a basin large enough for three people.

One day, she had prepared a bath for me and it was a pleasant discovery Lisa knew something about massage, herbs, and water temperatures associated with this ritual.

She had told me one of the countries where her father and the family had lived was Japan. She thought a warm bath and a nice rubdown always made life more pleasant.

My memories of this kind of situation were not quite like hers. When I was in Japan, while in the Army, my visits to bathhouses were for less than family-like purposes.

While they lived in Japan, the two women who came with the rented house had always insisted the whole family be given a massage after their baths. Soon everyone was enjoying this most luxurious of pleasures.

Lisa had learned how to give a massage, and I always felt like a brand-new person after she did it. She even managed to find old Japanese records we played while bathing, adding a certain peaceful quality to the whole ceremony.

The massage had to be done in a certain way. The body had to be treated in a very special manner to make sure the massage was most effective. Lisa believed the human body was an incredible work of art and creation.

I once tried giving her a massage, and she said all I did was tickle her so she never let me do it again.

Here in Prague, I felt so far away from her. I missed her a lot. Missed her in the simplest of things she did: her laughter, her rituals, her teasing me about my brooding, her desire to please me even though she knew that just being around her was more than enough for me to be happy.

I missed not being right next to her when she woke up in the morning, that I could not put my arms around her and hold her close.

I would miss not taking her to *Chez Berthillon* and buying her favorite exotic ice cream and *marron glacés*, those delicious glazed chestnuts she was so fond of.

I was sorry it would be a while before we would go see those wonderful Fred Astaire/Ginger Rogers movies, in which dancing was supreme or go and see *Casablanca*. She thought it was the best love story ever.

"I thought ours was the best," I complained.

"It is. I'm talking about a movie."

"Absolutely!"

And our beloved *Cinémathèque* where we had spent innumerable nights watching great films. It had sadly become another victim of the madness going on in Paris, as its director—Henri Langlois—had become embroiled in the protests.

The powers-that-be did not like him because he was a liberal supporting the students, so they fired him. It led thousands of people to demonstrate in support of Langlois. Lisa did not need to encourage me to go out and protest.

"You see, protesting against injustice isn't bad, is it?" she said, as we marched.

Though it is in Hollywood or in lesser-known places where films are made, it is in Paris that they are loved and appreciated in a very special way.

One can literally go and see a different movie every night of the year and not see the same film twice. Lisa and I enjoyed our share of great and wonderful films from around the world.

I would miss not going shopping with her. Now that she was pregnant, the looks on the men's faces at the weekly street market that had previously showed envy were different, not jealous, but with a deep understanding that nature was doing what she is supposed to do.

It was springtime in Paris, and love was its ultimate manifestation.

"They aren't jealous anymore. They understand what's going on," she had said.

"How do you know?"

"Just by the way they treat me. Listen to their voices. The words they use. They now called me '*Madame*.'" And she was pleased. This was true, and was not condescending. You could see how pleased they were as well.

I did not want to say much on the phone from Prague because it could not but make life more miserable. I thought of the things we did together in Paris. The galleries we visited. The plays we saw. The concerts we attended. The books we enjoyed reading to each other.

The small bistros where we sat and talked for hours and dreamed of happy things. The little restaurants we discovered. The excursions to the flea market at Porte de Clignancourt searching for antiques to decorate the apartment.

Our long walks by the Seine while holding hands, feeling secure, at peace and not saying much. Perhaps love is being together in silence yet knowing and understanding the other.

Lisa wanted to know everything about Paris. Nothing, however small, was insignificant. Her interest and her curiosity were abundant. We spent lots of time exploring the city.

When I first got to Paris, I also used to roam the city. I was fascinated by it, and I wanted to make the city my own. I discovered things that were important to me.

I remember reading that there was a café on Boulevard Bonne Nouvelle, I think it was where Baudelaire went to write his "*maudite*", or ill-fated poetry, which is absolutely brilliant.

I found the café and, bigger than life, there was a table with a little plaque on it stating that old Baudelaire wrote a lot of his poems sitting at the table.

It gave me a wonderful pleasure to sit at the same table. Lisa shared those sentiments. It was in the small details of living in Paris that one found out its true meaning; how to get the best of it no matter how silly or insignificant it may have looked.

One drizzling afternoon, she came home from her classes and wanted us to go for a walk by the river. I was in one of my funky moods and did not think much of her idea. But to be truthful, a few weeks earlier I had convinced her to go ride the motorcycle around Paris with me, while it was raining.

It was dangerous as hell, but we had so much fun and when we got home, we were completely soaked. Later, she had prepared a hot bath for us and afterward we made love.

When Madame Commère found out about our little bike-riding madness, she had not been pleased that Lisa had agreed to do it.

"*Vous êtes irresponsable tous le deux. Complètement fou!*"

She had been right. We had been totally irresponsible and completely crazy. But what the hell? When you are young and in love, you are going to live forever.

I had told Lisa that day when she wanted to go and walk by the Seine, that I was not feeling too chic and in all likelihood by walking in the rain, as she wanted to do, I would probably end up with a head cold. My arguments were ignored.

"So, it's OK to go riding the motorcycle while it is pouring, but just to walk by the river under a drizzle is not?"

Soon we were walking by the Seine under a fine mist. She had insisted that to her all of the things that had ever been written about lovers in Paris were true, even about walking in the rain. I did not get a head cold. After we came back, and after soaking up in a hot bath and drying each other up, we made love.

"Why did you really come to Paris?" Lisa had asked that day.

"It was a pilgrimage. Part of it was also a debt I owed."

"A debt?"

"Yes."

"To whom?"

"A couple of Army buddies I was in Vietnam with."

"What kind of debt was it?"

"Oh, it was something silly."

"Do you want to tell me about it?"

"I'd rather not."

"OK."

The one thing that always struck me about Lisa was that whenever she felt I did not want to discuss something she would never insist. Of course, this would get to me and more often than not, I would end up sharing it with her anyway. She had my number all right.

However, dredging up memories I wanted to keep from overwhelming me was never something I looked forward to with joy. Some recollections are best hidden behind the veil of our pretenses.

When a man has a woman in his life committed to him with everything she is it seems a bit disingenuous to hold back because one is afraid to reveal oneself. It is always a very delicate situation, no doubt about it. Many of us prefer to remain quiet.

However, how true can love be if one fears revealing one's own ghosts? There is no easy answer. After all, whatever one is now has to do with where one has been, with the human baggage one carries around.

"I didn't want to tell you because I didn't want to stir up sad memories."

"Were you afraid?"

"Yes."

"Why?"

"Not easy dredging them up. Anyway, who would want to know about them?"

"I would."

"Yes, but you're different."

"I'm not. Well, maybe because I love you."

"Big difference."

"Yes, but you can't let fear rule your life."

"I'm trying not to. Why bother with war stories? It's all in the past."

"True, though sometimes the present can clarify the past especially when such past has been bleak, and left us without hope."

"Do you think we learn from our past?"

"Yes. My mother says so," she said, seriously.

"Oh, that's OK, then," I said, laughing. "Are you sure you want to know about this?"

"Yes."

In Vietnam, while riding a chopper—in one of those senseless missions the Army is fond of planning because it has to get rid of bodies and its oversupply of gasoline—we had been shot down. The chopper spun out of control and down it went with dizzying and terrifying speed as it crashed-landed with a terrible loud bang.

The good thing was that we were just a little higher than tree level when we took the round that killed the pilot and injured the co-pilot. The bad thing was that out of about a dozen or so GIs, most of whom I did not know, only three survived the crash. I was one of them.

To this day, I still do not know by what miracle I survived. I remember going down, the panic, the rush, the shouting, thinking that I did not want to die, then the violent crash and nothing but blackness around me.

I woke up in a hospital with incredible pain in my face, horrendous, unbearable. I could not talk, and I could barely see out of one eye. In addition, my right arm was broken. I had lost five upper front teeth in the crash, but I was lucky.

I was alive—though when you are in terrible pain and you hear people saying that you are *lucky* to be alive, you sure as hell do not feel it. I had never experienced that kind of physical pain. At first, they filled me with morphine. Eventually, they reduced the dose and I had to get used to dealing with less morphine and more pain.

They evacuated me to Japan. Since I could not talk, I communicated with the doctors and nurses in a kind of chicken scratch. When I wrote, I wanted a mirror they would not let me have one. They kept saying I was going to be OK, but all I could think of was that half of my face was gone—the reason for the pain and why they would not let me have a mirror.

Gently Lisa touched my face. She kissed me.

"But in the hospital, there were other guys whose injuries were worse, so much worse than mine. Just horrible. Impossible to describe—" I stopped.

For an instant, I felt completely lost. I was not sure I could continue. Boy, it was tough. I was trying to control my feelings because I did not want to fall apart in front of Lisa.

I did not know why I was afraid of that. She saw my face, took my hand and held it. She did not say anything. She waited.

"I often wonder what happened to those guys. How are they coping? What about the doctors and nurses? How do they remain human after dealing with such an ordeal? The maiming, the hurt, the cries, the dying . . . that's why talking about those things is so incredibly painful."

"You don't have to if you don't want to."

"I don't want to, and yet if I don't try to deal with such memories, I feel like I'm a fake. I'm just pretending. I don't want to do that. I don't want to be so afraid. Do you understand?"

"I do." I did not doubt she did.

"To lift my spirits up they used to tell me I looked like the perfect Halloween pumpkin."

"Who said that?" Lisa asked, still looking and touching my face as if trying to guess how my injuries must have looked.

"The doctors and the nurses."

While in Japan still not being able to talk, as the swelling was high, to help me pass the time one of the nurses got me a tape recorder with some French audio language tapes. I spent most of the time there listening to them. Back in college, I had been interested in European history and in the French language.

The nurse thought listening to the tapes would get me out of my funk, forcing me to concentrate on other matters beside my pain, the fear my face was half gone, and that I would be deformed forever.

Europe had always been a mystery to me. I thought Europeans had some superior knowledge, a place in this world intellectually and spiritually higher, morally superior than Americans.

Obviously, I chose to overlook the horrible things Europeans had done to each other, to other people, over their long and complex history.

Finally, my arm was mending nicely. My eye and my face got better and I was wheeled to see a dentist who took all kinds of X-rays and measurements, imprints, and told me he would fit me with a bridge for my missing teeth, and nobody would know the difference.

They eventually gave me a mirror so I could see my face. It was the strangest of feelings. I was looking at me and I did not recognize me! I was staring at my face and the eyes seemed to belong to my father, adding to my sense of loss and spiritual dislocation.

"Your face welcomes you back," the nurse had said, grinning, when she saw my reaction.

"I know this will sound crazy to you, but I was surprised my face was still there," I said, to Lisa

"Really, why?" Lisa was looking at me and smiled.

"Maybe because I hadn't seen me for weeks. I had forgotten what I looked like. I don't know."

I had a couple of good buddies back in my unit in Vietnam and, as only those who are young and arrogant enough to think they are going to live forever, we had made a pact that when our military service was over, we would meet in Paris, drink champagne, and ogle those lovely French girls.

While recovering in Japan, I heard from them through the usual letters, ribbing me that "I was just a dirty yellow dog," that I was being a "fake" for pretending to be hurt when, in fact, I was not, just so I could get out of the hell-hole we were in.

Eventually, my face healed back to normal. The dentist fitted a bridge in the gap, my arm healed, and everybody declared I was as good as new. The Army then decided before shipping me back to Vietnam to send me on R&R—Rest and Recuperation—to Bangkok, where I was when President Kennedy got shot.

What I did not know was that in the meantime, my two buddies had bought the farm. When I got back to my unit everything about them was gone. I found two other guys in their bunks. I fanatically resisted the idea my buddies were gone from my life.

For days, I imagined they would come back alive from the field. Every time I heard helicopters landing, I would rush to the landing site even though I knew it was futile.

I fantasized, just like in the old days, about our usual needling of each other. About being full of crap, and hating the Army for what it was doing to us, to everybody; nonetheless, thankful we had survived another lousy, stinking day.

The bullets with our names on them had not found their intended targets; we had cheated the grim reaper.

At other times, I imagined they had finished their tour, had gone back to the States, were safe and sound, but did not want to let me know where they were just to bug me.

This fact helped me get through the interminable nightmares and days of walking around like a zombie. For the next few weeks, life was hell with very little awareness of what was happening around me.

Then I was literally plucked out of the jungle, and sent back to the States via Bangkok. My tour in Vietnam was over. It happened so fast that it seemed like I was in some kind of crazy dream. Things were blurred, foggy.

In less than twenty-four hours, I was taken out of the jungle and dumped right smack into the middle of the American scene as if nothing had happened in the previous twelve months.

I went from worrying about jungle rot—rain, leeches, humidity, mosquitoes, hot as hell, snakes, the Vietcong shooting at me, people dying, confusion, fatigue, ugliness, wretchedness, a sense of loss and innocence, the immense human brutality, the absurdity of it all—to walking in San Francisco and trying to remember when it was safe to cross the street.

It was freaky, a most bizarre feeling. I could understand why guys went crazy upon their return to the States from the war zone. I arrived in Oakland on New Year's Eve.

After processing us, the Army gave us two-day passes and told us to get lost. I took a bus to San Francisco across the bay and went to Market Street. Everything seemed completely out of proportion, people enjoying the end-of-the-year festivities, and here I was walking by myself and feeling miserable, empty, and lost.

I called my girlfriend back in Los Angeles, where she was going to graduate school, and she was shocked to hear from me as she thought I would not return until February. I told her I wanted to come and see her, that I could take a flight out of San Francisco that very night.

She said it was not a good idea as I only had a pass for forty-eight hours, and the flights were probably booked solidly due to the holidays.

As we talked, she kept asking if I had received a letter from her. I told her I had not, and it did not matter since I was back. We kept talking, and soon I heard the metallic voice of the operator, "Please deposit more quarters," which I did not have with me.

I gave my girlfriend the number, and she called me back. But it seemed like it was a long time before the phone rang. She had said "I'll call you right back," so I stood there waiting and waiting. Finally, the phone rang and we continued the conversation.

The delay in her calling back should have told me something was not quite right, because she kept repeating the question about her letter.

I asked her why the letter was so important, and she started to cry. Then, it hit me! I had seen GIs get a "Dear John" letter from a girlfriend or wife, telling them the show was over, that she now was pregnant by some other man.

Some guys went crazy with rage and jealousy. Before I left for Vietnam, my girlfriend and I had sworn eternal love for each other. The separation and the distance were not something we had truly understood.

It is hard to have a romance through the phone or the mail, and though her letters were always filled with wonderful thoughts and plans for the future, she had finally decided the wait was too depressing.

Who could blame her? On top of which the daily news from Vietnam was brutal. Would I come back changed, or a cripple, or worse, in a body bag? She could not bear the idea. I understood the sadness and emptiness of being alone and so far away from a loved one.

In the final analysis, what is important is to grab a bit of happiness when we can because we never know when the shit will hit the fan. Love's highway is littered with empty promises, broken hearts, and painful scars that time cannot expunge.

She kept crying and I kept saying, "OK, OK." I was trying to console her, and the more I tried the worse it got. It was as if I had been the one doing the dumping.

Eventually, it dawned on her that she was being the shithead. She then told me what the letter said. She had found some other guy; she was two months' pregnant; they were getting married.

When the phone rang, she had been getting dressed to go to a New Year's Eve party where they were going to announce that their wedding would take place in a couple of weeks in Las Vegas.

I felt so numb that at that moment I would have preferred to be facing bullets than a sterile telephone booth.

She regained her composure, and I could tell the shock of hearing from me and of her giving me the bad news had started to wear off. I was not angry or bitter. I was tired.

I felt guilty, my heart filled with emptiness. I thought it was my fault. She wanted us to keep in touch and wished me a happy new year. I did likewise, but I did not mean it.

Afterward, I walked around Chinatown for a while and, unlike many returning GIs, I felt no resentment toward the Asian faces I saw that evening. I took a bus back to Oakland and midnight rang while I was riding the bus.

The driver was in a good mood and sang "Auld Lang Syne" and wished to the half a dozen or so people on the bus a happy new year and a happy life. Some hell of a New Year's Eve!

Months later, when I was living in Paris, I happened to go by the American Express office one day and there was a letter from her. She wrote, she hoped, I would eventually get it, and she was now the happy mother of a baby boy.

She also wished me good luck and asked that I write to her. I never did. What would have been the point?

After I was discharged from the Army, I went back to graduate school, but I could get not behind the effort. Returning to school was such a shock because, though I was back in the classroom with people my own age, I could not fit.

They talked about frat parties, football games, pep rallies, getting drunk, and all I could think of was people getting blown away to pieces. I felt disconnected and filled with morbidity. I even missed my previous Army life as crazy as that now sounded.

History had been a favorite subject of mine, and journalism seemed to fall in the same ballpark. I thought it was a noble profession and a reasonable field of study. But like everything else in life, ideals are sometimes better in the abstract.

Much to my own dismay, I discovered I was not very good at it. The idea struck me as being too cold, too clinical, and too remote. In so many instances, journalism seemed disingenuous about what is reported. The truth is very often sacrificed to expediency. Too much sycophancy.

I was sick of the kowtowing behavior of many journalists to the people who signed their paychecks or their kissing politicians' behinds in order to curry favors from them, or the relentless invasion of innocent people's privacy in order to be the first one to write their bullshit stories.

Some journalists are nothing but vultures, like Big D. had said. I did not want to be part of that reality; too much hypocrisy. Besides, maintaining the necessary distance to report the facts was very difficult for me.

It did not take me long to realize I was not the same person as when I left to do my military service. During my undergraduate years, university life had been my refuge, now it offended me leaving me sullen and depressed.

"I don't mind telling you I also met a shy, lovely girl, and I was never able to truly express my sentiments for her and did everything I could to hide how I felt. I have always regretted it because I should not have been so afraid to speak the truth and try to become human again."

"I don't mind," Lisa said, with that wonderful, understanding smile of hers.

I had thought I would come back and pick up where I left off, but it was not possible because I was a lifetime older than the others around me were. What I had not realized was that learning about the world and how if functioned was no picnic.

What I knew about the world, about me, had been converted into something different. Life had intervened, screwed it all up and I did not fit anymore. I had gotten older before I had a chance to grow up.

I had always envied those who seemed to readapt well to their previous civilian lives. I could not do it. The more I reflected, the more I understood that I did not fit.

It was painful to see me stumbling around trying to establish normal relationships with others. Nothing was the same anymore.

My points of reference had disappeared, and I had become a total stranger in my own life. I did not recognize me. The only thing I knew was that I could not continue ignoring what was happening to me. I was a mess.

"That's why I regretted that I was not able to tell this girl how I really felt about her," I said. "In the loneliness and turmoil that I was living through, I was not able to accept many things in my life, even what I might have meant to her. I didn't understand what was going on. My spiritual reference points seemed to have abandoned me."

"Do you still have regrets?" Lisa asked.

"Yes, but in a different way."

Like so many things in our lives, we try this, we try that, we try something else and eventually we settle for what we can get. It is a joke to think we still have time to make choices, that we are indeed *able* to make those choices.

Very often, the choices we think we are making are already made; then, all we do is fit ourselves into this acceptance mode, and that is all she wrote. I could have become a travel agent, I suppose, and maybe would have been good at it. A friend of mine thinks I *should* have become a travel agent.

Like countless others before me, I came to Paris to live, to experience new things, to reflect and try to forget the heartaches, set some distance and hopefully find some answers that had eluded me. That there might not be any answers did not make the effort less worthwhile.

When you think about it, the more one digs into wanting to comprehend what was going on, the more the questions pop and the circle did not get broken but got bigger.

I had my doubts that at the end of my life I could be wiser than when I started this search for whose face was behind the mirror. On the contrary, it seems we start off wiser when we begin searching for the simple reason that we are new in the game.

Whereas when we finish all, we learned was that we did not know jack. We had simply attended a circus and we were the sad clowns.

Oh, I suppose arguments could be made about growing older and wiser. Yes, age and experience did count for something, but not always for what we needed them or when we needed them.

As an undergraduate in college, I had been attracted to the French culture, the history, the language as unique, exciting and poetic. I had no idea where my interest in languages came from. I liked the idea of other languages, other cultures, and other people.

That was one of the reasons living in Europe was exciting. Yet, I also firmly believed we should do away with frontiers. There should be only one race: the human race!

Eating Chinese food, visiting Italy, reading Tolstoy, climbing the Matterhorn, walking through the Black Forest, riding ponies on the desolate Pampas, watching Sumo wrestling in Japan, being thrown in jail in Africa, or mugged in Central Park in New York City, or whatever, should be done as a member of the human race. Not because we were Chinese, Italian, Russian, Swiss, German, Argentinean, Japanese, African, American, but simply because we are members of the human race.

I was a sucker for the sounds of other languages. They always invoked in me ideas, mysteries, and histories of lives I knew nothing about. I seemed to have a good ear for languages and this was a way of using such a facility.

I spent countless hours and hours studying French, wanting to learn to speak it like a native. I had a romantic notion I could do it—silly of me. The idea of living in Paris fascinated me, though, I did not know much about the French people.

I was intrigued by their history, their art, their culture, and by their contradictions. I thought part of the problem in trying to understand the French was we were guilty of wanting to romanticize them.

I fought not to do that as the reality turned out to be different, and often lead to anger and frustration. In the basics, of course, we were all part of humanity even if the French thought they were the ones leading the parade.

In graduate school, I barely lasted one semester. I had applied to the Sorbonne and when I was accepted, without any hesitation but perhaps more out of sheer desperation, I packed my suitcase, went to the airport, and *voilà*, I found myself in Paris.

My friend Gary was living here, and said to come and stay with him if I wanted to. I was not trying to get away from America. I only wanted to move toward something else. Paris has always seemed the magical city to me.

Then there were the promises I had made to my buddies. Back in Vietnam, after I found out they were dead, I picked up two small pebbles, which I had been carrying in my pocket ever since then.

Those two small pebbles were my connection to them, for in a moment of drunken cynicism we had made a pact that whoever came out of the fucking war alive should go to Paris and honor the other or others who did not make it.

I was the one had gotten through, and now here I was in Paris with a pact to respect and I could not quite figure out just what I was supposed to do about their memories. I had not had the courage to think about it.

We had talked about drinking champagne and pondering the gracefulness of Parisian girls. I could not bring myself to do either one. For the many months I had lived in Paris, I had pushed those ideas out of my head. I just could not do it. My heart was not in it.

"Remember I told you about la Closerie des Lilas?

"Yes, we've walked by many times," Lisa said.

"I know. It has to do with oysters."

"Oysters?"

"Yes. My buddies and I had read about Paris, Hemingway, and how he used to go to la Closerie and eat oysters. We thought it was cool. We made a bet, we would go to la Closerie, eat oysters, and drink champagne like Hemingway used to do."

"But when we go by you don't want to go in."

"The funny thing is that I don't think Hemingway ate oysters at la Closerie. But now it is too late for me to tell my buddies that."

"Is that why you don't want to go in?"

"They lost and I won . . . a rotten, lousy piece of shit bet. I can never go in." For a moment, I thought I was going to lose it. She saw that and held me closer to her.

"I'm so sorry, Alex, so sorry."

I felt guilty for having been the one left behind until, one day, I found myself walking down by the Seine. It was a beautiful day. The city appeared to be as attractive as she could get, with the sun shining and Parisians shedding their winter gear.

There was a feeling of happiness in the air, replacing sad sentiments. I sat by the riverbank and watched the few people who were there.

There was an elderly couple with a small boy, and the man was trying to teach the boy about fishing. There was much merriment from the three of them. The old man had so much patience with the boy, and the boy was trying so hard to learn what the man was showing him.

The scene was simple and honest, filled with love, innocence, and care. I watched them for a long time. At one point, the man washed the boy's small hands in the river.

It brought me back memories of another young boy in Africa, and how the old man sitting next to him had kissed his hand when the boy was trying to give him comfort.

Now here I was, in Paris, pretty much witnessing the same tableaux as I saw in Africa but in a more innocent setting, and it struck me as wonderfully pure and moving. I can still hear the woman calling to the boy.

"Yves Henri, Yves Henri, regard ton papie."

"Leave him be," the old man said.

The manner in which the man said to the woman to leave the boy alone, when she asked the boy to pay attention to what his grandpa was showing him, told a timeless story of older generations preparing the younger one for the day of replacement in the never-ending cycle of life.

The grandparent's words and the boy's laugher lifted my spirits. The tableaux seemed to belong to a time when life was free, pure, and not so painful.

I started thinking about those two crazy guys—Jack and Micky—and the small pebbles I had been carrying for the past few months. It seemed appropriate that now was the perfect time to toss them in the Seine. I reached into my pocket and took them out.

We had all agreed that when the moment came, we would not utter banalities and empty words. On the contrary, whoever was left standing would be just like we had always been—vulgar, gross, mocking—and not carry around the guilt of having survived the terrible ordeal.

We had promised that there could be no phony words or forced sentimentality. Whatever it was had to come from the heart and from the guts. We could not hide behind platitudes. It had to be just like we had been in real life.

It was the only way to honor our friendship. Life had to go on, to be faced, no matter how much she kicked you in the balls.

"I love you bastards," I said. "So here I am in Paris by myself, and I miss you like hell. I'm a hurting sonovabitch, but that's how the gods wanted to play it. It ain't fair. Not that you give a shit what I think. You never did! Thanks for the memories.

"What I miss the most is your laughter, your love, not having your ugly mugs around, and your friendship. So long. Let the nymphs of the Seine take care of your young asses from now on, and gently carry you instead of me. Since I'll never see you or hear your voices again, fuck you both . . . wherever you are . . . you lousy, no-good bums."

I held the pebbles for a long moment, rubbed them against each other, then without looking at them I threw them into the middle of the river one after the other. They went skipping across the water and sank to the bottom.

"I started to cry, bawling just like a baby. I was also laughing because it occurred to me that those two lousy bums were probably having the last laugh at my expense."

Here I was in Paris feeling like shit, and crying my sorry heart out. I could picture them calling me all kinds of names because I had let my emotions get the best of me.

"That was my farewell. That was the debt I had to pay. I've never told this to anyone before. I had wanted to write about it, and have often attempted to but it doesn't come out right. It seems to be missing something. I don't think I could ever write it the way I feel it. Maybe when I'm older. I don't know . . ."

"War is so awful, so inhuman. I'm so ashamed of what we're doing in Vietnam. I don't understand it. I can't imagine the fear you must have felt," Lisa said.

"There is no way to explain that fear. It invades every pore of your existence, and you can never clean yourself of it—the violence, the incongruity, the banality. It's funny how you search in your mind to make war 'human.'

"I know it sounds ludicrous, but that's how you try to keep your sanity. You want to relate it to something you understand like a tennis match, so that when the contest is over you shake your opponent's hand, and then you go take a shower."

"Is that the part of the book you want to write?"

"Yes. What is there to 'win' in a war or in Vietnam? Who 'wins' in such a terrible ordeal? The sad truth is that we lose by winning. It's so stupid. We are not equipped to get rid of our penchant for violence against our fellow man. We ignore the obvious lessons of humanness, of humbleness, and simplicity. A screwed-up world we live in."

Now it was my turn to look at Lisa desperately hoping she would explain things to me. Guide me. Protect me from my own fears and nightmares.

I also knew it was not fair to place such a burden on her. Yet perhaps airing out my sentiments would help unburden myself from such terrible feelings, and ugly memories.

"I'm sorry," I said.

"No, I'm the one who is sorry because I don't know how to help you."

"Your being here is all the help I need."

"I love you," she said, with tears in her eyes. "It's a beautiful story about your buddies. It makes me feel close to you. Thank you. You'll write it one day. I know it! You don't have to feel lost and lonely anymore. I bet they're happy because you're sharing it with me."

I knew she was trying to console me by saying that.

"Do you really think so?"

"Yes," and she gave me a wonderful smile that always made me feel good. She embraced me. "I must also thank them."

"For what?"

"Because if you had not made that pact, we would have never met. It's because of them that life made it possible for us to meet. Remember, I once asked you if you believed in the cosmos?"

"Yes."

"We have our proof. We can conquer life together."

"Do you think so?"

"I know so! You don't need to feel sorry for yourself or them. You're all free!"

"Maybe you're right. Knowing them, they're probably jealously watching because I'm sitting here with a beautiful girl and talking about them, and they would have been embarrassed and too shy to admit it pleases them."

"Do you think they would have been jealous?"

"Absolutely! Though they might hold it against you that you're not French," I said, teasingly.

"Really?"

"I'm just kidding. They would have been happy to meet you. I'm sure you would have liked them. They were good people."

"I'm sure of that."

"Anyway, they would also be giving me a hard time for not telling you the whole truth."

"And what truth is that?"

"You mean it isn't clear?"

"No."

"It's not obvious that you're one of the last few great broads left on this earth?"

"No. Sometimes we need to be told that and other things as well."

"Like what?"

"I'll never tell." Now she was teasing, giving me a taste of my own medicine.

"Going for your pound of flesh, I see."

"Why not?" She was smiling.

"That somewhere in all of this madness, you would come into my life, not break my heart, and I would love you until the moon falls out of the sky."

"That's lovely."

"Come on, you knew that."

"It's wonderful to hear you say that. You know, even great broads need to be told, occasionally, how much we're loved."

Her eyes sparkled. When I look back on the many reasons why I came to Paris, I must accept that love happens to you wherever you are. Search for self is search for love and what it brings to all of us. Men and women are not whole without it.

Living through this crazy and wild ride called life without one another is not easy. It is fraught with disappointments, missed opportunities, even danger, but that is the ticket.

Some of my friends always argue that finding a soul mate should not be such a hard and frustrating task. The image of Iris came into my mind in a flash, and then it was gone. Lisa must have seen something in my eyes, but she did not say anything. I was glad. The past was no longer important.

Her face was serene, and now I no longer needed memories of the other women I had loved. I tried to remember them, but it was hard to bring them into focus.

They all seemed just a jumble of memories, all blurred images, not interesting. I had, ostensibly, been looking for love and found none. It was love that had found me instead.

Lisa was the only reality that made sense because she was here in the flesh, and not some half-forgotten memory that no longer mattered. She was present with all of her faults sharing my faults. Somehow, through the eons, we had connected and had now become each other's reality.

It could be argued that as long as Lisa and I were "in love" things would be fine, and there was a great deal of truth to that idea; that is until the shit hit the fan. I knew about the shit hitting the fan.

I was more cynically in tune with that reality. Lisa was not. That kind of cynicism was not part of her baggage. Maybe she was too young or too inexperienced in the way life treats us all. I do not know.

She lived like the rest of us in this absurdity called life, and for some reason she made it look like anything but that. It was a gift that some people have. I sure as hell did not have it. She moved closer and started kissing me.

She put her hand on me and I got hard. Slowly she took me in her mouth. Her love and tenderness always overwhelmed me. She stopped and looked at me with those lovely eyes of hers.

"I want to tell you something," she said, smiling.

"What?"

"I don't know how to say it," she said, shyly.

"What is it?"

"Promise you won't laugh."

"OK, I promise."

"Let's make love . . . the other way."

Her request came from so far out of left field that I started to laugh, but she was serious.

"Really?"

"Yes," she said.

If now this took me aback, it was not because she had asked or that I thought it was something stupid, dirty. It was that the desire we have about exploring the unknown was never limited to purely abstract objects. A man and a woman's intimacy is splendid and unique.

"Are you surprised?" She asked.

"No."

"Who else could I ask if not you? You're my lover, my man, my master, my soul mate, my companion, my life. I'm yours, you're mine. You're so close to me. I love you so much. Sometimes, I walk around thinking nobody deserves the happiness I have in my heart because I found you—"

She stopped and looked at me and, for a moment, there was a look that came across her eyes, a look I hardly ever saw in her, fearful, doubtful, not the Lisa I knew.

Dear gods, please keep her the way she is. Lisa, please stay the way you are. Do not change anything about you, please. Do not let life make you uncertain or scared, or sad.

"Then at other times, I feel that I'm going to die before our baby is born. Do you think that's normal?"

"Fear is not limited to people like me." I said, trying to comfort her.

"Yes, but this is a new experience for me. I fear I'm not as strong as I think I am."

"There are so many changes going on inside you, physically, mentally, and spiritually. You have a life growing inside of you that will depend on you more than you can possibly imagine. I feel the same way, and I'm never going to carry the baby."

"Perhaps you're right. I envy you because you're always questioning your life, whereas I just accept mine and it seems vacuous."

"Is it?"

"I don't know. Of course, it isn't. It just seems that way."

"Are you unhappy?"

"No. How could I be? I have never felt as complete as I feel now with you. Yes, there are moments when nothing outside us makes sense. I wish we were the only two people living in our own world, that we didn't have to deal with all of the madness going on outside our window—"

She stopped. My erection was slowly disappearing. Serious discussions when you are about to make love is not likely to produce much mutual sexual pleasure. She saw that and touched me again. Then one thing led to another, and I did what she wanted.

I reached around and touched her, and the more I touched her, the more Lisa pressed against me and the wetter she got. When she climaxed, her whole body was shaking, and she was moaning and pressing hard against me.

"It felt like I was swimming, like I was floating. Strange. It hurt, too," she said. She turned around, kissed me and held me closer.

However, moments of uncertainty live with us even when we are not reflecting on them. Moments, when I was also overwhelmed by what was taking place outside our window.

So many of the things we took for granted were no longer safe and innocent. The currents that ran around the world were passionate, shattering, and often unyielding to reason.

Lisa's question that day about why I had come to Paris seemed very simple, but it was layered with all kinds of meaning and significance. It is hard to put into words the multiple reasons why Paris is such a magnet to so many people. I suppose, being bit of a romantic helps. Paris brings out the romantic in all of us.

Even if you hate the French, Paris always sounds sophisticated and chic, filled with such a powerful lure—no other city in the world does that to your soul. Coming to Paris was not a culture shock. Somehow, I fit right in.

Of course, there were ambiguities, banalities, and misunderstandings. All of the things we associate with facts that are not our own, that we are not familiar with.

"What about you?" I had asked her.

"We've lived in so many faraway places that America has remained the dreamland. Even after we finally settled in the U.S., in my mind it was where we went for vacations, like Disneyland. In many ways, it has remained that.

"Hard to explain. I mean, I love our country, but America always seems to be this mythical land. That's why I understand what José was saying about his gypsy friends and their mythical land—" she stopped again, searching for the exact words to explain how she felt.

"I grew up," she continued, "knowing that the world was large and that I could go anywhere and it would be OK. That's why I wanted to come to Paris and see for myself. I could go back to the States and be fine there, I suppose. But my life is here with you. The rest is too complicated, really. I'm only twenty-three years old. I'm not that complicated."

"You're still a baby," I said, laughing and hugging her.

"I'm not a baby, though sometimes I feel too young to deal with the world around me."

"Were your parents very adventurous?"

"In a way. My dad loved his job, so his natural shyness was overcome by doing what he loved best: helping other people. And my mother was always the practical one supporting what he did."

"They sound like great folks."

"They are."

"Do you think they'll like me?"

"They'll be crazy about you. I guarantee it!"

I hoped so.

Suddenly, I didn't want to be in Prague anymore. The political unrest back in Paris was getting worse. The Sorbonne situation was getting to be a *"bordel"*, like the French are fond of saying when things are disorganized, chaotic, out of control.

On this last day of April, the students were on strike and the situation was getting uglier. The unrest was no longer limited to the Parisian students, and now had spread to other campuses across the country.

It made me very uneasy. I also had the stupid impression the phone wires that were serving as the link between Lisa and me were now there to keep us away from each other. I found myself regretting my decision to come here in the first place.

The more I thought about what I was doing, the more it seemed I had been driven to come here by outdated expectations. What did I hope to accomplish? I was going to be just another bystander to an inevitably cruel and dreadful event over which

I had nothing to say let alone try to stop. I was a simple and banal witness of a dream's transformation into a nightmare. I hated these sentiments of despair that such thoughts brought to my heart and spirit.

The fight of the Czechoslovakian people had nothing to do with me or how I felt, or even any sympathies I may have had for their plight. However sympathetic I was, my involvement would not amount to anything at all.

I was surprised by my attitude, and I attributed much of it to the fact that I missed Lisa too damn much. The benefits to be gained by being separated did not equal the sacrifices she and I were making.

My attitude was not the best to have, that much I knew. In the past, my sense of futility, stupidity, and absurdity had been overwhelming but not totally hopeless when confronted with the nasty things people do to each other.

Now, this feeling of total hopelessness was fixing itself in my psyche, and I did not like it. I did not want to be in Prague—that was the real problem.

I was also torn by my belief that it is the actions of individuals that eventually make the difference in doing away with repressive, tyrannical people and governments.

It is individuals like Adam and his mother, like all of their friends, like anyone in this world who wants to be free, who make the difference. I could not deny this most basic of my own convictions even when I could see that hope was fading away for them, their lives, their country.

I did not want to dwell on the negative, but I found myself lost in thoughts of total helplessness and despair. I have a child on the way, I must snap out of this, I thought; however, the harder I tried the worse it got.

Perhaps Lisa was right and her ideal world of just the two of us living in some mythical island, away from this absurd world where no one else would be allowed, made sense.

I had never thought that by excluding the whole world life would be easier, but the idea did not seem so crazy or remote anymore. I knew that even though people brought out the worst in others, it was also true that people brought out the best in others.

One could no more renounce listening to Beethoven's *"Ninth Symphony"* or Mozart's *"Clarinet Concerto"* or read *"Lord Jim"* by Joseph Conrad, or enjoy looking at Monet's *"Déjeuner sur l'herbe"*, than deny the butchery that was taking place in Vietnam.

Or the daily violent demonstrations of American students against a very ugly and divisive war, or what was now taking place in Paris, or worse, what was in store for the Czechoslovakian people once the Russians moved in. Boy, I thought, it sure as hell was not the best of times.

"I'll sleep on your side of the bed tonight," Lisa said, toward the end of our phone conversation on that first evening. "I love you. I plead guilty," she added, and the line went dead.

Afterward, the silence surrounding me in that sterile hotel room in Prague was like a sharp stab to my aching, lonely heart.

ELEVEN

The phone rang several times before I realized it was in my room. I was not sure what time of day it was. When I looked at my watch it showed ten in the morning, yet I had the impression that I had just gone to bed. These past few days in, Prague, I had averaged a few hours of sleep a night.

The night before, I had been out chasing leads, and had come back to the hotel a couple of hours ago to try to get some rest. In the last few days, I had managed to get through to Lisa sporadically but our bits of phone conversations left us more frustrated than satisfied. For the obvious reasons, we feared that someone was listening.

Our static-filled phone talks were about as banal as they could get and totally inconsequential, with the result that they left me more depressed than if I had not made them. Lisa told me that the silence for her after hanging up the phone was unbearable.

I had wanted to suggest we should not call, but I also knew that I would be the first one to break the silence anytime I could. To hear her sweet voice was worth the long and frustrating waits by the phone.

The moment I was back in the hotel I tried calling Paris no matter what time it was. The last few days had also been hectic, tiring, and I was not at all certain I was getting anything worthwhile to telex to Alain back in Paris.

Everyone in Prague was paranoid. The euphoria of earlier times was slowly giving way to the awful truth the Russians were going to invade no matter what they publicly declared to the contrary.

A bit groggy I picked up the phone. It was Alain.

"Thank God I got through to you!"

From the sound of his voice, I immediately knew that something was wrong in Paris, very wrong. The sick feeling in my stomach made it clear and unambiguous. Now I was fully awake.

"It's about Lisa," he added.

My mind went blank. Hearing Alain's words wiped out all of my feelings. I felt numb, empty, sick and dead. Oh, please, let her be OK. The line was filled with static, and I pressed the phone to my ear very hard wanting to hear every word, every nuance.

"She was arrested last night."

"What?" Christ. "Why?"

"I don't know. I have everybody I know trying to find out. Things are so out of control here that it's next to impossible to learn anything."

Lisa in jail? God almighty!

"She's pregnant for Christ's sake. It's not possible. And the baby? *Merde*! This is crazy." I was scared.

"It is crazy. Also, the Sorbonne was taken over by the police yesterday late in the afternoon, and they closed it down."

"Are you kidding?"

"I wish I were."

By the sound of his voice, I knew this was a sad and terrible day for him. Lisa in jail, and the Sorbonne now taken over by the police. It was his Alma Mater as well. The Sorbonne is one of the oldest universities in Europe. It had seen and survived its share of repression and political turmoil.

Only twice since the university was created had it been closed. The first was back in the 13th century, and the second time was during the German invasion of France in 1940.

For so many French people, the Sorbonne was as sacred as an institution got.

"I'm sorry to have to tell you about Lisa."

"I've got to get out of this fucking place and return to Paris."

I was so stunned by the news of Lisa's arrest. I could not think of anything else to say.

"OK, I've tried booking you out of there on the first flight, and I can't get you a seat. I even tried getting you out through Moscow, and I'm not having any luck. I'm sorry. It's all my fault," he said, his voice filled with regret.

"Come on it wasn't you who arrested her." I could not possibly guess how terrible he must have felt. "Can you get me out on a train?"

"They are difficult to book from here. Milo called the American Embassy here and they're aware of the situation. He has a good contact and so do I, and we're working hard trying to find a solution. The embassy here also called the embassy in Prague, and there is a guy there by the name of Tubbs who knows what's going on here if you want to call him."

What could the embassy in Prague do? Cleo's face of dismissal when I suggested she call the American Embassy in Greece for Chris suddenly came to mind. What the fuck did they care?

"From what we've been able to put together, she hasn't been mistreated. I've spent half the night trying to find out what's going on. I tried calling you, and I couldn't get through. I thought you would know about the Sorbonne by now."

"I was out most of the night all over this city, and I really didn't pay any attention to anything else. I've just come back from one of those fruitless chases."

"I understand. I really feel terrible about Lisa."

I knew he was trying to comfort me, and for that I was grateful.

"Do you think she's OK?" I asked with trepidation.

"Is one ever OK behind bars?"

The whole thought of Lisa in jail was mind numbing. Not Lisa, not my Lisa. *Merde!* And the baby?

"I'll get cleaned up and see what I can do to get back to Paris right away. I hope I can get through to you on the phone for updates."

"I can't tell you how sorry I am about this. We're talking about France *putain de pays*—whore of a country—I'm so ashamed, you have no idea. I want you to know that I don't care what it takes. We'll get her out no matter what the cost is."

"Thanks, I know you're doing your best."

The line went dead. I was terrified! All kinds of crazy and wild thoughts were going through my head. What if they are beating her up?

What if they cause her to have a miscarriage? Would they force her to abort the baby? Why would they arrest her?

Alain said things were hectic in Paris; man, the whole country was going to hell. I should have known better. Why did I not anticipate something like this happening? I was too damn relaxed about the situation in Paris. I should have been more vigilant. It was all my damn fault.

The gods were teaching me a lesson, and I was not prepared for it. Man, now what? She never told me anything was wrong. I am sure she would have told me. I have to trust her on that. I held the phone in my hand. I was terrified, desperate, shaking very badly.

If I do not get ahold of myself, I am not going to make it, I thought. So slowly, I started to count and by the time I got to ten I put the phone down.

Where was Lisa now? The French police did not have a nice reputation for tenderness especially now that the situation was getting out of control. There were so many thoughts running through my head that it was impossible to focus on just one. What could she have been doing?

Slowly, I went over what I remembered and the only thing that seemed to make sense was the business with Adam and Ulla. How I wished I had possessed the clear presence of mind to ask Alain about Ulla and Adam. I thought, boy, this was all I needed.

I was tired, and I was not even sure what day it was. I looked at my agenda and saw it was Saturday, May 4, 1968. Wearily, I wrote: Lisa in jail in Paris. God Almighty! Why? I went into the bathroom and looked at myself. I looked like shit. I felt like shit.

My eyes had dark rings under them. My mouth felt dry, with a horrible taste. Everything seemed so hectic. It was true that in the last few days, I had not had much sleep, and it was catching up with me. I had also prolonged my stay in Prague for a few more days. I had been the one who had suggested it.

Lisa had not been keen on my staying longer, but I had managed to convince her it was OK. Boy, I wished I had listened to her. It was my fault entirely. Man, what the hell did I do to deserve this? In the last few days, I had not been able to see the people Adam and Alain had wanted me to see.

Everybody was afraid of meeting in the open. I had to use all kinds of subterfuge not to compromise them. It had been trying and heavy on the psyche. Everything had to be done with all kinds of backup plans.

If this does not work, you need to double back and wait at the usual place. If no contact is made, go back to your hotel and you will have to do the same thing tomorrow in reverse order at the same time. At the meeting place, when you see a man carrying a copy of Paris-Match *go back to your hotel and sit at the bar.*

Order a drink of Bailey's and stay there for twenty minutes, exactly. Then go immediately to your room and someone will come knocking on your door within five minutes. Remember, five minutes. Make sure you destroy any evidence. The rest will be easy.

Easy, right.

Though my heart had stopped beating at hundreds of miles an hour, the face in the mirror looking back at me was the face of a very scared man. I put my hands in front of me, and they were shaking like those of a drunkard.

I could not control the shaking. I turned on the cold water in the shower and stepped inside. What did I do that the gods would not protect her? This was the last thing I expected to happen to us.

The fear and uncertainty were the worst feelings I had ever had in my whole life, not only because I was so far away from her, which was bad enough, but also because I had not been there to protect her.

I was out here doing something that already seemed unimportant. What was I thinking? I could not remember when I had felt so lousy, lost, and isolated.

OK, OK, maybe I was being too hard on myself. I did not know how long I stood under the shower. I lost track of the time. Then through the noise of the water, I thought I heard the phone ring.

I was not sure. Yes, it was ringing. I came out of the shower, almost slipped and fell but, somehow, I made it to the phone and picked it up.

"Hello?"

"Alex?" It was Adam's mother.

"Yes."

"Bon jour. C'est Madame Suvadova, comment allez-vous ?"

The voice was flat. I knew it was a code. Normally, she introduced herself as being Adam's mother. She had told me that whenever she would introduce herself by using her last name, it would be a signal to meet her later because she had something important to tell me.

"I have seen better days."

"Yes, I'm sure. I wonder if you could drop by whenever you can today. I'd like you to have a look at the letter I wrote to Ionesco. I want to be sure my French isn't so banal."

She was a French teacher; she wrote better French than I did!

She knew something, and I was grateful to her, eternally grateful. I also knew she was taking a chance, for although her invitation seemed innocuous enough, you could never be certain what the powers that be knew, and what they intended to do.

"I was going to get some breakfast," I said, trying to keep the anxiety out of my voice.

"Perfect timing. Come over, and I'll prepare you one of the best breakfasts Prague has to offer for your help with my letter."

"I'd like that"

"Très bien. A tout à l'heure, alors."—Very well. I'll see you in a little bit.

"OK, et merci beaucoup."

I hoped my voice had not given away my fear. I was lucky to find a taxi right away, and with my heart pounding as if it was going to burst out of my chest, very nonchalantly, I sat back and looked at the city going past my windows and registered nothing.

She was waiting for me at the front door. Her demeanor and attitude gave away nothing. I truly admired her, for in a clear and most eloquent way, she was teaching me there was grace under pressure. She was something else.

We entered her apartment. It must have been the look on my face that told her that I already knew the bad news. She embraced me and held me close. I wanted to question her but, wisely, she put her fingers to her lips, turned, went to the kitchen, and wrote down something on a piece of newspaper.

Lisa and the baby are fine!

I was never so grateful to anyone, ever, in my entire life. She took the paper, tore it to pieces, set it on fire, flushed the ashes down the sink, and gave me a wonderful smile.

"I hope my humble breakfast will help you regain some of the energy you seem to have lost visiting our city."

"You don't know how I have looked forward to it since you invited me this morning. I'm very much touched by your kindness."

Once the breakfast was over, as was our usual routine, we walked outside and down the street.

"Yes, the baby is fine and so is she. A little tired but fine. Apparently, it was my son they were looking for."

"Why?"

"I don't know why. But he's a good boy. He's smart."

I saw how worried she was. I hugged her. It was the only thing I could do. Then I told her about Alain's phone call. Through my head spinning, I tried to imagine, once again, what it must have been for Lisa to face the police in the middle of the night.

I cursed myself for having left her alone in Paris. I had promised to protect her from all harm. Some promise! Her Ethiopian tribe would soon be over looking for me with murder in their hearts. The thought gave me a slight moment of respite and levity.

"I'm afraid the French government has committed a major blunder regarding the Sorbonne. It is inconceivable they would do it." Adams's mother was clearly dismayed.

"I told Lisa they would do it, she never wanted to believe it."

"I never thought they would."

"Do you know why they took Lisa?"

"No. The French police can arrest people, keep them for days without telling them why they are holding them, and with all the events going on the situation is not clear. Perhaps it is not as bad as in this country. *Mais toujours est-il que je suis vraiment déçu de voir le gouvernement français agir comme ça.*" Her voice sounded bitter, sad, and distant.

She was clearly disappointed over the French government's actions and also knew more about French police tactics than I did. The situation in Paris was reaching a very critical point. Many workers had now joined the students.

This was no longer a student protest but something closer to a full-blown revolt and dangerous, very dangerous. Somehow, Lisa had been caught in the middle of the madness, and I still had no idea where she was or why she had been arrested.

My feelings of horror, fear, and helplessness could not have been worse. I vaguely knew about the French system holding people for as long as the police felt like it. It was beyond my comprehension that it would happen to Lisa—and in France of all places!

How in the hell would I know what was in store for her? My mind was racing about the way our legal system in the U.S. works. Talk about futility.

"Where is Adam?"

"I don't know. He's a practical boy and won't try to contact me directly for the time being. The news I got about Lisa came from another source."

"What about Ulla or José?"

Here she smiled and for some reason her smile comforted me a bit.

"I don't know anything about José, but Ulla was also arrested; however, it appears the Swedish government is preparing to demand an official explanation from the French government at a high level."

I had to laugh. Sweden—not a large country—in fact one of the smaller ones in Europe, and was already on the ball. How come the U.S., one of the two superpowers in the world, would do diddlysquat for one of its own citizens?

I was also impressed with the fact that whatever network Adam's mother was part of, it appeared to have up-to-date information, and this was to the good. Living the way she did, she had to trust her sources and, therefore, I had to trust her.

"I just hope Lisa and the baby are fine," I said. It sounded so futile.

Her eyes told me she understood my fears, and she understood them far better than anyone else could at that moment.

"We must have faith," she said. Her voice was so firm that I felt guilty about betraying my own fears. She had a son to worry about, after all. She held my hand. "You love her very much, don't you?"

"Yes, she is my life! I'm so afraid something bad is going to happen to her or the baby. And I'm not there."

"We must be strong." She put her arm through mine and we kept on walking in silence.

I wanted to be back in Paris in the worst possible way. Distance, fear, and ignorance about what was happening to a loved one play tricks on you. I wanted everything to be the way it was before I left Paris for Prague. I formed an illusion that all I had to do was wish it and things would be back the way they were.

I felt so damn inadequate and regretted to no end my decision to come here. I wanted to just close my eyes, open them, and, *voilà*. I would be back in Paris protecting her.

Here I was, hundreds of miles away from where I should have been. I knew absolutely nothing about what was happening to her or why. And the baby—our baby! Man, talk about being at the end of one's wits.

Can French police, when everyone hates them, still be nice to pregnant women? The situation in Paris was a mess. I thought I had better stop driving myself crazy and plan to get out of Prague. It was my first and only priority.

"We must never give up," Adam's mother continued, "the information I received this morning told me the baby was fine. Lisa was fine also, tired, but fine."

My passport! The Holiday Inn had asked for my passport when I first checked in. They had said they would hold it until I left. This was not unusual since it happened in other countries as well. Now that there was a connection made to Adam and his mother here in Prague, the situation was not as simple as I wanted.

I could not afford any further complications. The paranoia level could easily rise. I must be careful, I said to myself. OK, Lisa and the baby are fine. My next goal, my only goal, was to get back to Paris by whatever means necessary.

"She will be fine. She's a strong and courageous girl. My son tells me so."

After telling me she would keep in touch and pass on whatever information she got, we embraced, and I left grateful for the positive news. Where to start? I needed to get my passport back. I needed to book a flight out of here immediately.

I also knew there were not many flights out of Prague to Paris. Money was no problem as I had a couple of credit cards, plus enough traveler's checks, and some cash.

I also knew that in the last few days, I had done a great deal of dodging in and out of taxis, buses, and tramways. If someone had been tailing me, they would have enough to make my life unpleasant if they chose to.

Why would anyone do that, though? The answer was obvious: I was visiting a repressive society and to the authorities in their fucked-up logic of political repression, an American probably represented a far more serious danger. I was only a symbol, but in this part of the world such a symbol was not to be permitted.

America stood for freedom. Repression was not part of what America was all about in spite of the turmoil she was now experiencing. I found a taxi right away, which I took to be a good omen—that was how desperate I was that finding a taxi made me feel like I was finally getting things under control. When I got back to the hotel, I told the assistant manager I was checking out.

"By the way, I wonder if I could have my passport now, and could you tell me how much I owe." I was trying to be as nonchalant as I could, though my heart was beating at two hundred miles an hour. The assistant manager opened a file and started looking at it. There was no passport in it.

"Do you want to check out now?"

"Well, when I can get a flight out of Prague."

"It would be best to get yourself a flight first so you're confirmed to leave Prague. Your passport will be handed back to you then," he said, rather dryly.

He was looking at me in a way that suggested I should not insist too much on this issue. He had been very friendly and helpful these past few days. Perhaps, I should not push my luck.

"OK, that's fine. In fact, could you see if you can book me a flight to Paris, or London, or Brussels, or Amsterdam? I would be eternally grateful."

"I will try."

"I'll be in my room."

"Very well."

I went up to my room. I wanted to believe so much it was only a matter of hours before I would be back in Paris and the situation would be OK. Would Lisa be worried that by now I would have known what happened, and that would end up worrying her even more?

Man, life can get so screwy. How did she feel at this moment? Was she sleeping? Had she eaten? Was she cold? What if she got sick or had a miscarriage?

I had never felt so alone in my life. The situation called for some unique powers and I was not sure I had them. I had to be strong for all of us and I sure as hell was not feeling any strength. I went into the bathroom and washed my face in cold water.

Though I now knew Lisa and the baby were apparently doing fine, I felt worse than this morning. Could someone have said she was doing fine just to mislead me? What if she were injured—or dead?

The phone rang. It was the manager.

"There are no available flights to the cities you wanted. I've asked them to put you on standby on flights to Vienna, Milan, and Munich, as well, and to let me know of any cancellations."

His voice was strained as if afraid of someone listening to the conversation. He hesitated and this did not give me any comfort.

"Also, someone from the State Security called earlier looking for you. They asked where you were. My colleague didn't know so he told them so."

"Thank you. Did they say what they wanted?"

"No," The tone was tense. Not a good sign.

"I'll appreciate anything you can do to get me on the first flight out of here. I have to go back to Paris immediately."

I did not know if I should have said that. On the other hand, if State Security wanted to talk to me my travel plans would not keep them from dropping in to pay me their "courtesy" visit.

"I understand," he said, before hanging up.

So the vultures were now circling the prey. For some reason, the fear the cops wanted to talk to me balanced the fear I had about the events back in Paris. All of this sobered me up.

I carefully checked my belongings in an attempt to determine if someone had come into the room while I was out but saw nothing suspicious.

Everything was where I left it. I stood by the window looking outside trying to project myself into the consciousness of the people I saw walking below.

I wanted to be part of their immediate destiny. I knew that could never happen. Once again, the absurdity of life assailed me. Who in the fuck are we kidding?

Were the people I saw on the street going home? To the pharmacy? To spend another day at the office? To a lovers' rendezvous? To look for a plumber? To find toilet paper?

To stand in line at some store because there was a line already there, not knowing what was being sold but whatever it was, it was better to buy it now?

I was not like them anymore than I had been like Mohammed back in Yugoslavia. They had been living in this crazy nightmare called communism for so many years.

I did not know how I or anyone else who had not actually lived like they had, for the last twenty-five years, could possibly understand what their lives had come to.

It was always easy for me, for Alain, for the others who did not live here to come and tell them we were in solidarity with them, with what they were attempting to do.

They had our blessings and respect, but for all practical purposes, they were pretty much on their own, though we wished them well.

Looking down at the people crossing the street, I wondered just how many had faced having a dear one thrown in jail for "suspicion" of being a dissenter, a so called "enemy of the people" and unable to defend himself or herself, in a system that was brutally efficient in getting rid of those it did not like.

If Adam came back and was thrown in jail, would his mother call every person she knew and ask them to intercede for him? Of course, she would. All of her life's work would be put on the line. What choice would she have?

What choice did anyone living in this society have? In a most vicious and insidious way citizens of this country, and all of the other countries under repressive governments, had been forced into accepting a terrible, corrupting choice.

A choice that gave them some modicum of material comfort in exchange for their own moral degradation, loss of their dignity, and annihilation of their personal integrity.

What a fucked-up world we have constructed for ourselves.

Adam's mother knew and understood that for the sake of her son, she could not drop out of the system and choose an alternative simply because there was not any.

She was lucid enough to know that to survive she had to accept spiritually prostituting who she was as a person, and in the process destroy her moral integrity, the very idea of her own self-worth.

That insidious process was what made it so degrading. Yet, paradoxically, it was that very same moral degradation people had to engage in to exist that always presented the greatest threat to the survival of tyrannical societies.

That was why repressive societies were paranoid, and had to be on guard against people like Adam and his mother, at all times. This is such a fucked-up way of living, I thought.

I was not depressed about what human beings did to one another— we had been doing it for so damn long we took for granted it was never going to change.

Would the Czechoslovakian people, or any people living under cruel and tyrannical governments, ever be left to live their own lives as they saw fit and be like everybody else? Was it possible?

It was not even a question of my cynicism finally controlling me. It was more the recognition of the total absurdity of our lives, and how the evil in us constantly tries to trample others and take advantage of their fears and their insecurities to gain, but gain what?

Yeah, fuck our neighbors.

The phone rang again. It was Alain. I was so grateful to the gods for the phone working.

"OK, the news isn't so bad. Dr. Brisson saw Lisa about an hour ago. She and the baby are doing well. Lisa is more worried about what you're going to do than about herself." I laughed. My lovely Lisa. It did not surprise me.

"Milo got an attorney, very prominent guy, well connected, who's right now trying to figure a way to get her out of jail. It's Pete we're having a tough time controlling. He wants to storm the police station," Alain said, half-amused, half-concerned.

Good old Pete, I loved the man. This gave us a chance to chuckle a bit.

"Why was Lisa arrested?"

Alain had not said why, though Adam's mother had given me a general hint that it had to do with some kind of political action Lisa and Adam were part of, but what political action?

One was free to pretty much do what one wanted in Paris as far as politics was concerned. France has always been one of the most traditionally liberal countries in Europe.

On the other hand, I could not discount that things were pretty hectic in France right now. With the students on strike, and now the powerful unions getting in on the act there was bound to be some circles within the government clamoring for tighter measures and less tolerance.

"It's not clear. I found out that Ulla was arrested, too," he responded. I did not tell him that I already knew about Ulla from talking with Adam's mother.

"They weren't looking for her, but she was with Lisa. It seems Ulla made such a row about Lisa getting arrested the cops decided it was best to take Ulla in as well."

"Bless her."

"The Swedish government is preparing to lodge a formal protest."

He allowed himself a bit of a laugh.

"I don't think *les flics*," and here he used the French slang for police, "know what to do with these two women."

"Are you sure that Lisa is fine?"

"Dr. Brisson told me there is no immediate danger. Of course, the longer Lisa remains in jail the greater the risk for something going wrong," he said, certainly not the kind of words I wanted to hear.

"Do you think they'll torture her?"

"Alex, please. If that were to happen, I won't wait for Peter to storm the jail. I'll do it myself, and I'm sure Milo will be one step behind me if not ahead of me!"

I knew he meant it. Briefly, I brought him up to date on my efforts to get out of Prague. I did not mention meeting Adam's mother. Nor did I share with him the news about Czechoslovakian state security's interest in me. He had enough problems as it was.

Besides, somebody could have been listening. We promised to keep in touch at all costs. I thought of calling Lisa's parents, but even if I got through what would I tell them?

"Hi, this is Alex, your daughter and granddaughter are guests of the French government in some dismal Parisian jail, and I'm calling you from Prague, but other than that things are OK."

Yeah, that would be just dandy. Another level of anxiety was not what I needed now.

I also thought of calling José, but seeing the trouble I had getting through on the phone it would have been another exercise in futility. The only thing I knew was that I had to get back to Paris at all costs.

The train was the other possibility. Overnight to Germany, and from there take a flight to Paris. I wanted so badly to be back there. I would have given anything to get back.

I needed miracles, and I silently prayed for one, though I knew the gods were not predisposed to granting me anything. Nevertheless, I prayed for one. Something told me the manager's words about state security looking for me were far more ominous than they appeared.

I was not afraid for me. I could see myself telling them to go fuck themselves. But it was one thing to think of doing it in the abstract, and quite another to finally be confronted with it and what could happen if I lost my cool.

I realized that, like all the people I had seen here, I was scared, very scared. Under the present circumstances, it would serve no purpose to play the tough guy role. It was better to keep my mouth shut and remember my manners.

Lisa's words while we were in Normandy about something happening to me while I was in Prague came to my mind, but it was to her that something bad was now happening.

The gods knew that for Lisa, I would give up everything that I was. She now represented what my life was finally coming to something resembling normalcy that had meaning and not a mere accident. I could no longer just try and get by.

Not this time, in fact, not anymore. What I had experienced with her these past few months had touched me very deeply. It was true that I did not completely understand the change, but I was not fighting it anymore.

This sense of wholeness, of belonging, was new to me because I did not have to pretend. I did not have to feel that I was an outsider. Was that what Cécile had meant when she said that I was "too self-centered"? I never thought I was, though, I could see why she had said it.

I never experienced with her, or with any other woman, what I had found with Lisa. Suddenly, it was there. Lisa could look me in the eyes and tell me her heart was mine without ambiguities. I needed to work harder to come to such a similar grace.

She did not have to go through all the contortions that I went through. There was no need for her to do that. Lisa had brought the simple message that love existed. It was not some crazy dream or something reserved for just a few.

I knew with time things could change, life could change, feelings could change—change is inevitable in all humans—but what now existed in my life was true.

I had found someone who loved me, pure and simple. She did not impose conditions. She just gave me whatever it was that love is supposed to give—no need for explanation. In love, what is required is to stop making excuses. Lisa had done that.

I was working to do the same, and it was not easy. Perhaps, that was what the gods were showing me: I had to work hard if I expected to become worthy of her.

"When I love, I give," Pete had said upon giving her the painting.

Lisa had not said that to me, but she did not have to, and it was because of this that she was free. I was still struggling with that idea, and I had seen glimpses of it. I could not deny it.

My weariness and fear belonged to another time, a time when Lisa did not exist. Now everything was different. Lisa existed. There was a baby, our baby, who existed.

Perhaps, later, we would laugh about me stuck in the middle of a workers' paradise while they languished in some Parisian jail, though today it sure as hell was not a laughing matter.

The facts were clear: Lisa was in jail in Paris with our baby; I was stuck in Prague without my passport; the cops wanted to talk to me. A nice fix I had gotten myself into.

Did I have an ace up my sleeve? No, and these were not the times to try to be brave or foolish, for if I screwed up, I would not see Lisa for a long time. I had to prepare for any eventuality. The question was how? I needed to act and not react—easier said than done.

I wanted to walk out of there with no fear that at the last moment someone would tap me on the shoulder and ask me to step back for there was still another question that had to be answered.

What I needed was the same thing I had seen Demetrios do in Athens for Chris. I wondered how he would have done it. It was through him that I met Iris, and it was also through him I had met Lisa. The thought had not occurred to me before.

It was a coincidence that had taken place and for some reason, out of the blue, it had now dawned on me. I had not had any news from him, and I also wondered if he had received the copy of the article I had sent to him, the one I had written about him that he thought had made him "famous." I laughed.

What was happening to those crazy Greeks? Thinking about these things momentarily took me away from feeling lousy about Lisa and what was happening to her.

How did she feel at this very moment? I love her! Does she see it? What if I never saw her again? It was not morbidity that made me think of that. My hands were shaking. Had the gods heard my prayers?

In the past, I had been scared on many occasions, but then I had been alone and had nobody else to think about. Today was different. I could not pretend to be brave when I had a pregnant lady waiting for me.

I needed to get some perspective about my present situation—without it I was nowhere. It was not as if I had never been in tight situations before. I had and had managed to keep my cool.

Back then, however, I did not have the agony of thinking of a woman I loved in jail, carrying my baby and with me so damn far away, from where I should have been to begin with.

Would I be as strong as Mohammed was when he learned his baby had died, or Big D. facing the moment when he had to kill another man? Or Pete knowing he and Roxanne would not have a child they so much wanted?

These are things that life had brought to us without any logical explanation. Was this one of those decisive moments? How could I tell? I seemed to have very little room to maneuver. A strange calmness washed over me.

The security police were on my tail, no doubt about it. From what I knew, their tactics did not augur well for anyone caught in their web. I just had to keep one step ahead of them. But how?

To pretend otherwise was phony, and the last thing I wanted was to fail Lisa and the baby. That was not an option. People often say things happen for a reason. I could only hope that whatever happened would be for a good reason.

I thought back to difficult situations I had faced in the past, and tried to extract from such memories what had sustained me through those trying moments. Would such experiences be of help in my present predicament? Maybe. But, then, again, maybe not.

My thoughts took me back to Istanbul, sometime ago, where I found myself in the middle of two well-armed sides buying and selling heroin. Alain had asked me if I would try to do an article on drug trafficking in this part of the world. Like a fool, I told him yes.

I thought, what the hell, I can do this. A contact he had in Istanbul introduced me to Johann, a German guy who lived there and knew his way around this dangerous world. Alain's friend warned me not to trust Johann and not to say anything about what I was doing.

Thus, I found myself, late one evening, after a series of detours—in a large and dimly lit garage surrounded by old and abandoned American cars—witnessing a big drug deal conducted by two heavily armed groups. Johann spoke a little French, and needed someone to translate from French into English.

Very innocently, he had asked me to come and meet some of his "friends." This meeting was not about friendship but about business—hard-core drug business. Right off the bat, I could tell both sides distrusted me.

Nevertheless, there followed a negotiated contract for the delivery of the purest form of heroin. The Turks talked to Joann in German. He would translate it into French for me, and I would explain it in English to the buyers.

The man in charge of the buyers was a black American whose accent was unmistakably New York: Brooklyn. Quantities, deliveries, dates, were discussed and the prices quoted were amazing!

The delivery would take place in a few days. The exact time and place remained one sticking point. It was the most civilized business meeting. The American guy was loose and cool.

But as the haggling got serious, I realized he guessed I was not just a friend of Johann's who happened to be there to translate. I had other reasons for being there. I saw it on his face.

I do not know how he guessed it. His distrust of me was immediate. In this most bizarre, dangerous, and crazy situation, he now seemed to weigh every word I translated with careful and long silences.

He avoided looking directly at me, which did nothing to calm my nerves. It was probably the only time in my life that I wanted to trust my instincts completely, but the notion scared the hell out of me. I am not an instinctive person.

I realized, I could end up with my body riddled with bullets if I lost my cool. I knew he had guessed my feelings, but I was lost about what his feelings were.

Then, there was one Turkish guy who kept looking at me in an odd way, finessing me with his hard, evil stares—dangerous, very dangerous. He was sweating profusely. My fear upon realizing I had to be cool about what I was doing made me even more scared that I now had become part of the story.

No money or drugs were exchanged. One would have thought the deal had to do with buying Dutch tulips rather than hard drugs.

After some very tense moments, due mostly to making sure all of the details of the deal had been ironed out completely, and having to wait for the translation to take place, both sides expressed satisfaction and the meeting ended. I wanted to get the hell out of there as fast as I could.

"Haven't I seen you somewhere before?" the American said to me casually, too casually. Everyone stopped to look at me. I froze.

"I don't think so." I finally managed to answer.

"Your face looks familiar."

I was scared with a primitive fear one cannot easily control. The looks exchanged between the two groups were murderous. The whole place became as silent as a tomb.

I was trapped. The look in this guy's eyes said to me that if I got killed it would not have made any difference to him.

"You've been to Istanbul before?" He continued.

"No, it's the first time."

"Are you visiting or for business?"

I thought the bastard wants my head on a tray like a pig, and probably with my balls stuffed in my mouth. I knew he was doing this on purpose. He was just getting even. As scared as I was, I also knew I had to keep my cool.

I was not about to let this bastard browbeat me. I knew he could get me killed, but I was not about to let him think I was going to be a pushover.

"I'm supposed to meet a friend of mine who is in the Peace Corps here in Turkey." I tried to keep my voice from letting him know I was scared shitless. It was probably wishful thinking on my part, but I tried.

"Really. A good friend, I imagine."

His words were not hurried or threatening. It was a pleasant conversation between two normal people, except there was nothing normal about what had just taken place, and nothing normal about what I was risking if this asshole decided to do a number on me.

"Where is he stationed?" he asked, a moment later.

Perhaps he was going to drill me like this for his pleasure before he decided to turn me over to the Turks. The rest of the people were carefully following our conversation.

The tension in the air was intense. I was not sure whether I was putting my buddy's life in danger if I explained he was stationed in a town called Antalya, which was true.

My good buddy Hank, from college, had joined the Peace Corps and had come to Paris for a visit not too long ago, telling me about his work in Turkey. I had written to Hank that I was coming to Turkey and asked him if we could meet, but I had not gotten a response from him yet.

"It's near Izmir. I can't remember the name of the town," I lied.

There was some murmur from the Turks. One of them said something to Johann. It did not surprise me that the Turks understood English.

"He says he knows about the Peace Corps work. He's heard they are helping the people," Johann said to me, in French.

"What did he say?" The American asked.

"That this guy knows about the Peace Corps helping people in Turkey," I translated for him.

My mouth was dry. I was not sure if I had peed in my pants. I am sure that if I had reached down to verify, I probably would have found that my balls had shriveled to nothing. There was a long silence.

The American was looking at the Turks as if expecting them to say something. On the other hand, the Turks seemed to want him to make some sort of decision. He was silent for what seemed like an eternity. Finally, he stood as if tired of the whole charade.

"Well, tell your friend to keep up the good work," he said.

I translated for Johann, which he translated into German for the Turks. They all shook hands and the meeting was over. I waited a moment to move because I did not trust my legs.

When Johann drove back to the hotel, he seemed keen on confusing anybody who might have been following us. It took over a couple of hours to get back.

We literally toured Istanbul at night. Though I understood the precautions, it was nerve wracking. We did not say much.

I felt stupid and guilty because I had participated in an illegal transaction, and I was not pleased. I knew I was trapped and could not have done anything to prevent what had taken place. I had to wrestle with my own conscience about what I had witnessed.

I also knew, the authorities were not very benign to people involved with drugs, though, I had only served as the hapless translator. My press card would not be of much help and like a fool, I had taken it with me. Alain had warned me not to carry it, especially in such situations, but I had forgotten to leave it at the hotel.

Johann had wanted to pay me for translating, but I had turned him down. Nevertheless, I thought it wiser to start thinking about getting out of Istanbul. I pretty much had all of the material I would need to write the article for Alain.

Back at the hotel, Johann seemed in good spirits and was chatting away as if nothing out of the ordinary had taken place. I did not trust him, but I was also fascinated by the way he acted. His youthful face and demeanor betrayed nothing, and I wondered how many secrets he kept.

He followed me into my room. He wanted to continue the chess game we had started earlier in the evening, but I was not in the mood. I was thinking of asking him to leave when, abruptly, the door to my room flew wide open and half a dozen men stormed inside with their guns drawn. They smelled like cops, and they were.

They immediately grabbed Johann, slapped handcuffs on him, pushed him against the wall, and started talking to him in German. One of the cops stood by my side. I did not dare move. They wanted Johann.

It was almost as if I did not exist. As they were taking him away, the black guy walked into the room with a big smirk on his face. The son of a bitch was a U.S. drug agent!

"You're good," he said. "I couldn't have pulled it off the way you did, and I'm good at what I do. Have you ever thought of becoming a cop?"

I wanted to kill him. He looked at me with a slick smile on his face as if the exercise of the previous hours had been a walk in the park. The bastard had just about had me killed. I was pissed. He knew it.

"You prick," I said.

"It was supposed to be a compliment," he said, laughing.

"Yeah, well, don't do me any favors."

"Relax, it was either that or both of us would have gotten it."

"You figured out why I was there. You did it just to bust my balls. And it wouldn't surprise me if you speak German."

"I do, and my Turkish ain't bad either. Anyway, reporters are scum."

"Well, I hate pricks like you, too.

"I'll try to remember it for the next time."

"Yeah, you do that."

"What are you complaining about? You saw the way that guy kept looking at you."

Yeah, I remembered.

"He's a bad ass," he continued. "Yeah, I've got to hand it to you. You didn't blink—or maybe you're just lucky."

Yeah, lucky. Right. His voice did not sound too sarcastic anymore.

"Your friend has vouched for you," he continued.

They had done their homework! Jesus. I wondered how they had found Hank so fast.

"Izmir," he muttered, then smiled and shook his head as if disappointed because I had lied, or perhaps it was his desire to feel superior for actually having caught me in a lie.

Now he wanted to have the last word about the whole episode. For some reason, I felt he wanted me to laugh with him. I was not in the mood.

"Why didn't you tell me your friend is a brother?"

I hated the son of a bitch even more for bringing into the conversation that my buddy Hank is black.

"It's none of your goddamned business. Furthermore, he ain't your brother."

"Anyway, he says to say hello," he said, with a smirk.

"Go fuck yourself!"

"Temper, temper, temper. I'll take a rain check on your invitation. I'd like to extend one of my own: You ought to consider getting out of this place, like, pronto. I hear you live in Paris. It must be nice at this time of the year.

"Say, I'm due for some vacation. If I come to Paris for a visit, can you give me a tour of the hot spots? Also, make sure that if you write any shit about what happened tonight that you get my name spelled correctly."

He knew, I would never reveal his name even if I knew it, which I did not know it.

"Yeah, right. Mr. H-o-o-v-e-r, that's how you spell your name, isn't it."

He started to laugh again, a rich, sonorous laugh that sounded cool, relaxed, and not indifferent—more like the joke was on me, and I was being a bad sport about it. I started to shake in pure anger.

It was a good thing I did not have a weapon for I probably would have done something stupid. He walked over to the chessboard on the table and stood looking down at the game, studying it.

"I believe white will check mate in three moves," he finally said.

He looked back at me, laughed, and walked out of the room. I walked over to the board and studied it. The bastard was right.

I never did get together with Hank. Later, he wrote me he had read my article in the local newspaper about a big drug bust, though, I had made no mention of any American drug agent. Sometimes, I wondered if the guy ever came to Paris.

It probably would not have taken him but a few phone calls to find me given the kind of work he did. After I got back to Paris, Alain suggested, half-seriously, that I should stop making Turkey my favorite vacation spot.

Had I been scared in Istanbul? Yes, absolutely! But through it all, I had somehow managed to overcome my fears and lived to reflect on it. I was not certain if the memory was strong enough to guide me and hold me through what I was now facing here in Prague.

Yet when one is desperate, as I was at that moment, there is no other choice but to try to conquer those fears. Lisa trusted me, and that feeling gave me hope and lifted my spirits.

Maybe all the mind games I was playing would turn out for naught, but at the point where I was, something, anything, was better than nothing. The phone rang. It was the hotel's reception desk.

They had not yet found a seat on a flight to Paris for me. I asked them to please send a telex to Paris, to Alain, informing him of that. They said they would try.

TWELFTH

Suddenly, I heard a loud banging coming from somewhere within my drowsiness. It was hard to determine its source. I tried to shake myself out of my sleep, but I seemed unable to do so. The banging continued, relentless, loud, and unfriendly.

I thought I must put a stop to this; it is keeping me from getting some rest. It is probably the maid wanting to get into the room to clean. Maybe I should call the reception desk.

The banging would not stop. This is ridiculous. Who the hell do they think they are? I heard my name very loudly, coming from a woman's voice. There was a dull echo to it like it was in a tunnel or underwater.

I thought it was Lisa's voice, but then, again, I was not sure. Now I could hear it clearly. It was my name. I could hear it distinctly; however, the woman's voice I did not recognize.

It was not Lisa; whose voice was it? Adam's mother, perhaps, but it was not hers, either. Then a man's voice also called me. The voices were calling me by my first name.

This was surprising because the reception downstairs had never used my first name to address me. Maybe I told them that it was fine, and I forgot. I racked my brain trying to remember if I had given them such permission, and I could not find it in my memory.

Oh, well, it was no big thing, really. I saw faces. They seemed wan, tired, listless, and they felt sorry for me I could tell. Now all of us shared a secret. We had something in common. We were in the same boat going nowhere, though we had to stay together.

That was the thing. My name again, loudly. A man's voice. Loud. Banging. Loud. I woke up. I sat on the bed, scared, and I looked around me.

There was a photo of Lisa on the nightstand, smiling, looking at the camera with her hand over her tummy and showing off her pregnancy. Was this the photo we sent her parents? What was it doing here in Prague?

I did not remember taking a copy with me. So, what was it doing in this hotel room? The banging and the voices calling me continued; then, I knew.

I was back in Paris!

I stumbled out of bed trying to focus. The familiarity of my own apartment seemed to jump out at me and confuse me even more. In a daze, I recognized the furniture and the other stuff.

In a rush, I put on my robe, hurried to the front door and when I opened it, standing outside with worried looks on their faces were Madame Commère, Peter, Roxanne, and José.

"I'm sorry, I was having this crazy dream someone was calling me," I said, still in a fog.

"It wasn't a dream," Pete said. "We've been banging on the damn door forever. Are you all right?" He kept looking at me trying to make sure.

"Yes, I'm fine, it's fine, thanks."

Now I understood where the noise, the banging, the calling of my name came from. Madame Commère had tears in her eyes. She did something she had never done before, she hugged me, which took me aback; turned, and walked down the stairs.

"Can we come in?" Roxanne asked.

"Please come in. I'm sorry."

I stood in the middle of the room trying to get my bearings. Roxanne hugged me, then she went into the kitchen, and soon I could hear her making us some coffee. I noticed she had a couple of fresh baguettes with her.

"You, OK?" Peter asked, again.

"Yeah, I'm just a bit bummed out. I couldn't sleep last night at all. I think I fell asleep when the sun came out. How did you find out I was back?"

"Alain called," Pete said.

"You look like shit," José said, and he pointed to my robe. In my rush to get dressed, I had put it on inside out! Everyone laughed. I took it off and put it on properly.

"I know. Don't ask me how I feel."

"Yeah, how do you feel?"

He was trying to be funny. His face was tired, his eyes were bloodshot, and he looked like he needed some sleep.

"I have seen better days," I said, and gave them each a big hug.

Yes. I had seen the sun come out in the middle of the Egyptian desert, a giant ball, yellow, bright, powerful, eternal, and the giver of life. I had seen a superb production of *Aida*, at the Caracalla Baths, in Rome—unforgettable.

I had seen surfers riding giant waves in Wamea Bay, Hawaii, and experienced the thrill and fear those of us watching felt. I had seen and heard Maria Callas sing *Tosca*, unbelievable.

I had stood in Red Square during Christmas Eve looking at the vast blanket of freshly fallen snow, listening to Christmas music, and wondering why everybody thought Russians did not celebrate this most Christian of holidays. I had rafted down the Grand Canyon, an experience of a lifetime.

I had taken Lisa to an incredible concert by Jacques Brel, the best poet and singer of French music, though not French, but from Belgium, and with an amazing musical sensibility and talent. Lisa had fallen in love with his music and lyrics, as I knew she would.

I had also seen the face of a woman I was so worried about because of what was happening to her. I had seen her happy face when she was looking at me and teasing me about my madness. When we were making love,

I had seen the way she seemed so intent on making me her own. Such a lovely face and now in the nightmare we were going through, the face was as clear, fresh, and immediate as if I had been looking at her in the flesh.

She had brought to my life something that went beyond the love a woman has for a man. Lisa had shown me a sense of decency about relationships. In her own unique way, she had brought an incredible sense of truth about love, about herself, and about me. She forced me to look directly at who I was and not hide behind a mask.

"Look, nothing can come between us except us." She had said one day while we were walking by the Seine. "All things must be equal between us. Everything I bring to you is within me. You can take all the superficial stuff, the signs, the symbols, the masks most of us hide behind, and you will find that I left them out of our relationship."

"What brought that on?"

"It's my heart speaking, that's all."

If truth were told, I was afraid more for me than I was for her. She was stronger than I was. I thought back to the idea of some people going through life and not being tainted by its ugliness; rather, they touched life and made it better for the rest of us.

Somehow, the cosmos in its wisdom had anointed certain individuals with this gift and you either had it or you did not. So many of us spend our lives looking for it, condemned never to find it.

Lisa had i!

I wished the gods had been more patient with me, more tolerant, more accommodating but, alas, that had not been the case. The stardust from which I had sprung would never form such a mold as the one from which Lisa had emerged.

I was a prisoner. She was free. Now that a baby was the result of her love for me, that reality was so complex and mysterious I still had trouble dealing with it.

I was scared; of course, I was scared—she was behind bars in some dismal Parisian jail. I was scared I had not been wise enough to fully understand my relationship with her.

There was no yesterday, only today and tomorrow and forever. Do people love forever? I did not believe it. Why should it be any different for me? But for Lisa it was different.

The past few days, back in Prague, had been exhausting and without end. I had been unable to get a return flight to Paris. All I could do was sit and wait. That was the hardest part. I was a prisoner of my worst nightmares—an anxious, ugly, and depressing situation.

The lowest moment of my life!

Not even the fact that I witnessed their May Day Parade, boisterous, filled with enthusiasm, gaiety, took away my anxiety and fear about what was happening to Lisa back in Paris.

I was watching thousands of people march by with giant banners; all full of hope for a better life, free, with no longer an oppressive government controlling their destinies. Looking forward to a brighter future for themselves—their families. And all I could think of was that my own personal life was not looking bright at all. Lisa's plight was the only thing I could concentrate on.

Being in Prague and witnessing these events was exceptional, yet I also felt that I was absent, just going through the motions. I felt guilty about my sentiments.

The parade was tumultuous and it did give the people attending a sense that maybe, just maybe, their lives would change for the better. I could not really concentrate on what was taking place around me. I hated to feel this way.

That weekend of May fourth and fifth was the longest and loneliest weekend I ever lived through. Since getting the news from Alain about Lisa's incarceration, my mind had been racing at hundreds and hundreds of miles an hour trying to figure a way to get out of Prague.

Always imaging the worst. That Saturday night, I did not sleep at all. I tried to get through to Paris for almost twenty-four hours with no luck.

I was reaching the end of my rope when late on Sunday afternoon, in sheer desperation, I decided to call Adam's mother and asked her to come and join me for some coffee downstairs. I needed to talk to someone or I would go crazy.

She graciously agreed to come immediately. It was a gutsy move on her part. When later I said so, she dismissed my concerns with a wave of the hand. She was something else. I told her that the state security agency was looking for me.

"That's serious," she said.

"I feel dumb sitting here waiting for them to come back."

"Oh, I don't believe they work on weekends," she said, bringing a bit of levity to the situation.

I appreciated her sense of humor. The truth was that I did not know just how much time I had. I needed her help in the worst possible way.

"I have to get out of here, fast. I can't wait until they come for me. If I take a plane or train, they can stop me at the last minute. They know where I am. They can keep track of me. The solution is to go by car to Germany or Austria. I need to disappear and try to cross the border before they realize I'm missing."

"It's risky."

"I have no choice."

"For that you need your passport."

"I know. Helping me is probably riskier for you."

"It's my business," she said forcefully. "Your passport? The hotel won't give your passport back?" Her question brought into focus how desperate my situation was.

"I haven't really insisted. I wanted to talk to you first."

We were sitting in the lounge and had a clear view of the reception area. She looked in that direction. She looked back at me.

"What does the night manager look like? She asked.

"What do you mean?"

"Physically, what does he look like?"

I was somewhat taken aback by the question.

"It's the guy with the glasses, tall, with gray hair. He seems to have a bit of a limp," I managed to answer.

She sat quietly mulling over my desperate request. The way she looked at me reminded me of Cleo back in Athens: Looking at my face, studying me, and searching for clues about whether I was worth taking a chance on.

Did I merit the risk involved? It felt like she was trying to make up her mind. I knew I was asking for something dangerous, and I felt damn incompetent. Her face was totally blank. She would make a perfect poker player, I thought.

Then she appeared to have reached a decision. Quietly, she instructed me that around midnight I was to leave the hotel. Just take my shoulder bag and all of my notes and papers. She said that I was to take a taxi to a nightclub; she wrote down the address.

There, someone would start a conversation with me at the bar and I was to follow his directions to the letter. She asked me to give him enough traveler's checks to pay for the hotel, she would see to it later. I did not ask her how she intended to do that.

"How would he know me?"

"*Il vous a déjà suivit.*"

She saw my reaction and smiled. I had suspected I was being followed, though I was not sure by whom. Now I knew. I had been very careful at the hotel not to leave any papers around.

Once, I thought that someone had been in my room because I detected my dictionary had been moved, but it could have been just my imagination or the cleaning woman.

It was no secret that the maids were suspected of being government agents. I knew I was being very careful, so I took comfort via that fact. In any event, since I had nothing to hide and I always took my papers with me, which had its own risks as well, I just had to play it by ear.

Either way they had the upper hand, and driving myself crazy with worries about it was not going to change the reality.

"*Le problem c'est votre passport,*" Adam's mother continued. That was the only hitch: How to get my passport back.

"Do you believe in the cosmos?" she suddenly asked. Lisa had said something similar once. I did not know what I believed in but where I was at that moment, I was willing to believe anything.

"Sometimes, it's the only thing that makes sense. Of course," she added, with a wry smile, "a few dollars can sometimes work miracles—even in a worker's paradise."

Women do see the practical side of life probably more often than men do. I embraced her, and she held me closely. I did not ask her if I would see her later. My heart told me I would not. I went back to my room. The conversation with Adam's mother had lifted up my spirits.

I do not know how many times I walked around the room, looking at my watch, wanting for midnight to arrive, and at the same time wondering how in the hell this thing would turn out. Talk about being a prisoner of one's fears; I was!

Finally, I stuffed all of my notes inside my shoulder bag and stood in the middle of the room with a knot in my stomach, still unsure of what would happen next or how soon before I would see Lisa again, when I became aware that something was being pushed under the door of my room.

It was my passport!

Someone was sliding it under the door. Was this a trap? I sat on the bed and looked toward the door for a long time. I did not want to open it. Very gingerly, I finally walked over to the door and stood looking down at the passport.

I put my ear to the door, but I could not hear anything outside. I was afraid that if I pulled it into the room someone would bust the door open, and who knows what would happen next.

But I was running out of time. I had to be at the club as Adam's mother had instructed me. Holding my breath, very slowly, I finally got on my hands and knees and after looking at the passport very carefully, I started pulling it in little by little.

It was jammed tight between the door and the floor; however, I managed to free it. I held my breath for what seemed like an eternity, waiting for the knock on the door. My hands were shaking and I was sweating.

All the weight of my fears was riding on this being the miracle I had asked the gods for, though, I also thought of the sacrifices the gods expect for such favors.

I stood and slowly walked to the bathroom and turned the light on. It *was* my passport all right. I recognized a stain from accidentally spilling ink on it a few years back.

Adam's mother! How had she done it? She had mentioned that dollars always bought anything, anywhere. The thought occurred to me that it would probably be downstairs where something was going to happen.

There I would be stopped by the security cops just as I was getting out of the hotel. Such a spectacle would be more dramatic for them.

What the hell, I thought, I have come this far, so I might as well face the music. To get out of Prague was the only priority. I had to take the leap into the unknown.

To get back to Lisa, at whatever the cost, was the only decision I needed to face. I left the light on in the room and my other belongings all over the place as if I were coming back. The hallway was empty when I came out of the room.

The elevator seemed to take forever to go down. There was nobody waiting for me in the lobby. I dropped off the key at the reception counter, as I had done many times. I did not detect anything unusual.

The night clerks looked up at me indifferently. Resolutely, I walked to the front door and out of the hotel, but I was shaking.

As I stood outside waiting for a taxi, I looked back and through the glass door, I saw the manager looking in my direction with what I thought was a bit of a smile. It was probably my own feverish imagination. I was afraid to smile back.

The taxi took me to the club's address written on the paper Adam's mother had given me. I glanced back and did not see any other car following us. I still was not sure how this thing would turn out, but I felt a little relief.

In less than ten minutes, after having to walk through a dark and dank basement leading to a trap door and back through a small courtyard and another door still, and after handing a man who met me at the bar several traveler's checks—more than enough to pay for the hotel—I got into another taxi to be driven to the German border.

The man at the bar had explained that going to Germany was less risky and simply do what the taxi driver said to do. Another taxi would be waiting for me on the German side. I tried hard to remember if I had seen the man at the bar before but he was totally unfamiliar.

He wished me good luck. I tried to relax a little, but the strain of the last few hours had taken its toll. Even concentrating on Lisa's plight was not easy.

There was a set of car headlights behind us that really shook me up. The driver kept looking in the rearview mirror and muttering to himself, which added to my fears, but he kept his cool.

He drove through several neighborhoods, and after what seemed like long and interminable moments, the other car turned off.

The driver and I breathed rather audible sighs of relief. He still wanted to make sure no one was behind us so we did an hour's long night tour of the outskirts of Prague. Nobody followed us. He turned the radio on and it was playing *Madama Butterfly*. He started to hum along to the music.

Private Cooney! That was his name. In Bangkok, in transit after my tour in Vietnam was over while waiting for my flight back to the States, I started talking to him. Cooney would be best described as American as corn from Iowa.

Much to my surprise, he did not want to go back to the States. In fact, he told me he was going over the wall and would never return to the U. S., never! He seemed so distraught at the prospect of going back. He was smoking like crazy.

He was looking for someone to help him get an ID card so he could get off the base. He kept repeating that he was not going back. He had met and had fallen in love with a bar hostess in Bangkok, and wanted to marry her.

The Army had said no. He was given his orders to ship out, and he had not shown up at the airport. The plane left without him.

The Army busted him from a sergeant down to a private for being A.W.O.L. His ID card was taken away, was ordered to stay on the base, check with the dispatcher every hour, and be ready to ship out at a moment's notice.

He wanted to get off the base, and needed an ID to do so, so he asked to borrow mine. He said that I could declare I had lost it. He was so despondent and showed me a picture of a girl who had a simple face, and very kind and soulful eyes.

They had fallen in love just like that. He had rented her a place and had given her money so she would not have to work bars anymore. They had lived like this for over six months, but now his tour was up.

He tried to extend it, but the Army was not buying it. He had tried to get the chaplain to marry them; however, upon finding out what the girl had done for a living, the Army had denied his request.

"I told them the whole truth," he said, still innocent about the ways of the world. "I didn't want to lie. She told me not to say what kind of work she had done because she knew the Army would turn us down.

"I told her I wouldn't lie, that the fucking Army wasn't marrying her, I was marrying her! Then bigger than shit, they did a number on us. I wished I had listened to her." He stopped and lit up another cigarette. His small hands, heavily stained with nicotine, were shaking.

"She got pregnant but had to get an abortion," he continued. "The Army says girls get pregnant on purpose so GIs have to marry them just so they can go to the States. But she didn't get pregnant for that.

"She got pregnant because she loves me. The abortion was so tough on her, and she was all alone when she got it done. She wanted that baby so bad. I couldn't go see her because I was out in the field trying to kill people." He started to cry.

"Man, I know she loves me . . . fuck the Army! I ain't going back to the States, and that's that. Of course, she's now afraid and tells to me go and send for her later. Shit, if I can't get her out while I'm here what do you think her chances will be when I'm gone?"

He was so earnest. His story made me think of what Monique had told Lisa and me about Billy, her GI, and the graves in Normandy we had seen at the American cemetery. The Army chews up guys like Cooney as cannon fodder, and spits them out without any further thought.

"Look, I know you may get in trouble if you give me your ID," he said. "I have no choice but to beg you for it. You know how they fuck with your head. I'm getting off this base. If I can't get me an ID, I'm going over the wall and probably get my ass shot. I've got to take a chance to go find her. There is no other choice. She needs me."

"Suppose I give it to you. What are you going to do next? Eventually they'll find you."

"They'll never find me. Me and her are going back to her village, which is in the middle of nowhere, and we'll settle there. I grew up on a farm, and I know how to work the land. I know how to survive; I've done it all of my life." From his looks, I guessed he was barely twenty years old!

"You can't hide the rest of your life. What if the Thais decide to boot your ass out of here?"

"Well, I ain't gonna worry about that now. All I know is that I've got to go find her and take her away from here. Are you gonna help me or not?" His tone was beyond desperation.

"What if you get caught at the gate? I mean, if the MPs decide to look closer at your name, and you are in possession of my ID, then what?"

It would have taken a blind man not to see that his looks did not even approximate mine.

"I'll cover your ass. I'll never tell them you gave it to me. That'll be dishonest and stupid. I don't want to get you into trouble. I give you my word of honor."

"I don't know, man, I just don't know. What about your family back in the States?"

"Just me and my mom. I know she'll be crazy about Naree. I know it. My mom is backing me up a hundred percent. I've told her what I want to do, and she said to go ahead. All the Army wants is for me to go out and kill people. I don't want to do that anymore.

"I'm sick of it. America is fucked! Look what happened to Kennedy. All we do is kill good people. I don't want to go out there and kill those simple peasants. They're like me," he said, finally with a sad and distant voice.

I did not give him my ID. And whenever the music of *Madama Butterfly* came on the radio, I would switch it off. Puccini's tale is about personal betrayal; life, the Army and I had betrayed Naree and Cooney.

Two modern day star struck lovers, in their anxious search for happiness, for their dream to be together so they could make a life. In the taxi, I did not want to be reminded of my dismal failure back in Bangkok, but I could not shut off the driver's humming or the radio.

"Man, I wish I could help you," I had said to Cooney.

"Don't wish it. Do it. Have you ever been loved like that by a woman?"

A woman had never loved me like that, not until Lisa. I saw how stupid I had been with Cooney. We make incredible mistakes in life and we pay the price for them afterward, because life sucks!

"It's everything," he added softly. "You don't give a fuck what others say. I know some of my buddies think she's ugly with her slanted eyes and her English ain't from Harvard, but I don't care. What the fuck do they know? I'd like to see them try to learn her language.

"Man, it's what's inside that counts. She is beautiful. Her heart is so pure. She is kind, decent, loving, sweet, and so innocent. Don't you see? If I leave her here, I don't know what she'll do. I love her. She loves me. She's all I've got."

He stopped and wiped the tears from his sad and distraught eyes.

"She's the best thing that has ever happened to me. Why can't the fucking Army understand that? I hate these pricks for breaking her little heart and making her so sad."

Frantic people do desperate things. I now understood what Cooney had been saying. Back in Bangkok, I had been too stupid and insensitive—vulgarly insensitive—to understand his despair.

Now, here I am in the middle of Czechoslovakia doing something similar to what Cooney said he was going to do.

I am going over the fence, as it were, with my guts in an incredible turmoil. Terrified of getting stopped, fearing unfathomable consequences if I got caught but still determined to save my loved one.

It all told the same story: people trying to be everything for the one they love—no matter what. I did not have the balls to give Cooney my ID or the heart to understand his hopelessness.

I should have understood it!

All Cooney had wanted to do was rescue and protect the woman he loved. And I had not helped him.

I needed to go to the bathroom. When I came out, he was gone. At the time, I thought the fact he had not waited for me sort of got me off the hook. I also felt guilty for my lack of courage. I had been driven by strange reasons in not wanting to give him the ID.

Yes, I could have declared it lost. It would not have made any difference to the Army or me, but it would have made all the difference in the world to Naree and Cooney.

Many times, afterward, I fantasized about his having gotten away with his crazy plans, but I also knew I was playing mind games to feel less guilty about my poor, cowardly, stupid, and fucked-up behavior.

I did try to find him later but to no avail. I never saw him again because I got shipped out back to the States later that night. I knew I had miserably failed Cooney in his most desperate moment.

Can we be anything significant at all to another human being? I hoped with all my heart that he had managed to succeed. I wanted to believe it because I had been a damn coward.

Marty had said to me, back in Yugoslavia, that I would go to paradise for my attempt to help Mohammed and his baby. I do not think Marty would have been proud of my shameful failure to help Cooney.

I had told the story to Lisa, who tried to console me by saying that she would always believe in her heart and soul that Cooney and his girl had gotten away with it; that they were probably living happily in some farm country in the middle of Thailand, surrounded by lots of babies.

My experience—and my sense of guilt due to my failure to help Cooney—told me otherwise.

As we got closer to the Czechoslovakian/German border, after what seemed like long and incessant hours on the road, hours filled with anxiety impossible to describe, the driver got quiet, turned off the radio, and stopped the car.

He got out, opened the trunk, took out a bottle of vodka, and signaled for me to get out. Then he sprayed some of its contents on me. I was surprised at this. He took a long swig and passed me the bottle. I nearly finished it!

He threw the bottle away. He asked for my passport. I reeked of cheap vodka when we got to the border.

The driver got out of the car and started talking to the guards and, from what I could sense, explained to them that he had this crazy drunk American in the car.

He showed them my passport and the officer in charge told two young guards to walk over and have a look.

I pretended that I was drunk without too much drama, and I even opened the door and stumbled a bit trying to get out of the car. The guards held me steady and put me back inside the car.

They walked back to the guard station, talked to the officer who picked up the phone, and dialed.

I got really scared. The officer was having problems with the line because he kept shouting into the phone. The look on the taxi-driver's face led me to think that if we failed with our charade our asses would end up in some Siberian gulag.

The driver then started pointing to his watch and to me. He was arguing with the guards about being late.

The guards had a discussion. They were young, inexperienced, and probably tired, but still unable to make up their minds. The officer sent the two young guards back to the car.

This time I pretended I was asleep. One of them tried to awaken me, and I had to concentrate hard faking sleep, yet at the same time not show them I was shaking pretty badly.

If these guys got cute, I might have had to make a run for it, I thought, which would have been idiotic as hell—talk about desperation driving you insane. I could see the German border post a couple of hundred meters away.

The guards went back to the office, talked with the officer, and he finally stamped the passport. The driver walked back, got in the car, and we drove into Germany getting a cursory glance at my passport from the German border police.

I could not stop shaking. I needed a drink in the worst possible way. The taxi driver saw the shape I was in, and kept saying, "OK, OK, OK." He was just as shook up as I was. He took a small flask from his glove compartment, containing cognac, and handed it to me.

I took a long drink handed it back to him, but he did not have any. He then drove to the nearest town and found the taxi waiting for me.

I gave the driver two hundred dollars in cash; he was surprised. He shook his head and handed me one hundred dollars back.

"Too much."

"No, please, take it. Please!" I pleaded with him.

He shook his head.

"No, it is OK."

He kept shaking his head as I kept pushing the money toward him. He would not take it.

"*Merci, merci, vous étés libre,*" he said in French, with a sad look on his face.

I was free, but he was not. His words brought to me, once again, how innocent people's lives can be destroyed by politics, and scumbags. I had a choice, but he did not. We both knew it.

I embraced him. He had saved my ass from a gulag in Siberia, and I could not return the favor. Even in my own crazed state of mind, at that moment, I realized money had very little meaning—a humbling experience.

A clear lesson to me about the decency and honesty in people even under the most trying circumstances. He had tears in his eyes and so did I. Man, how I wished I could have taken him with me. I thought of Adam and his mother.

The German taxi driver spoke a bit of English, and he drove me to the Munich airport where we arrived just as the sun was beginning to emerge from its long sleep. He took my dollars without any problems. I spent still more hours waiting and trying, literally all day, to get a flight back to Paris.

I was bleared-eyed and tired but relieved that I was on my way back. I called Paris, got through, and left a message for Alain that I had made it to Germany.

Because France was now in the middle of a general strike, there were no flights that connected directly to Paris. The closest I could hope to get was Brussels.

After what seemed like endless waiting, I got on a flight from Munich to Brussels by way of Vienna and London, which is like traveling from Los Angeles to Alaska by way of Las Vegas, Hawaii, and Houston. OK, I am exaggerating, but it felt that way. Talk about an odyssey.

There were only a few trains running between Brussels and Paris, but I finally got a train to Paris where I arrived past midnight at La Gare du Nord. I stood in the aisle the entire trip, as the train was very crowded.

I had called Alain from Brussels, and he told me he would pick me up at the train station. A great sense of relief fell over me as the train rolled into the station.

I had been up and running with very little sleep for four days. I was beat; and I reeked of cheap, stale vodka, cognac, and human fear. No wonder my fellow passengers on the plane and the train did not act with kindness toward me, but I did not care.

I was coming back, though, I did not relish walking into an empty apartment knowing Lisa was spending another night in prison.

I hated it. It depressed the fuck out of me.

Alain did not look like he had gotten much sleep, either, and as he drove, he brought me up to date. The situation in France was getting crazy. Now that the workers had joined the students, *en masse*, matters had become very risky, and the government was unable or unwilling to restore order or to accept the changes the protestors were demanding.

The city was rife with rumors of an impending and violent crackdown by the police or worse, *a coup d'état* by the military to overthrow the sitting government. Alain was jumpy and nervous.

"How bad is it?"

"I've never seen the French act this way," Alain said. "Earlier today, the students and the riot police got into it with each other in a big way. It was bad, probably going on as we speak. I don't know what's going to happen. The workers' joining the students is a serious problem for the government. De Gaulle doesn't understand what is going on. He's lost it, I think."

His words worried me a lot more than ordinarily would have been the case for I had only one concern: "How will this affect Lisa's release?"

"I don't know. I really don't know," he answered, after a long pause.

The apartment smelled of her. As I opened the door, I had a vision in my head that Lisa would rush into my arms, but the place was empty, quiet, and forlorn.

Some homecoming! I poured Alain and me some pretty strong whiskeys. The burning of the alcohol going down my throat made me feel a bit better. As Alain had driven through Paris, the city seemed eerily quiet in this early month of May.

He said most of the turmoil was taking place in the Latin Quarter around the Sorbonne. We talked briefly about the material I had brought back with me from Prague, and he said it could wait, that now the only thing for us to concentrate on was how to get Lisa out of jail.

Dr. Brisson had seen her earlier in the day, and she reported that so far, they seemed to be treating her correctly. There was no sign of anything being wrong with Lisa or the baby. I was greatly relieved.

Dr. Brisson also told Alain the people in charge were now having second thoughts about keeping Lisa behind bars due to her pregnancy. The American Embassy had finally taken some action. Some official had met with Lisa and, apparently, a formal protest had been lodged.

Based on the information Milo's friend had been able to gather, the authorities were trying to find a formula under which Lisa and Ulla would be released without losing face.

I stood in the middle of the living room and wondered about my crazy life. If someone had said to me a few months earlier that due to my going to Greece I would be facing what I was now facing, I would have said they were totally, positively, and certifiably crazy!

Yes, back then, I had felt the need for change in my life, but absolutely nothing had prepared me for my present circumstances. I remembered what Sophocles, one of the great playwrights of Fifth Century Athens, had written: "But life takes sudden twists."

I was back in Paris, in my own apartment, alone, sick with worry, and wanting with all of my heart and being to be next to Lisa. I excused myself and told Alain I needed to soak up and get rid of the grime and smell. He understood and left.

We would talk early in the morning. I sat in the hot tub with a second glass of whiskey. I considered taking a bath with all my clothes on but decided that would not be so practical—besides, Madame Commère would not have approved.

The whiskey had no effect on me. I was tired, but I was fully awake. How in the hell did this whole ordeal come about? I had not discussed with Alain the political angle surrounding Lisa's arrest. I was not in the proper mood to try to unravel the mystery at two o'clock in the morning. I just sat in the tub and soaked.

The International Herald Tribune I had bought in Germany had brought me up to date on what was happening in Paris. It was apparent, the government and de Gaulle had been unable to put together a plan to deal with the student unrest.

French society was undergoing a tremendous and violent upheaval, and nobody seemed to know how or where the events would end. Nothing like this student revolt had ever been experienced before, certainly not on such a large scale.

While the government seemed adrift, its opponents were keen on bringing it down and, as a result, the country was now risking total paralysis. All of the public services were in great disarray, not a good sign.

The private sector was also suffering the consequences of the riots. Gasoline was being rationed. There were long lines at gas stations. There were also stories of empty supermarket shelves.

Alain had said that it would not be a bad idea to stock up as much as possible. Images of wartime France with people hoarding everything came to me. Thinking about them made me sad.

"Do you think *a coup d'état* is likely?" I had asked Alain.

"It is unthinkable. We can't be like some small African country."

"Well, things are really crazy around here."

"That's where the danger is. The government and the students going at each other could lead to total chaos, and in that scenario the military taking over would not be so far-fetched. There are Army troops stationed outside Paris.

"The cops and the CRS—the riot police—are tired. The government is talking about declaring martial law. There is plenty of talk about bringing the Army in to make sure there is some kind of government control around here."

"The Army coming into Paris would be extreme."

"Of course, but with all the chaos and order crumbling the government may not have another choice left. We're looking at the beginning of a total revolt, and unless the politicians running the show do something this is going to explode and there could be serious bloodshed."

He sounded gloomy. It was unusual. Alain was not given to overstatements. He always had a sunny disposition, but seeing him down, I did not doubt his concerns were real.

"Do you think this thing could go that far?"

"I don't know. A serious miscalculation by one side or the other, and there is no telling what will happen. Both sides have to be careful. The students and the workers know they have the government over a barrel. The government, however, still has all the power and these guys are not without the usual hard liners who are just waiting for the word to go into action."

It was hard to believe that France and its people had come to this. Not too long ago, there had been all sorts of newspaper editorials about how France had been "spared" all the turmoil taking place in other countries.

"I think *vieux pépère*," Alain continued, meaning de Gaulle and employing the words often used by the French when referring to old guys, "has to be clear as to what he's going to do. He can't fuck up this one. He's already shown some weak spots. And let me tell you: that is all the mob needs to know to take him on. It's bad out there."

"Who's in control, then?"

"Good question. The Prime Minister, Pompidou, has been trying to hold off both sides before they start seriously hurting each other. He still has the confidence of de Gaulle, but I'm not sure if he has the confidence of the opposition, and he needs the confidence of the people as well. I'm telling you, *c'est la merde*."

"Does Lisa know that I was heading back?"

"Dr. Brisson told her."

"What was her reaction?"

"Dr. Brisson said Lisa smiled and told her she knew you would come for her."

That night as I sat in the tub, I wondered what Lisa might be thinking. She had once said that she trusted me never to fail her in a moment of need. I did not quite understand what she meant then. That moment was now, and I hoped I was up to the task.

How to proceed? Alain had said that I had to call Milo first thing in the morning because his connection had more access to the authorities than Alain's.

He also said, after much reflection, that neither he nor Milo felt Lisa was in immediate danger. It was not comfortable to be in jail, but they did not feel that even under the present trying circumstances the authorities would be so reckless regarding how they treated a pregnant woman.

Now that the U.S. government was finally getting into the act, the situation was bound to improve Lisa's chances of being released as soon as the French bureaucracy got its act together.

"I will need you out there in the streets. I hope I can count on it."

"First, I've got to get Lisa out of jail."

"Of course. Get some rest, and we'll talk in the morning."

I could not have asked for a more supportive friend. Still, Lisa was in jail and nobody knew why; furthermore, nobody knew for sure how long she would remain there. That is how things stood at the moment.

After the bath, I went and sat on the bed and marveled at the looks of the room. Nothing was out of order. Lisa, as was her usual wont, had always made sure of that.

She always argued with me to be practical, and I was not. Since living with her, however, I had come to the conclusion that bringing a bit of order around me was not such a bad thing after all. I did try, and while not always successful, I knew I was improving.

Before I left for Prague, she had made me promise that upon my return I was to explain everything that I had done, felt, and thought—every detail—even the most trivial and unpleasant ones.

What I had pictured coming back from Prague was, that she would be waiting for me at the airport, then we would go to our favorite brasserie, l'Île Saint Louis, and she would tell me every detail of what *she* had done during my absence.

I, in turn, would do the same and share all the juicy tidbits about the people I had met, what I said, but mostly what they said. What were their faces like? How had they sat? Were they fat, old, young, thin, men, women?

What words they used? How were they dressed? Where did I meet them? Were they full of hopes? Did they believe in what they were doing? Did they believe in themselves?

"You're a slave driver, aren't you?"

"Not true."

"You sound worse than Alain does when I turn in the material."

"Come on, he demands more because he's paying for it."

"OK, how much are you going to pay me?"

"A lot."

"How much is that?"

"My grandfather set up a trust for me and Robin. I'll give you a part of my share."

"Shouldn't you save that for the baby?"

"You'll give it back to her, won't you?"

She pretended to be aghast at the prospect of my squandering our baby's inheritance.

"It sounds like you're just transferring money from one account to another, while I still have to work giving you all those juicy details of what happened to me," I lamented.

"Then, I'll give you all that the trust has."

"You can't give me what belongs to Robin."

"OK, I'll give you my entire share."

"That may not be enough. I'm expensive."

"I'll borrow Robin's share as well."

"Do you think she'll let you have it?"

"Yes, she's my twin, remember?"

"I'll think about it."

"Come on, I'm giving you our child's dowry."

"I don't think she'll need a dowry. If she turns out to be like her mother, she, herself, will be the treasure."

Lisa gave me a long look as if she were seeing me for the first time. Her eyes suddenly filled with tears. I thought maybe I'd said the wrong thing.

"Alex, that's so beautiful. I can't tell you how overwhelmed I am. I'll never forget what you just said. You don't know how rich you already are."

"That's why I need you, so you can remind me."

"I will, I promise you. For the rest of your life, I will!"

The homecoming had been anything but happy. I was back in Paris, but I was also alone. I walked to the room Lisa had stayed in when she first came to live in the apartment. It was now going to be the baby's room. Lisa had wanted to paint it and the concierge had promised her nephew would come and paint it for us.

Lisa and Madame Commère now spent a lot of time making plans for how this room was going to look. No detail was spared. The silent room seemed so forlorn and empty. I tried to picture what it would be like with a new baby and baby furniture, but the images were not clear. Lisa's incarceration was the only thing I could concentrate on. I needed some answers.

Lisa and Ulla were in jail, and I had no idea where Adam was. I did not even know where he lived. Calling José at two in the morning was not practical, either. The whole situation was crazy and confusing.

I looked at some of Lisa's notes from school hoping to find some clue, but the notes were about her classes and assignments so there was not much help there.

I walked back to the living room and stood in front of Lisa's painting. The little girl straining to hear the water running down the creek was sheer poetry, harmonious, ethereal in the manner Peter had painted her.

And though I was feeling lousy waiting for the night to give way to the day so I could start doing something, anything—and it was hard to imagine just what I was going to do—looking at the painting, I felt a sense of peace and quiet.

The loveliness and innocence the little girl represented gave me hope for what I needed to face in the morning. When the sun finally came out, I fell asleep only to be awakened by banging on the door a couple of hours later.

Standing outside, were Peter, Madame Commère, Roxanne, and José with anxious looks on their tired faces. Then Madame Commère embraced me, which surprised me, turned around and walked downstairs.

I had noticed they had brought with them a couple of freshly baked baguettes. It occurred to me that even in moments of crisis the French still remember the basics.

Fresh bread with butter—*tartines*—with a cup of hot coffee for breakfast was one of them. Roxanne had prepared the breakfast for us.

"Can you guys fill me in on what happened?"

"There isn't much to tell," José said. "That night Ulla had decided to come and stay with Lisa. When I called here the next day there was no answer. I waited and waited. Ulla was supposed to have called me in the morning.

"You've got me so paranoid with your story about Yugoslavia and Mohammed's baby that I finally rushed over to find out what was going on. That's when the concierge told me what happened. I called Pete—"

He stopped. The feeling I got was that we were all embarrassed about Lisa's arrest. In our most lucid state of mind, we had never considered that the French, that nebulous idea of a people, would act in such an offensive manner, and we took it as a personal affront.

We had been slapped on the face by someone or something we had loved so much and so blindly. It was sobering to think the French could be so offensive to us who had respected the idea of France.

I did not want to personalize what had happened, yet I had no other choice.

"These fucking frogs," said Peter.

I understood what he meant. I also understood that he did not mean Roxanne, who happened to be French. The *other* frogs had let us down.

"Yes, the fucking frogs," Roxanne said, in her lovely French accent.

We started to laugh at her words, her accent, her anger, and the manner in which she repeated Pete's words. It seemed kind of funny she was separating herself from her fellow compatriots. She was French, but not the ugly kind.

"What are we going to do?" she asked.

I had no plan of action. I did not even know where to begin. Getting Lisa out of jail as soon as possible was the first order of business— but how?

"I don't trust this guy that Milo has been talking to," Peter said.

"Why not?" I asked.

"He's a whore. One day he is pro-government, the next he's against them."

"That may be in our favor if he has contacts on both sides," José said. "If we need a whore to get them out, so be it."

"I thought Ulla was supposed to have been released?" I asked him.

"That's what the cops led us to believe. I don't know. Now they're saying they were acting in good faith and it's Ulla and Lisa who are making things harder for them. Who knows?"

"What was Lisa doing that the cops came and got her?" Pete asked.

He seemed angry. I was not sure if his anger was aimed at Lisa for having done something he disapproved of or at himself for getting angry at something that was not his business. Or was he angry with me?

"She *has* the right to protest if she wants to," said José.

Pete did not look at José.

"You're right," said Roxanne.

She was not excusing Pete's words; I was certain of that. It was that the tension we were all under could cause tempers to flare up and she, with a great deal of tact, was trying to avoid our getting into an argument.

"I know she has a right," Peter finally said, softly.

José sensed that Pete's words were aimed at diffusing the situation.

"I was in jail once," said José, laughing at the memory.

"I didn't know you've been in jail," I said.

"You don't know everything about me, do you?"

Of course, I did not. As I sat there trying to clear my head of all the different emotions and thoughts, I looked at the three of them and was grateful they were with me sharing the concern and the anger over what was taking place.

I was appreciative of their support. I could not have asked for better people to share this emotional and trying moment.

"Why were you in jail?" Roxanne asked José.

"I ran away from home," he said, sheepishly.

"Did you run away to join the circus?" Pete asked.

José started to laugh, a good belly laugh. It was so contagious that soon we were all laughing. Somehow, the moment of levity provided by Pete's words was what we needed and it made us relax.

"Are you psychic or something?" José asked.

"No, but you look like someone who would run away to join the circus," Peter said.

"How can you tell?" asked Roxanne, who seemed a bit surprised at Pete's words.

"In America, everyone wants to run away to join the circus," Pete said, smiling at her.

"Is it true?" she asked, looking at José and me.

"Well, kind of. I thought about doing it once," I said.

"That must be the Tom Sawyer in all of you," she said.

"Well, he didn't really run away to join the circus," Peter said.

"I thought he did," she said, sounding disappointed if it turned out to be otherwise.

"OK, babe, we'll make old Tom run away to join the circus. And even if he didn't, I'm making it official that he did. What the hell, I like that version better, anyway," Pete said.

"I think the justice system in this country is terrible," Roxanne said. Her words brought us back to reality.

"France, among the more liberal and humane countries in this world, has a pernicious and sometimes backward system for administering justice," Pete said. "The state has too much power in this domain. It can do what it wants, and the citizens have very little to say about it. So damn hypocritical."

"Still, what do we do now?" Roxanne asked again.

She had brought us back to the nagging question. Given how the French legal system works, and given the fact that the country was now in the midst of a rather grave crisis, it was going to be hard to figure out what to do.

"I need to talk to Milo so he can explain to me what in the hell is going on here," I said. "Talking to Alain last night left me more in the dark. He wasn't very optimistic. Maybe he was too tired. We're all tired. I know I am."

I looked at their faces, and in spite of the levity of a few moments ago, I could see the fatigue. Pete's face was very sober, and for some reason it gave me more to worry about, not necessarily about Pete doing something foolish, but that he may have been sensing something far darker than the rest of us could possibly imagine.

Did Peter know something the rest of us did not? It bothered me. Was Lisa in more danger than we had been led to believe? I did not want to dismiss my gut feeling about Pete.

Yet I did not want to end up getting so paranoid that I would be unable to figure out what needed to be done. For the time being, it appeared that Lisa and the baby were not in any immediate danger.

But could anyone guarantee their safety? What if she got an infection or started bleeding, or went into premature labor like

Mohammed's wife? Would someone think of calling a doctor? Could the cops force her to have the baby in jail? It was unimaginable. It made me sick to think about it.

Lisa and I had been sitting at La Coupole one early spring evening just when the student revolt was evolving in a more dramatic and violent way.

"Our baby is truly going to be a baby of the revolution," she said.

We had not been back in Montparnasse since the first day when she had come to visit me. We had walked by the small hotel where she had stayed, on rue Delambre, and on down to Boulevard Montparnasse.

I also showed her the Hôtel de Blois. We went in, but the receptionist was not anybody I recognized.

"We should have rented a room," she said, as we came out.

"Rent a room? Why?"

"The man seemed a bit disappointed that we hadn't booked a room," she said, and started to laugh. "Actually, we should move to Montparnasse."

"You don't like where we live?"

"I do, but I also like the idea of a home café. Where we live, we really don't have a home café like this one."

It was true. On the other hand, finding an apartment as good as the one we had in Trocadéro was not so simple. Where we lived were mostly residential buildings. There were a couple of cafés down the street, but none seemed ideal to fit the sense of a home café that I so dearly loved.

It was probably my own fault because I had never made an effort to establish a new one. For me, and by extension for Lisa, the only home café was back in Montparnasse, at La Coupole.

"Maybe we can ask Milo to help us find a place," she continued.

That night had been one of those wonderful occasions that gives Paris its charm and makes you love the city more. Lisa had gotten tickets to see Nureyev dance in the ballet: *Le Jeune Homme et la Mort* and it had been a magnificent and most memorable experience.

Montparnasse seemed calm, and people were going about their usual business on the boulevard, sitting at outside cafés, chatting with friends, making plans for the weekend. We had gone there for a nightcap after the show. The appearance was deceiving.

The students had been restless for several weeks and the situation did not seem to be going well for anybody. It was not hard to see that the government and the students were digging in.

Whenever I talked to Lisa about the dangers of her being at the Sorbonne if the police decided to tear gas the place, she always said I was exaggerating. She preferred to think that the police would not abuse the traditional reverence France held regarding the Sorbonne.

We decided to walk to rue de Rennes and then turn and walk down to the Latin Quarter. I was not sure I wanted to do this for the quarter was where the student demonstrations were taking place.

She said it would be OK. We would not walk where they were happening. It was cold but bearable. We would grab a taxi to take us home if she got tired.

"I bet you the government will order the cops to move in. Governments do not like to be told they are wrong, and they do not like to give up their power," I argued.

"To go in just to throw out a bunch of kids won't be worth what it would cost the government."

"Why do you seem so sure about that? All kinds of governments, whenever they feel threatened, react in violent ways. The French are not above this."

"They're not, but they're also practical people. I don't see them making such a mistake," she said.

"You just don't want to believe that when push comes to shove the French, just like the Americans or the Haitians or whomever, will do what is necessary to keep law and order intact.

"The police and the authority of the state are hardly ever questioned here. When it comes to law and order, the French government leans pretty much to the right."

"I know. Why don't we just hope for the best?" she finally asked.

She put her arm through mine, and we walked down toward Saint-Germain-des-Prés Boulevard. With her red bonnet, flushed cheeks, and her growing belly, Lisa looked like the perfect *Parisienne* out for a night stroll on this nice but still cool evening in the spring of 1968, waiting for her baby to be born.

"For someone raised on hot dogs and peanut butter you are much more political than most Americans. Why is that?"

"It's the exuberance of youth," she said, smiling. "Maybe if I were back home, I would not be protesting. I would not be pregnant, that's for sure."

"How do you know that?"

"I just do."

"Wait a second, I seem to remember we've already had this conversation."

"That's true, but my reality is here not back in the States. I was supposed to be here and be part of this event. I was supposed to meet you and have your baby. So that's what I'm doing," she said, firmly.

"You know, you have a way of making lots of stuff seem so simple."

"Sometimes."

"So why the politics?"

"My parents have always told me that when there is injustice you need to fight it. It has to do with being part of history, of something big, momentous. I want to be involved in what's taking place right here; it's a reflection of what's happening in the rest of the world.

"You can't be afraid to stand by your convictions. I wasn't raised that way. I know it sounds trite, but it just happens to be the truth."

"Shouldn't you be more concerned about making sure that nothing happens to you or the baby?"

She looked at me as if I was protesting for nothing and, of course, I was. I had no reproach to make regarding her taking care of herself while pregnant. Her genes and upbringing would produce a healthy and lovely baby. I was sure of that.

Yet I feared and fretted she might be taking unnecessary risks for issues that had very little to do with her. I was torn between accepting that she was free to pursue what she wanted to do, and my own desire to protect her and act like I knew what I was doing so she would listen to me.

I guess, I was just acting like a typical male who thinks his woman should listen and believe everything he says. It was the ego thing acting up on me. I knew it was silly, as I did not want to be dictating her life.

I also felt responsible for her safety and wellbeing. I was not trying to impose my will; I just did not want anything bad to happen to her. I would never have forgiven myself. She put her hands on her belly and rubbed it softly and slowly, looking down at it.

"She's fine. Aren't you, sweetheart?" We walked silently for a few more moments. "I talk to her all the time, did you know that?"

"No."

"Well, I do."

"What do you talk about?"

"Oh, just girl talk. Sometimes, when I'm playing the piano, I swear she likes the sound of a certain kind of music. I can feel her moving inside me. Oh. There she's doing it again."

We stopped and right in the middle of the boulevard, I put my hand on her belly and rubbed it. People walked by and kind of raised their eyebrows. Lisa and I just laughed. It was wonderful.

The first time I saw the baby moving, I was scared and thrilled, touching and seeing the ripples on Lisa's belly.

"What kind of music does she like?"

"Mozart, of course! Then the Russians. The other day I was playing Grieg's 'Piano Concerto' and she seemed to like it a lot. Beethoven seems to trouble her, I don't know why. Of course, she also adores Sinatra, Aznavour, Brel, Becaud, the Beatles, Simon and Garfunkel, and American jazz.

"All them 'cats' as José calls all jazz musicians: Davis, Hancock, Adderley, Mingus, Brubeck, Evans, Parker, Mulligan, Coltrane, Dizzy, Bechet, Ellington, Gillespie, Monk, Rollins. The list is endless. I told José she really likes Miles Davis' version of '*Concierto de Aranjuez*,' and he was impressed."

"Oh, yeah, what did he say?"

"'My kind of broad,' he said." She smiled.

"If she likes all that I'm impressed, too."

"I'm telling you, she's something else. When I play Debussy, she calms down and gets very intrigued."

"Oh boy, more frogs."

"I don't know if she's going to be a frog!"

"She's going to be born here. What does that make her?"

"Half of you and half of me."

We are half of our parents. There are no two ways about it— regardless of where we are born.

After Peter, Roxanne, and José came knocking on my door early that morning, we were all sitting in the apartment drinking coffee and eating the *tartines* Roxanne had prepared, while trying to figure out what was the next step to get Lisa out of jail as soon as possible.

"Should I be calling Milo? Do you think it's too early?" I asked.

"Call him now," Pete said. It sounded like an order. Roxanne winced but said nothing. José did not make a comment.

Suddenly, the phone rang. It seemed so loud and impertinent that we all froze, and it took us a moment to figure out it was ringing. Roxanne, however, had the good sense to pick it up and answer it.

"Hello, Lisa? Lisa!"

We were all shocked. Roxanne, her face really worried, handed me the phone. My hands were shaking.

"Lisa, are you OK?"

"I love you more each day. God only knows why."

"Where are you?"

"Well, we're in an office surrounded by all types. We were awakened very early and we're being let go when the paperwork is completed. Can you come pick us up? Ulla called José, but he's not home."

"He's here."

"Oh, good, then come get us."

An immense feeling of relief and doubt came to me at the same time. I thought if the gods are going to make me pay later so I could have her back, what the hell, I was willing to pay the price. To be together again was the only thing that mattered.

Then she passed me to some guy from the embassy who told me where they were and that I could come get them. I had enough time to throw on some clothes, and José and I rushed downstairs. Pete and Roxanne said they would wait for us in the apartment.

The taxi drove us through early morning traffic to the Prison de la Santé. Neither José nor I said much. Both of us were too damn worried about them. How do I describe my feelings upon seeing Lisa? What my heart felt? Words fail.

There were moments in life when what was not said was far more eloquent and precious than all the words in a dictionary. Both women were a bit pale, but seemed in good spirits. We all embraced. Lisa held me against her for what seemed like a long time.

"I told myself that I would not cry, and I won't," she said, and I saw how hard she was trying to keep her promise.

José and I were so eager to get them away from that place we hardly listened to what the men from the embassy were telling us. I excused myself, and promised I would call them as soon as I could.

They said they understood. We shook hands with the French police. Again, the scene made me think of the time when we got Chris out of jail back in Athens.

THIRTEEN

Lisa wanted to take a warm bath after returning home from prison, and was now sitting in the tub luxuriously letting the warm water bathe her. I sat on the edge of the tub scrubbing her back.

"I feel like I spend half of my life getting people out of jail," I said.

"It's not half of your life."

"Maybe not. In any event, I seem to hang around jailbirds, and I never had that problem in my life before."

She laughed her rich, lovely laugh. All the way back from the jail, she had held my hand and would not let go. José and Ulla took another taxi back to their place. We promised to talk later.

There was something José said that suggested he knew more about what was going on. I did not pursue it, it could wait.

Lisa did not say much on the way back from prison, except to make comments about one of their jailers, how he was doing everything possible to make their lives miserable, a mean game he played with them. Pete and Roxanne had stayed with us for a bit.

Madame Commère came, cried, embraced everyone, and left. I had called Milo and Alain and told them the good news and to thank them for what they had done.

"Were you afraid for me and our baby?"

"Yes, and how," I said.

Those terrible feelings of helplessness were still there, raw, on the surface.

"That's nice. Can you imagine? *J'étais à l'ombre!*" This was French slang for being thrown in the slammer.

"No, I'm having a tough time with that."

"Why don't you take your clothes off and join me?"

"I thought you wanted to take a bath?"

"Well, yes, but it isn't as if we haven't taken baths together before."

I undressed and got in the tub with her.

"They did let me take a shower last night, but I just wanted to relax in warm water with you next to me."

"How do you feel?"

"Strange. When we were in the taxi, I was looking at the streets, the trees, and the people. Everything seemed very bright, harsh, and the colors weren't attractive. They were indistinguishable, like in those black and white films with lots of shadows. I don't know.

"It's hard to explain. I knew I was out but I didn't believe it. I was afraid to be out. It sounds crazy, but as we were walking out, I was afraid to go, and I was also afraid they wouldn't let me go.

"You say how all of us can get used to anything, even terrible things. I was thinking about that because I hope I never get used to the horrible things we do to one another."

Her words were soft, and had been expressed in a kind of monologue, disjointed. She looked at me with a distant, sad face, and my heart felt lonely and heavy for I kept wishing that she could have been spared such a terrible ordeal.

Again, I felt guilty, and I wondered if the memories of what had happened would ever disappear from our lives.

"The apartment seems strange, kind of big," she continued. "It's weird. It's familiar and yet I feel like I don't belong here, as if I'm dreaming, that being here with you isn't real. I fear someone will come to wake me up, and you and everything will disappear, and I'll be back in that awful place."

"My love, you're here with me. You're back. Nobody will hurt you or take you away from me, never!"

"Thank you," she said, softly.

After I sat in the tub, Lisa straddled me.

"Oh, I see," I said, laughing.

"I love you so much. I missed you so much. Just hold me and promise me you'll never leave me alone again, ever!"

"I promise you."

Later, she went to bed. I sat on the floor right next to the bed, and she held my hand as she fell asleep. Eventually, she let go of my hand. I went into the living room to disconnect the phone. I tiptoed back into the room, and she was sound asleep, curled up in a fetal position.

I sat on the floor and watched her. She seemed so fragile, so vulnerable, and yet there was so much strength in her. The image of Lisa and the first time I saw her sleeping came back to me.

Now as I watched her sleep how I wished to be a poet. To have the soul, the heart, and the sensibility of a poet so I could invent magical and wonderful words that would tell her what my heart felt.

To describe those amazing feelings she had brought to me by her presence, simply by her being, so her love for me would echo through the eons of time, and I would always hear that echo.

I was so overwhelmed by her. By the way she looked at me and by how she felt toward me. By how she had touched the very core of my own existence. I had never known such feelings. I thought of how unprepared I had been to receive her love, to have the courage to reciprocate such a love.

I wanted to go back to day one, to the beginning of life's genesis, to the innocence of being, so that we would not be tainted by so much sadness, cynicism, and absurdity.

I longed to create a world for her where love, laughter, and happiness were the only things that mattered, and where her life would be happy and as pure and innocent as her sleep was at that moment.

I thought of her love, beautiful as a bright, warm summer day, one that I wanted so damn much to be worthy of. I would give her mine, and I would no longer be afraid.

Her love—only the gods knew its origin—that had now changed my life, and how! Her love: True and beautiful like a delicate bird. A love filled with desire and dreams that brought tears to my eyes.

A love that had made me fearful and shy, but no longer. I wanted to capture my innermost feelings and engrave them in her heart for always, so she would know that until the moon fell out of the sky, she was my destiny.

I wished to freeze in time and for eternity how my heart was filled with her being. I felt so inept in matching her love for me. I was not among the lucky ones who have the incredible gift of saying eloquent and simple words that convey feelings, revealing the very essence of who we were with images of poetry, love, and tenderness.

I longed to be an artist like Pete who could take a simple view of a stream and transform it into a lovely creation, then give it to Lisa because of who she was. I did not have such grace in my life. Without her, I felt banal, crude, overwhelmed by my own fears and ineptitude.

I wished for a magician's wand that would make all of the despair, and ugliness of the world disappear with just one simple stroke. I wished for her a just and happy world surrounded by beauty, love and integrity.

One of optimism, decency, not one of anguish and deceit. I wished for her a world free of human phoniness and sadness. I wished . . . I wished . . . I do not know how long I sat there watching her sleep.

I had unplugged the phone so she would not be bothered. Earlier, I had called José and he said Ulla was out shopping. It made me laugh—life and living had to go on. I lost track of time. I was lost in some kind of dream world.

The quiet of her breathing, in the semi-darkness of the room, was giving me an incredible feeling of comfort and security. It was as if she and I were the only people living in this world, after all.

I wanted to wake her up and share my thoughts with her because I knew it would touch her, but if I woke her up it would not be the same. Perhaps, it was better that she slept through my reverie.

In spite of what had happened, of my own shortcomings, my life also felt complete and in harmony. I had found Lisa, she was mine, and I did not have to wish it anymore.

At that moment, it felt as if the apartment was my impregnable fortress. It was silly but that is how I felt. I wondered if she dreamed of babies or of jails and jailers—too damn repulsive, unpleasant and hard to understand. I had her back and nobody, but nobody was ever going to harm her. No way!

Earlier in the day, I had felt depressed because of the guilty feelings I had about what had happened, and relieved because we were back together. We were sitting in the kitchen. She had regained some of her color, some of her old self with the bath we took and . . .

"Alex, it wasn't your fault. You had nothing to do with it. The fact that you weren't here doesn't make you guilty," she said, when I told her about my feelings.

"I know, but I still feel bad."

"We're together. That's all that matters."

"I know, but—"

"But nothing."

She sat on my lap and put her arms around me. She smelled delicious.

"Do you remember when we first met?" she asked.

"Yes."

"Where was it?"

"At Cleo's. You and Robin came with Big D. in the middle of the night. I thought, this guy's lucky he's got a couple of good-looking broads with him."

"You didn't even pay attention to me," she smiled and hugged me. She was not reproaching me.

"I did, too."

"Well, maybe to my sister."

"I paid attention to somebody. How was I supposed to know it wasn't you?"

"Because I smiled at you and you ignored me."

"That's not true."

"I think you were busy with other matters," she said, with a big, wide smile. I knew she was just teasing me.

"I was?"

"Maybe not. It was probably my own imagination."

"Yeah, I would say so."

We laughed. In another sense, it was one of those secrets—old loves—couples have that in time loses all its significance.

"You know when I was in jail, I talked to our baby all of the time." For a moment, Lisa seemed overcome with grief, but she managed to control it. "I explained everything to her. I didn't want to hide anything."

"Everything?"

"Well, almost," she said, "I explained to her how I came to Paris to find you. I told her I had been afraid to come and see you because I didn't know if there was someone else in your life."

"Really?"

"It's true. And remember my haircut?"

"Yes?"

"A confession . . ."

"What?"

"I did it because of you. I wanted to look different to you."

"You never told me any of this."

"It's the truth," she said, and her face shone with a soft, loving look.

I hugged her. I could not believe she had felt that way. Strange what we do not know about people we love—what we imagine. And what we later discover about them comes as a surprise that often leaves us humbled.

"And then, in some strange and mysterious way," she continued, "you had not gone to Spain as you had planned. It was as if you were waiting for me, for her. I took that to be a sure sign that you would be her father. I was certain and happy she would be proud to be your daughter."

I loved this woman to the end of time. What Lisa had said was such a gift to me, so simple and all encompassing—a gift whose origin would be unknown to me no matter how long I lived.

"I want to tell you something," I said.

"What?"

"It's a kind of confession, too."

She looked at me half-serious, half-amused.

"Remember when you came to see me here in Paris for the first time?"

"Yes?"

"After I dropped you off at your hotel, I had some strange and conflicting emotions. I had been afraid to show just how happy I was that you had come to see me. I mean, I wanted to act cool, tough, to pretend.

"But when I didn't hear from you, I resigned myself to the idea that I'd never see you again. I wanted to go to your hotel. Then I thought, if she's gone I prefer that time will show it to me. I don't want some hotel clerk telling it to my face."

Tears came to her eyes. She understood.

"Then when you came back with those flowers, that was something, that was really something—" I took a deep breath and stopped.

What makes a man and a woman intimate? It has to exist beyond their physical connection, though that is how intimacy is often manifested. But what is it? We use all kinds of names and perhaps it is all in the names we use. Perhaps, it exists in another time dimension.

Or perhaps it is more like the rainbow, magical, mysterious, there, but not there. The reality is that no one knows. The only thing we know is what we experience, and yet we cannot touch it. It exists all by itself outside our own reality.

"I was so overwhelmed, and scared, too."

"Why?"

"I didn't want to hope. I have such a hard time imagining you could love me. And when you used to get phone calls from other guys, I told myself that it was none of my business, but my heart also told me to stop pretending and admit how I felt."

"Really?"

"I knew I had no rights, and I often felt sad, lonely, and jealous. I longed to tell you, but I was so afraid I would lose you."

"You never suspected I loved you?" She looked at me, and I could see that now it was her turn to be surprised.

"No," I said.

She had asked me that question already, and I was no more prepared to answer it now than before. Somehow, she expected me to have some creative brainpower I obviously lacked. I also recognized that in matters of love, I am always lagging behind.

"You're a dummy," She smiled, kissed me, and held me against her.

"That I am. Even long after your return," I said, "I was still afraid. Then remember the night when you danced for me? After you said 'no' when I asked if you were a daydreamer? I thought, if she doesn't daydream how can she love me? I represent nothing. I'm nothing. Then you danced." The memory was lovely.

"I wanted you to see me the way I see myself," she said. "I longed to show you that little girl who had danced by herself, in the middle of the night, so many times and so many lives ago, was here with you and she loved you with all of her heart.

"That's what I wanted you to see. I didn't want you to be afraid anymore, because I knew you were. Yes, the dance was about dreams—our dreams. I was hoping so much you would see that. Who needs heaven when we have each other?"

"I was so touched by what you had done. I can't tell you how my heart felt that night."

It was fantastic to have her back. To be together again; to look at her face; to touch her; to smell her; to be part of her existence—just to know where she was.

"Have I ever really confessed just how much I love you? Really, truly, love you?" I asked her, after a while.

"Not lately."

"I love you the size of a couple of hundred billion galaxies."

"Really?"

"Yes, and that's only the beginning."

"There's more?"

"You have no idea."

"Boy, that's big, huge!" Her face was beaming.

"Yes, big, very big."

"I'm sorry," she said.

"For what?"

"For putting you through all of this."

"You are who you are and I don't want to change that. I don't want a different Lisa."

"You won't be ashamed that the mother of your child is a jailbird?"

"*Jamais!*"

"*Je t'aime.*"

She smiled, and those wonderful eyes of hers looked at me with a clear and loving gaze. I opened her bathrobe and rested my weariness on her lovely breasts, now larger with the coming of our baby into this crazy world, and I wanted her in the worst possible way.

Suddenly, I woke up in the middle of the night. Lisa was having a nightmare and in some primitive, subconscious way, I sensed she was about to wake up, so I did before she did. I reached over and held her close. She was shaking.

"It's OK. You're fine. You're safe. We're together. You're back home. It was just a bad dream."

She started to cry. I felt so powerless for I had no way of making her life return to the way it was before. Lisa had felt a little dizzy earlier in the day, so Dr. Brisson had come by to examine her, declaring that baby and mother were doing fine.

Lisa told me she was afraid to be alone in the apartment, something that would have been unthinkable in the past. Everything had changed. I felt sorry and longed for the previous innocence I knew was lost, and would never come back. I felt betrayed.

After she woke up, Lisa wanted to talk about her ordeal. She had been arrested with a bunch of other people, mostly students. The cops had been rough and nasty, calling them names and making terrible threats.

"The worst part was the lack of privacy. Imagine being in a room not much larger than our kitchen with ten other people—all of us scared out of our wits. The others with me were really nice, especially when they saw I was pregnant."

"Did the cops say why they were arresting you?"

"Not really. I guessed it had to do with Adam and Daniel."

Daniel Cohn-Bendit. Danny the Red, as he was now being called. Born in France of German-Jewish parents, he had found himself at the head of the student movement. He had not been interested in either being part of or leading it.

By the sheer force of his personality and political convictions, he had eventually found himself one of the leaders of the movement. As a result, Daniel had become the *bête noire* of the French government.

He represented, for the students and for the government, the very symbol of what was right and what was wrong with the educational system in France.

When the police invaded the Sorbonne, Ulla had called Lisa to share the bad news. Apparently, Cohn-Bendit had been there earlier that afternoon and had made some threats that the government had taken seriously.

The cops closed off the streets leading to the Sorbonne, then went in and pushed the students out with some phony pretext. As the students filed out, the paddy wagons were waiting and took them away while the police stayed inside the building.

Lisa's first reaction had been to join the protest. But then she thought of what I had said, about my fears of how dangerous it could be, and was not sure what to do. José argued vociferously against the idea for he also thought it was just too dangerous.

Ulla was less concerned, but eventually agreed that José and I were right about Lisa not exposing herself to gratuitous dangers, and had to be careful due to her pregnancy.

"I was so sad to see this great university, my university, fall into the hands of the police. The funny thing is that I don't know Daniel at all. I've seen him a couple of times. I talked to him briefly. I liked him. He and Adam are good friends."

"But why didn't they go after Daniel if he was the target?"

"It's intimidation. Adam knew it would happen. The French government wants him out of France. They want Daniel out of France, too, except he was born here of German parents and has lived here most of his life. So, there is this technical problem: Is Daniel French or German? They can't catch either one of them, so they went after their friends."

Adam had wanted to turn himself in when he found out the cops were after him because he feared for those who had helped him. Lisa and Ulla told him that it was out of the question; they would go to jail rather than give the police any information.

"It was an accident that Ulla was spending the night here. I guess they selected me first figuring that since I was pregnant, I would be an easy prey. Boy, were they wrong," she said, with conviction.

"Lisa you *are* crazy."

"Well, maybe a little. Anyway, I had made up my mind not to talk to the police no matter what."

"The cops never told you what they wanted?"

"Not really. They kept asking about Adam and Daniel. I told them I knew nothing other than Adam and I were in the same class. Of course, they knew he had stayed in the apartment."

"Did the cops ask about me?"

"And how!"

"Are you serious?"

"At one time this guy—*Monsieur Tabac* Ulla and I called him because he smoked like a chimney and reeked of stale tobacco smoke—wanted to find out where you were, and when I told him you were in Prague that seemed to intrigue him a lot. In fact, I thought they were after you.

"I told *Monsieur Tabac,* I would not talk to him unless he stopped smoking in my presence because it made me ill. He didn't like it, but he never smoked around me after that. Ulla thought the guy looked like Dracula. Actually, Dracula was better looking."

"Did they say why they wanted to find out about me?"

"No."

"This is crazy."

"I know. They seemed to know a lot about many of us. It was scary. I was so afraid, afraid for our baby, afraid for you—"

She stopped, suddenly overcome with the emotion of recalling the terrible ordeal. I put my arms around her and held her close. She embraced me. It made me feel how awful and lonely those moments must have been for her.

I wanted so desperately to erase those ugly memories from her existence, pretend nothing had happened.

The gods did not grant such wishes.

I wanted to pretend I would have known how to deal with this madness had I been there. That it should have happened to me and not to her. I longed to change places with her so she would not have to carry such an ugly burden. I wanted to suffer in her place, though I knew it was not possible to erase the hurt. Lisa saw how angry and sad I was feeling.

"It's OK," she said. She kissed me; it was her turn to comfort me. We held each other for a long time just listening to our hearts silently seeking relief and warmth from each other.

"I was so afraid you would call here," she continued, "and there would be no answer and you would go crazy with worry. The police had awakened Madame Commère before they came knocking on our door. She was downstairs. As we were leaving, I asked her to please call Alain. She was mad. Do you know what she called the cops?"

"What?"

"*Sale cons,*" Lisa started laughing.

"You're kidding."

"She was something else. I'm telling you."

Calling Parisian policemen *sale cons*—dirty cunts—is never a good idea. I was not surprised Madame Commère had dared insult the cops using coarse words. Tempers were flaring up all around.

"What did the cops say to her?"

"They called her: *vieille pute.*"

"Oh, no!"

"I thought she was going to hit them."

I could picture the concierge, standing tall with all her Gallic arrogance and pride, even after the cops called her an "old whore,"—her feet wide apart, her hands on her waist, her double chin thrusting forward, glaring, daring them to take her in. Lisa laughed at my description. Her laughter was such a welcome relief.

"How did you find out I was in jail?"

"Alain woke me up. He had been trying to get through to me since the night before. After I finished talking to him, the thought of you in jail was so painful. I never felt so powerless, so lost, so alone and so far away from you. My life suddenly became ugly. What if I lose her and the baby, I thought.

"What could I do? Where could I go? In Vietnam, I had been terrified. The fear I had, in Prague, about losing you and the baby was beyond anything I had ever felt before. I thought I was going crazy. I didn't know what to do—I was helpless!"

Once again, an incredible rush of anger, fear, and confusion overpowered me. The images and memories of my feelings while I was in Prague assaulted me, clear and devastating.

She took my face in her hands and kissed me. She was so tender. Women can be so intuitively strong and yet tender when it comes to moments like this.

"You're wonderful. I know how you feel. I know it! It's OK," she said, smiling to keep from crying.

I took a deep breath. "You talked about others in jail with you."

"Yes, they treated them badly. There was this girl and the cops—" she stopped. I saw fear in her eyes like I've never seen before. "They beat her up. I threw up and maybe that got them worried, they stopped. I never saw her again, but her face was always in my mind. I thought they would do the same thing to me. Then they wanted to release Ulla only. It was a pretty low moment."

"You don't have to talk about it anymore. It can wait."

"I want to tell you everything so you won't feel guilty about what happened."

"I don't know that I'll ever get over this sentiment of culpability."

"I'll help you," she said. "When Ulla refused to leave, I was so proud of her. It got the cops all upset and they accused us of not having any respect and that we didn't appreciate what they were doing for us—they were serious. It was humorous, but it really wasn't.

"We told them, we didn't want any favors from them. It's strange about being in prison. What kills you is the routine, and yet it's the same routine that keeps you from going insane—"

She stopped again, and pulled me close to her as if afraid someone would suddenly come and take her away again.

"I don't know if I can forgive those frogs," she finally said, laughing at herself.

"Well, you said you thought you were ready for them."

"Yes, but this is ridiculous. Wait until I tell my parents. They'll send us airline tickets to come back *tout de suite*—immediately! My mother always says that if I'm not wanted anywhere, to come where I'm wanted no matter what."

"Do you know what Roxanne called the cops?"

"What?"

"Fucking frogs."

"She is so polite and so proper. I'm going to hug her and kiss her next time I see her," Lisa said, laughing and shaking her head in disbelief.

"How did *they* find out?"

"José came over because when he called here there was no answer. He talked to Madame Commère who told him what happened, and he called Pete. Alain told me that Pete was ready to storm the police station when he heard you had been arrested."

"He was going to do that?" There was a look of surprise from her.

"Yes, but not just Pete. Alain said that he and Milo would both raise hell if they found out they were mistreating you—they were not joking!"

"Like *The Three Musketeers.*"

She shook her head at the thought of Peter, Alain, and Milo turning into a modern version of Alexandre Dumas's characters in his novel, *Les Trois Mousquetaires*, storming into a French prison—one for all and all for one!

"That night, José took Ulla and me to dinner. We were so upset about the Sorbonne being invaded by the police that at the last minute, I asked Ulla if she wanted to come and spend the night here. We would just try to console each other.

"Anyway, José felt kind of left out, but he was a good sport about it. We dropped by their place. Ulla took some stuff with her and we came here. Little did we know that her packing an overnight bag would come in handy later on."

Lisa was sitting in the middle of the bed, her oversized nightgown giving her a lovely look of softness and radiance. I sat on the floor; exactly on the same spot, I had sat earlier in the day to watch her sleep.

"So how did it happen?"

"Ulla and I were just sitting in the living room talking and commiserating, when there was a loud knock on the door. We thought it was José. When I opened the door, there were these four men and a woman.

"They said they were police—halfway flashed their badges and kind of barged in without an invitation. They were surprised to see Ulla. It was a bonus for them to find her here—" again, she stopped and seemed afraid and lost.

"You don't have to continue."

"I want to. I know I'll feel better afterward."

The cops wanted to know about Adam. When Lisa told them she did not know where he was, they got upset and searched the apartment without asking her permission.

"I was arguing that they had no right to invade the apartment. It's funny now that I think about it, because I kept asking if they had a search warrant to enter the apartment. They went through all of my papers and yours, and when I asked them what they were looking for they just ignored me.

"They didn't appreciate it when I told them that if I had a secret plan to overthrow the government, the apartment would be the last place where I would keep it."

She laughed, and I thought how deeply ingrained national traditions and character are in all of us. Requiring a warrant by the police to enter someone's apartment is part of what we grow up with back in the U.S.

"One of *les flics* said that this wasn't America, and stop telling them what to do. They didn't have to have permission from anybody to bust into the apartment. What I hated the most was that they were using the *'tu'* when they spoke to me. It's crass and offensive."

In French, there are two ways when addressing a person: the *tu* and the *vous*. The *vous* is formal, polite, and normally used when people meet each other for the first time.

Though the *tu* is the more familiar term, it can also be used in an insulting manner, to diminish a person's dignity, to reduce that individual to the lowest common denominator—to put her in *her* place.

Then the police told her they were taking her in, and when she protested and asked why they simply told her to shut up and do as she was told. They had a discussion, among them, about Ulla for they apparently knew who she was, but had no orders to pick her up.

Ulla demanded that they take her in as well and there followed an angry confrontation between her and the cops.

"You know how Ulla normally sounds when she speaks French, with that soft, wonderful Swedish accent of hers—calm and cool. Well, you don't want to get her mad. She wasn't going to take no for an answer.

"In fact, she stood blocking the door, and dared them to physically drag her out of here. It convinced the cops she was serious, so the head guy finally said: 'OK, let's take them both in.'"

"Did they put handcuffs on you?"

"We wouldn't let them. I told them in my condition, I would be a fool to make a run for it. Besides, I hadn't done anything to be arrested. They barely let me throw some stuff together in a bag, and we left. That's when one of the cops made a comment about Ulla's bag. He said something about it being apropos or something like that."

She seemed a bit more relaxed now that she was able to share those horrible memories with me.

"What did you think, while it was happening?"

"I only thought about you," she said, quietly.

"Really?"

"Yes. I mean, I knew you would be so worried about the baby and me once you found out. You would feel guilty because you weren't here, and I didn't want you to feel that way."

"I don't think I have ever, in my whole life, felt so totally helpless and alone."

In a way, reliving the nightmare was positive because it would perhaps free us of its sheer terror. The first night had been terrifying for her and Ulla. There were other students who had been arrested, and the cops had been very cruel to them. For Lisa, it was the first time she had been exposed to such intimidation and abuse.

"Do you still want to live here after all of this?"

"Yes." My question surprised her. I do not think she had thought about it. "You can't say that everyone is like those thugs that came here. If I leave, they win and I don't want them to win. Monique isn't like that. Or Pierre, or Roxanne, or Milo or Alain, or Madame Commère, or Dr. Brisson, or the others who were in jail with me. They won't run me out of this town, that's for sure."

As she said this, she laughed that wonderful, rich, deep laugh of hers that always made me feel good.

"I told them that if something happened to my baby, I would hold them personally responsible no matter what. I don't think they were interested in being nice to me, but the baby had them worried.

"They brought in a doctor who asked me if I was feeling OK, and wanted to examine me. I told him, I would only permit Dr. Brisson to examine me."

He took some notes and the next morning they let Lisa see Dr. Brisson.

"It was only for a few minutes; boy, was I happy to see her! She had a big argument with the police for arresting me seeing that I was pregnant. She was so angry. Not a good idea to get Dr. Brisson upset, that's for sure. She demanded she be allowed to come and see me whenever I asked for her.

"The cops weren't pleased, but finally agreed when they saw how angry she was. She became my contact with the outside world. She was great! She called the cops: 'une bande d'imbéciles,' right to their faces!"

"It's a good thing they didn't throw her in jail, too," I said, laughing.

"Let me tell you, Dr. Brisson and Ulla are what José would call: 'tough broads'," and we laughed at that thought.

"I'm going to name our baby after them," she continued. Dr. Brisson's first name was Céline. "Here in France, you can give the baby three or four first names if you want to."

Eventually, the American embassy had sent someone to see her. Lisa felt more protected.

"You know, it does seem strange that you end up around people who go to jail," she said. Earlier, I had told her José's story about his jail experience.

I got up and sat right next to her on the bed, and we embraced. It felt good to be sitting right next to her, in the middle of the night, just listening to her, sharing details of her ordeal.

Then the police had wanted them to sign a statement, and Lisa and Ulla refused. The situation had become a bit sticky for the French authorities in that now they had two governments officially complaining about what was happening to their respective citizens.

From that moment on, they had been treated better and had been left alone. The conditions of the other inmates, however, did not improve. And Lisa said she saw people being insulted and treated with no respect.

When she told the guards she would go on a hunger strike if they did not stop, that got the authorities very worried. The next thing she knew, they had awakened her and told her she and Ulla were being freed.

"Would you really have gone on a hunger strike?"

"I was scared, but I knew that if I made the decision, I would have done it. I thought about my father who has such moral decency. Then I thought about you. I only hoped that if it came to that and something bad happened to the baby or to me, that you would have understood," she answered, after a long pause.

Her face was pensive, and I could not read anything in the way she looked. I knew it was not a fair question to ask about wanting to go on a hunger strike, though, I had not asked it to be unfair.

"I've been thinking about those people still in jail," she continued. "What's going to happen to them?"

"I don't know."

She was looking at me as if expecting me to come up with the answer.

"Remember the story you told me about the young boy in Africa?"

"Yes."

"When you're in jail, you discover what liberty means. You come to appreciate and value the things you took for granted. I know now how he must have felt, being robbed of his freedom, made prisoner, not knowing. It takes away your dignity. Perhaps, it was the reason he made the decision he did; at least, he could control his destiny."

"We'll never know the answer."

"Why do we do such horrible things to each other?"

Her face and eyes shone with a sad clarity that made me even more depressed, with the realization that life kicks you in the solar plexus, whacks the wind out of you, knocks you down for good measure, and when you get up you are not the same person anymore.

Your innocence and integrity just go to hell. Everything changes. You can no longer go back to the way you were. It is so damn sad we cannot protect our loved ones from the meanness of others, from their ugliness, and hate, from their sick and tortured selves. From their stupidity and from the disgust we feel due to their evil nature.

Camus had once written about not loving the human race but rather loving only certain individuals and their wonderful human qualities, hoping he could take those qualities, cut them in millions of pieces, and spread them all over the place so he would always find a bit of those whom he loved in everyone else.

Then I told Lisa how Milo and Alain had worked so hard to find a way to get her out of jail. I told her of my own anxieties and tribulations back in Prague, and how courageous and magnificent Adam's mother had been.

"She told me she had information that you and the baby were fine. I trusted her."

"How did she find out?"

"I never asked her. I don't think she would have told me. All I cared was knowing you and the baby were OK. You have no idea how relieved I was when she told me."

"I want to meet her. She sounds wonderful!"

"She's incredible. She's really something else. I can see where Adam gets his backbone."

"We must invite her to come and visit us. We will pay for her ticket, *d'accord?*"

"*Oui, absolument!*"

It pleased her.

"The best news was when Dr. Brisson told me you were on your way back. My heart felt so full. There was never a doubt in me about you not coming back to find us, no matter where we were. Even if it took the rest of your life! I could never imagine you just giving up. Never!"

She shook her head. Her words were soft and seemed so full of dignity. Her eyes were beaming. I did not know what to say. Is that what love is? To have no doubts at all about the other person's promises to you?

"How do you feel," she asked me.

"I feel like I've just come back from the worst nightmare of my whole life. And you?"

"Actually, I feel so much better. I have you back. Our baby is safe. We're all together."

After talking some more about having to call the embassy to see what they wanted to know, she told me she would be grateful and delighted if we made love the way we used to. I obliged with all my heart.

Alain called the next day. He had been monitoring the situation and said he needed my help. The whole world was now focused on what was going on in France.

Business was picking up a lot. I was eager to help him out, but I was not too eager to expose myself to gratuitous dangers. Dr. Brisson's visit the day before had made Lisa feel better. She was optimistic, filled with confidence, and secure.

The talk the night before had made a big difference. However, in the back of my head there was this nagging sentiment: I was not sure if the cops would come back and arrest Lisa again.

"Why would they have let me go, then?"

"Can you guarantee they won't come back?"

"If they wanted me, they could have easily kept me behind bars. Yes, the U.S. government was putting pressure on them, but you know when the French don't want to listen to anybody, there's nothing to be done."

"We should move to someplace where nobody knows who we are."

"That's running away. I don't want to do that."

"OK, how about getting away from Paris just for a few days? Maybe go back to Normandy. I'm sure Monique and Pierre will welcome us back."

I looked deeply into those big eyes of hers. Her pregnancy was working such wonders on how she looked and how she acted. When she first told me she was pregnant, I thought of the countless stories about pregnant women with their morning sickness, of their craving certain foods. In Lisa's case, the morning sickness lasted for about two weeks, and she never craved special or exotic foods.

"I'm telling you, I'm a normal, healthy person. I don't even remember the morning sickness. Are you sure it wasn't you who got sick?"

"Maybe you're right," I said,

Thinking that given all of my anxiety about what was happening, it was a miracle I had not been the one who suffered morning sickness.

Now she was beginning to have trouble with her back and sleep was not as comfortable, yet she never complained about her discomfort. Her desire to experience her pregnancy was not limited to dreaming about her baby or imagining our lives after the baby.

It also included suffering through the pains and discomforts of her pregnancy. I realized how physically trying her time in jail must have been. She leaned over and hugged me.

"Alex," she said in response about getting away from Paris and going to Normandy for a while, "do you really want to leave when probably one of the biggest stories in our lives is taking place here in Paris? We have front seats, and you want us to miss it?"

I knew when I was beaten.

The reports in the regular press spoke of an exhausted police force. Of students' changing tactics and getting more confrontational, more daring, and thus more dangerous.

Since the police had occupied the Sorbonne, there had been talks of organizing the students to go and take the Sorbonne back by force. It was both stupid and romantic and about as good as Don Quixote fighting windmills.

Alain said that under the circumstances the only thing left for me was to go out and cover some of the events. This was the big story in the news. The whole world was focusing on it. The rent still had to be paid.

"I hate this *bordel de merde*, but we've got work to do. I need photos, lots of them. I know you're also good with the camera; so, get out of your lethargy and go out and earn your keep," Alain said.

Lisa, not surprisingly, agreed with him.

"What if I get my head busted?"

"You won't. Think of the stories you'll tell your grandchildren."

Paris was a *bordel de merde*—a shitty place—as Alain was now claiming every moment that he could.

Since my return, and Lisa's release a few days earlier, there had been riots and constant fighting between the police, the students, and workers—all taking place in the Latin Quarter.

The newspaper headlines, in big bold letters, told of a whole country paralyzed, not sure of itself, of a people who had somehow lost the incentive to correct the problems.

Of a government scrambling to understand and come up with possible solutions. Of General de Gaulle—wartime hero, leader of a disunited France—determined to hang on to power with just as many of his fellow citizens committed to getting rid of *him!*

It was a situation fraught with danger for everyone. France was now in the middle of an incredible social upheaval. This was an historic event; there was no way to ignore it. Alain and Lisa were right.

I had lots of material from the work I had done in Prague, and to give Alain his money's worth was going to take a bit more time to organize it.

However, the situation in Paris was more immediate—Prague could wait—and trying to guess the outcome was proving hard and frustrating. Alain had said he needed me. I was torn between going out to cover some of the events and taking care of Lisa. Easier said than done.

Adam had also reappeared. Lisa had said that Adam felt so terrible, was so ashamed and so fearful something would happen to her again; he preferred to keep in touch only by phone.

At first, I thought maybe the phone was bugged, but upon further consideration I dismissed the idea as just too paranoid—even for me. Thus, the Latin Quarter became my beat.

There was a pattern to the students' behavior. It would begin with clusters of them just ambling through the quarter with no specific goal in mind. Slowly, the numbers would increase until it grew into a mob.

Then it would take on a personality of its own, with just a few *"anarchists"* in the mob beginning to agitate for some action.

As the tempo of the physical confrontation with the police increased, so would the tools and tactics of the students. The first thing was the chant against the police: *"CRS, SS, CRS, SS."* Tying the Gestapo (SS) to the French riot police (CRS).

Eventually, one would hear the famous French cry that has become the permanent fixture of French history: *"Aux Barricades!"* Followed by the digging of the famous *pavés*—cobblestones that have been such an integral, historical, and physical part of Parisian streets—and the barricades would be built.

After which the cobblestones began to fly, and before long it was a free-for-all with *pavés* flying in one direction, and tear gas and concussion bombs flying in the opposite direction. Fire hydrants were knocked over and tons of water flooded the streets bringing more chaos and danger.

Anything the students could carry, break or use as a weapon was used. Nothing was too heavy or too awkward: Cars, *pavés*, trucks, trees, heavy chains, bottles, trash, trashcans—were used to thwart the advance of the police and to build barricades.

Then the police would bring their water cannons, and these high-pressure hoses did their dirty work against the students.

One night, I saw a bulldozer manned by the police pushing debris down Boulevard St. Michel, while hundreds of students were pushing debris up the other way and pelting the cops with *pavés*.

The whole spectacle seemed hilarious except, that there was nothing humorous about both sides trying to gain the upper hand in this bloody fight.

The students were well organized in long human chains. As the *pavés* were dug out, they passed them to the front of the line so that the barricades could be built. Then after cars, trees, trucks, trashcans, and anything else that was combustible was built into a giant barrier, someone would pour gasoline over the whole mess and set it on fire.

No one was safe from the danger, as I found out on my third night in the Latin Quarter. Press passes were a joke for all of the journalists covering the events. The police did not think journalists could or were neutral.

I got a billy club shoved into my ribs with so much force that I doubled over in pain. Some people half-dragged me away from the danger. My press pass was not going to protect me.

This seesaw battle continued throughout the night ending at dawn when students, tired and dwindling in numbers, scattered into the side streets to go home, get some sleep, recuperate, and be ready to come back the following evening to start all over again.

Throughout all of the chaos, there was also the constant wailing of the civilian ambulances carrying the wounded to hospitals. The students used regular cars with Red Cross flags draped over them to help evacuate the wounded, which was how I found out José was doing the same thing.

One evening, after getting more tear gas in my system than I cared to breathe, I decided to visit a makeshift emergency first-aid center to see just whom the cops were bashing.

Great was my surprise when José walked in helping carry a wounded girl. I was surprised without being surprised, really, as I had a vague notion, he was more involved in the protests then he was letting on.

"What the hell are *you* doing here?" I asked him.

"Just helping out, man."

"How long have you been 'helping out?'"

"I don't know . . . since the thing started, I guess . . ."

I started to laugh. We both stood laughing, while the others around us did not understand what our hilarity was all about.

"Did Adam put you up to this?"

"Not really. We did talk a little bit. But the idea was mine."

"Your idea, right. What about our women?"

"Oh, they know," he said, nonchalantly.

"So you were holding out on me?"

"No, but you've got enough worries of your own," he said, as he left to go back and bring more injured to the aid center. José had a car and was using it as an ambulance.

"We didn't tell you because we didn't want you to worry," Lisa said later, when I asked about what José was doing.

"All of those secret conversations you, Adam, and Ulla were always having had to do with the student rebellion?"

"Kind of."

"You know this is pretty foolish." I laughed. But it was not funny, but what could I do?

She smiled. It had now been a few days since her release, and Lisa was back to the way I had known her: happy, loving, making plans for the baby, for her life, for us. We *were* going to be a family. The whole notion was still strange to me.

I had gotten her to promise not to go out to demonstrate against the government. I had put my foot down on this. She had agreed, though not without protesting.

"I feel like I'm letting them down," she said, referring to her classmates.

"How can you say that? Come on, you have a baby coming. Do you want to take chances?"

"No, but—" she was obviously torn by personal loyalties.

"Ask anybody. Ask Ulla, or José, ask Adam," I said, trying to find supporting arguments.

"I know. They've already told me. I mean, everybody's telling me to take it easy. I feel fine."

"Look, I know how much you care about this thing. But it's just too dangerous to be demonstrating with what you are carrying in that big belly of yours. You would never forgive yourself if something bad happened. Come on, I'm the one who's supposed to be impractical."

"I don't know why I love you so much." She smiled, embraced me, and held me close.

"So, there are more important things, right?"

"Absolutely!"

Lisa was committed to the ideals of her fellow students, but she was no fool. A baby was on the way and in the final analysis that fact ruled our lives. Of course, that did not keep her from spending an excessive amount of time on the phone.

She acted like she was operating the switchboard for the whole damn revolution. The phone never stopped ringing. It was so busy that I had been ordered not to use it unless it was a matter of life or death.

I obeyed. What could I do? Alain was upset he had a hard time getting through to me. I did not tell him why, though, I suspected he guessed the reason.

FOURTEEN

The Latin Quarter became a giant urban battlefield. There always seemed to be more students than police. I saw tired and grim faces, eyes bloodshot. The police had to work over-time with very little sleep or rest.

Tempers were shot, frayed, with the police distrusting anybody young enough to resemble a student, but neither side—government or students—willing to reach some kind of compromise.

It was funny for around that time the peace talks to end the war between the Americans and Vietnamese started in Paris. I had talked to Alain about covering this event, and his sentiment was that those talks would last long after the student revolt was over.

"It'll be a couple of years of talks. Once the North Vietnamese overrun the south, they'll settle. Americans are clever, but they won't outfox the North Vietnamese," Alain said.

On this particular night, the Latin Quarter around the Sorbonne was eerie with the residue of tear gas hanging in the air creating an awful, nauseating effect. Hundreds of students were just lingering around, waiting, expecting something to happen—looking for something to happen.

It was obvious the students were not happy with the presence of the riot police. I walked from the Luxembourg Gardens, down Boulevard St. Michel, past the café where Lisa and I had spent time talking that first evening we were together in Paris.

The windows in most shops on the first floors of the buildings were safely boarded up. The boulevard was filled with pockets of people arguing heatedly, everyone having an opinion—mostly against the government.

People were fed up. They were against the police, the school system, the country's elite, and the entire political structure.

What was not clear was whether the negative attitudes against the government could or would translate into positive sentiments for the students by the greater public. There were, nevertheless, voices saying the students were right to want to bring the whole system down.

The extremists argued that the entire Latin Quarter had to be torched to prove to the authorities that changes had to be made in the system. I passed by Place de la Sorbonne now occupied by hundreds of riot police, and walked down to the corner of St. Michel and St. Germain Boulevards.

The next thing I saw were hundreds of people rushing up Boulevard St. Michel. They were yelling and screaming, most of them with wet handkerchiefs or towels over their eyes and noses.

The air was thick with tear gas fumes, strong and sickening. There was no way to escape it. My eyes and throat burned like hell. I could see that something very big was taking place near the Luxembourg Gardens.

I decided to go around through rue St. Jacques, which also runs parallel to Boulevard St. Michel, and up toward the Luxembourg Gardens.

Lots of students were running in the same direction. When I got to the intersection of rue St. Jacques and rue Gay-Lussac, all hell had broken lose. Cobblestones, trash cans, the heady metal grills placed at the base of the trees, concussion grenades, trees, dozens of vehicles of every size and shape, and everything that was combustible was now burning on top of the barricades.

It seemed as if the anger and madness of both sides could no longer be controlled. The CRS—the infamous riot police—were beating the hell out of anybody they found in the way, and the students were using every weapon available—*paves*, metal rods, wooden clubs, heavy chains, golf clubs—to fight them back.

The anger of both sides was sobering and dangerous. It was a mob out of control, with the police outmatched and literally battling for their lives. I had never seen an urban riot before. It was ugly.

This was no longer a simple protest by the students for school reforms or for minimal changes in the whole political system. The game had become serious and bloody.

The chaos it was bringing to the lives of Parisians was very scary. It spelled total revolt to me. Civil war could not be far behind. I saw battles in which police and students showed brutality and ferocity against each that was very frightening.

Lisa wanted to see the aftermath of the rioting at the Luxembourg Gardens, so I took her there the next day. The remnants of the burned-out cars still smoldering on top of the *pavés*, and the smell of tear gas hung in the air a bleak reminder of what had taken place the night before.

The street looked like a lunar landscape: desolate, foreign, forbidden, except that this was Paris and maybe it was populated by a bunch of lunatics, after all. Lisa was shaken by what she saw.

All of the logical arguments, the discipline, the classical education with its pride about intelligence and lucidity, the elegant and diplomatic words the French language is capable of inspiring in those who speak it eloquently, had vanished.

What remained were the insults, the incredible anger, and the violence that seemed to have no limits. It was a sad and sobering experience. I did not like it. I felt so disappointed. It was the same feeling I had experienced when Lisa was arrested.

I could not accept that these things were happening in the city I had come to love and respect. I felt betrayed by the ugliness. Lisa shared the sentiment, though she argued vehemently that the government had been obtuse in not listening to the protestors.

She said that had the students been given some sense that their complaints were legitimate and would be seriously addressed, all of the madness could have been avoided. I was not sure.

I had decided to nurse my bruised ribs that evening and Lisa, José, Ulla, Pete, Roxanne and I had joined Milo in his apartment for dinner.

"Don't you see? We have to make demands," Lisa said. "If we don't, they'll divide and conquers us. And it'll be back to the way it was . . . nothing will ever change."

It was hard to figure out what was right, really. The confusion we all felt was palpable. Of course, educational reforms had to be made but would the political body be willing to make those changes when violence was the order of the day?

"If there's no pressure then nobody does anything," José said.

"That's true, but when we push each other to extremes it brings out the worst in all of us," Milo said.

"What would you have the students do, then? Continue with the status quo?" Ulla asked.

"I don't know. I really don't know," Milo said.

"Nobody knows anything," Roxanne said.

"The government can't continue to ignore the problems," Ulla said. "I know what's going on at the Sorbonne, a great institution but lacking so many facilities. The students have to go to a crowded café in the neighborhood to do their homework, because there are no decent study halls for them to work in."

"The lectures are zoos," Lisa said. "Three hundred people crammed like sardines into small lecture halls, and teachers hiding in their ivory towers. I don't blame people for being fed up. I didn't realize how things were before I came here. It's shameful."

"But is violence the solution?" Pete asked. "The other night was pretty scary. People caught up in this frenzy of hate and violence. I'm not saying the students are wrong. I just wish people would settle their differences in a peaceful manner. It's always dangerous to settle on extremes."

"The government is screwing up in a big way," I said. "You're right when you talk about extremes. Frankly speaking, I don't know of a social revolt of this magnitude that has been resolved with flowers and kisses."

"That's always the experience, isn't it?" Roxanne said.

"It's true," Peter said." But more than that, it's the danger always hovering over a revolution that if cooler heads don't prevail the revolution will devour its own children. I wonder if the students will remember that historical reality."

"We French aren't very logical," Milo said. "We get caught up in the fantasy of it all, and the result is that we end up killing each other. Look at the commune: How many Parisians got killed by other Parisians?

"I'm not proud of the students, but I don't give much credit to the government either in spite of what Pompidou said last night. I'm not sure he's gone far enough to meet the demands made by the students. It may be too late," he added, not without an air of sadness.

"Neither side can be proud of what happened at Gay-Lussac," I said.

It was the prime minister, Pompidou, who the previous evening—after the bloody riots by the Luxembourg Gardens I had witnessed—had spoken on television promising to pull the police out of the Sorbonne, and also promising to give in to most of the students' demands. I had not seen nor heard the speech.

Lisa told me about it when I got home in the early morning. She had stayed up waiting for my return. I protested when I found her still awake, but she was having none of my objections.

"You smell awful," she said.

"I feel worse than I smell," I said, holding my side.

"Oh, they got you. How can I trust you now *mon cher petit Alexandre*. You're not supposed to get hurt. You're supposed to report what happens but not become part of the story."

Whenever she wanted to humor me, she would imitate Milo's French accent when he spoke English, and pronounced my name in an exaggerated manner just to be pompous. I started to laugh, which made my bruised ribs cry out in pain.

"That's what you told me. I just wished the message had been given to the guy who stuck his *matraque* into my ribs."

"Were you throwing *pavés* at *les flics*?" I knew she would have been very happy if I had been throwing cobblestones at the police.

"No."

"Why not?"

"Alain isn't paying me to throw *pavés* at *les flics*."

"Are you sure?"

"Yes."

"You didn't even throw one for me?"

"No, not even one."

"I'm going to have a serious talk with Alain about this," she said, laughing. "Come on, a warm bath will do wonders for you."

As I was taking off my clothes, she leaned over and kissed the welt on my ribs.

"There, that should make the pain go away."

I stood naked in the middle of the bathroom.

"Oh, the smell. What did you do, take a shower in the tear gas?" she asked, holding her nose and pushing my clothes away with her foot.

"Yeah, it feels like it. Anyway, tear gas was not meant to give you a nice, sweet smell of a rose garden in full bloom."

"Yes, that's for sure."

While she prepared the bath, she told me about Pompidou's speech. She was happy and thought what Pompidou had said was the beginning of a victory for the students.

Pete asked no one in particular, that night when we were at Milo's house, "so you think they'll pull out of the Sorbonne?"

"It's laughable," Ulla said.

"That's just to gain time—*c'est du bidon*—it's phony," Lisa said.

"You're right," I said. "It's ridiculous and phony. Getting out of the Sorbonne was a good political move, and it really doesn't cost the government anything. With everybody on strike and no classes, what does it have to lose by pulling out? The police will go back soon enough."

"We just can't give up. What about the unions?" Lisa asked.

"The students and the unions are social enemies," Milo said. "The workers are communists for the most part, and the students in this revolt remain pretty bourgeois. How do you get these two social classes to agree? I can't see it. It's water and fire."

"I always think the French are sheep so maybe the students will make the rest of us act with courage and honor," Roxanne said.

"We should make love and not war," José said. We all applauded and cheered.

"Merci mon cher José. Incontestablement l'amour c'est un phénomène un peu excentrique, mais saine, tout á fait pratique, et satisfaisant !" Milo looked around the room, and we all cheered again.

"Absolument," José said.

"Are you sure you're not French?" Milo asked José in that charming, thick French accent of his.

Then we toasted and drank champagne to lovemaking—a little eccentric, sane, practical, and certainly a most satisfying phenomenon!

Workers' unions in France were powerful and well-disciplined, and up to this point had refused to join the students' protest. Part of the students' argument had been that this was a social revolution on behalf of the unions and the workers; however, in typical French fashion, the students and the unions distrusted each other.

Now, with the government fearing an alliance of these two distinct and different groups against itself, the situation was beginning to resemble a three-ring circus without a ringmaster. The newspapers had analyzed the events, and the criticism for the political body was heavy and sarcastic.

It seemed everyone had hidden motives except the students, who in their idealism had not yet factored in cynicism in their quest for a better system and a better life.

Union leaders also faced the problem that younger members would end up having more sympathies with the students, and thus prove much more difficult to control. The unions then called for a general strike with the intention of bringing Paris to its knees.

The strike did nearly paralyze Paris. No Métros running, no postal service, no trains, no taxis, no buses, no trash collection, no banks open, people stayed home from work.

"Leave it to the frogs to screw things up," Pete said.

The strike was coupled with one giant manifestation in the street of Paris on this Monday the 13th of May. It was a powerful statement against the government. Lisa and I managed to make it to the Place de La Sorbonne that day, where we stood as the people in the parade walked by in silence.

Pompidou had promised the police would withdraw from the Sorbonne. It now stood empty, still, and abandoned.

We were watching the thousands of people walking on Boulevard St. Michel when Lisa spotted Adam who was standing just behind us talking excitedly with other students. He saw us, and I could tell his hesitation.

Lisa went over to him and embraced him. He was very emotional about seeing her. She put her arms around him like a mother consoling a child. I did not go and join them. I saw Lisa talking to Adam to reassure him.

She said something to him, and he started to laugh, and soon the others joined in the laughter. Finally, Lisa brought him over. He was shy.

"Je suis vraiment désolé," he said.

"Pourquoi?"

"I'm really sorry because I failed Lisa and you."

You didn't," Lisa said.

"I could not protect you," he said. "I should have turned myself in and you wouldn't have suffered." He was so earnest.

"I don't think it would have made any difference to the cops," I said.

"Do you think so?" he asked, somewhat relieved of his imagined burden.

"That's what I told him," Lisa said.

"She's right," I said.

"I hope so," he said, wanting to believe us but still not sure.

"Look, all of you had to do what you had to do. There is no one to be blamed. Don't worry about it," I said.

"My mother says to say hello," he said, shyly.

"Well, thank you. I'm so grateful to her. You have no idea. Everything OK back home?" I asked, apprehensively in asking questions about his mother, but I also wanted to be sure.

"Yes, though the only thing she said to ask you was about the clothes and suitcase you left at the hotel."

The three of us laughed.

"Oh, my god, she didn't go and pick them up, did she?"

"No, she was just wondering."

"Tell her to forget about them."

"Yes," Lisa said. "I hope the hotel gives them to the Good Will Society. Do you have such a thing back home?"

"Good Will?" Adam had apparently never heard of such an institution.

"Never mind, buddy. Don't worry about it. As long as everything is OK with her," I said.

"Yes, she's fine. No problems." All three of us knew what that meant.

"Great. Give her our love," Lisa said. "We owe her so much. I think you have the most wonderful mom."

He was beaming. You could tell he was touched by her words and sentiment behind them.

"Adam, I'm going to tell you something, but you must promise to keep it a secret for a while, OK?" she said.

"OK," he said without hesitation, which made me laugh.

"Alex and I have decided to invite your mom to come visit us here, and we'll pay for everything."

At first, what Lisa had said did not register with him; suddenly, he understood and he was stunned. He looked at me, then back at her, completely without words.

He wanted to say something but it was obvious he could not. His eyes started to glisten, and he kept shaking his head.

"*Oh, mon dieu*, oh my God, *ce n'est pas vrai ça ?* It's true? *Oh, ce n'est pas possible.*"

He started to giggle like some kid who has suddenly learned he has won the gift he has longed for and yet he does not believe it.

"Yes, it's true. We want her to come and visit us and stay as long as she wants, right?" Lisa turned to me.

"Absolutely."

I had never seen Adam short of words. He embraced Lisa and shook my hand profusely.

"*Merci, merci.* OK, I promise not to say anything to her. She'll die when she hears the news, I promise you." And all three of us laughed because we knew and understood.

He had a faraway look, one of those looks so seldom seen in people's faces. One of wonder, embarrassment, excitement, all combined because when you hear such wonderful and unexpected news it overwhelms you completely, and all kinds of emotions are felt and registered.

"I'll call her and tell her," Lisa said.

"Lisa, yes, please. I only wish I were there to see her face," he said. Then in a very serious manner he added, "OK, I promise to keep such a fantastic secret. As José says, 'mum's the word!'"

He put his index finger to his lips to indicate silence. We all laughed and he embraced us.

"OK, I must go, something big is coming up," he said, a moment later. His eyes had a mischievous look.

"What is it?" Lisa asked.

"I'm not supposed to say anything," but his eyes said, if you want to know all you have to do is ask.

"I thought we were all in this together," Lisa said, taking his visual cue.

When it came to how much he adored and trusted her and Ulla, no secret would be safe with Adam if they wanted to know what it was. He looked around in a conspiratorial manner and drew us closer to him.

"We're going back into the Sorbonne!" he announced proudly.

"When?" Lisa was ecstatic.

"When this demonstration is over. We're staying no matter what. The Sorbonne belongs to the people."

Lisa had the widest smile on her face that I had seen that day. She could not contain herself. She embraced Adam. So it was that Adam, Lisa, and I, were among the first dozen, then hundreds, then thousands who later that day entered the Sorbonne once it was back in the students' control. This was a real victory. Their faces told it all.

We managed to squeeze inside the magnificent *amphithéatre* that was bursting at the seams. Lisa was enthralled, but it was just a bit too confining so we decided to get out before the crush of humanity became too much.

In her condition, she was not safe in this sea of people. Everyone who stood right next to her tried, without much success, to give her a bit more space.

We walked through the hallways and into the courtyard. I loved the old building.

"So many memories," I said. "I can't believe I'm here with you. If someone had told me a few years ago, that I would find myself walking in here with a beautiful girl, whom I love like there is no tomorrow, gorgeously pregnant, and about to be the mother of my child, I don't know what I would have said."

"Now we'll have our own memories to treasure," she said, as she hugged me.

I remembered when I had first walked these hallways. I had been shocked when I had gotten the answer I had been accepted to come and study here. Walking along these long-hallowed corridors now—so familiar from years ago—and holding Lisa's hand was a wonderful moment.

Looking at the people around us, their happy faces not quite believing what they were doing; hearing but not really listening to the chattering everywhere; still fearful that something might go wrong; not wanting to trust their senses in what they were experiencing and living through; but determined to continue with the struggle. It was quite an experience.

"I will remember this for the rest of my life," Lisa said. "Nothing can replace what I feel being here with you and walking around this place. So much of my life has changed since I met you." She rubbed her big belly.

"Is that good?"

"This is the best of times for me. I love you. I love life. I even love these crazy frogs," she said, laughingly.

"Boy, if you love the frogs, things must really be good."

We stopped and kissed. We were like tourists visiting ancient ruins recently discovered and in awe of what we see, in awe of the fact we also happened to be in the right place at the right time.

That moment gave us a greater understanding of our basic human values, and the simple beliefs in something to make our lives worthwhile. We had to believe change for the better was caused because individuals made a difference.

We did not have to dance with the devil to have rights to our personal dignity, integrity, to our self-respect. Some truths were eternal. The individual had won a victory.

What we learned in moments like this remained imprinted in our souls for the rest of our lives. We could go and become nothing but at this particular instant, we were special. We knew it and everyone else knew it, too. I saw it on Lisa's face.

We held hands and walked around savoring what we both felt. Once in a while, we would stop and she hugged me. This was ours; it truly belonged to all of the students, and their supporters.

We lingered for a long time, probably longer than was practical since she was getting tired. There was no need to say anything. We just let this sense of euphoria bathe us and carry us. We wanted to stretch the wonderful sentiment of victory for as long as we could.

No one who lived through that experience could easily forget. The individuals, as represented by who was there that day, had prevailed. *Extraordinaire!*

Yet the word *guignol*—puppet—also comes to mind when I considered those events for the truth was nobody really knew what was going on. No matter how optimistic and resourceful the students were, the government did not appear to be listening.

It had enormous power, and whoever controls the power controls the outcome. The government, cynically wanting to give the appearance that it was listening, played this game of puppetry with the student population.

The powers-that-be insisted that nothing out of the ordinary was going on in France. The pursuit of France's grand objectives was the most important task and duty. And the students, feeling superior because they were again occupying the Sorbonne, now thought they could set the rules.

The two sides, no matter how you looked at them, could never converge to find common ground. The situation was maddening. Both sides were angling for different results.

Both were caught up in their own rhetoric and tactics, believing destiny was on their side. The occupation of the Sorbonne was probably the highest point for the students and the workers who were involved in the revolt of May 1968.

I wanted to think of it as the best of the events that took place in Paris that month of May, for other events brought much pain and sorrow. Nobody was spared. There were extremes on both sides, and the blame had to be shared by everyone.

Lisa and I returned home later. She was tired but elated. For her the turn of events in the struggle—getting the Sorbonne back in the students' control—seemed to augur a better future, probably not a practical thing to hang on to, but as usual the heart always hopes.

I called Alain to tell him what I had seen, and he wanted me to go back to report on what was happening at the Sorbonne.

"I'm so happy we went," Lisa said.

"Me, too."

She put her arms around me and held me close to her.

"I love you," she said.

"Really?"

"Yes!"

"The rumors going around are true, then?"

"Do you still have doubts?"

"Yes," I said, just to tease her.

"If I have not convinced you by now, then you're totally hopeless," she said, smiling.

"The only thing I know is that I'm totally and hopelessly in love with you."

"All is not lost then."

"No, all is not lost."

"OK, when you come back you need to wake me up. I want to know everything."

"You need your rest." I protested.

"I'm fine. Remember when you used to wake me up to make love? And that night when we went to get onion soup at Les Halles?"

Lisa, who normally slept like a log, had suddenly awakened me in the middle of the night. She was looking at me with a serious look, "OK," she said without any explanation, "but do you belong to me?"

"Of course, I belong to you. I want to belong to you. I need to belong to you."

"Good."

"Is that why you woke me up?"

"No, I'm hungry?" she said, and embraced me.

"Go make a sandwich."

"I want *soupe à l'oignon et pommes frites.*"

"Onion soup with French fries? At this time of the night?"

"Everybody in Paris goes out to eat *soupe à l'oignon et pommes frites* in the middle of the night. When you live here you do like the Parisians do."

So we had gone to the same restaurant my friend Gary had taken me on my first night in Paris. We ate *soupe à l'oignon et pommes frites* and watched the crowded restaurant with the other patrons, boisterous, loud, and enjoying the night's *ambiance.*

Then we walked around Les Halles, which at that time of the night was buzzing with all kinds of nocturnal people.

"I love a night like this. I wonder what all of these night people do during the day," she said.

We came home just as the street cleaners were beginning their daily task.

"And then you wanted to make love, remember," she added.

"Wait a second, that's not the way I remember it."

"Sounds like somebody is complaining."

"Who could that be?" I asked.

"I don't know."

"It's probably someone with a very short memory."

"Yeah, what do you expect?"

"Do we know who she is?" I said, to tease her.

"Not she, but he."

"Who?" I asked knowing she knew I would not forget.

"I don't know."

"Will you ever forget?"

"Never!" She answered before kissing me goodnight.

Thus, it was back to the Sorbonne for me. Only a few hours since Lisa and I had been there and now the whole place was different. It was as if the lights had come on in this dark, musty, forbidden place, where the doors had been thrown open and fresh air streamed in and everything was bright, colorful, filled with youthful enthusiasm.

The cobwebs of the famous French bureaucracy were being swept away by a tidal wave of newfound freedom.

There were flags, posters, and signs of every color and size silently shouting their slogans in a torrent of anti-government rhetoric—students everywhere. There were marathon discussions. Everyone was encouraged to participate, to share experiences.

The talks were endless. It was easy to see why the French were so in love with their language. The students could talk, and talk they did with incredible clarity, elegance, eloquence, and passion.

Every conceivable point of view was aired, considered, discussed and not just political theories but practical things, too: How to get organized, the task of daily living in the old building, the needs bound to crop up and how best to take care of them.

But the main goal was the need to bring changes not only to the educational system but also to the entire French society. Theories abounded about how to change it, improve it, and make it respond better to the needs of those who were part of it—how best to take advantage of the new freedom.

One of the speakers was Adam, and I experienced his eloquence and intelligence. I saw why people believed in him. I was very proud of him and, not for the first time, I wished he were not facing such a terrible future back in his own country.

Committees were set up to deal with the myriad problems inherent in the changed situation now that the Sorbonne was back in the students' control. The level of sophistication by the students was high and filled with youthful energy. Other students brought food, and it was shared. There was an incredible sense of community among everyone.

Given how French society was structured, it seemed that what was happening at the Sorbonne was the practice of the words you see everywhere that have come to symbolize France: *Liberté, Egalité, Fraternité!* Words that are for the most part vacuous and disdained by the populace that knows the score.

Balzac had once written, "We have Liberty to die of hunger, Equality in misery, the Fraternity of the street corner." For some reason, in this setting, the words: *Liberté, Egalité, Fraternité,* did not seem as cynical as Balzac's words.

This May 13th, 1968, at the Sorbonne in Paris, was indeed a day to remember. People were polite to each other. They went out of their way to show compassion, to show they cared. No one was made fun of.

It probably came as a shock for—normally and as a rule—Parisian students and, Parisians in general, tend to be rude and somewhat indifferent, but what I saw that night was exactly the opposite.

It was as if all of the rules of good behavior that *papa et maman* had tried to instill in these students had not been in vain. Now that it was time to put them into practice, they were being recalled with a great deal of common sense and feeling.

French parents would have been happy and proud to see the cream of French youth acting intelligently and politely. To see the students changing their arrogant way was a treat.

The goal of the student movement was clear: change the system! Change to bring tangible transformation, not just for the students but also for everyone else. This was a revolution meant for the greater France.

The old ways had to be replaced with new ones. In their discourses, some students drew parallels between their May revolution and the original French Revolution.

It seemed all of the frustrations and unhappiness accumulated over years and years of passivity were finally released and this had led to a giant *ras le bol*, another of those famous French expressions difficult to translate. The closest that I can come to is, one has had enough! One is fed up!

I also suspected that somewhere behind letting the students have the Sorbonne back, the government was making a cold and well-calculated move to diffuse and neutralize the anger that just about every sector of French society felt.

I feared that by pulling the police out of the Sorbonne, the government was not responding to the needs of its citizens but simply buying time, like Lisa had said.

Deep in my guts, I had the sensation that in spite of their energy, enthusiasm, idealism, and commitment the students in their naiveté would end up with nothing to show for the incredible leap of faith they had taken. I did not share these fears with Lisa, however. I preferred to keep them to myself.

Only time would tell. No matter how much one supported the students' hard work, in the final analysis, the people who had the power were never interested in giving it up or sharing it with anyone else.

I got home at dawn the following day. I did not wake Lisa up although she had left me a note reminding me to do so when I got home.

"I have to tell you something that will make you laugh," she said, later that day.

"What?"

"My sister called last night just after you left. She wanted to find out how things were going. They're very worried about us with all of the bad news coming out of Paris."

Lisa and I had discussed what she would say to her parents when they called. We did not want them to be worried.

"What did you say?"

"I told her we're fine, we're just following events."

"And she believed you?"

"Of course, she didn't believe me."

She stopped and started to laugh. I had no idea what the laugh was about.

"What's so funny?"

"OK, you don't know my sister, my wonderful sister. So responsible, organized, polite, and well-mannered. I mean she knows everybody's birth dates, anniversaries—you name it. She remembers them all. Well, she got arrested on the same day that I did."

"You're making that up."

"I'm not. She really did."

"Don't tell me she got arrested for protesting against the government."

"It was a parking ticket."

"A parking ticket? Come on, nobody gets arrested for a parking ticket."

"Well, she did. Apparently, she had gotten a ticket a while back and forgot to pay it. It's so unlike her to forget something like that. She got pulled over by the police on a routine traffic control, and was put in jail because there was a warrant for her arrest. I told you twins have things happen to them that are similar. It's weird."

Giggling, she told me her parents had gone to bail her sister out of jail. The judge had been sympathetic and had reduced the fine and gave Robin a lecture. When Lisa told Robin what happened to her, both sisters laughed about it. Lisa got Robin to promise not to tell their parents about her ordeal for fear they would worry.

"OK, you told me about similar things happening to twins. Is she pregnant?

"No, but she's working on it, I'm sure," she said, with a gleam in her eyes.

"Just what kind of family is this baby of mine going to be born into, anyway?"

"The best!"

"Yeah, a bunch of delinquents."

She laughed at my silliness.

Then only one day after the students took the Sorbonne back, de Gaulle went to Romania—talk about hubris. With *Le Grand Charles*, as he was sometimes referred to, there was never any chance of deviating from previously established plans. Like every Frenchman, de Gaulle saw a much greater role for this country than the realities allowed.

"Les *émeutes*," or revolt or "*les événements*," as the newspapers euphemistically called the students' insurrection, were not going to interfere and derail what de Gaulle had in mind for his own self-aggrandizement.

He was not about to be deterred from pursuing the grand designs he had in mind for France, and, thus, for himself. A few soreheads were to be expected. After all, with over 365 kinds of cheeses, how can the French be expected to rise above their pettiness and be unanimous about anything?

One thing de Gaulle always said about his compatriots and Roxanne had mentioned already: "The French are sheep." De Gaulle thus acted toward his fellow citizens accordingly. The body politic, in the elected members of the national assembly, was expected to follow the general, and it did.

If de Gaulle thought it wise to leave the country in the midst of a great crisis, then it was fine by them. If the big guy was not worried, why should they be?

"This is total insanity," Milo said.

"Why?" I asked him.

"You just don't leave in the middle of this mess. It goes to show you the contempt he has for everybody and everything."

"I thought you were a Gaullist," I told him just to give him a hard time.

"I'm not. Granted, he did pull us out of Algeria and so far, he's kept the Brits out of the Common Market to which they don't belong to anyway. And if they join, one day they'll leave. That's how they are. Still, the trip, the timing—it's all wrong."

"Maybe he knows something we don't."

"No, he's just acting like he's always done: imperial and cavalier," he said, not without a hint of admiration.

For de Gaulle, going to Romania was a rendezvous that could not be put aside, postponed or, God forgive, canceled. Other lesser mortals could change their plans or make excuses, but for *Le Grand Charles* it was out of the question.

I had to admit that French politics was something only the French understood. They were just waiting for the head guy to tell them what to do, even if he treated them as his personal property.

"We're just like the children who want our *papa* to tuck us into bed every night, and read us our favorite bedtime stories of how the ancient *Gaulois* beat the enemy of our *patrie*," Milo said, with contempt. "That's how we've always ruled ourselves."

Sometimes, it is easier to understand why Americans are different from the French. We got rid of our king a long time ago, when we separated from England. The French guillotined their king and queen, but they still seem to accept the idea of being ruled by some form of monarchy—monarchy of the republic, I called it.

The students were also using a phrase that again defies translation, that was, however, symbolic of what was happening in France; *chienlit!* It is an old expression. The polite translation was: Fouling the nest. I much prefer the Parisians' version of it: Shitting on the bed.

There were signs everywhere in Paris with these words. I did not know if they referred to de Gaulle or to the students or both. Given what was happening in France, I would have said it was applicable to both sides: French shitting on each other.

As the birth of our child was getting closer, I asked Lisa, "don't you think we should get married before the baby is born?"

"Why?" My idea seemed to surprise her.

"Well, am I not the father of this baby?"

"You know you are."

"Do you want her to carry my name?"

"She will. Here in France if you go to the *Mairie*—city hall—and register our baby when she is born, she'll get your name even if we aren't married, that's if you want to."

"Stop being silly. Of course, I want to. But are you sure?"

"Yes. You'll have to go and register her."

"How do you know all this?"

"Madame Commère told me."

"You don't mind?"

"Mind what?"

"That we're not married?"

"I'm married to you."

She had said that before, but she had never brought it up again. I must say that the idea of not being "married" to her bothered me. I did not need to be married to accept the notion of responsibility and honor. My question had to do with children being the result of a union the law recognized and accepted.

Maybe my own liberal attitude about live and let live had not advanced far enough to be applicable to my own life. I was willing to accept that the times were changing, but not so much for me.

"Now you're the one being silly," she said, after a moment of silence.

"Why?"

"Because you give so much importance to a piece of paper, as if that's going to make any difference to me."

"It doesn't?"

"No," she said. "Oh, I know my parents would disagree. I guess a child needs to be perceived by others as having a 'legitimate place' in society. To me, our baby's legitimacy is the result of us being in love and not because of a piece of paper that codifies or formalizes our love."

"You're not afraid of what people are going to say about having a child without being married?"

"It's my life. Anyway, it's kind of late to be worried about that. You know, Madame Commère told me the French accept the legitimacy of the child without such stupid conditions. A child has a mother and a father. She's legitimate whether her parents are married or not."

"What will you say, though when she asks about it?"

"We'll tell her she was conceived in love. Yes, we were not married, but what matters was that we found each other, respected each other. You loved me, and I loved you because somehow the cosmos made it possible for us to meet.

"When a man and a woman are in love, very often, it results in children being born from such love, and that we love her with all of our hearts. So, there's no need to worry about it. We'll get married later if you want to."

"This sounds so much like when you asked your mother about her and your father."

"Well, it comes from the same family. It's wonderful don't you think?"

She was right. It was hard for me to imagine wanting my life to be different. My life was here, now, not in some strange future whose outcome was very far removed from my present reality. My life could not get better.

I suppose, I could have taken a trip to the moon and that would have been special, but I did not want to go to the moon. I did not want to live in any other place, or at any other time, or to have any other life than the one Lisa and I were sharing.

I desperately wanted to believe the wonderful things Lisa had brought to me were real. She had said so many times they were, but I always suspected that was not the case.

I had carried these fears for so long. I had to keep working so they would not overwhelm me. It seemed there had to be a thunderbolt from the sky, some signal telling me my life was fine, or a messenger, maybe a Hermes, who would come and say I had nothing to fear.

It was so damn hard to get rid of old fears and demons, to clean out our spiritual closet of its emotional skeletons hanging inside.

Pete came over to the apartment late Friday of that week. He wanted to find out what the students were up to. Lisa was out taking her walk. The doctor had recommended a daily walk. I had gone with her often, but today she wanted to go by herself.

"I thought you didn't care what the students were doing."

"I've never said that," he said. "I just think the French in general are not ready to make the changes this country needs to make life better for everyone."

"Have you heard from John and Juliette?" I asked.

John had gone back to London taking Juliette with him. He did not want her to be arrested. There were rumors that rightist groups with police cooperation were keen on making life miserable for people on the left, and Juliette was a member of the communist party.

"Yeah, they're fine. I told him to stay there, and make sure Juliette doesn't come back to try to be a hero."

"How did you end up in France?"

He hesitated before answering. He was quiet for what seemed like a long time. When he spoke, he sounded weary not because he was keeping a secret but more like the memories were too far away to recall them.

"Living in France was probably the furthest thing from my mind a few years ago. I lived in New York. Believe it or not, I was a lawyer."

"A lawyer? You?" I could not have been more amazed.

"Yes. Does it surprise you?"

"Well, yes."

Nothing about Pete or his demeanor would have told me he was a lawyer. You could have knocked me over with a feather.

"I was. I was married and—" he stopped.

For a moment, I saw his face go from a relaxed to a hard look, as if whatever memory he was now thinking about was not very pleasant. I suddenly realized that recalling such remembrances *was* painful for him, and I should not have asked him why he was in France.

"I was in love," he continued, "very much so. She was the love of my life! I remember so clearly, when I met her. I went to a reception—" he stopped again. I could see he was struggling to find the right words, more to explain to himself than to me.

"I can still see her wearing this long, soft, pink dress, a picture of such loveliness and innocence that when I first saw her my heart skipped a beat, literally. An incredible feeling came over me. It was like an electric shock. I never believed in love at first sight, but I immediately knew it was that. She was exactly the woman I wanted in my life."

He walked to the fireplace and stood looking at the painting he had given Lisa. His face now had a warm smile.

"Lisa was very much touched when you gave her that painting."

"The pleasure was mine. I told her it was waiting for her."

"She told me that. Does Lisa remind you of your ex?"

"Yes, in many ways, yes. I think Lisa sort of makes me think more of the daughter I never had. I'd like to think she would have been as lovely, wonderful, and spunky as Lisa is. She loves you, you know. You're lucky—" he stopped again.

His face was softly bathed in a mixture of pain and resignation. His eyes were misty, with a faraway look. He continued in a kind of monologue as if he were talking to himself.

"It's hard not to long for those days with an old man's regrets and wonder why it didn't work out. I'd like to think Patricia loved me, but I don't know. I came home one evening and, well, she was gone! Had taken all of her stuff and just up and left.

"No explanation. No reason. Nothing. It was like she had never been part of my life. The whole relationship seemed to have evaporated into thin air. It disappeared. . ."

He looked at the painting again as if to clarify his thoughts. After a long silence, he continued with a rueful smile on his face.

"She was young and came from a wealthy family, I didn't. I used to work long hours because I was afraid, I would never make enough money to show her she hadn't married a guy who wouldn't give her what she was used to. I was stupid.

"I should have understood she needed love and not money. Then later, when I went to see her parents, the explanation I got was that people in their position sometimes exceed; yeah, that's the word her father used. With money comes 'certain privilege,' he said. I didn't want to ask what that meant. I guess such privilege created its own morality."

Pete's voice was down to a whisper, soft, disconnected, distant. There was quietness to his whole demeanor. This was not the guy who threw wine bottles at windows in crowded restaurants.

"I didn't understand that," he continued, but more like talking to himself. It seemed like he had forgotten I was there.

"I blamed myself for what happened. I still do. I never went back to the house. An attorney friend of mine handled the divorce. I didn't contest it. I sold everything that was mine that I had accumulated through my efforts, and left.

"I had a childhood friend who lived in Hawaii, and he invited me to come and stay with him. I didn't care one way of the other, but I went anyway. Then we took a trip to the South Seas. Tahiti to be exact, and that was essentially my first exposure to the French.

"I found them to be kind of exotic and strange because in my head I have always identified the French with medieval churches and not with huts and half-naked people running around. My friend also used to come to Paris, once a year, and suggested I come with him—"

Once more, he stopped and looked at his hands. He seemed to be examining them with a great deal of interest. I did not know why it struck me in such an odd way.

Peter had well-sculpted hands, and he kept them always clean, with none of the traces of paint one usually associates with people who did the kind of work he did. He was very meticulous when it came to his hands.

"Again, it didn't make any difference either way so I came to Paris with him. I liked Paris right away, so I stayed. If truth were told, I don't think I could have lived in Hawaii forever, too much paradise.

"I was getting what mainlanders call 'rock fever.' Painting was a hobby of mine, and I was kind of good at it. I went to the Beaux Arts School here in Paris, and learned discipline. It took a while to get settled into my own style. I'm not a great painter, but what I do is mine, and I like it.

"I don't paint to make money even though some of my paintings have sold well. I'm more interested in trying to capture something—a sentiment, a glimpse of truth, something honest—however small, before my time runs out . . ."

His voice was still soft. Since I had met Pete, I never knew him to be someone who liked to share personal things with others. Yet I also found him to be a lonely man. Maybe lonely is not the right word.

More lonesome, always looking in from the outside, never quite comfortable where he was. This sense of not quite fitting in was what I found interesting in him. Perhaps, in another sense, I resembled him a lot. I am never quite sure how I fit in.

When he started talking again, his voice now was stronger. He seemed to have regained his old-self.

"One day, one of the professors at the school gave a *soirée*, and out of boredom I went. Roxanne and I met that evening. I hadn't wanted to be social as I hadn't been to a party for a long time. Anyway, I was a bit shy at first, but she was very decent, kind, and honest.

"We've been together ever since. I told her about Patricia. Actually, I never thought I'd learn to love or trust another woman. I love Roxanne, and I trust her. She made it possible for me to do that."

"She's quite a lady. Do you ever wonder about your ex?"

Pete seemed surprised at my question "Who doesn't wonder about past loves? Yes, I do but it passes, though in some strange way I'm here because of Patricia. Why do you ask?"

"I always wonder about that fork in the road. What if we had not taken the road we did, where would be now be? And what about the things we didn't do that we should have done? Lamenting those others who aren't part of us, who are now faded memories.

"What became of them? Where are they? Are they happy? Do they think about us? What do they remember about us? Do they even remember us at all? What about the longings for the innocent moments back then, infinitely regretting not having said what we should have said?

"I often wish I had been more honest, that I hadn't hidden my true feelings for fear of getting hurt. It's crazy the price we pay for our own spiritual shortcomings."

"If you don't want to go mad," Pete said, "you'd better stop thinking about those things. It'll keep you awake for many a night."

"Is it all about fading memories and regrets?"

He did not answer right away. He seemed to be looking for an answer. "Sometimes," he finally said.

"Do you think you'll ever go back to the States?"

"No. And you?"

"I don't know."

"This is where I belong. This is my home; this is my life!" He said, cheerfully.

Pete decided to join me in the Latin Quarter that evening and as fate would have it, it turned out to be one of the worst riots going on nightly in the Latin Quarter.

It all started at the Gare de Lyon, one of the major train stations in the city, where hundreds of students were milling around after a demonstration earlier that day. The police moved in, and a pitched battle took place between them and the students.

It seemed that everywhere you turned there was destruction and riots. The madness of the police and the rioters was without limits. Both sides allowed incredible violence—bloody faces attested to that.

I needed to drop off some papers and rolls of film at Alain's office, so after lingering for a while around Place St. Michel, Pete and I walked along the Seine and toward rue du Louvre where Alain's office was located.

We left the stuff with his concierge, and as we started walking back to the river, we saw about two hundred people milling around the old building of *la Bourse*—the Paris stock exchange—right smack in the middle of Les Halles.

There was something very unsettling about the mob being on this side of the river. I could not tell if all of the people there were students or workers. They were indistinguishable from one another. No cops were around.

It was not too far from the Latin Quarter, but far enough that it had not occurred to me that any trouble was brewing here. Most of the people I saw had probably marched from the Gare de Lyon.

It did not take much brainpower to see that *la Bourse*, the ultimate symbol of greed, indifference, and selfishness, stood unprotected, like a giant whale beached in enemy territory—defenseless.

I had been inside the building—the interior was classic—a couple of times with Alain, because he knew some people who worked there, and his office was just a couple of blocks away. Pete and I watched the people as they silently roamed around the building.

The tension in the air was thick, defiant, and menacing. What better statement to make against this symbol of capitalism, corruption, slavery, than to destroy the building of the stock exchange?

"What do you think they're going to do?" Pete asked.

"I don't know. With some of these people you never know what to expect."

It seemed like the mob had the whole place to itself. This was not very helpful. Some people had large iron rods, chains, clubs, and other heavy weapons, and they were brandishing them in the air, arguing and shouting among themselves.

I decided to go near the building to get a better sense of what they were proposing to do. Pete stayed where he was.

"You go. I'm kind of old for this madness," he said, a bit apologetically.

You could tell just by looking at the faces of the people there that they reflected hate and violence. As I was milling around the crowd appeared to be loose, but there was organization and leaders.

These people knew what they were about to do, gathering force and determination in a very lackadaisical way, as they joked among themselves.

Then in a kind of a rush—like water from a broken damn running down a hill gathering momentum and power, and with a monstrous roar—the crowd surged forward in a well-coordinated effort.

Jumping over the old wrought iron fence around the *Bourse*, there more for decoration than for protection, the mob shattered the large glass doors and burst inside the building. The smashing and destruction inside were vicious.

The wooden structures, desk, fences, walls were no defense against the attack. It was a malicious ballet choreographed for complete devastation and mayhem. Then gasoline was poured over the mess. The smell told you what was going to happen next.

I did not see who ignited the fire, but given the gasoline it was not hard to guess what the final outcome would be. Everyone started to rush out of the place. The flames reflected eerily on the euphoric faces of the mob.

It is fascinating to watch something so large go up in flames. I felt a rush of emotions. I could understand how the participants must have felt.

"Why are you doing this?" I asked a guy who was standing right next to me.

"Why not? Does it bother you?" He looked at me as if I had just arrived from Mars.

"I'm just curious, that's all."

"It's kind of amusing, *non*? In any case, *je m'en fous*."

A very French attitude and expression: *Je m'en fous*—I do not care. Sometimes, I think the French character is reduced to this pernicious expression: *Je m'en fous!* With his innocent air, I could not tell if he was a student or a worker.

He shrugged his shoulders, smiled, looked at me one more time, and walked to join his friends, *très décontracté*—relaxed—very French. This guy will have no trouble sleeping tonight, I thought.

For good measure and not to take any chances, barricades started to go up on the streets leading to the building in order to keep any police and firemen from reaching the blaze.

It was the final act of a well-prepared plan. Everything that could be uprooted, moved, crashed, thrown in, was added to the barricades, making me think of military tactics employed in war.

Even in this madness, I felt a sense of sadness because, though trying to burn down the building was indeed an act of protest, it also showed to what extent violence was now leading Parisians to anarchy and maybe civil war.

The reality was that such violent acts would make no difference in the end; they only added fuel to the harsh measures the government would eventually take to stop the mob from destroying law and order.

I stood watching the building being consumed by fire. The crowd thinned out, and I went back across the street looking for Pete. He was standing right next to an overturned car talking to Alain.

"Where in the hell did you come from?" I asked Alain.

"I came by the office and saw the flames, so I rushed over. I didn't think you'd still be around here"

"We were at Place St. Michel, but since I had some stuff to give you, we walked over."

"Yes, my concierge told me you had come by."

"This is crazy," Peter said.

"Can you believe it?" I asked.

"Well, maybe it was a good thing after all," Pete, said.

"What was?" Alain asked.

"Trying to burn this damn building down," I said.

"Why do you say that?" Alain asked.

"In this country," I said, "there is such a gulf between the rich and the poor. The social classes are rigid. People are fed up. You can't blame the students or the workers for wanting to destroy a system that oppresses them. Putting the torch to his place pretty much tells de Gaulle what his fellow citizens think of his latest offer."

De Gaulle had addressed the nation earlier in the day. He had come back from Romania earlier than planned, promising to make radical changes in the way society operated. He had committed to making French society more open so that everyone could share in it.

He had asked for a vote of confidence—a referendum—in which voters would approve his proposals.

"So you don't think this referendum will work?" Pctc asked.

"He's done it before." Alain answered. "It's worked because of the way he does it. He gives us a stark and, to his eyes and the eyes of many of my compatriots, a simple choice: *Moi ou la merde!*"

"And he'll get away with it," I said.

"As always," Alain said, quietly, with disappointment in his voice.

"The master trickster at work. You've got to hand it to him. He knows his business, and he knows his co-citizens," Pete said.

The big question remained, however, whether French society would buy de Gaulle's plan? Or would they reject it, as it appeared they were willing to do, based on the riots that had taken place here and were taking place in other parts of the city, and around the country even after he spoke of making changes in the educational and political systems.

"Stay tuned," Pete said.

There were not that many people around when the riot police and the firemen finally showed up. The firemen started working to save the building. It seemed a difficult task and from where we stood, I could hear they thought they would not be able to do so.

The policemen, however, were in a foul mood. We made a hasty retreat through a small adjacent street. We did not want to push our luck.

"Do you get combat pay around here?" Pete asked me.

"I should," I said.

"*Il ne faux pas lui mettre des idées dans sa tête,*" Alain said, giving me a stern fatherly look while warning Pete not to put ideas into my head.

Pete and Alain left. Pete because he had enough of this madness for one day, and Alain because he needed to go back to the office to monitor the events from the people who were keeping him up to date. I went back to the Latin Quarter.

It was a night of total chaos, terror, and brutality. It was next to impossible to decide which night could be considered the worst so far in the revolt. The escalation of violence was out of control.

Nothing seemed to make people pause to reflect on what was happening. I had given up saying and thinking things could not get worse—but they did.

The riots along with the strikes were completely out of control. It was another night of madness, bloodshed, and cruelty with the police beating people indiscriminately.

They made no attempt to figure out who was a rioter and who was not. Everybody got the same treatment. It was also a night when, according to official sources, over two thousand people were injured. Hospitals were overwhelmed with the injured.

The authorities had managed to expel Danny the Red from France, and he had tried to come back and was stopped at the border. This only enraged the students and more demonstrations were organized. The word of the movement was: Strike and change your life!

France was now undergoing a giant social experiment comprised of violent protests. Living in France gave you the right to go on strike. If you were not striking against something—anything—you did not understand a damn thing about what was taking place.

Alain and Milo thought the whole country was going down the toilet. Physically I was exhausted. Lisa found me sleeping over the typewriter a couple of times. I had been chasing the revolution all over the city, mostly at night, and slept whenever I could in the daytime while trying to cram as much information as I could in the photos I gave Alain or wrote afterward.

I felt like a stranger even in my own apartment, as it always seemed to be the meeting place for still another group discussion, another idea, another plan.

Though Lisa was still supporting her classmates, I could also detect a certain degree of disillusionment. It was frustrating to see the people who came to our place were really a bunch of romantics and so impractical.

An ingenious plan to end it all, had it been devised, would have been debated *ad infinitum* resulting in nobody agreeing on what to do next. This fact reflected the reality of the youth and inexperience of the participants, for their lack of focus and immaturity worked against them.

There were sharp disputes among our revolutionaries. I could not help but think what Peter had said about revolutions eventually destroying the people who bring them about.

Lisa had a tough time admitting that no matter how much she wished it to be otherwise, the only tangible result had been the hardening position from both sides.

The weekend of May 25 resulted in more bloody days, more bloody riots, more bloody nights, more protests, and more manifestations. De Gaulle gave still another speech. He said he would not resign after all.

Then, as predicted by Milo, people descended on the streets. This time thousands upon thousands of people were demonstrating, not in support of the students but in support of de Gaulle. It was the old principle of the French being sheep that I had heard so often expressed, over the last few days.

I was in Alain's office when Milo showed up. He was in a foul mood.

"What in the hell did you expect?" Alain asked him.

"I don't know," Milo responded. "I expected something more than a whole bunch of idiots acting, well, like idiots. I'd like to know how this whole thing came about. Where did all these thousands of people find gas for their cars or the buses to come to the manif? Where did they get the gas? I'd just like to know."

"Come on," I said, "people got together over their back fences, talked things over, and then decided to share their gasoline so they could all meet on the Champs Elysées."

"Our French cynicism seems to be finally taking root in your psyche," Alain said. "We'll make a Frenchman out of you, yet."

"Are you crazy?" Milo said to Alain. "He'll become worse than we are. You know how impressionable Americans are."

"Well, at least I could claim I was taught by the best," I said.

"I have no doubt," Alain said, "the speech, the meeting, the people, the gasoline, the march—they're all tied together and it doesn't take a genius to find the thread and follow it. There is only one man who could pull it off."

"*Le General*," Milo said, gloomily.

Later that night in the Latin Quarter, the noise, the yelling and screaming of people who had been injured—along with the unnerving wailing of the sirens from the ambulances, and the horns from private vehicles as they rushed through the streets taking the injured to the hospitals—only added more confusion, and madness to what was taking place.

This was not the Paris of beauty, charm, and worldly sophistication that Lisa and I had come to think of as ours. The Paris filled with our feelings of love, fantasy, and hope. The Paris of good things in life for us.

It sure as hell was not the Paris of the song: "I Love Paris Every Moment of the Year." This was a city plunged into ugliness and violence, sad, and unrecognizable. Nothing charming about what was going on here, I thought.

I went home anxious and depressed as the sun was just beginning to appear. I saw no end to what was taking place. There were so many things that were not clear anymore. Actually, the end I saw coming was going to be bad, very bad—ugly. I was now pretty much convinced the protests by the students were just exercises in futility.

Reading the newspapers about what was going on with the government and with de Gaulle was not pretty. There were cries from the political opposition demanding to pass a motion of no confidence trying to force a change of government.

The left was now openly telling people not to listen to de Gaulle. Again, civil war was not far from the surface. This was scary. Did I want to stay here with Lisa pregnant? Could I force the issue with her?

I knew she was a practical person and, so far, had kept her part of the bargain. She had not gone out to dig the *pavés* from Parisian streets. But what if the whole country suddenly ignited in a frenzy of hate and violence? I would have to start thinking and planning about a way out of here.

Milo had reminded me that we could go back to Normandy, and I had mentioned it to Lisa several times. She was never enthusiastic about it. Her parents were now calling literally every day and begging her to leave Paris. I had talked to her mother as she was having a hard time getting Lisa to listen.

"Alex, you must insist on it. With the baby coming it's just not safe. We think you should go to England or Germany. I hear they have wonderful maternity clinics," she said.

"So do the French," I said, not without a tinge of exasperation in my voice.

"Of course," she said. "It's just that with the things going on, Paris may be a bit unsafe at the moment. Besides, other than you she has nobody else there. I hope you understand our fears."

"I do. And I hope I count for something. Anyway, Lisa argues that you gave birth to her and Robin in Ethiopia, right smack in the middle of the bush, and you handled it pretty well."

"Yes, that's true, but there were no revolutions going on," she chuckled. "I was terrified. But I had no choice—you do."

"Well, revolution or no revolution Lisa is not terrified, and she has made a choice. We're not alone here. She has a great doctor she trusts and lots of people she can count on."

"We know how much you both love Paris. I just think it may be wiser to leave Paris just for the birth. Try to convince her. She doesn't want to listen to me."

"If she doesn't want to listen to you what makes you think she'll listen to me?"

"She loves you. She swears by you. You're the most important person in her life. You're the father of her baby. Talk to her, please," she said, not really convinced I would be any more successful than she was.

Love, the cure for whatever ails mankind.

"Lisa tells me she and Robin take after you in their stubbornness," I said, just to tease her.

"Well, that's what their father always claims," she said, laughing.

Her laughter was just as rich and wonderful as Lisa's. I was looking forward to meeting her parents.

As I rode my bike back to the apartment, the smells in the empty streets told me that no trash had been collected for days. Even Lisa had begun to have doubts about the wisdom of what the students were doing, though she was not ready to give up.

"This is crazy. There is no way the students are going to win. No way," I said.

"I know," she said, sadly.

"Look, you've told me how important the events here are to you, to me, to the baby. OK, I understand, but I suspect that what Milo says is true. It will all be for naught. Summer vacation is coming up, and I can't imagine the French willing to sacrifice such an important happening in their lives. You might as well ask them to give up their wines, their baguettes, their cheeses . . . sex . . ." she laughed.

I sat across the table from her. Though she had tried to explain her feelings about the students and their protests; nevertheless, Lisa's attitude remained a bit of a mystery to me. I understood personal convictions. I understood principles.

Because of that, I wanted to understand what she felt, how she felt. Lisa had a degree of innocence and bravado, but it was not phony or a fad. She really believed that individuals did make a difference. She desperately wanted to see that difference take place during her lifetime, and not in some distant nebulous future.

However, given the fact that she was also facing the birth of our baby, a baby she wanted and waited anxiously for, her own common sense ruled that anything she could do to help Adam, Ulla, and the others, would be in spirit and not in practice. This drove her crazy.

"Can you imagine? Here I am right smack in the middle of two great events in my life, and I can participate, truly participate, in only one of them," she complained.

"So?"

"I want to do *both*. I mean this is 1968. Women burn their bras. We're supposed to make our own choices. We're free," she said, laughing at herself.

"You want to be written up in the annals of revolutions and student protests as the only pregnant lady who stood up to these horrible, nasty, mean, politicians, risking it all?" I said, laughing at what we both knew was an impossible situation.

The realities of Lisa's own life, besides me, were simple: She was pregnant, and in spite of lofty desires, her baby was the only thing that mattered. I understood the contradiction. Hell, my whole life had been made up of attempts to deal with contradictions.

"It's not fair, but I know there's no other choice," she said.

"Do you regret it?"

"Never, though it would be terrific to think that I could do both."

"You can think it as long as you don't do it."

"It just isn't fair."

"Maybe during the next revolution our child will take up where her mother left off."

"I guess there are far more important things in life than rioting and digging the *pavés* from the streets of Paris," she finally said, not without some faded hopes in her voice.

"You guess?"

"Have no fear, your child is well taken care of, and her mother will do nothing to risk her wellbeing."

Lisa got up from the table and came around. I stood and put my arms around her. What doctor Brisson had said about Lisa and her abdomen getting bigger was now taking place. The weight was well proportioned.

She sparkled in those mysterious and magical ways pregnant women do. She was calm and complete. Very often, I felt as if she really did not need me anymore. She had said that I was silly to have these feelings, but I could not help it.

Lisa would be talking when, suddenly, she would get quiet and softly rub her belly, as if giving comfort to the life she was carrying inside her. There was this amazing connection of mother and child, and it was lovely to observe.

Whenever she got quiet, I would just sit there and look at her, drinking it all in from such a well of beauty and harmony. Then at other times, she would take my hand and put it on her, and I could feel the baby moving. What a thrill that was.

"How does it feel when the baby moves?"

"Well, she's moving."

"I know, but like how?"

"It's hard to describe. You have this child, this tiny life inside, and she's moving. I don't know how to explain it except to tell you that I feel so connected to her. Because of that bond I feel so connected to you."

She took my hand and placed it on her abdomen, and I started to rub it softly. I wanted to have the same connection Lisa had to the baby. When Lisa spoke again, her words were beautiful and moving.

"She is me, and I am she. She is you, and you are she. She is she, and we are she. Through her, you and I we will always be one and the same!"

No truer words had I ever heard in my life.

Lisa was now totally convinced we would have a girl. Madame Commère also believed so. She had once said seeing the shape of Lisa's belly made it clear Lisa was carrying a girl. I thought the certitude was all pure nonsense but, of course, what the hell did I know? I was only the father.

Madame Commère had solemnly declared it to be so, and that was like the Pope passing judgment on the scriptures. On the other hand, I was very touched when Madame Commère said she had asked God to protect Lisa and the baby from all harm.

"You see, she isn't that bad," Lisa said.

What could I say?

Lisa made life seem simple, real, and true. Is that what life was supposed to be all about? Two people in love. Dreaming and sharing an unknowable but exciting future; anxious and uncertain yet able to discover each other; prepared to learn from each other; taking care of each other; believing in their common destiny; no longer afraid to reveal to each other who they are.

Willing to receive and able to give to each other; joining in this mad adventure called life; taking the leap of faith and ready to open up the vast reservoir of love and affection residing in the human heart; looking forward to the wonderful surprise life brings.

Would the gods allow me clear sailing? What if they were waiting to play tricks on me? Oh, boy, I thought, I had better get rid of these crazy thoughts.

"Tu veux faire l'amour?"—do you want to make love? Lisa asked.

"Tu veux?"

Afterward, she told me a wonderful story about her parents.

FIFTEEN

A couple days later, Lisa and I attended a rally at L' Odéon Theater in the Latin Quarter. The theater, another historic landmark in Paris, had been taken over by the students about a week before. Much to the surprise of everyone, the police had not interfered—another carrot from the government.

Actually, the word that I used was *miett*—crumbs—the authorities were throwing the students. Lisa, Ulla, and José did not agree with me. José had come by and told us about the takeover of L'Odéon.

He and Ulla had attended a dance recital by an American dance company, as José knew some of the dancers from his New York days. When the show was over, students came in and claimed the theater was now the property of the people.

José said the American dancers, though surprised by the event, were in solidarity with the students, and he was recruited as a translator between the students and the American dancers.

"This is wonderful," Lisa said.

"It's great!" José exclaimed. "Do you know how expensive the tickets are in that place? Only the fat cats can afford to go there."

"What are the students going to do?" Lisa asked.

"I don't know. Maybe put on shows for the people who won't have to pay through the roof to see," he said.

"OK, you guys tell me what all this can accomplish?" I asked.

"At least, people will have a chance to enjoy themselves without having to pay an arm and a leg for it," Lisa said, echoing José's words.

The rally at L'Odéon had been another marathon of sorts, and the place was crammed with people. Because Lisa, Ulla, and Adam had helped organize the event, we got seats inside the auditorium.

Earlier in the day, the place had been electrified by the presence of Jean-Paul Sartre, a one-time professor and a Nobel Prize winner in literature.

Sartre was a great hero of the left because he had refused to accept the prize when it was awarded to him. The triumphant faces of the students told it all. I saw why Lisa was caught up in this movement.

It was the event of a lifetime! Lisa was greeted by some of her classmates with tears, embraces, and jocular comments about the fact she was a "veteran" of the movement. Her time in jail had earned her stripes and she was now, "*Une ancienne combatant*," an old warrior.

"At my age, can you imagine that. I wonder what'll happen when I get to be thirty," she had asked, laughing at herself.

"You'll be leading the legions to conquer hunger, disease, poverty, making this a better place for mankind. *Aujourd'hui, la France! Demain, le monde!*"—Today France, tomorrow the world!

She laughed at my attempted cynicism, because she knew I was very proud of her.

"No, I'll probably be staying home and taking care of a house full of our kids."

"How many is a household?" I asked, in trepidation.

"Oh, I don't know. I haven't figured it out. Anyway, didn't you promise my parents lots of grandchildren?"

"Lisa, Lisa! Remember me?"

A pale young woman pushed through the crowd toward us. We were standing outside after the meeting was over. Her face was bandaged, and both eyes were blackened, though on their way to healing. She seemed filled with good spirits and tenacity. After a moment's hesitation, Lisa recognized her.

"Sophie!"

The two women embraced. Sophie was crying, openly. Lisa started to have tears in her eyes. "How are you? Are you OK?" Lisa asked.

"Well, other than these black eyes I'm feeling much better." Sophie regained her composure and was looking for a handkerchief in her purse. I gave her mine. She looked at me and smiled. "*Merci,*" she said, wiping her face. When she touched her eyes, she winced. "What about you and the baby?"

"We're fine," Lisa said.

Lisa introduced me to the girl. "Remember I told you about a girl whom the cops were pretty horrible to? It was Sophie!" Lisa was still marveling at finding her among the hundreds of people at the rally.

Sophie embraced me. "You're Alex. She talked about you all the time. I feel like I know you so well. Lisa was amazing! If it had not been for her. . . I don't know—" She stopped.

Lisa and Sophie put their arms around each other, again.

"She was so brave," Sophie continued. "We were so scared, but she fought for us against *les flics*. She was never afraid of them."

Sophie took Lisa's left wrist, looked at the bracelet, shook her head, then turned to me.

"*Les flics* wanted to take this away from Lisa, and she wouldn't give it to them. They were so mad. I thought they were going to hit her, but she never compromised. Never! Alex, she's a rare individual, *dans la grande tradition d'un Voltaire, défenseur des opprimés!*"—Sophie compared Lisa's behavior to Voltaire, the defender of the oppressed.

Lisa was clearly surprised by Sophie's words. She had never mentioned this incident and looked at me as if to say "Don't listen to this. She's overdoing it."

"Lisa kept telling us not to be afraid. She told them they were cowards to treat us like that. I told her she was my friend for life. No, more than a friend—she's now my big sister. Never afraid. *Extraordinaire!*" Sophie embraced a very embarrassed Lisa, once again.

"I think she's exaggerating," Lisa said.

"I'm not. Ask the others," protested Sophie.

"Alex, it was Sophie who was incredible. The cops didn't do anything to me, but you should have seen her. They were so rough with her, and she never cried. She had so much courage. I was in awe of her. Revolutions are won by people like her."

These two young women had lived through an experience that would never disappear from their memories. When you see real people struggling, fighting for what they believe in, for their personal integrity, the human spirit soars and we do not have to make apologies for who we are.

"It was Lisa, also. Can you imagine? To have *une Americaine*—and pregnant to boot—fight for us? That was something, really something. We called her *La Pionniere*. *Les flics* didn't like her. They weren't kind to her."

The passion behind what Sophie said did not surprise me. Lisa had not shared some details of her ordeal with me, and I felt that perhaps I should not have been there listening to what Sophie was saying. Not that I was not proud of Lisa; I was, and how.

It was just that the sense of modesty, of not wanting to toot her own horn seemed so basic to her, and what she believed in. Lisa was moved by Sophie's words.

She looked at me a bit guiltily as if by not having shared the information she had withheld a secret. Now that it was out in the open, she felt embarrassed.

Perhaps, the only answer to the nastiness we humans inflicted on each other was to realize we were also capable of wonderful deeds, of helping others—even when we were at the breaking point.

I envied Lisa and Sophie for having lived and shared such rare moments of truth and integrity in their lives.

The image of the Czech taxi driver who had refused to charge me more than one hundred dollars to get me out of Prague, and saved my ass came back to me.

I had told the story to Lisa, and she wondered if we could find out who he was through Adam's mother.

What has remained deeply etched in my memory from those days, was the incredible sense of freedom, of self-worth the events gave to everyone. The feeling that if individuals took the initiative, they could bring about changes to their societies, significant changes.

Changes for a better life, for a better tomorrow for themselves, for their children, and for everybody. Sophie, Ulla, Adam, José, Lisa and the others had demonstrated that.

The world still had a chance to be a better place when people like them fought for their convictions and personal integrity.

France was undergoing a vast experiment in direct democracy and as chaotic as it was—the French were known for their crazy ways—there was electricity in the air, and that good things were about to happen.

Yet the feeling of uneasiness in my guts about our personal situation, in addition to the events happening around us, was also never far from the surface. I did not want to be faced with Lisa getting arrested again. There was no guarantee the cops would not come back in the middle of the night looking for her.

I had called the American embassy and while the situation was quiet, as far as Lisa was concerned, they also made it clear that conditions were dangerous and we had better not get further involved. With Lisa, it was easier said than done. I understood they were just doing their job, but I resented the advice.

Not all French society was in tune with the student revolt, however. The sons of the bourgeoisie were indeed taking part in the protests. In fact, they may have been the guiding light of the revolution, though many parents were not wholeheartedly accepting their demands. There was violence. Sophie's battered face proved it. Matters could get worse.

My fears were that the next time the cops would not just inflict black eyes but be far nastier. Yet I also knew asking Lisa to leave Paris was out of the question. I had tried already and had gotten nowhere.

Finally, when I considered everything, I did not think I had the right to demand she leave or give up what she so fervently believed in and hoped for. She had the right to pursue her own destiny, but I did not like it one bit. Again, I was caught in my own damn contradictions.

I have to be very careful with my own ambiguities, I thought. I was not trying to be noble or brave, but I also understood that as much as I wanted to decide where my place was in the scheme of things, Lisa was also trying to define her own place.

We were different, and we were also the same. The line separating men and women, as far as personal, philosophical, and political convictions were concerned, was getting blurred. Yes, "The Times They Are a-Changing," as Bob Dylan, the bard of our generation, had so succinctly put it in his famous ballad.

Lisa and Ulla had by now regained their passion for the situation, and there was a constant stream of traffic in and out of the apartment. I did not know most of the students. They would come and have endless conversations at all hours of the day and night.

The apartment was large enough that Lisa and I could still have our privacy. We slept in the back bedroom, and away from all-night discussions that seemed to have no end.

One fact that was quite striking to me: Nobody smoked while in our apartment. In France, smoking by students is almost *de rigueur*—a must—but everyone knew smoking was not healthy for Lisa's pregnancy. So they went outside to smoke.

I was touched that all these tobacco addicts refrained from smoking while they visited us. I could only guess what fits of nicotine withdrawal they suffered.

We found ourselves hosting crazy and exciting group discussions about the role of government in today's society, and the place the students would occupy in this new world. About the New Man!

Listening to these baby faces say the only thing that made sense was complete anarchy, followed by the establishment of a different system—one that would always conserve and guarantee individual freedoms—was sobering and exciting.

They called themselves the "revolted," accusing France and its privileged class of wanting only to protect their perks, not giving a damn for the students let alone the workers.

Though I feared the cops would come and bust us again, I was also caught up in the excitement of being part of this unique and historical event. What was also remarkable was the incredible depth of debate the people who came to our apartment were capable of.

Very sophisticated and complex ideas were aired out. Ideas that only those still innocent about the world could espouse without fear or embarrassment. Someone had brought us a mimeograph machine and the damn thing was running day and night, printing tracts and posters against the government. Some of them were quite artistic and droll.

The students had organized themselves very well. They looked after each other with care and concern. The network they had formed worked smoothly.

What was also interesting was that Madame Commère seemed to be of two minds about what was going on in the apartment. She did not approve, nor did she disapprove. It struck me as totally out of character given that she always had strong opinions about everything.

"Aren't you tired?" I had asked Lisa one day.

She was sitting at the kitchen table working on a stencil. She had smudges of black ink on her face, and had I not known what she was doing, I would have said it was an art class assignment.

"Oh, just a little bit."

I stood by her, she continued for a few moments, stopped, looked at me, got up, and kissed me while holding her dirty hands away from me.

"We're a pest, aren't we?"

"Yes! What are you going to do when this thing is finally over?"

"Go back to being your woman and wait to have our baby, hopefully be a good mother, and . . . I don't know. Why?"

"You can't be a revolutionary all your life."

"I don't intend to. You know what I'd really love to do is work for UNICEF or some other organization that helps kids around the world. Children are better than adults because they're very sensitive and not corrupted like their parents."

"Yeah, but if you work for one of those organizations, you'd be running all over the place, I'd never get to see you."

"I'd come home on weekends," she said, smiling.

I put my arms around her. Somehow, all the work she was doing gave her an inner strength, and she seemed lovelier, healthier than she had the right to be considering the crazy hours she spent helping her friends.

"Anyway, have no fear, the baby is fine. I've told you that I come from good, healthy, dependable, solid stock."

"What does all this mean to you, really?"

"Well, right now it means I have to finish this thing so we can run it," she said.

"Of course."

Ah, yes, Lisa was never one to neglect the immediate or practical side of life.

When I look back on those days of May 1968, the emotions they evoked fill me with longing for a time that is no longer possible. We were all innocent, untried. Everything seemed conceivable then.

We could look at the lives of our parents, and we knew that we did not want to be like them. They had given us a world where the balance of humanity's sanity was centered on having more atomic bombs than the other guys.

We longed for a world of reason, humanity, freedom, and self-respect, not a world of phoniness, of spiritual emptiness, unable to move beyond the status quo. Stuck in its ugly and depressing cycles of violence and man's inhumanity to man.

And for us, Americans, certainly not a world of the Johnsons, McNamaras, Nixons, Westmorelands, and all their minions.

We wanted to grow old, serene, and leave behind for our children a world of peace, respect, human dignity, and justice. Was that possible given humanity's proclivity for screwing things up?

That was why the Paris events—but also events in the U.S. and everywhere else—were so important to those of our generation who experienced them. We were all moralists, every one of us. We wanted to change the world for the better. We dreamed of a world of honesty and human decency.

We were all part of a protest movement, a social revolution, that touched all aspects of our lives—*a gigantesque ras le bol*, as the French would put it; a way, of simply saying that we had had enough of the bullshit around us!

For Lisa, Ulla, Alain, José, Milo, Adam, me, and countless others, May 1968 in Paris, France, was but a small contribution to help our generation move forward in its desperate search to find its place in the sun.

There were so many events that occupied my life during those few days. And it was just a few days that became the focus of everyone's attention. This was not an event that had lasted for months and months.

After Alain had asked me to go out and snoop around, I did much to my own regret, in many instances, especially when the tear gas was as thick as early morning fog and my throat and nose were raw from breathing it in.

Some of what I saw in the streets of Paris did not make me happy I was living in France. The police acted brutally against the students. Not that the students were always correct, they were not. Everyone has to share the blame.

There were days when I really did not sleep much, when I came home early in the morning to crash, and had to be up a few hours later to go out on the street again. And always, I had the uneasy feeling in my guts that Lisa had to be careful for her own and the baby's sake.

Many times, I dreaded going out, or worse, I came home fearing Lisa had been arrested again. Whenever I tried calling the apartment the damn phone was always busy. It was mad!

"If you want to be true revolutionaries," Milo had said, "maybe you should move out of your place and find another one to hide in. Every revolutionary does it. The cops know where Lisa lives. They won't hesitate to come back and get her."

"Come on, we're not revolutionaries." I protested.

"Well, *les flics* won't be pleased if they pay you a second visit and find that mimeograph machine in your place."

"I don't have another apartment. I don't want to hide, and Lisa wants to stay."

"Either she's brave, or she's crazy."

"Or she's right."

He looked at me and smiled in a way that suggested that for the time being he was not about to argue my point. I could tell, though, that his indulgence was not unlimited regarding how Lisa and I were now living.

"Anyway, she's caught up in this thing. She keeps saying that it'll shape people's lives for a long time to come," I said, trying to justify Lisa's feelings and her commitment to the cause of the students.

"OK, here is what I want to propose: You move to an apartment my mother owns. There's even a maid that comes with it. Don't tell anyone else about it."

"You know Lisa won't just crawl into some hole not to be heard from again."

I could see my words were not making him too thrilled.

"*Bien*, but promise me that if the situation gets too hot, you will seriously consider it. Here's the key."

He handed me a key insisting I memorize the address, which I actually did.

"Yes, I promise you. Hell, I'm more scared than you are."

"You have a rather peculiar way of showing that, with all those cowboys running in and out of your place as if it was some kind of O.K. Corral. The police probably suspect it's a big center of conspiracy."

"It is not, and we're not 'cowboys.'" We laughed. "But I don't know what else to do. I don't want to have to fight her on this. Anyway, as scared as I am, I think the students are right. Besides, I don't know how I could prevent your mother's place from becoming another 'O.K. Corral.'"

He did not answer. I suspected that Milo, in spite of his doubts was rooting for the students but hating what was happening to his beloved Paris.

Milo also told me his mother was very upset about the events, and that contrary to what the rumors said, a lot of the traditional French were willing to make the changes the students and the workers were demanding.

Milo felt, however, that many supporters of the revolt were doing it for their own personal gain and not because they were in solidarity with the students.

There was Milo again, holding two views: agreeing with the students and the workers in their fight for reform while hoping that it would all take place, by some kind of miracle, in another time dimension that would not involve any changes to his privileged class.

I was always trying to convince Lisa that Milo was right and that we had to be careful. My protests fell on deaf ears. In fact, she seemed to have become a kind of "clearing house," always on the phone, receiving and passing phone messages, coordinating things. As usual, I fretted over this.

"They're not coming back for me. They don't want me."

"How can you be sure?"

"I can't, but they want the bigger fish. I'm not really a priority for them."

"I don't feel secure. I mean, I don't want our child to be born in some Parisian jail," I protested.

"You're exaggerating. She won't be born in captivity. Can you imagine? We'll soon be parents!" she said, beaming.

I could not imagine it. Though I was anxious for time to move forward, I also knew that the time for just the two of us would be lost, never to be regained, and I was unhappy about that.

I looked forward to the baby, of course, but I was also fearful of the changes that would come about. We would soon be three and if, in fact, it turned out to be a girl I worried how I would find it in my heart to truly love Lisa and the baby.

"How can I possibly love two women?"

"Your heart is big. You've learned to love me. You'll learn to love her, and if my father is an example, you'll love her more than her mother."

"Do you think I'll be a good father?"

"Yes, otherwise I wouldn't have selected you," she said, with finality.

We had talked about the mate selection that occurs in life. I had always believed it was the female who made the final choice, and Lisa had simply agreed with a heartfelt: Amen!

Then the whole of French society got in on the act of rebellion. Maybe there was something to what Roxanne had said about the French behaving like sheep.

"These fucking frogs are totally insane. Do you believe this shit?" Pete said.

Every sector, every class, every level of French society went on strike following the students' lead.

Doctors, dock workers, actors, bus drivers, delivery companies, theaters, newspaper vendors, post office workers, workers at giant auto manufacturers, restaurants, government ministries, gas stations, bakers, butchers, fishermen, trash collectors, workers at city halls, taxis, street sweepers, maids, small companies, telephone workers, stock brokers, big companies, banks, the national gas and electric companies, sanitation workers, hotel clerks, insurance agents, train conductors, prostitutes, train station workers, border police, ambulance drivers, workers at toll gates, tax inspectors, customs agents, social workers, teachers, radio announcers, TV newsmen, film producers, directors, the Cannes Film Festival, electricians, plumbers, lawyers, judges, nurses, writers, musicians, dancers, singers, workers of the old and venerable opera house in Paris, the nude dancers of the Moulin Rouge, Casino de Paris, Folies-Bergère, newspapermen and women, young and old, students from all levels of education, housewives, individuals, entire families—you name it, even the winos and the *clochards* went on strike.

"Do you think those two *clochards* we met that night at Place de la Contrescarpe are also on strike?" Lisa asked.

"Why not? It's a free-for-all here. It would not surprise me if those two hobos aren't standing on some street corner protesting against the government and demanding their rights."

"Demanding their rights?"

"Absolutely, their right to be *clochards*."

"Of course," she said, and she laughed.

About the only two segments of French society not on strike were the firemen and the police, although there were rumblings from their unions that maybe they should also go on strike. The black market for goods, mostly gasoline, flourished, immensely!

Milo and Alain were appalled at the extremes people went to in order to secure gasoline. People were tired of standing in line for hours to get just a few liters of gasoline for their cars because it had been rationed by the government. Sometimes, it made me laugh because the entire country had become a giant practitioner of *"Système D."*

"It's what has always saved France from falling on its own sword," Milo had said.

"You can't hope to survive and be a viable country or a European power if this thing continues," I said.

"Don't worry," he said, "eventually all of this madness will start getting old. Keep in mind that summer vacation will soon be upon us. And no matter how much revolutionary zeal my fellow compatriots have, summer vacation is an imperative.

"No Frenchman worth his salt would ever give up the right to *Les Grandes Vacances"*—the four weeks of paid summer vacation every working French citizen is entitled to—"*C'est sacré!* Besides, *Le Tour de France* is also coming up. How can that be postponed? You might as well try to postpone the end of the world."

Le Tour de France was the annual bicycling event that took place in the middle of the summer, during which dozens of cyclists rode around France for hundreds of kilometers. The French were fanatics about it.

Thousands of people lined up the roadsides just to get a glimpse of a bunch of guys riding their bicycles at top speeds. Entire towns went crazy if the tour organizers selected them to be part of the spectacle.

"To deny us such God given rights as *le Tour,*" Milo continued, laughing "is to deny who we are. It's just not done. By July and August, what is happening now will only be a banal piece of memory for most of us."

Milo was not being cynical; he was just being French. There was a sad but true logic to what he was saying. It was a reality that made the French so exasperating, so infuriating to understand, and so interesting as hell.

There was an internal logic, unique to the Frogs, contradicting and defying what the rest of us mortals did or thought. I suspect the French act without ever thinking how it will affect the other person. This attitude is almost genetic.

The criticism aimed at them that they are much too individualistic for their own good, that they do not care or that they are unfriendly, does hit the nail on the head. Yet it still does not seem to make any difference. It has nothing to do with them! The typical response when they are criticized for such behavior is always: *Quoi, moi?*—who, me?

"This attitude is like leftover radiation from the Big Bang," Milo said. "It'll be here for as long as we breathe, shaping how we view each other and the rest of the world. You should be a bit more tolerant of us. We're much older than you yanks. I suppose like old people we have our quirks, aches, and complaints, but it's all mostly for show."

"So, it's not honest?"

"It depends. Let's face it: Our days of great glory are long past. We're no longer in control. It's the same for the Brits and the other Europeans. You Americans are the top dogs running things now and for the foreseeable future . . . indulge us a bit, it's not so bad."

Then Thursday, May 30th, turned into the biggest rally ever seen or staged in Paris, in support of de Gaulle. He was back in the thick of the action with determination. He asked people to rally for him, to show "those losers" he was in total control and that he had *le peuple* behind him.

He was the only guardian of their *Liberté, Egalité et Fraternité*. I had sat at home with many of Lisa's friends listening to the radio address. It was a great performance.

"*Il nous a eus,*" one of Lisa's classmates said at the end of de Gaulle's speech. Which can be best translated as: He stuck it to us!

You had to hand it to de Gaulle. He knew which buttons to push and how far to push them. We all knew the jig was up. Like everything else in their lives, the students knew that de Gaulle had made changes in the government, but the changes were a sham.

This eccentric, aging man, whose time had passed, would never address the substance of the students' complaints and yet still controlled, if not ruled, their lives in ways that were of the past.

I could sense that in the spirits of Lisa's friends the air had been let out of their hopes and dreams. The reality was hard to take because the changes they had all fought for, had so passionately argued and hoped for, were suddenly looking more like pipe dreams, like mirages seen by thirsty men in the middle of the desert. I felt their disappointment.

Seeing Lisa's face, I realized, and not for the last time, how the lessons life teach us could make anyone cynical and bitter. I did not want that to happen to her or the others.

The image of Adam's face when he was trying to convince himself that one lone American showing up in Prague would make a difference, came back to me.

Did we ever really learn from our experiences without having our spirits broken? Are we destined to always struggle, and lose—accept it as inevitable?

Then, as predicted by Milo, people descended on the streets after de Gaulle's speech. Thousands and thousands of people were demonstrating, not in support of the students, but in support of de Gaulle. The Champs Elysées was the focal point for the huge demonstration.

The old principle of the French being the sheep and de Gaulle the shepherd, and that they were lost and he knew the way and would lead them back to a safe, warm place, was still operating.

I had gone to the Champs Elysées, and to see the mass of people showing support for de Gaulle was impressive, bringing back the memory of the May Day Parade I had seen in Prague. Afterward, I went to Alain's office. Milo was there. They were both in a foul mood.

"We've got no balls," Alain said.

"What the hell did you expect?" Milo said.

"It's so disgusting," Alain said, "we finally have a chance to really make changes, to show ourselves that we have courage, that we're free. And what do we do? We wait for the others to do it first. Let them stick their necks out, that's our way.

"So, we continue to bitch and moan. That's what we are: A nation of complainers—*raleurs par excellence!* We're good at that because that's the only thing we know how to do. We should all be shot for having no courage. What a waste. *Quelle honte*—what a shame."

Alain's words came out softly and slowly. I had never seen him so down. Here was a guy who had done his dirty service for France as a soldier

341

in Algeria during the war there—he was still carrying a piece of shrapnel in his right shoulder—a guy who loved his country deeply, yet who was also very lucid about his society.

The French, in general, are not patriotic in the same way we Americans are. It would not occur to them, for example, to put their hands over their hearts when their flag was passing by or to sing "La Marseillaise" before a sports event, or to put a flag out on their balconies to celebrate their country's founding.

"One of your few enlightened compatriots—Mark Twain said"—Milo was fond of quoting, "that supporting your country all of the time was fine, but the government only when it deserves it. I agree. Anyway, in France, there have been too many damn governments and regimes to keep track of."

Milo repeated this whenever I brought up the subject about the French not being patriotic. Yet, that reality did not negate how fiercely proud the French were about their country.

"So that's how this May of 1968 will end?" I asked them, "with the French having their fling at attempting to change not only their educational system but also the roots of their social and political system, during this beautiful spring, and all for nothing?

"Just waiting for the summer to arrive so they can pile up the kids, the dogs, their mothers-in-law in their Renaults and Peugeots? Then take off for *Les Grandes Vacances* and tie up the nation's highways in those giant traffic jams? Then come back at the end of vacation or *à la rentrée*, as you say, to face the same problems that they are facing now, not much wiser, but most definitely well-tanned? *Voilà la France.*"

"Bravo, you seem to have finally understood us," Alain said.

"Yes, we don't always walk on water, you know," Milo said.

I had come to appreciate and love these two guys. There was so much I had learned from them and the way they looked at the world, at their society, and at their place in it. They could be cynical, ornery, hard, and unsentimental but also had a great deal of humanity, humor and understanding.

Always tuned in to the idiosyncrasies of existence, to its absurdity, and to its contradictions. Lucid about the fragility of life, about themselves, about their fellow men, about their society, without forgetting that in the final analysis, it is all about human behavior and that as such the whole exercise was always teetering on disaster.

I was proud to be their friend, and I knew our friendship would never disappear. It made me feel good to have them be part of my life. They could be full of nonsense too, but who is not? Lisa was crazy about them. They both loved and were devoted to her. She was their little sister.

Another day and another rally. Lisa argued that we should attend yet another student protest in the Latin Quarter. I argued against it but without success.

She wanted to do it and seeing her determination, I did not think I could have kept her from attending without causing all kinds of problems. The lesser of two evils was to accept that I was in no position to keep her from doing what she wanted to do.

She knew this, and I suspect she would have gone without me. I was not upset about her wanting to do it as much as I was fearful that it was a hell of a risk. The cops had an ample supply of tear gas and concussion bombs and they never hesitated to use them. As usual, my arguments were ignored.

"We'll stand on the edges. We won't go and get caught up in the middle. At the first sign of trouble, we'll leave. I promise you that. I promise you," she said, to pacify me.

"What if you start having contractions right smack in the middle of some riot?"

I was already imagining myself in the middle of the Latin Quarter, with the students and cops beating each other up, and me helplessly watching our baby come into this world.

"I won't. I've talked to Dr. Brisson, and she said it would be OK."

"What the hell does she know? She's just another quack."

"She is not!"

"She doesn't go out and throws *pavés* at *les flics*, does she?"

"Actually, she told me she was pretty active during the Algerian War."

"What is this? My life is totally crazy. I'm now surrounded by a pregnant anarchist and a delinquent doctor."

"You're not. The baby is not due just yet. You know I won't do anything foolish. Come on, please! Come with me if you want to."

"What do you mean *if* I want to? Do you think I would let you go all by yourself?"

"I didn't think so. Anyway, I told you that just to make you go crazy."

"Is that nice?"

"No, but I'm running out of weapons to use here."

What could I do? She came and put her arms around me, happy I had agreed to her madness.

"I knew you would understand. Besides, you've promised Alain you'd check out a few things for him."

"Yes, but not with your hanging around looking like the rear end of a double-decker London bus, and with your waddling."

"I do not waddle!"

"Yes, you do."

"It's not true."

She walked away from me to show that she did not waddle. Of course, she did. I did not know of a pregnant woman who did not waddle. I was sure I would waddle if I were carrying a baby.

I often wondered how pregnant women manage to walk when their center of gravity is out of whack due to their pregnancy. She was silent for a moment.

"So, I waddle?

"Well, just a little bit. It really isn't that noticeable," I said, trying to keep a straight face.

"Liar!"

"I still love you even if you do waddle like Donald Duck."

"You'd better. It's all your fault that I waddle."

"It's not."

"Yes, it is."

"What did I do?" I asked, pretending to be innocent.

"Oh, now you're going to say it was all my doing?"

"No, it's my fault, you're right. I should have never agreed. I should have let you go back to the States."

"Do you mean that?"

"Of course not. I would have cried my heart out and would have never forgiven myself. I didn't want to wake up years from now and regret that I had not had the courage to accept that I had come to love you like I had never loved before.

"I didn't want to live my life with this thing in my guts that I was not brave enough or honest enough to tell you about. I already regret so many things. Sometimes, it feels like my entire life has been a big excuse. I didn't want to have any regrets about you and about my love for you."

"That's nice, but do I really look that big?"

Her response made me laugh. Here I was telling her how important she was to me, exposing my heart and soul—no holds barred—and she acted like it was small potatoes compared to the bigger issue at hand: How big she looked.

"You didn't hear what I just said?"

"Yes," she said, and gave me that wonderful female look that said: Boy, this guy does not truly understand what is at stake here.

She went into the bedroom to look at herself in the mirror, and I followed her. She was a very pregnant lady, no question about it, but she also looked beautiful. Her face, her eyes were filled with a magical, mysterious and tranquil look. The gods allow only pregnant women to own such a look.

"If you looked any bigger people might actually begin to notice you."

"I do look big, and I don't care. I'm pregnant, and I waddle. What do you want from me? I feel fine, and this is a beautiful day. Besides, I need to take my daily walk. Are you going to sit here and criticize my waddling or are you coming with me?"

The weather was sunny and warm. There were plenty of students marching, and Daniel Cohn-Bendit was leading the parade. He had snuck back into France from Germany, and was now parading in a kind of counter-demonstration in response to the rally that had taken place the day before in support of de Gaulle on the Champs Elysées.

We did not see Adam. Adam had, a few days before, promised me he would arrange an interview with Cohn-Bendit.

Then when Alain found out that Cohn-Bendit had also promised every other journalist working in Paris the same thing, he decided that he did not want me to go. He was looking for an interview and not a circus, Alain said.

I never got to meet Daniel Cohn-Bendit. Adam said that he would try sometime later but by the time we were able to agree to the conditions, Cohn-Bendit was no longer making headlines.

As we stood by the sidelines watching the people walk by, you could tell the students were beginning to show fatigue and disappointment. De Gaulle had stolen their thunder and had undermined their struggle.

Like everything else in life, the people they had meant to help and lead were also tired of the ordeal and were no longer as committed and dedicated as they had been in the previous weeks.

The reality was that the students had encountered one of the most rigid educational systems in place controlled by a rather pernicious—and powerful bureaucratic mind.

This combined with the natural apathy that invades all of us when we do not see immediate results—from the things we so passionately believe in—was bound to be disheartening. Very often, I thought the revolution of May 1968, in France, was really more of an intellectual exercise.

It was true that physical damage had occurred, that people had been injured, but the battle seemed to be going on in the endless discussions that took place everywhere you went.

It would take more than words for this revolution to change anything. I really did not think the greater French public, after considering and seeing what had taken place the past few weeks, had any stomach left for pushing it to an all-out civil war. Not this time, anyway.

There was now a sense of resignation settling in that nothing would ever change. In this new reality, the students were showing maturity, but preserving the status quo would also lead to more bitterness and cynicism. In the final analysis, those in charge probably could not have cared less.

It was a long weekend, the end of May 1968. The beginning of June felt tired already. The Métro and the buses were still not running, and the taxis were hard to find. José came to pick us up, and we went to their place for dinner.

On Monday, public transportation was still not working. So Parisians, in typical French logic, took their cars to the streets, creating what many people categorized as total gridlock, pure and simple. No one could move.

What depressed so many people was that things were reverting to the way they were before the students rebelled. The movement had run out of steam, and everyone felt it.

Millions of workers, who had taken over factories and offices around the country and had occupied them for weeks, now found themselves outwitted by the mostly empty promises from the government.

Even the union leaders were falling over each other striking compromises with the government, and with the companies just so they could retain and protect their own privileged positions.

The workers understood that the jig was up and started to walk away from the places where they had stood, in vigilance, safeguarding what was theirs to lose. They came to realize that in spite of a change of government, the situation would not get better.

They had been, once again, outwitted by de Gaulle and his cronies and betrayed by their own leaders. The students also felt their failure to bring about the changes they so desperately wanted, was a bitter pill to swallow.

There is no better recipe for apathy and deception than seeing your efforts dwindle to nothing. There had been a good chance for a change, but those who held power were not about to give it up or the manner in which they were exercising it.

After all, the so-called mandarins of the French government's bureaucracy were part of a system that gave them incredible privileges and they were not about to shoot themselves in the foot. The changes the students had fought so hard for would have to wait for another time, perhaps another revolution.

José and I were sitting at le Fouquet's Café, on the Champs Elysées, that last weekend of May 1968.

"I thought it would work, man. It really felt good to think that new things would happen. I really believed it. What a fucking shame, man," José said. He was clearly disappointed.

Lisa and Ulla had decided, at the last moment, to go shopping for baby clothes while we waited for them.

"Pete had it right. The French ruling class doesn't have the balls to really make the changes. They don't give a shit. It's all about protecting their perks and privileges, isn't it?" he added.

"Yeah, I guess so," I said, not really knowing what else to say.

He was silent for a moment, and then he pulled a piece of paper from his pocket and showed it to me. It was the third notice from his draft board back in the States. They wanted him to take his physical for possible Army induction.

"What are you going to do?"

"I don't know. Ulla tells me to go to Sweden and stay there."

"Do you really want to do that?"

"I don't know. Do you think they'll ask the French to arrest me if I don't go back?"

"With all the stuff the French have to deal with here? I doubt it."

"My parents said I should just stay in Europe."

"What do you think?"

"It's such a screwed-up world. I don't see myself killing people. I'd rather make them happy than cause them pain and misery." He sounded troubled and wounded.

"I know what you mean."

"You went."

"Yes."

"Were you sorry?"

"Yes." It was true. I had come to regret my tour in Vietnam immensely.

"Would you do it again?"

"I don't know. I've asked myself that question before and I don't know." That was also true.

"You never talk about Nam."

"What's there to talk about?"

"I don't know—all the shit that's happening over there."

"You've got that right. It's all shit."

"I hear guys are into drugs and stuff."

"There's a lot of that."

"Did you ever take any?"

"No."

"Why not?"

"I just wasn't interested. The Vietnam thing was so fucking crazy that drugs were not going to make it better or keep me from getting my ass shot. What about you?"

"I have, but I also discovered that it bores the shit out of me, and sort of de-sexualizes me?" José laughed when he said that.

"*De-sexualizes* you? What the hell kind of word is that?"

"I don't know. I lose interest in sex."

"That can't be good."

"It ain't. I prefer sex to drugs any day."

"*Excellent choix, mon ami*, as Milo would say," I said. We both chuckled.

"Anyway, it's not that I'm afraid. It's just that I don't believe in this fucking war, that's all," he said.

"Maybe you should pull a Yossarian number on them."

"Yeah, but if I told them I was crazy, then they would know for sure I wasn't, and they would draft my ass up in no time."

"Catch-22!"

"You've got that right!" he said.

"Follow your nose, man. Your personal convictions have to stand for something."

"Yeah, my old man says that."

"It's just a physical, maybe you won't even pass it," I said.

"I know. Anyway, it's not a fair question to be asking of you or anybody. I'll just deal with it when the day comes. I still have time," he said, putting the paper back in his pocket. I did not envy his position.

"Look," I said, "I can't advise you on this, really, but anytime you want to talk about it you know where to find me."

"Thanks," he said, and then he was silent for a long moment. "Did you know that Adam is going back to Prague?"

"Really? When?"

"Soon, but he hasn't told Ulla or Lisa about it."

"How do you know?"

"He told me. He also asked me not to say anything to them. The other day he said he was in awe of both of them for not talking to the cops when they were in jail. 'They have balls, José,' he said."

And José and I laughed as he imitated Adam's Eastern European English accent.

"Adam is really very fond of those two broads," he added.

"Yeah, I know he is."

"Well, his mother will be happy to have him back or maybe not."

"Oh, I'm sure she will," I said, though I suspected that whatever he decided would not be easy for either of them, and for the things they believed in.

"I know he's struggling with it. Life can be so screwed up," José said.

"If he goes back, I'm sure one day we'll see a photo of him astride a Russian tank either throwing a Molotov cocktail or handing the Ruskies some flowers."

"I hope it's the first," he said, with much conviction in his voice.

"When is Ulla going back?"

"She hasn't decided."

I vaguely remembered what Lisa had said about Ulla's parents asking her to come back to Sweden, especially now that the school year had been wasted.

He was not sure if Ulla would return to Paris to try to finish out the school year. José and Ulla were planning on joining her parents later in the summer at her parents' house in Costa del Sol, Spain.

To think about people leaving us is hard—a difficult change to weather when you are in the middle of such an intense life—living lives of passage, especially in Paris, and especially due to what was now happening around us was not a picnic.

People moved into our lives or we moved into theirs and this gave us the impression it was going to be that way forever. Then the clock struck one minute before midnight, and everyone had to scramble to go back to the same spot where the clock had found us in the first place, except it was not the same spot anymore.

We all knew it was not permanent, yet we clung to the idea that we would make it so or at least we would make it last just a little bit longer—squeeze it to the last drop hoping against hope that midnight would not strike its dreadful toll.

The reality was unambiguous. People came to Paris and became part of our lives with no stated goal that it would be the end of the road for them, and with no desire for permanence. A sojourn that by its very nature had a time limit.

We all come to Paris, especially to Paris, to find something of ourselves, but not necessarily to find that someone special to love us or for us to love. I accept that no one comes to Paris just for that. However, it does help if it happens while you are in this great city.

Yet as I had once mentioned to Lisa, that if I had not been looking for her, for someone special to complement me, I would be denying a force that is truly human: the desire for order, for happiness, for self-awareness.

And yes, even for the reproduction of the species however unromantic and banal it sounds. For me and Lisa, the gods had granted us the favor of meeting and falling in love. I was very grateful.

We had constructed a world, and it was our life here in Paris today, not tomorrow and certainly not looking forward to going back to whatever it was that others went back to. It was the end of the line for me in many ways. Peter had more or less said the same thing when we last talked.

For Lisa, however, it was the beginning. I had asked her if she thought one day, she would find herself missing her family, getting homesick, and perhaps think she had to go back.

"I can't read the future," she had said. "I don't know what's in store for us, and I'm not afraid of changes. One day we might decide to go back or maybe we'll never go back. I'm not worried about it. My life is here with you. If tomorrow you decide you don't want me, I'll pack my bag, take my baby, and go back."

"And you would leave me here with my broken heart?"

"Only if you don't want me anymore."

"What if it turns out that *you* don't want me anymore?"

"That'll never happen," she said, categorically.

"How can you be so sure?"

"Trust me. I know what I'm talking about."

The choice had been made. I had only to trust her and in the future. Chris's words came back to me, once again, and I prayed to the gods he was right.

We were all strangers. Yet we wanted to believe that even in a state of flux we could live normally until we died. We wanted permanency in our lives. Having to bid farewell to those we loved, to people who had come into our lives for this flicker of time and with whom we had lived such intense moments, was nearly impossible.

To remain on some lonely railroad platform or in some antiseptic room at an airport, as those people walked out of our lives forever, was heartbreaking.

To be the one left behind was always unbearable.

When we lose a loved one to death, life does present us with a *fait accompli*. However cruel or unexpected our human helplessness is, it cannot be negotiated. We have no choice. There is no other way. We die with them.

But when people go back to where they came from and out of our lives, our routines, to pursue their own lives, and because we have shared with them special moments, to believe we can change the rules of the game and lessen the impact of their separation from us, was brave but foolish.

Of course, there was something to be said about the resiliency of the human heart. One cannot compare leaving to the death of a loved one; nevertheless, having someone just up and walk out of our lives because time ran out was no picnic, no matter how clever and brave we believed we were.

So, who's got it made?

José seemed down that morning, as we were sitting at le Fouquet's Café. It was unusual to see him this way.

"You think that Ulla will go back?" I asked him.

"Yes. There's too much shit going on." He sounded gloomy.

"Why don't you ask her to stay here?"

"I don't think she wants to. Her life's back there. I'm just her Parisian connection, man. You know the flavor of the month, or whatever."

He sounded cynical. It was not the José that I had come to know and appreciate. I also understood his feelings. I could easily identify with them.

"Come on."

"Well, it's true."

"Have you really asked her to stay?"

"Yes, but it's not like you and Lisa. Ulla came here to study, and she wants to go back. Her parents want her back. I understand that. It ain't easy, but I understand it."

"Do you love her?"

"Do I love her? I don't know what that means. I really don't. I suppose I do. But I'm not ready to make plans. I don't think she's ready to make plans. I'll let time do its thing, I guess."

"Maybe she'll come back." I did not really believe that.

"I'll just take it one day at a time. I have no regrets. I don't think she does, either. We'll see what happens."

Much later, Ulla went back to Sweden, but she kept in touch with him until José met another girl from Sweden and started living with her. I laughed about it afterward.

I kidded him that he had been infected with *the Swedish* bug, as he seemed to have girls from Sweden hanging around him all the time. I used to call him the foremost expert on Swedish affairs.

He laughed, and one day he told me that from time to time, he talked with Ulla on the phone, and she understood. "A man cannot sleep alone in Paris," she had told him.

Our apartment then became less crowded. The parade of Lisa's classmates started to dwindle. The *ambiance* became down and sad, not as frenzied anymore. The old mimeograph machine that had worked literally every day and sometimes at night became silent.

For me, it was a good thing because that meant the police would not necessarily be thinking of Lisa, and I was glad for that. She, of course, was unhappy about the turn of events.

"Do you think anything good will come out of this after all?" Lisa's voice was filled with disappointment.

On this Sunday, Milo had invited everyone to lunch at his country house, the same house where Milo and I had once had dinner with five half-naked Japanese guys. Milo had told everyone the story, and we all had a good laugh about it, though in telling it, it seemed less silly than it had been.

None among the group who were there that day—Milo, Ulla, Adam, José, Sophie, Peter, Roxanne, Alain and Catherine, his lovely wife whom we had never met before, John and Juliette who had come back from England and I—really knew how to respond to Lisa's question.

We all sensed that if anything was left undone, it would not change anything. We had pretty much lost the struggle.

Sophie, the girl whom Lisa had met in prison, had joined us. Lisa had asked Milo to invite her, and we could see that Adam and Sophie were quite taken with each other right off the bat. In his eyes, she was another heroine who had fought for the ideals that were important to him.

And Sophie, in return, clearly admired Adam for what he had done. She responded to Adam's interest with the usual French female charm. Later, I kidded Lisa about them.

"You're becoming a yenta, now?"

"Don't be such a cynic. They looked so sweet together. I knew they were going to like each other."

"The Czech-French Revolutionary Anarchist Mutual Admiration Society."

"And what's wrong with that?"

"Do you think he'll ask her to go with him back to Prague?"

"It's most likely that she'll suggest it," Lisa said, giggling. For some reason, I suspected Lisa was hoping for a romance to come about.

"You're a romantic, aren't you?"

"Look who's talking?"

In the last few days, the situation in Paris had peaked, and there was an undercurrent of sentiment that seemed to be signaling that the revolution was no longer controlling people's lives.

In fact, Alain had said he was now looking forward to reading what I had brought back from Prague, as the situation over there was starting to look far more ominous than ever. The dream of the Czechoslovakian people

350

to create "socialism with a human face" for their society was not in the cards.

Adam had announced his plans to go back to Prague, and this time neither Lisa nor Ulla had made an attempt to talk him out of it. In another sense, the cooling down of the French situation made me feel less apprehensive.

But I was also saddened by the fact that the students were going to lose the small gains of the past few weeks. There was a sense of mental and spiritual exhaustion from all sectors of French society.

There were still pockets of resistance around the country, but now even the workers were making deals with their companies, and it seemed that everybody—management, workers, government—were all trying to cut the best deal possible.

"*Après moi, le déluge,*" Roxanne said, quoting an old historical French expression.

SIXTEEN

Alain called and woke us up early that morning with the sickening news of another of those insane events that are beyond the limits of human comprehension.

"Bobby Kennedy has been shot!"

Some dates would never disappear from my life. It is not that I want to remember them. It is just that I cannot forget them. June 5, 1968, Paris, France, is one of them, a case of *déjà vu* and sickening.

Alain did not have all the details, but the reports were certain that Bobby would not survive if he were not dead already. Bobby had been gunned down during a political rally back in Los Angeles, where it was still the evening of June 4th.

Jesus, what was this world coming to? The empty feeling in my stomach; the nausea rising; the sense of life being completely out of control; incomprehensible; the extreme madness of someone who could do such a thing in cold blood; the fear that there was no place to hide—all of that was too much to bear.

"Bobby Kennedy has been shot," I told Lisa.

"That was Jack," she said, not quite awake, suddenly confused about the awful news because it was just too overwhelming. There had to be a mistake.

"No, babe, Bobby he was in Los Angeles."

The blood drained from her face. She looked as if expecting me to stop everything, to freeze time, to not let it continue, to go back, to run the reel backward.

"Is he dead?"

"I don't know, probably."

"Bobby? Oh, God, and he leaves his kids and his poor wife. What's going to happen to them?"

"I don't know."

Lisa took my hand and held it. Our confusion and pain could not have been more devastating.

"Remember you told me about meeting him?" she said.

My brief encounter with Bobby Kennedy, which I had always treasured, came about in a rather banal and simple way. I had been in New York on an assignment from Alain, and decided to go to Los Angeles for a few days to visit a friend before I went back to Europe.

Bobby Kennedy was going to speak at a student rally on the campus of the University of Southern California. As my good luck would have it, my friend worked at the university in the department responsible for setting up the sound system for the rally.

I asked him if I could help him set up the P.A. system the day Senator Kennedy was coming to speak, as I was very much interested in hearing what he had to say. Bobby was touring the country giving speeches and many people were encouraging him to run for president.

We set up the sound equipment on the steps in front of the Doheny Library, at the university, and eventually Bobby Kennedy showed up. The actor Robert Vaughn accompanied him.

As Senator Kennedy started to speak, the microphone went dead, no sound. Someone had accidentally unplugged the wires, and there was the Senator talking to himself. There were about twenty or so yards between Kennedy and where my friend and I were standing by the sound equipment.

I got on my hands and knees and worked my way through countless legs until I found the unplugged wires. I plugged them in, stood trying to find some room to wiggle around, and there was Bobby Kennedy right next to me.

For his whole speech, I literally held the microphone wires afraid that they would come unplugged again. I remember one phrase he said that day that stuck in my memory because I wanted so much to believe it.

"I'm here with *The Man from U.N.C.L.E.*"

This was a reference to a popular TV show at the time—where the good guys saved the world from the bad guys—with Robert Vaughn playing one of the good guys.

"I have nothing to fear!"

The accent was pure Boston. The laugh that his words received from all of us standing there came from the heart because we thought that if he wished it, that it would be so.

Earlier in 1968, *The Man from U.N.C.LE.* had not accompanied Martin Luther King, Jr. when Reverend King was killed not that it would have made any difference.

When the rally was over, Senator Kennedy thanked me for being there and helping him. We shook hands. I have always treasured the memory.

As I sat right next to Lisa, that tragic June morning in Paris, an incredible emotion of confusion, and defeat came over me. Throughout most of my life, I had tried to find out a reason as to why people kill others. I found none.

Something was wrong. So very wrong. I searched within myself to find some reference, some fact, some kind of moral and spiritual anchor, something that would help me keep focused as to what was important in life. I always come up empty.

I knew that another agonizing truth would never leave us. Lisa moved closer to me, and I put my arms around her. Nothing made sense anymore.

I often wonder about the vacuum created by such premature deaths; premature in the sense that at first glance these individuals presented us with a vision that things could change, were going to change for the better, and then these people were snuffed out.

"Please tell me why things like this happen," she said. "Please, try to explain them. Lie if you have to. Please, lie and I know that it'll be a lie. But I don't care because I don't want to believe the truth. Make it go back to the way it was before." Her voice was so wanting and incredibly sad.

"I wish I could do that."

We turned the radio on and listened to the announcer give the grim details. I got up and opened the curtains to our bedroom. I looked outside the window. Everything had changed, and yet it all seemed as it had been before we went to sleep.

The early morning traffic below our window was deathly silent. Normally, I always heard its faint hum, not this time. The cars seemed to move slowly as if in a *cortège*.

It was going to be a beautiful June day here in Paris, which somehow was not right. When someone is gunned down in such a cold and murderous way, the day should be gray, disgusting, and distant.

Lisa sat on the bed, and very softly, she kept rubbing her belly as if seeking comfort from the tiny life that would be arriving in just a few weeks. She had tears in her eyes, and she seemed so lost.

I walked back to the bed, sat right next to her, and I started rubbing her belly. The baby responded a couple of times, but it was more as if we had awakened her and she was not interested in the adult world that she was about to inherit so she went back to sleep. I could see Lisa was gaining some comfort from this.

The emptiness created in our hearts and souls by such tragedies was so overwhelming. There were individuals who give the rest of us a glimpse of something good. A hope, even if it were fleeting, that things could change, were going to change, and would show us where to go, where we needed to be.

Such ideals always seemed to be cut short. It felt like we had been betrayed by something ugly, incomprehensible, inhuman. Like a locust destroying everything in its path, the inexplicability of the cosmos invades time and everything went dark.

Was there a more benign meaning than simply saying that the whole ordeal of life was but a fool's fantasy, persisting and continuing to persist in driving us crazy since the beginning of time, and we had no other choice than to live with the charade instead of thinking of something else to do?

But, do what?

Once more, I felt like I was an orphan and the reality of the tragedy made that feeling even worse. I did not know what to tell Lisa. What kind of world would our child—any newborn, inherit? Was there any hope for a better future, really?

I thought about where I was when I heard the news of President Kennedy's death. Would the young barmaid back in Bangkok who had cried with her GI Joe find it in her heart to light another candle?

"I'm afraid," Lisa said.

"I know . . . I know . . ."

The phone rang again. It was José.

"Man, the country is going to shit. It's not right, it's not right." He sounded so despondent. "I'd bet you that fucking Johnson did it again."

"Come on."

"Well, you can't convince me that Johnson had nothing to do with Jack's death, no way. That son of bitch did it!"

There had been so many crazy conspiracy theories about Jack Kennedy's death, and the sickest was that Johnson had been behind it. At that moment, José really believed it.

"Get off that crap. It'll drive you nuts. You know that's not rational," I said.

When our hearts were made to suffer in such a brutal manner, our sense of loss, our hopelessness, our moral and spiritual helplessness—our feelings that we have been abandoned in such an uncaring world—can turn us into idiots and even the most sensible person can lose perspective.

Again, with such human tragedies, life's ledger continues to be unbalanced, still on the minus side.

"Man, Bobby had so much to give, that's why they killed him. I bet you. He was one of us! Man, we kill the best in us. The country is fucked. It really is. I ain't never going back! He was the only guy who could stop this fucking war." José's voice sounded sad, angry, and so wounded, and he was crying.

I looked at Lisa, and she was just staring into space while rubbing her belly. For some reason, I felt like she really did not need me anymore. It was the weirdest of feelings. I did not know why I felt that way.

It must have been that I really had no words that I could use to comfort her, or José, to ease their pain. I felt empty, tired and, not for the last time, I just wanted to crawl into some hole, go to sleep and not have to deal with all of the madness and sadness around me.

What were the lessons of life? What did we learn? At what moment did the lessons of life become part of our psyche? Was it upon reflecting on our past, on our history, that we gained some insight that could help us deal with the things we had to do to survive?

What if reality always leads us to a dead end, terrifying, dreary, and lonely? A place that had no exit, a *cul-de-sac*, and we could not back out of it? What if we really did not have a chance?

What if at the end of the day life was just a random event, second-rate, or trivial, with no more significance than a gnat's fart? Every day we made things up so we could get through it.

I lived inside my head, really. I was a private person. Lisa understood that. But she also said that I could not remain aloof, detached, that I had to be involved. That I could not renounce life.

The more I thought about it the more I felt my own helplessness, confusion, and fear. I wanted to change my attitude, understand the greater sense of who I was but the more I thought about that the more remote things appeared to be. News of Bobby's death only reaffirmed how little say we had over anything.

We were just puppets being dangled about at the whim of some inane idea of destiny or fate. We got up every morning, and we went and stood in line hoping that it could lead us to a better place from the line we stood in yesterday, and the day before and the day before that.

And the more we wanted to exercise control over who we were, on the world around us, the more it was obvious we did not count for much. We were superfluous. Who the fuck were we kidding?

I wrestled every day with those fears and, presently, with an even greater notion that someday Lisa would get tired of me, get tired of who I was, or what I was not. Get tired of her life with me. During those moments, I dreaded so much what the future would bring.

Sometimes, I felt lost in a sea of angst and despair without the necessary tools needed to combat life and its vicissitudes. Often, the mockery of it all was so sharp that my spirits literally denied me the simplest of pleasures.

Inside, I was still struggling with my demons and I could not honestly say that I was free of them. I suspected I had just simply pushed them aside for another time, another day, when they would rear up their ugly heads to strike me once again rendering me helpless just as the news of Bobby's death had done today.

More often than not, most of us ended up doing the same things repeatedly. We were creatures of habit. Adam's mother had said that the evil we knew was sometimes better than the evil we did not know. We were comfortable with that evil.

It was so much safer to stick to what we knew even if it brought us nothing but pain. Thus, we tended to deny our capacity to dream, to have a bit of fantasy, to soar. I remembered reading about Einstein saying that the fantasy in his life was far more important than all of the physics he knew.

Yes, the reality of life was scary but I also saw the need for dreamers in this world. Yeah, we needed more dreamers in this crazy world. Lisa was right. We needed the Adams, the Josés, the Sophies, the Lisas, the Ullas, the Milos, the Peters, the Alains; humanity needed all the dreamers!

"I'd like to go to a church and just sit there for a while," Lisa said.

Notre Dame was filled with tourists, but a kid saw Lisa's big tummy and gave her his chair. Lisa and I had once attended a concert there when an organist from Russia had played Bach's "*staccato in D Minor*," and it was just beautiful.

The music soaring through the magnificent building, filling it with sounds of delicate beauty. The sounds also reaching into every nook and cranny of the human heart and spirit of those of us who were there listening that day, and creating a magical, mysterious, and harmonious surrounding.

There was something peaceful and soothing about going in today and thinking about Bobby Kennedy. And not only about Bobby Kennedy, but also about everybody on this whole planet who had been the victim of man's inhumanity to man.

Such suffering had no borders, no race, no gender, no religion, no nationality, and no age. It was a human tragedy, and all of us were its victims and its perpetrators because we were all the same.

Mid-June arrived, and I was looking forward to spending a simple weekend hoping that the situation in Paris would, somehow, get better. Lisa always thought that weekends brought an end to things that were most unpleasant.

She argued the coming of the weekend gave respite from the troubles one encountered during the previous weekdays. Once the weekend arrived, the troubles were over.

Then when Monday came around, the problems we had to deal with were brand new and had nothing to do with those of the previous week.

"No, the problems are the same," I would argue with her.

"To me they aren't," she would argue back. "These are new problems. How can you say that they are the same? Are the days the same? No. So the problems are different. Problems don't last more than a week. That's all."

She would say it to bug me and make me stop worrying too much about the uncertainty of it all. Lisa and I would argue about things, and she was passionate in her beliefs and convictions, but we did not get into fights. One day, I asked her about it.

"You've noticed that we've never had a fight?"

"What's there to fight about between you and me?"

"You know, couples fight and stuff."

"I'm not interested in a fight with you. Peter and Roxanne don't fight. You said you admired them for that."

"That's true."

"Do you think we should have a fight?"

"No, that's not what I meant."

"OK, if you want a fight," she said, and smiled, "I'll put it on my agenda. We'll set the time, the place, the reason for the fight, and we'll do it."

"That's a very interesting idea."

"We'll program our fights. That way we'll know ahead of time all of the particulars, and we'll go at it. No holds barred. Should we also program who is going to lose?"

"I'll probably be the one to lose."

"That's a very wise thing for you to keep in mind," she laughed and embraced me.

The fights were by other people and other things and the weekend of June 19, 1968, turned out to be the bloodiest yet, and the most vicious that the student revolt produced. The fighting and rioting went on everywhere you looked!

It was as close to complete anarchy that Paris had seen. Everywhere you turned, there was fighting between the police and the rioters. Covering the events was a marathon into the void.

Going from one quarter to another became like a seamless journey into the abyss that now seemed so imminent and real. There were so many medical aid stations set up by the students everywhere that it was next to impossible to know for certain just how many people were injured.

The medical aid stations were saturated with the injured. The whole city of Paris had now entered its own twilight zone.

Some parts of the city's heart would probably be lost forever and with it some greater part of ourselves. So many of us hoped, against hope, that these sad times would not become the only memories to carry for the years to come. It was hard to imagine that our spiritual scars would ever heal.

Paris was a total mess!

But there was another feeling in the air as well. The city had now seen the worst student rebellion ever, and it felt like Paris was looking for a way out of this madness.

Lisa was less certain that all she and her friends had hoped for would be accomplished. There was a sense of exhaustion of spirit and soul, pervading everything. Everyone had reached the limit—so had I!

My work for Alain had become a matter of surviving the tear gas, the *pavés*, the water cannons, the *matraques* of the police, and my own fatigue.

I was sick of so much anger, violence, and destruction. Lisa understood that, and had now become more focused on what was going to be the biggest event of our lives. I had also come to believe that Milo had been right all along about his prediction.

It was only a matter of weeks, days, actually, when the proper summer vacation would begin and already the mood in Paris seemed to be swinging toward that.

With the arrest of nearly fifteen hundred people a couple of days later, my bet was on the government to finally gain the upper hand. The Prime Minister, Pompidou, made a formal announcement that he was granting the police more power to arrest anybody caught in the act of rioting or of inducing others to riot.

The change in the law did nothing to assuage my fears about Lisa, yet I could sense that she was no longer any priority for the cops. They may not have forgotten about her, but she was no longer a target.

"You see, we don't have to worry about it anymore. If they had really wanted to arrest me again, they would have done it when they arrested all those other people."

Lisa had called Adam's mother with the invitation to come and see us. She was absolutely delighted, completely surprised and overwhelmed by it. She could not believe it! She also told Lisa she would prefer to remain in Prague, at least for the near future.

Lisa told her the invitation was open, and whenever she felt it was possible for her to make the trip to let us know, and we would take care of everything.

"She was very emotional when I told her. I could hear it in her voice," Lisa said. "Thank you for agreeing to invite her."

"No, thank you for suggesting it."

Adam knew that he could not stay in Paris any longer. He now saw the need to go back and become part of what was happening in his own country. The news from there was not positive. The political game the Russians were playing was becoming more dangerous by the day. They were going to play hardball.

Everyone expected them to move in at any time. It was only a matter of when, not if. Adam had come by to say goodbye and Lisa, Ulla, and he had a long and tearful evening together. Ulla was also going back to Sweden, though she wanted to stay until the baby was born.

"I was here at the beginning so I want to see whether the result is good work," she would joke. Ulla and José now seemed to have accepted that she would be leaving never to come back. He had not mentioned his Army physical again.

Lisa and I were sitting in the apartment watching the news. It was a bit strange to see how quiet the place had gotten. There were no more group discussions until the wee hours of the morning, no more noise from the mimeograph machine.

Someone had come by and taken it away. The phone was not busy. The parking on the streets was easier. The baby's room had been painted and decorated with its proper curtains and baby furniture.

Despite the madness taking place in the city, neither Madam Commère nor her nephew had forgotten that he had promised to paint the room, and he had done a wonderful job. Life has to go on.

Madame Commère had also knitted beautiful baby clothes and most of them were pink. I was very touched by her doing this. As I have said before, I do believe concierges set the rules and the rest of us just have to live by them.

Though, I still thought that it was quite mad of Lisa to have asked that the room be painted a slightly soft rose color as, in my view, there was no guarantee we were going to have a girl.

"But what if we have a boy? A boy with a pink room, and dressed in pink isn't too swift. They'll make fun of him. They'll call him a sissy."

"It's not going to happen. We'll have a girl, and you might as well get used to the idea."

I guess since she had made up her mind that it was a girl we were waiting for, soft rose was the color. In addition, Pete had come and painted on the walls an abstract mural of animals in a forest, which added a sense of tranquility to the room.

With just a few colors and lines, Pete had created a pastoral effect, and it was just magical. I would find Lisa sitting in the room enveloped in such a lovely setting.

"How do you feel?"

"Tired, but wonderful! She moves and kicks a lot. I think she'll be a soccer player. She anxiously wants to come out and start kicking the ball," Lisa said, still marveling at what was happening inside her body.

It was true. By now, I was used to putting my hand on Lisa's tummy and feeling the baby move. It never ceased to amaze me. Lisa's pregnancy was at her peak. She was big, did waddle, but she was still beautiful, serene, and complete.

Her parents had accepted that she would not be leaving France for the baby's birth, that in any event it was too late and much too dangerous for Lisa to travel. Frog country would have to do for the birthplace of their grandchild.

Dr. Brisson was more than satisfied about everything, and she had made the arrangements at one of the maternity clinics in Paris for the baby's arrival. She was not sure she would be delivering the baby as she and her family had long-standing plans for their summer vacation.

Pete and Roxanne had also made plans for their yearly trip to the south of France. Yeah, all activities in France must take a back seat to *Les Grandes Vacances*.

Milo had been right about the vacation exodus.

The Sorbonne's situation had now begun to look like a nightmare. The old building was filthy and unkempt. Factions had broken out among the students and the unanimity about shared goals of the previous weeks was gone, now replaced by the usual petty jealousies and personal interest. The place was a beehive of divisions, intrigue, and more discord.

It had been nearly a month since the students occupied the Sorbonne, and the atmosphere had changed from the day when Lisa and I had walked the hallways and marveled at how wonderful this victory had been; now, it seemed hollow and sad.

Radical groups were fighting each other, and it was only a matter of time before the police would come back and reoccupy the place. This time there would be no common resistance against *les flics*.

A small and somewhat insignificant incident—someone got stabbed inside the Sorbonne, and the police were given permission by the student leadership to come and investigate it—became the catalyst that broke down the barrier and with it the back of the students' uprising.

Before anyone knew what had taken place, the Sorbonne was emptied of students, and it was back in the hands of the police. The glorious effort by so many people to get rid of the bureaucracy that ruled their lives came to a whimpering halt.

I happened to be in the Latin Quarter that Sunday when it happened. Once the word got out that an impending takeover of the Sorbonne by the police was expected, it brought hundreds of students back to the streets.

The government told the students that if things calmed down, they could have the building back.

That in the meantime, it needed to be cleaned and repaired and it—the government—was the only entity that had the means to do it and do it right. It made sense, but it was a con—*c'est du bidon*—like Lisa had once said. We all knew it.

The revolt would not die without a last-minute resurgence of violence. Negotiations between the students and the police continued, and more students came and made preparations to man the barricades and defend their last bastion of protest.

Sometime late in the afternoon, it was apparent to everyone gathered in and around the Sorbonne that an assault was imminent. After surrounding the building and making sure they had all of the manpower needed, the police cut off all of the locks the students had put on the doors and stormed back into the building.

The students fought back gallantly, valiantly, but it was like Custer's last stand. The tear gas flowed and flew and both sides used the same brutal tactics. I spent my time going around trying to avoid getting more tear gas than was necessary.

But it was obvious even to the most dedicated, fanatic, and committed of the students and their supporters, that it was too late. The Sorbonne's occupation would no longer be tolerated.

Quietly and slowly, most of the students decided to stop fighting but still crying from either the tear gas or from the realization that the end had arrived.

They came out of the building and gave themselves up to the police. Most were allowed to go free and the occupation of the Sorbonne was over.

The so-called May of 1968 student revolt, in Paris, would now be another chapter. A long and important one, to be sure, in the often disconcerting and strange odyssey that all of us who were in Paris during these events had lived through. Time felt empty, tired.

The uprising in Paris would probably be best remembered for what it might have been rather than for what it was. We had seen the best and the worst. We had seen hopes come alive. Then we had seen hopes dashed to nothingness.

We had lived intense moments and we had also seen the futility and absurdity of it all. We had lived with our fears, and we had controlled them a bit, but we had not overcome them. We had loved, we had cried, we had laughed. What had been accomplished?

Yet something had changed. Something had invaded the psyche of the French soul, and I only hoped that it would not just disappear in the dustbin of deception and disappointment. The students had been magnificent, real, and true.

They had all been touched by this event. Lisa was right. The event would remain with them for as long as they lived, though, I was less certain it would shape their lives the way she had so passionately argued.

They would remain scarred and would carry those scars with them for the rest of their lives, but it would not mar what they had to do to continue living in their country, in their society.

There would be some changes. It was impossible to imagine that a whole country, a whole society, could undergo such a traumatic experience and not be deeply touched by it. Changes would come, at what rate and how substantive nobody knew.

One could only hope they would be large and significant enough because so much pain and suffering had gone into the effort to make those changes come about.

More often than not, the effort put into something worthwhile does not produce the best results. Yet the heart always hopes. My cynicism and fatigue made me less enthusiastic about any permanent changes, big or small. Lisa, of course, disagreed with me.

"It doesn't matter if the changes are small," she argued, "they're there. We didn't have them before, but it's a victory. Not the victory that Adam and the others wanted or that I wanted, but they're there. It's the tiny pebble that causes discomfort and governments, like people, eventually have to do something about this tiny thing disrupting old, tired routines."

"Yes, but it's easier to stop the machinery, find out where the pebble is, get rid of it, and continue as if nothing has happened," I would argue back.

"You're right, but it's not the same anymore no matter how you look at it. Something has changed! It can never go back to the way it was before."

"Forget the government. What about the people? Will they change for the better? That's the big question for me."

"Yes, I have to trust their collective wisdom. I just can't accept that all of this was for nothing. I just can't, and I won't!" She would always look at the glass as half-full and not half-empty.

She was right, of course, she was. A world without hope is a dead world. The main streets of the Latin Quarter—Boulevards St. Michel and St. Germain—were eventually covered with asphalt for ever!

The old *pavés* that had been there for hundreds of years were now given a new, shiny, and permanent coat of asphalt. The cobblestones would never serve for anything useful, again.

It was such a great loss to Paris, but then maybe it was a good thing. I was not sure, though no *pavés*, no revolutions. New generations would never experience the sheer pleasure of throwing *pavés* at *les flics*!

The Latin Quarter became inundated with police, in civilian clothes, keeping a close eye on the young people, wanting to make sure that no surprises would appear.

I stopped going there. Keeping tabs on *les flics* was not my thing.

The revolution was over, though there were still a few clashes that took place between the authorities and students and a few workers.

About the only thing left was to reflect back on it with disappointment, bitterness, and sadness about what it might have been. Lisa and most of her friends were hurt and tired.

But like so much of what we hope for and never get, what they had experienced these past few weeks had been real. Though the revolt had not turned out the way they wanted, this rite of passage had also made it clear to them the work they still needed to do to change their society and make it better—and that in itself was priceless.

As for me, well, there were some wonderful things in the future. The baby's arrival was getting closer and closer, and preparations had to be made for that day. For the first time, the idea of a family was no longer an abstraction. It was just around the corner.

Vito and I had long phone conversations about his film project, and he said that he wanted to postpone any serious work until the beginning of next year. In fact, he had invited me to come to Rome in the spring and work on it.

"You see, good things do happen to you. We'll go and spend the spring in Rome. That'll be wonderful," Lisa had said when I told her the good news. She was so happy for me.

"Wait a second! He didn't say to bring the whole family."

"Don't worry. The other day when he called back and you weren't here, he said he would be delighted if we came and that he would insist that you take us along. I don't think you have any other choice."

She said, laughing and already looking forward to going to Italy. She knew I could never see myself going to Rome without them.

"You see, you'll get your Italian trip after all," she said, triumphantly.

The translation of *L'Étranger* was coming along fine. I was finding a sense and clarity from studying the text that seemed to move the translation in the right direction. Lisa and Milo were pleased with what they had read.

"This should put fire under your *derrière* to start thinking about the book you're always talking about writing," he said.

"That's what I keep telling him," Lisa said.

Alain was also talking about the possibility of publishing a bilingual magazine in Paris, and he wanted me to help him. No one had ever attempted to do this before. Milo was very high on the idea. I was not sure what it would mean, as I had never thought of publishing a magazine even in my wildest dreams.

Milo said he had some good contacts in the banking and business world, that he saw no problem in getting people interested in financing the venture. Milo also let us use his summerhouse, and Lisa and I were able to escape the heat of Paris, at least for the month of July.

Lisa's parents and Robin were now just waiting for us to call them with the news of the baby's arrival so they could make the trip to Paris.

Lisa's father was doing great, health wise, and the news made Lisa feel the whole world was a wonderful place after all. I had to agree with her.

I spent a lot of time arranging the notes on my trip to Prague, and waiting patiently for the baby to arrive. I had also started sketching out some ideas about the book I wanted to write.

Lisa, in her subtle way, had been making sure that I would not push it aside. Yes, there was wonderful stuff for the future. It could almost make me a believer, after all. I still had my bike, as Lisa did not want me to get rid of it.

Perhaps she was right about my keeping it. Alain was now certain that Prague and the Russians would be the next big world conflict, but he knew better than to ask me to go back. I would not have done it. I had more personal things to attend to.

SEVENTEEN

Our baby arrived at 4:59 in the morning. I fell in love immediately! Yes, it was a girl—a beautiful girl with a set of the biggest, brightest, and most sparkling eyes!

I wondered what they saw. The eyes were set in a round, lovely face, with apple cheeks that somehow seemed young and old at the same time.

I had seen her come out of her mother's womb and for that split of a second, it felt as if I were seeing my own birth. She did not make a sound. I panicked. Then she started wailing, her lungs now filled with the air that would sustain her from here on.

They put the baby on Lisa's chest, and the baby calmed down. It is said babies recognize the sound of their mother's heartbeat and know the smell of their mother. Ours was right on target.

August 15, 1968 was a radiant day for me.

I would always remember it. I wanted to remember it. As I was walking out of the clinic, the sun was shining. I even detected smiles on the Parisian faces I met on my way out of the clinic. Maybe it had to do with this one being a maternity clinic.

Perhaps, all it took was just a little smile to have the world smile back at you. There had been a summer downpour the night before, and the rain had given way to a beautiful Parisian summer day and sun with its effulgent face. It was going to be hot, but I did not care. The trees were all green and filled with summer leaves.

I was tired, but I had never felt better in my whole life. I wanted this feeling to stay with me forever and ever. It was foolish to think that it would last, and I wondered why it should not be so. Why could life not be always sunny and bright?

I had just left Lisa and the baby no more than a couple of minutes ago, and I already missed our daughter. The doctor said that it had been a normal routine delivery. Routine for him, but nothing routine about it for me.

Our baby's birth was the most magical moment of my life!

I looked up at the blue sky, and I thought about dying. How curious it was that just a couple of weeks ago I had received the news of Chris's death. I had debated sharing the news with Lisa and when I happened to mention it to Pete, his advice was that sometimes it was better not to say anything at all. Telling Lisa would not change the reality.

I was not being callous or insensitive about my buddy Chris. I cared very much about him, but with death, there is no hope. With the birth of a child, there is hope and more hope, and at the end of the day hope is what keeps us going to face another day and another and another still.

"There is plenty of time for bad news," Pete had told me. "You should concentrate on life right now and not on death."

I do not know why, but I thought of his decision not to tell Roxanne about her inability to bear children. I was not sure how long I would keep the news about Chris from Lisa. I did not know what the best solution was. In the end, I decided to follow Pete's counsel.

Telling Lisa the sad news now would not change anything. I wanted the birth of our daughter to be the only event ruling our lives at present. It was what made Lisa and me look forward to the future.

Yes, I could reflect on the cycle of birth and death, but I was less pressed to dwell on the latter at, least, for now. The logic of such events, birth and death, was impeccable. The timing of the first one was joyous. The timing of the second, not so much.

Both realities were as easy to see as the sun shining on that clear and bright summer morning. The more important reality was that the birth of the baby had already changed everything!

The birth of this child was not the proof I was going to die; that was a given. The birth just illustrated the beginning of still another cycle of life, and I knew such cycles always ended—always. It was OK to have fears, doubts, confusion.

Fear and doubt were part of living. The quest for life's answers would never end. Finding out who you were, the search for your own voice, would keep you busy until that last breath. *Know thyself* was the ultimate truth!

I was so grateful to the gods that Lisa was fine and the baby was healthy. So now, I had two women in my life who really belonged to me, and I belonged to them in return. Our daughter resembled her mother more than she did me, and for that, I was thankful.

I mean, who would want to go through life with a mini mug like mine? Lisa was so happy and relieved more for me, really, that everything had gone according to schedule. The baby had arrived on time.

"On time? I don't know about that." I said, yawning. "Why couldn't she have waited for a more civilized hour like tea time or something?"

Lisa smiled that wonderful smile of hers. I thought, I hope with all my heart that our daughter inherits her mother's great smile.

"Isn't she just lovely? And so healthy, I knew we would have a girl. You see, I told you that I come from good, healthy, dependable stock. And she has those beautiful green-blue eyes just like my mother," Lisa said.

"How can you tell?"

"Look at her."

I could not tell.

"You mean she has one of each color?" I asked just to make fun of her.

"Maybe you better get some glasses."

"Well, it's hard to tell."

"It's not," she said. End of story.

She had been right about us having a daughter, so I suppose she was probably right about the color of the baby's eyes.

Earlier in the morning, before the baby was born, there had been a big argument with the doctor about letting me stay with Lisa in the delivery room. Dr. Brisson was out of town, so she had made arrangements to have one of her colleagues deliver the baby.

Lisa did not mind, and since I had learned to trust Dr. Brisson's judgment, it never occurred to me this doctor would not let me stay to see the birth. He objected. It just was not done. He was acting as if I had had nothing to do with the baby. I was pissed!

Ulla and José, who had come to join me when I called and told them Lisa was in labor, took the doctor aside and had a long and mysterious conversation with him. I did not know what they were saying except that the doctor looked at me once or twice and finally relented, but I could tell he was not happy about it.

With his Gallic, supercilious attitude, he practically ignored me the entire time I was in the delivery room. I did not care. It was Lisa and our baby that I cared about.

"What did you say to him?" I asked José and Ulla afterward.

"Nothing," José said, smiling.

"Come on, you must have said something."

"Well, we told him that if he didn't allow you in the room with Lisa," Ulla said, "that with your history of madness as shown by the many paintings Mr. La Coupole has in his office, and your background as a mercenary . . ."

José started to laugh.

"I'm not a painter. That's Peter's history. And a mercenary? Where in the hell did you get that, you lousy bum?" I laughed.

"I didn't know what else to say," he said, smugly. "Painters and mercenaries are all I know!"

"We told him we couldn't guarantee his safety," Ulla said.

"Oh, no! You said that?"

"Sure as hell did," said José, a smirk on his face.

"And he believed you?"

"Well, the proof: You were in the delivery room with Lisa when your baby was born, weren't you?"

"The doctor absolutely believed him," Ulla said, and not without some smugness of her own.

"You guys *are* crazy!"

I embraced them. Yes, they were both nuts, they were our friends, and I loved them.

No wonder the doctor seemed to have suddenly changed his attitude, and had become a little more polite after he talked to them. He probably thought: That was par for the course for these American barbarians; violence was in their mothers' milk, no telling what this wild man might do.

"*Ils sont dingue!* They *are* crazy," Lisa, said when later I told her about what José and Ulla had told the doctor.

"Certifiably." And we laughed.

"I'm so happy you were there."

"Me, too."

The nurse took the baby to a table right next to Lisa's bed and started to clean her up. I went over to the table and took particular care to look at the baby's hands and feet, counting her tiny fingers and toes. Lisa and the nurse saw me and they both laughed and shook their heads. I knew it was silly of me.

Then I pressed my nose against her tiny nose, looked into those big, wide-open eyes and stuck my tongue out at her, and bigger than life her tiny mouth opened, and I saw the tip of her pink tongue as she stuck it out back at me. I swear it!

It was so wonderful, really. I do not know if this was my imagination but I would swear for the rest of my life that she did it.

"Of course," Lisa said, a moment later when I made a comment about it, "babies are not just dumb little creatures."

"Men don't know anything," the nurse said, when Lisa translated what we had been talking about. She and Lisa shared a look of female complicity.

I wondered why Lisa seemed so much wiser than I. She had a handle on life that was simple, direct, and practical. During her pregnancy, she had put earphones to her growing belly and would play music—and the baby had responded!

I could see the small ripples that she caused on her mother's belly as she moved. I did not know why this image came to me at that moment.

"Elle est magnifique!"

The concierge had cheerfully and formally declared when she finally saw the baby.

To translate the marvelous sentence Madame Commère had said would do a great injustice not only to her, but also to the French language. She had shown up at the clinic just in case Lisa needed someone, she said. I guess my presence was not good enough.

I found myself agreeing with what the concierge said about the baby in spite of the fact that I now foresaw this woman taking over, and perhaps not even letting me change the diapers. I wanted to do that. Apparently, in France, that was not something fathers normally did, but I wanted to be a good father from day one.

I saw Lisa's face smiling and took her hint and did not sit there and discuss openly with Madame Commère why American fathers could be different from French fathers. I would have lost the argument, anyway. Cartesian logic, Pete would have said, making fun of me.

Would Madame Commère let me hold the baby once in a while? It was not too terribly hard to imagine she would hover over me to make sure I did it in the proper manner: *à la Française!*

"We should name her Champagne because of how she sparkles. She's so bubbly with those beautiful shining eyes," I said, in jest. I thought that was kind of appreciated by the concierge—or maybe not.

Lisa wanted to name her after her two grandmothers: Daphne and Amanda. I thought both were beautiful names. She then added Ulla and Céline. Madame Commère had pronounced herself pleased with the choices!

I had never held a newborn so close to me with her smooth skin and her soft, light brown hair. I ran my hand over her silky stubble of hair. It felt so lovely, so delicate, and so fragile.

It brought to mind the memory of Mohammed's baby and the fact that I had not held her.

The purity and the innocence of a newborn were incredible. When you thought about it, all babies were beautiful and innocent. The struggle of life was to find out what happened after we were born. How come so many of us turned into monsters?

What happened that we got so corrupted, so uncaring, so out of touch with our feelings, with our humanity? I still did not have the answer and I seriously doubted I would ever find it.

Those questions were in the domain of the constant and everlasting struggle to understand who we were, and where we were in the scheme of things. Those questions were born with me, with Daphne-Amanda, with Lisa, with everyone else.

There was no escape clause in this contract. The most important fact for me, as I walked out of the clinic, was that even though my life had been completely transformed, it was still OK to feel overwhelmed by questions without answers.

I thought of the monk back in Athos. He had said that at the end of the day, you had to look at what you ended up with, for after everything was said and done what you ended up with was yourself!

Battered by life surely, but hopefully a bit wiser, and most definitely more humble. Still struggling, questioning, unsure, still seeking. The search would never end. There was no escape. That was the way life was.

In that recognition, in such awareness, there was fantasy, magic, hope about who we were and what we were seeking to find and to become; however chaotic the whole process was, truth had to prevail. There could never be falsehood for we had to face our destiny with dignity and honesty.

As Camus had written: We had to live an authentic life! For life, to be worthwhile, had to be examined, the process beginning anew every day. Answers, if any, would be as fleeting as a passing thought. Nothing was guaranteed.

Nevertheless, the journey was still worthwhile to undertake, and there was nothing wrong with being afraid, lost in a state of confusion. It was fine to confront those contractions—but it was also fine to think about other things that made our lives worthy of someone, worthy of love—in our primitive desire to be in complete harmony with the cosmos.

Lisa's love was truly a gift from the gods and now that Daphne-Amanda—D.A. is what her friends would call her, I was sure of that—was its ultimate manifestation of such love, I hoped and prayed this love would endure.

Maybe it was just my heart blinding me to the fact that humans change, and change could be and often was catastrophic and painful to our hearts and souls. Lisa had taught me about hope and about the nature of love.

I had to give my new life a shot. I had to because it would help me become a better person, a better companion for Lisa, a better father to Daphne-Amanda. I wanted to do that. I did not mind admitting it.

I would invent for D.A. all kinds of stories. Stories of magical, mysterious, and enchanting forests, of kingdoms inhabited by the kindest people and the nicest animals. I would tell her stories about love, courage, and happiness.

She would know tales of young maidens with long hair softly blowing in the wind, galloping on white horses with golden wings, coming to the rescue of young men—boys. I would tell her stories of little girls standing by windows, and listening with all their hearts and souls for sounds of the river.

She would also know everything in her life was possible. I would tell her no lies. She would have a mother and a father who would adore her and would never stop loving her, never!

She would bring joy and immense happiness to a set of grandparents and an aunt who would soon be coming to meet her. I knew they would be crazy about her. With a bit of luck, she might end up getting a brother or a sister. I certainly hoped so.

By a simple favor of the gods, and an unenthusiastic French doctor, I had been present when she was born. One day I would tell her that. I knew she would want to know all of the details, and she would want to hear them from me.

Girls were that way. And when she wanted to know how her mother and I met and fell in love, I would leave that to her mother. Women were better at such things.

I knew that Daphne-Amanda would be part of a much larger family. Pete, Roxanne, Alain, Catherine, Milo, John, Juliette, Ulla, Adam, José, and his gypsy friends would all adopt her, come to our place to do their magical ceremony to banish all the evil spirits, and that Lisa would approve and would entrust D.A. to them.

I also knew that, sometime in the future, Lisa would insist that we take her back to Ethiopia to be blessed by her tribe the same way she had been. I would have to ask D.A.'s grandmother about this. I also knew, however reluctant I was to admit it, that Madame Commère would substitute for faraway grandmothers when the time came.

What the hell, I thought. What about my parents? I wonder if the news would bring as much joy as it had to Lisa's parents. I did not know. Should I write and tell them? I was not ready to deal with that issue, yet.

Lisa had said that I was a bit silly to harbor such antagonistic feelings toward my parents. Instead of forgiving them, I was the one stuck with my anger and resentment, with my cynicism. She was probably right.

I was going to call Lisa's parents back in the States as soon as I got back home. I had called them when Lisa had gone into the clinic. Now this phone call would be with wonderful news: They had a beautiful granddaughter and that mother and baby were doing just fine.

As I walked toward the Métro station, I saw it was filled with people rushing to work so early in the morning. The revolution was all but forgotten by most Parisians. Those in Paris, on this hot day in August, were mostly tourists and Parisians who had gone on their summer vacations in July. Everyone seemed tanned and relaxed.

I decided to take a taxi instead, telling the driver to take me down the Champs Elysées. It seemed appropriate that I should be driven down this beautiful avenue on what, for me, was the most magnificent of mornings!

Perhaps, in the back of my head, I was unconsciously remembering it was down the Champs Elysées I had been driven the very first time I had arrived in Paris.

It was also at the top of the Arc de Triumph that Lisa had first told me about Daphne-Amanda, just about nine months before. However, I did not ask the taxi driver to take me around the arch three times, like I had once done with Lisa.

So many thoughts came into my mind that morning, and I wanted to keep them fresh. I found myself imagining writing a letter to D.A., but what would I say to her? How would I say it?

I would tell her that I loved her, that my life was now full! A great circle had been completed . . .

This morning, when I saw your face for the first time as you were coming out of your mother's womb, it was a most magical moment of my existence. I was transported into a world of such purity and clarity.

An innocence of such intense feelings beyond anything I have ever experienced or been touched by. So overwhelming, I wanted to cry but was ashamed that I would end up embarrassing you and your mother. This goes to show you, I still have a long way to go to be completely honest and true.

For the rest of my days, I will treasure the incredible image of your birth and that beautiful face of yours and, yes, those apple cheeks. In that instant, I felt like I was seeing myself being born.

Such images will remain forever etched into my heart and soul. When I die, the image will not die with me but instead will travel back across eternity to join its point of departure.

Since that moment when I first saw you, the question in my heart has been: Who are you? I do not mean that you are a stranger to me; you will never be such a person. For to want to know others, to seek to understand them, to discover them, is a lifetime commitment.

A lifetime-quest—especially for those we truly love, and that in turn may lead us to a glimpse of our own individual souls and destinies. You will see this as you grow and meet others on the journey that you have now started.

For make no mistake: By your coming into this imperfect, crazy world, you have embarked upon a long journey that will be exciting and frightening at the same time. I am as certain of it, as I am certain that the taxi is taking me down the Champs Elysées.

So many unpleasant things are happening around us at the present moment in this city, that one could be excused for not wanting to have any hopes. But that is giving up, and not one of us is allowed to do that. The gods will never forgive you for such cowardice.

In your life, there will be disappointments, anger, hate, yes, hate. Hate for the horrible things humans do to themselves, to others, that are so despicable and evil.

But you will also learn to love the beauty that exists in others, their patience, their love, their innocence, their goodness, their simplicity, and their laughter.

I cannot pass on to you a message or a formula for living. There is no such thing. However, there is one thing that you can count on and that is that the truth is within you. It does not exist outside.

It is like a bell that always rings with beautiful sounds inside of your heart and your soul. You must listen for it. A very wise woman once said that to me, and it has always made sense.

You will be you and all that your mother and I can do is to make sure that you are not us. You must always remain true to yourself. And

370

one thing you can be convinced of: You will never find, in this crazy world, two people who will love you more!

Your mother brought me the gift of love, and you are the gift of life to me. One day I will die, as I must, for that is how all human journeys end. In life's blueprint, we have a timing device programmed in a finite way as someone much older and wiser once said to me.

Thus, we ought to use such precious time wisely, in the matter of living, and not be selfish and worry about dying.

For when that day arrives, I do not want you to be sad or feel sorry for me or for the things that I did or did not do. It does not matter. It will not matter. What matters is that you have come into my life and I am grateful, so grateful. I could not tell you how much even if I lived to see the sun die.

What will also matter is that as you grow older, wiser, and you will be wiser—how could you not be with a mother like yours—you must commit to seek the best and always be filled with what is best, with what is virtuous, kind, and decent in you.

Seek out what is best in others, and it follows that you will find what is best in you. Yes, seek out the nobility of the human spirit and reject its banality. It is your moral imperative. You will never be wrong in your search.

There are no promises that everything will turn out the way you want or the way you hope. Sometimes it will happen; at other times, it will not. Nothing is guaranteed and everything is uncertain.

You will learn to accept that and you will also learn to deal with it, but the struggle will make you stronger and wiser. Again, there is no formula for living. We just do it. You are a child of love! Remember that. Always remember that!

Love will find you one day! You can count on it but it is not the final answer. I do not know what the final answer is. Though now I know that love is the genesis of this great mystery called life.

All we can do is learn to appreciate that such a magical and splendid force has touched our hearts, for at that moment we are one with the cosmos.

One of your mom's favorite French writers is Antoine de Saint-Exupéry, who wrote an amazing book: Le Petit Prince. *I am sure it will delight you when your time comes to read it.*

Your mom loves what the fox character in the book says to the little prince, that she quotes all the time: "on ne voit bien qu'avec le cœur."— We can only see with the heart.

It is such a magnificent idea: To see with our hearts!

It is so simple and so true that even dummies like me can understand it. Yes, to remain open with a heart that is pure and innocent, and to not let the reverses in your life push you toward resentment, distrust, and indifference, that is a most worthy goal to pursue in your life. I am certain you will not be sorry you did.

Happiness will come to you, but happiness will always seem very elusive. Do you want to know something? I have learned that happiness is a task that constantly requires work but it is within us. You must commit to finding it.

You must fight against your worst instincts to deny its place in your heart. Cultivate it in your soul because with it comes spiritual freedom, and a clear vision of what is possible.

Yes, it is a constant struggle and hard to obtain. If it were otherwise, we, in our pride and excess, would not learn to appreciate it. There cannot be a life empty of happiness. What a bleak and desolate existence that would be.

I do not know what your life will be like when you get to be my age. I hope to be there to see you turn into a beautiful and wonderful human being, as I am certain that you will.

I also hope and pray to the gods that they will be kind to you and protect you. You will make your life the way you see it. Oh, I know that many times in the future, you will think that your mother and I are too old-fashioned, out of touch, stuck in the past.

You will be right simply because times will change against your mother and me. I am also sure, there will be other occasions when you will think we are embarrassing you with our old-fashioned ways and faulty memories. You will probably be right, as well.

My heart feels as if it is about ready to burst. You have no idea of the joy that is now deep within my soul because of you. I cannot imagine anything so pure, so strong, so sweet, so real, and so true. I was fearful of your coming, would you believe it? Yes, I was.

It was fear of not being able to find it in my heart to love you. How silly can your old man be? Your mother, in her usual manner, dismissed my fear with some simple words:

"I'm sure you'll love her with love beyond reason!" She said.

I know now how true that is.

You have only been out of your mother's womb for such a short period of time and, yet, it seems like you have always existed in my life. I just did not know it. I was busy looking the other way—the story of my life.

This may sound a bit strange to you, but I cannot remember anymore what my life was like before you arrived. Would you believe it? So, I am going to take a deep breath to calm down a bit.

I have never had this kind of experience before, so you must forgive and indulge me if at times I seem too sentimental and rambling all over the place. There is so much that I want to say. I love you more than I can possibly imagine or find the words to express.

I have loved you since your mother told me you were coming. I was just too chicken to admit it, but I do not mind admitting it to you now. You will understand my silliness, and I am sure you will forgive me.

You have no idea how strong that makes me feel. The simple fact that I love you is enough to make me want to stop the taxi, get out, and dance in the middle of this avenue.

But that would surely not be very practical and would probably lead to my arrest for disturbing the peace, so I will not do it. Believe me, I want to do it, but I also do not want to embarrass you so early in your life.

I wish I could dance like your mother does. One day, I will tell you about the night when she danced for me. It was absolutely beautiful, *magnificent. But, alas, no such gifts do I possess. I will, instead, dance with my heart only. I am sure you will understand.*

There are no messages or secret codes that I can pass on to you that will, somehow, make your life and your own existence clear, definite, easier.

There is a classic Latin expression that your mom taught me, that I have been trying so hard to make part of my life, to live by it. I want you to remember it: Carpediem. *It means, seize the day!*

Your mom lives by that belief. I admire and honor her so much for that. I want so desperately to live like that. You must also make it part of your life. It is such a fantastic inspiration: Carpediem!

If you are to remain true to yourself in the struggle to understand who you are, your own nature, seeking out your own destiny, your place in the cosmos, your quest will not be less worthy than mine or your mother's or anybody else's for that matter. You will find some answers. I have to trust the gods that you will.

So much has taken place these past few months in my life here in Paris. It brings to mind another city, Prague, also in Europe, where its citizens are fighting for what is just and honorable.

One day, I will tell you about that and I know you will learn to honor and respect the valiant struggle of those people to be free, just like you are. I feel like I want to tell you so much and yet I know that I do not need to explain everything. You will find it out for yourself. I have no doubt about it. I trust you.

Paris is very special to me and to your mom. We love Paris! And we also love her people however crazy they are at times. It is your city now. You own it. You have a right to it. Paris is such a lovely city.

A very special place and not the least because you were born here. I hope I can help you discover its soul. You do not know yet of the many sad things that have taken place here lately; but still, it is the best city in the world!

I cannot think of any other place I would rather be at this very moment. It seems that I have traveled far and long, but if such a journey led me to your mother and to you, I would do it again, and again, and again. I love your mother. I love you!

You know what, I think I will go to my home café: La Coupole. It is your mom's favorite home café and mine, and I'm sure one day it will be yours. And I will order a café-au-lait this early morning. Come to think of it, I can call your grandparents from there.

That might impress your grandma. On second thought, instead of coffee with milk, I will order a bottle of their finest champagne; yeah, that is a wonderful idea!

And If I get a little tipsy, I do not think the waiter will mind. As a Frenchman, he will know that the reason for such mad behavior and caprice on my part so early in the day has to do with women, love, and happiness.

I will most definitely tell him, just to impress him, that I am in love with two beautiful women and that I am certain of their love for me. And he, in typical French, male fashion, will think how lucky I am and, of course, he will be right!

Sweet dreams, D.A.

EPILOGUE

A few days after Daphne-Amanda's birth, the Prague Spring was over. On August 21, 1968, the Russians invaded Prague aided by several of their Eastern European minions. The world just stood by and let the people of Czechoslovakia and their land be raped, once again.

In November of 1968, Richard M. Nixon was elected president of the United States.

There is also a French version of this book: *A La Fin Du Jour*, for those of you who are Francophiles. Your comments regarding this novel are most welcome, and I hope you have enjoyed reading it. Also, be sure to check out my other novel: *Long Time Passing*.

edlevesko@gmail.com
www.edlevesko.com